SORCERER

By

Chris McMahon

Sorcerer

Published 2013 by Lanedd Press, an imprint of Pop & Top Publishers.
www.popandtop.com.au
Please direct all enquiries to the publisher at:
publisher@popandtop.com.au

ISBN: 9780992299446

Cover Artist: Daryl Lindquist
Edited by: Tracy Seybold

National Library of Australia Cataloguing-in-Publication enty:

Author: McMahon, Chris, 1965-
Title: Sorcerer / Chris McMahon
ISBN: 9780992299446 (paperback)
Series: McMahon, Chris, 1965- Jakirian Cycle ; bk. 3.
Dewey Number: A823.4

Chris McMahon's website: www.chrismcmahon.net

This novel is dedicated to my wife Sandra, for her love, support and unfailing faith in me.

Acknowledgements

Thanks to all the people who contributed over the years to the final work that the Jakirian Cycle became. Getting anything into print really is a team sport. Special thanks to my editor Tracy Seybold, cover artist Daryl Lindquist and critique partner Gary Kemble. Thanks to all the very patient readers of the first *Calvanni* edition in 2006, who have waited some time to see what happens in *Scytheman* and *Sorcerer*.

A Note on the World of Yos

Yos is a world where all metal is magical, and cannot be forged, appearing as *glowmetal*. The weapons and armour are either constructed of natural materials or a special class of composite ceramics developed for hardness or the ability to hold an edge while maintaining strength and flexibility.

Glossary

Bakta - A clear alcoholic spirit distilled from the baal cereal crop.

Calv - A long knife made of lanedd.

Druid - Magic user who relies on the Essence of Heaven, which varies according to movement of the suns and moons. Ability common.

Druidin - Class of Druid that gives no allegiance to the Temple of the Sisters.

Eathal - Natives of the vast cavern complexes of Kelas and evolutionary cousins to humans. Male and female known as thal and thel. Thickset and hairless, with sensitive eyesight.

Glowmetals – A naturally occurring blend of light, energy and metal. Arising in all sizes, shapes and combinations, they can neither be created nor destroyed, but can be manipulated to store and release their native energy.

Greatscythe - Staff-like weapon with twin concealed lanedd blades, one at either end, operated by a mechanism central to the haft.

Heat - Biological mechanism triggered by the extreme cold of Storm Season. Gives life-giving warmth, but releases inhibitions and makes self-control almost impossible.

Kelas – Continent formerly ruled by the Bulvuran Empire.

Lanedd - Specialised ceramic that can be cast into a blade, which holds a razor-sharp edge that can be sharpened.

Mought - Heavy cast ceramic used in armour, blunt weapons and fortifications.

Priestess - Wielder of Earth Essence, which flows only in certain locations. Ability to access Earth Essence rare in men (Priests).

Sarlord - Ruler of a Sardom by right of royal birth.

Scythe - A short pole weapon with a single lanedd blade.

Sisters - Yos' two suns, Larus and Uros, also worshipped as goddesses by the people of Yos. Larus, the Yellow Sister, and Uros, the Red Sister. Larus is the larger of the two.

Sorcerer - Wielder of magical Fire. Ability derived from hereditary and extremely rare. Practice currently outlawed by the Temple of the Sisters.

Storm Season - Sudden drop in surface temperature and subsequent violent storms that arise twice a year when Yos' two suns, Larus and Uros, eclipse.

Sundar - Supreme ruler of the Eathal of Yos.

Suul – Class of ruling nobility in Yos. Also Suulvey, senior peers and Suulqua, nobles of minor rank.

Temple of the Sisters – Dominant religious force in Kelas.

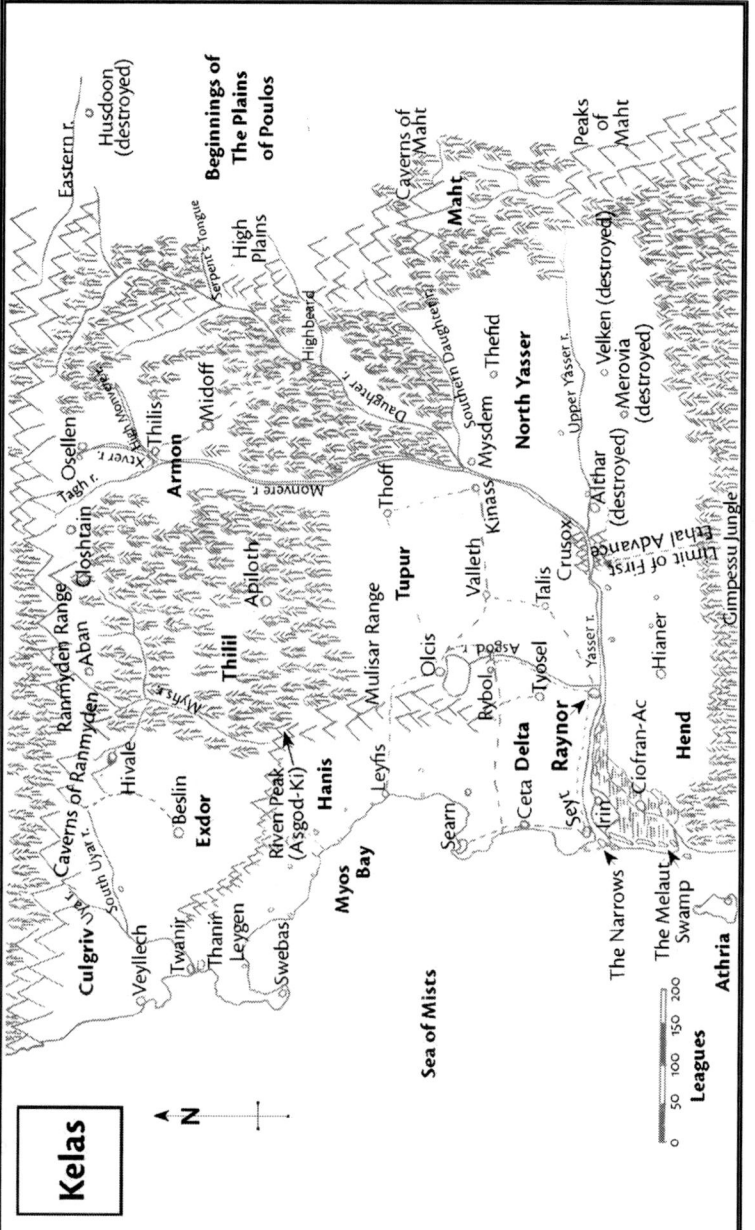

Kelas

N

Leagues
0 50 100 150 200

Prologue

Three days after Asic's Blessing
Cedrin Cinanac recognised as Scion by Kranor at Olcis

Faivel drew gently on the reins. He halted his jakkund on a low hill overlooking the Asgod River. The mount gave a low trumpet, dancing on its long, sleek legs. Its big ears swivelled as it scanned the ground ahead, alert for danger. Faivel squinted against the painful glare of Larus, adjusting the fall of the hooded scarf that blocked most of the yellow sun's savage light.

His detachment of fifty jakkund-mounted Eathal lancers formed a neat line behind him. His scouts were out of sight, ranging out almost a league.

'Warriors approach, my Lord,' said Huntmaster Arud.

'Ah, yes. I see them.' Faivel had yet to get the knack of coping with the light of the suns. Arud had more experience of the upper world than he did. As Hukum's second son, Faivel had escaped military duty – at least until his ferocious older brother had been slain by the human mercenary Raziin. The supreme leader of the Eathal had demanded justice for the death of his favourite. Faivel's comfortable life of scholarship had ended overnight. Whether he had desired it or not, he was now the Sundar's heir.

A line of dark-clad figures marched down by the river. Faivel channelled the Fire into the Lens Matrix. The view leapt into sharp relief. The marching lines resolved into ranks of Eathal clad in leather armour, with heavy hammers and shields slung across their backs. Like Faivel and his warriors, they were heavy-set and hairless, with heavy brows and thick, inflexible hips.

'Legion foot soldiers. Moving fast,' muttered Faivel. Arud remained silent, well used to his master's Sorcerous tricks. He scanned the lines, searching out the standard. A lean yellow teremb – the solitary hunter of the caverns – running on a dark background. 'Teremb legion. Lord Tynan. Why would Yeffrij order him north?'

'Shall we tell Sorcerer-Lord Tynan that Olcis is in the other direction?' asked Arud. Faivel smiled at his aide's wry humour, but rapidly sobered. He released his grip on the Fire.

They had pushed the swift jakkund mounts to their limits on their run south. Faivel's eyes flicked to the spare mount where the body of Raziin's warrior was ripening in the rising heat. The human's black leather armour was stained with old blood. Faivel wished he could have cut the foul thing free long ago, but he knew Yeffrij would need some tangible proof if he was to grant him the trackers and efreet messenger bats he needed to follow the renegade Raziin through the dense Thilil forest. He might be the Sundar's heir, but in the field Faivel ranked as Talonmaster, four levels of command below General Yeffrij. Hukum was determined that he would earn his place.

What he had learned from the dead warrior could change everything. He would need Yeffrij, his father's former apprentice, to reach Hukum across the Bridge of Minds and communicate the development directly to him.

'Let's find out what has drawn Lord Tynan so far north,' said Faivel.

The long-limbed jakkund flowed into eager motion, despite the sweat that lathered their dark fur. He felt the muscles in his mount's shoulders ripple beneath the saddle as he steered it down the hill to the river. The mouths of the jakkund worked like a bat's, uttering sounds pitched too high even for Eathal to hear. Their ears twitched as they sensed their path.

Faivel's men had picked up Raziin's trail outside Olcis and pursued him north into Tupur. They had clashed twice, but both times Raziin and his men had slipped his net. Their last battle had been on the edge of the Thilil forest. Four of Raziin's men had sacrificed themselves in a rearguard action, blocking a narrow defile against their pursuit. The last had survived – at least until Faivel's men had put him to the question.

The distance closed rapidly. Soon the outward elements of the Teremb legion met them, elite forward units equipped with stabbing spears and heavy shields.

They bowed to the Sundar's son as he passed, then continued north. Soon Faivel and his men had passed through the front lines of the advancing legion.

'There,' said Arud. The Huntmaster indicated with an outstretched arm.

Faivel pulled the light scarf from his face. He could see a small group of jakkund cavalry surrounding the Teremb standard. In a force comprised almost exclusively of footsoldiers, only a Sorcerer-Lord of the Eathal warranted the protection of the elite jakkund lancers.

Faivel held up his hand to halt his warriors and advanced on his own.

The Eathal warriors of Tynan's entourage eyed him without expression as their Lord turned to the newcomer. The Sorcerer-Lord wore the finest jakka-hide armour, inlaid with gems. His bald dome gleamed with fine oil.

'Lord Tynan,' said Faivel.

'Faivel,' said Tynan. As son of the Sundar, Faivel was entitled to being addressed as Lord. Tynan was taking the opportunity to enforce his senior rank as Sorcerer-Lord and General of the Teremb. The thal was a devoted follower of Hukum. Even so, it was no secret Faivel and his penchant for scholarship had always put him at odds with his father. He let the slight pass him by.

'Your forces are further north than I anticipated,' said Faivel.

Tynan's heavy brows creased in irritation.

'Since when does the strategy of Yeffrij's inner circle concern you?' snapped Tynan.

Faivel clenched his jaw in irritation. Tynan had always been an officious fool, but his connections were good. The command was a reward for his support of Hukum's faction in the Junta. Even so, his father had not included his legion in his crucial strike west to the human capital Raynor, sending him north with Yeffrij instead.

Faivel changed tack. 'My apologies, Lord. We have travelled from the north and scouted much of the way along the Asgod. Perhaps if I knew your purpose, I could given you information of value?' he said in a more conciliatory tone. He was used to appeasing witless fools.

Tynan glared at him for a moment more, then his pique was replaced by a smug excitement. 'We are in pursuit of the Olcis legion. The fools attacked our emplacement last night. We routed them easily and they fled north. No doubt in fear of our superior numbers.'

'They felt the wrath of Breathstealer,' said Tynan's aide with patriotic fervour. The Sorcerer-Lord's inner circle laughed in grim amusement.

Faivel's eyes flicked to the bulky shape of Breathstealer in the centre of the lines. The glowmetal was being drawn by jakka-drawn carriage. Each of the Eathal legions was proud of their offensive glowmetals. No two were alike, and they varied in power. Faivel had studied them all. In truth, Breathstealer was the merest of them, and the only glowmetal that Teremb boasted. The Sundar's Black Drakon legion carried nine glowmetals west to Raynor, including the Wallbreakers. All were formidable.

'Congratulations on the victory,' said Faivel smoothly. Their spies had reported that Lempar commanded the human legion of Olcis. He was an experienced general and would know better than to attack an Eathal legion at night.

'My Lord. I must report we have not seen any signs of a large group of human warriors,' said Faivel.

Tynan's face twisted in contempt. 'No? Why does that not surprise me?'

Faivel was speechless. His men were elite warriors. His scouts second to none. Before he could muster a response, Tynan had dismissed him and turned his entourage north to follow the main body of his troops.

Faivel sat motionless on his jakkund as the warriors of Teremb legion flowed around him. His anger quickly abated, replaced by uneasiness.

'My Lord?' Arud was at his side.

'South. Quickly.'

They moved out of the lines of the Teremb and raced south in its trampled wake. As the suns rose to the zenith, the heat became oppressive. The stench of the rotting corpse was a constant reminder of its presence. Faivel remained silent, alert for what lay ahead. Their scouts returned, and he sent them out again, more cautious than ever.

They turned west. When they reached the outskirts of Yeffrij's main camp, they came across the heaped bodies of human dead. Some one hundred warriors, their faces bluish-grey, eyes bloodshot and unseeing. The work of Breathstealer. Tynan's men were not simply boasting. Yet there were so few enemy dead. This hardly constituted a major attack.

They were challenged by a small squad of Eathal infantry. The Talonmaster bowed when Faivel identified himself.

'Where is General Yeffrij?' asked Faivel.

'The general is advancing to Rybol with the Red and Grey, my Lord. Hunter and Teremb defend the flanks.'

Faivel and Arud swapped a quick glance. The Teremb legion was far north of the flank. The idiot Tynan had broken formation in his eagerness to close with the humans.

'To the river,' Faivel ordered.

They passed through the deserted camp. Thousands of hide tents were set in neat rows. There was no faulting Yeffrij when it came to organisation.

They followed the main road towards the bridge of Rybol – a major artery connecting the province of Tupur to the vast human city of Olcis. As they neared the last rise, they saw a tall plume of smoke rising into the still air. He could hear the roars of Eathal in combat, mixed with human voices and the muted clash of arms.

Faivel crested the rise and drew up short.

The Red and Grey Drakon legions filled the plain to the river. The bridge at Rybol was in flames. As he watched, the main span collapsed, taking an advance detachment of Eathal with it. He winced. Eathal did not swim.

He saw shapes in the water and quickly enhanced his sight. Through the Lens, he saw they were rafts – running swiftly downstream. The saboteurs shot south, guiding the rafts with long poles. In a flash, he realised how the 'Olcis legion' that Tynan was chasing had escaped him.

It took him a moment to realise the sound of combat was coming not from the plain in front of him, but to the south. He turned his mount and raced along the ridge with his men.

It was to the south that the real attack was occurring.

Like the Teremb, the Hunter legion had been drawn away from the main force. Yet where Tynan was chasing ghosts, the Hunter legion had been drawn into an ambush among the maze of hills beside the river.

A full human legion – ten thousand men – engaged the Hunter legion. The Eathal force had been cut into three. The human phalanxes plunged deep into the disorganised Eathal ranks, while human javelin throwers, archers and slingers assaulted them from carefully concealed positions on the high ground. Faivel knew Kyan, the Hunter General, as a level-headed thinker. He could see the Eathal troops trying to draw back and re-form, but human cavalry thrust through the formations before they could coalesce. The Eathal, accustomed to fighting in darkness, had no missile weapons to speak of. What dart-throwers they did have were south with Hukum.

Even as his heart sank at Kyan's predicament, Faivel had to admire Lempar's masterful strategy. Without a doubt, the human general was the man behind this. He sought him out on the field, using the Lens, but all was confusion. He did find Kyan, standing with his banner-holders next to the Hunter legion glowmetal, Stomach Churner. Bolts of Force shot from the Eathal Sorcerer's hands, hammering into the human ranks, but the terrain gave him little scope. The whole combat had splintered into smaller engagements in the small valleys and defiles. The humans were fighting at the time of their strength – when the suns were at their brightest – while the Eathal were almost blinded.

Faivel felt a strange pressure sweep across him.

On the field, one of the detachments of human cavalry fell in confusion, men clasping their heads and stomachs. *Stomach Churner*. It was not enough though. The Hunter legion was taking heavy damage.

'Should we join them, my Lord?' asked Arud.

Faivel could hear the strain in his aide's voice. The warrior longed to join the combat, to take the fight to the humans. He himself could do much damage in the human ranks with his Sorcerous powers, but what he had learned from the dying human warrior stopped him. He would need Arud, and all his warriors, if he was to stop Raziin from reaching Ranmyden – and the prize he sought. 'We must hold here, Arud. Yeffrij will not desert them.'

'Yes, Lord,' answered his aide in a harsh whisper.

Time and again Kyan sought to reform, to manoeuvre, but Lempar always anticipated him. The human cavalry was unstoppable, sweeping through the valleys and down onto the Eathal. Like Teremb, the Hunter was one of the newly-formed legions. The elite Eathal legions were the Drakons, named for the fearsome hunters of the caverns. The inexperience of the Hunter warriors was showing.

After an agonising wait, Yeffrij's Red Drakon appeared on the horizon. With methodical slowness, the disciplined forward units swept south in a solid front of heavy shields, short spears stabbing forward with deadly precision. Yeffrij gave the human legions no room to manoeuvre. They overtook the beleaguered Hunter legion units, relieving them, and continued on, forcing Lempar's Olcis Legion into retreat. A dome of darkness formed across the front lines. Faivel smiled grimly as he imagined the panic in the human lines as they found themselves fighting blind. The Darkness was a potent glowmetal, and Yeffrij was using it with precision. Eathal could see heat. The shape of things was revealed to them, even where the light of the upper world never penetrated.

Faivel relaxed his grip on the reins of his jakkund, realising only now what sitting out of the fight had cost him.

A wedge of purple light rippled over a hill of human archers as the Door of Kallor was unleashed. A moment later half were down, others standing disoriented as the Red Drakon swept them to oblivion. The tide had turned on the humans.

A horn sounded across the battlefield. A human signal. Lempar's legion fled to the river.

'He is trapped,' said Arud.

'It cannot be that easy,' muttered Faivel under his breath. Lempar was too wiley to leave himself without a line of retreat.

Faivel channelled Fire into the Lens. *There.* The river bank was lined with rafts. Hundreds of them. The human cavalry reached the river first and crowded onto rafts. Even in retreat, Lempar was thinking clearly, preserving his most useful units. They pushed out into the Asgod and were quickly swept from sight. The rearward elements of human legion turned to form a shield-wall bristling with the long spears, giving the others room to organise their retreat. Behind them, warriors crowded onto the next wave of rafts. The crowd along the river bank thinned, but not before the Red Drakon reached the human rearguard. The fighting was fierce. Once more The Darkness was unleashed. Small whirlwinds buffeted those on the edge of the dome. *Secondary effects.*

When the dome of darkness faded, the human line was still standing. Behind them, the last of Lempar's fleeing legion escaped. Then the Door of Kallor was unleashed again. Its purple light swept across the human defenders. Faivel could hear men scream. Others dropped their weapons, staggering forward onto the spear-points of the Red Drakon, their eyes fixed on private visions of bliss or horror.

As the suns dropped in the west, the last defenders fell. Lempar's gambit was at an end. Perhaps half the Hunter legion had fallen – five thousand Eathal warriors against little more than six hundred of Lempar's men. Yet they had set back Yeffrij little more than a few days. His engineers would rebuild the Rybol bridge and the Eathal legions would roll inexorably towards Olcis. Lempar's single legion could do little but sting their flanks.

Without a word, Faivel led his mounted warriors down to the river. He steered his jakkund to the Red Drakon standard, knowing Yeffrij would be there. Now he had to convince Yeffrij to give him what he needed, persuade the Eathal General to contact Hukum and tell him the unthinkable. He swallowed, anticipating his father's reaction. Hukum was obsessed with the Destruction – the ancient cataclysm that destroyed the once widespread Eathal culture and drove the survivors into refuges like Maht. A destruction made possible by the Spear of Carris, a Sorcerous artefact of unparalleled power believed to have been lost long ago.

He looked back at Raziin's dead warrior. The man had endured much pain before he broke. He told them of Raziin's quest north, seeking to seize the Spear of Carris before the Cinanac heir, Cedrin, could claim it. If it was true – should either human take up the Spear – the Eathal would suffer a stunning defeat. Hukum's legions had left the refuge of Maht and its defensive glowmetals far behind them. They were stretched over hundreds of leagues now, vulnerable as never before in two thousand years.

Faivel shivered. He still could not believe it. Yet his men were experienced torturers and even to him the words of the human had the ring of truth. *Gentle Lidu, give me strength.* This was no longer about appeasing his father or vengeance for his brother Staraz. He had to destroy Raziin and this Cinanac heir, then seize the Spear for the Eathal. Anything less would spell disaster for all of them.

Chapter One

Ellen sat easily in the saddle of her amelak. The ache in her lower back had receded to a dull, ever-present throb.

'Herath. At last,' said Cedrin.

She turned and smiled at him, her heart doing a small flip as she looked at his serious face and intense grey-blue eyes. Even though they both rode the same woolly, long-necked mounts, he sat almost a head taller than her. A rough growth of stubble covered his cheeks and she longed to touch it, to feel the sharp roughness against her palm. The ever-present warriors who surrounded them, always watching Cedrin, stopped her.

Ahead lay the small, walled city of Herath. Set into the base of the Mulisar range, it specialised in gems, tints, rare minerals and glowmetals, all mined from the Mulisar. Most importantly, it was independent. At last they were outside Tupur – and beyond the reach of the Temple. Herath had grown from a collection of ancient mining camps into a financial powerhouse, ruled by the House of Herath and the many other trading guilds based there.

'I can't wait to get a decent shot of bakta,' said Skye, from the back of his narsiit. He towered over all of them. Where their amelak were so fatigued they were prone to miss their footing, Skye's winged mount was jittery with suppressed energy, ready to run for leagues.

'You can tell a lot about a man from his sense of priorities. I, for one, want a bath and a change of clothes,' said Marken, a hint of amusement in his golden eyes. His long golden hair hung lank around his shoulders. His once fine blue silk shirt was stained with dust and sweat.

Skye laughed. 'And once you are nicely perfumed, my Lord, would you care to join me in the common room?'

'With pleasure,' said Marken.

Kalyth, riding beside Cedrin, was silent. He rode straight in the saddle, his lean body as unbending as his mind. His dark-blue eyes were coolly assessing, fixed on the battlements of Herath as they drew closer. As always, Bovosan rode behind Cedrin, the heavy brow-ridges and leathery ears of the minitil half-breed concealed by a dark, hooded cloak.

'Ruus. Kanis. Take six men and go into Herath and find us an inn – nothing too conspicuous. Let us know when all is secure. We will wait outside the gates,' said Kalyth.

Osterac pushed his amelak forward. 'If I may, Kalyth?'

Ellen suppressed her annoyance as Osterac manoeuvred his mount closer to Cedrin and Kalyth, forcing her to pull up short. The former Olcis Suul and pretender was simply too eager to please. He was contrite now, but she could not forget the unbelievable arrogance he displayed in Raynor as false-Scion.

'Go on,' said Kalyth.

Osterac smiled pleasantly. 'I know Herath well. Let me go in with the others. I know an inn that will suit us.'

Kalyth nodded his assent, his expression unchanged. The warriors galloped to the gates and entered the city unchallenged. From here, the battlements looked deserted.

They drew up within bowshot of the walls of Herath and dismounted.

'Is this really necessary, Kalyth?' asked Cedrin.

'It is, my Lord.'

Cedrin winced at the formal address, but nothing on Yos could convince Kalyth to relax. Once Cedrin had been revealed as the son of Riin Cinanac, the last Emperor of Bulvuran, everything had changed. If the tall former-calvanni was frustrated at the restriction on him now, it would only get worse.

The warriors, all from Kranor's mercenary company, were sworn to Cedrin. Each of them wore the phoenix tattoo of the royal bodyguard, which Kranor had adopted for his company's

18

sigil. They took their vows to protect Cedrin seriously. Although there were only thirty of them now, more were en-route to Herath to form a full company of the One Hundred. Xyanthius, Kranor's second-in-command, travelled with them.

Ellen sought out Raphal. The nine days of hard riding since Olcis had been punishing, with only brief rests and a few hours of snatched sleep. The Priest's face was grey with exhaustion, his body stiff as he struggled to dismount.

'Here, let me help,' said Ellen.

Raphal gave a tight smile. 'I would have been happier getting off this damn thing in Herath.'

Once safely on his own two legs, the old Priest arched his back, wincing in pain at the stretch. She knew he would never complain and would endure far worse to be a first-hand witness to the unfolding of the Scion prophecies. He had defied the Hesguit and was as much a fugitive as any of them.

Salis Cintor, tall, blonde and stately, led her amelak over to Ellen and Raphal. Amid the mass of unwashed warriors, all intent on their new duty to the Scion of Bulvuran, Ellen was grateful for the presence of another Suul lady.

'Not long now,' said Salis, her pale-grey eyes gently meeting Ellen's. The Tree totem tattoo on her left cheek was beautifully detailed and had been retouched recently.

Salis' fluid grace always made Ellen feel awkward and plain. Her eyes seemed to look straight into her. Like Raphal, she was skilled in Earth Essence and was a gifted Truth-teller.

Ellen felt a court mask settle over her features, almost against her will, like a defensive reaction. 'It will be pleasant to wash off this dust.'

'I'll race you for the bath,' said Salis lightly.

Ellen smiled, unsure what to say. More than twice her age, Salis was an intimidating maternal figure. She had never been anything other than friendly, and as Kranor's wife, her allegiance to Cedrin was never in doubt. Ellen's own mother had died giving birth to her, and her isolated life growing up in the Athrian court had never included an older female confidant. Those women who cared for her as a child were low-rank servants, removed from her life as soon as she was old enough for her tutors.

Cedrin was standing with his friends Marken and Skye, smiling at some joke. She longed to go to his side but did not want to ruin the rare moment he had with his friends. The burden of leadership weighed heavily on him, and the continual presence of the bodyguard chaffed at his innate independence.

'I'll keep Raphal company if you want to go to him,' said Salis.

Ellen's heart beat fast at the sudden feeling of exposure. *Larus.* Salis seemed to read her so easily.

'We will be in Herath soon enough,' said Ellen, her voice even.

Salis eyes filled with concern and she reached out to Ellen, but something in her expression made Salis stop.

'Of course,' said Salis.

Raphal sank to the ground to rest. Salis sat beside him, folding her legs in one smooth motion.

Ellen looked around at the warriors. The men were familiar by now, some had even been part of the caravan she and Cedrin had travelled north with. She had posed as a simple traveller then. Now she was Ellen Cintros, Suul Sorcerer and consort of the Scion.

The suns dipped below the Mulisar range to the west and a vast shadow engulfed them.

Ellen looked up at the peaks above, awesome and majestic as they marched north. The light of the suns glittered off the snow on their western faces. Each was smooth, except for the last and greatest of them – Agod-Ki – Riven Peak. It loomed over them, shattered and broken. Even from here, Ellen could see the ancient ruins below the snow-line. A city vaster than Ciofran-Ac had once thrived there. A Verial city. It was hard to believe the bird-like beings were now little more than a myth in Kelas. She knew better. Erioth, a master of the Fire who had finished her Sorcerous training in secret, was a Verial. Now he was trapped in the deep caverns of Ranmyden, a prisoner of the Ward of Jykor, the magical construct that defended the Spear of Carris. And with them was the Behemoth, a dark creature linked to the Spear.

As the shadow deepened, the broken peak of Asgod-Ki seemed to blaze brighter. She shivered as a wave of cool air rolled down off the mountains. The Behemoth was the one they truly had to fear.

* * *

Cedrin raised his glass. 'Here's to new times!'

Skye and Cedrin downed their bakta in a single gulp, while Marken took his in two delicate swallows.

All three of them had washed, changed and shaved. The feel of air on his clean cheeks felt wonderful. The pace on the road had left little time for anything. Certainly no privacy. He looked over to the stairs, watching for Ellen, even though he knew he would not see her for hours yet. Olcis and the days that followed had been a whirlwind, one that had picked them all up and put them down in some strange new place. He was looking forward to some time alone with her. Of all the things that had happened, his relationship with Ellen was by far the most miraculous. Like some delicate flower he dare not touch for fear of destroying it.

Skye frowned at Marken's yellow silk shirt. The colour was bright and flawless. 'Is that new?'

'Yes. The other was ruined. I told the bath attendant to take it away,' said Marken.

Skye and Cedrin exchanged a quick look. Only Marken would think of discarding a silk shirt.

The inn, like many in Herath, was sandwiched between warehouses. It was non-descript, plain stone and timber, three storeys tall. The common room had been all but deserted when they entered it less than an hour ago. Now it was filled with Kranor's men. No. *His* men. Others were arriving though. The tavern crowd steadily grew. Perhaps it was the evening trade.

Kalyth, sitting alert at a nearby table, gave a command. Kanis, a dark-skinned and vicious warrior, and six other warriors unslung their greatscythes and formed a line across the centre of the room, effectively claiming half of the common room for their company. They eyed the crowd with ferocity, ready to defend him to the death. He had done nothing to deserve that allegiance. Kanis had once taken a personal dislike to Cedrin – a dislike that had ended in a near-lethal combat – before he was the Scion. The powerful warrior still bore the sign of his defeat – Cedrin had cut off part of his ear. Now he was fanatically loyal to him and carried the disfigurement like a badge of honour. It baffled him.

He looked across the room to where Bovosan sat silently with the warriors, his hood drawn down over his face. The minitil's hammer and shield lay close by. He was always watching, yet so quiet it was easy to forget he was there. Cedrin would not forget that the strange creature had saved him in Olcis.

Skye reached for the bakta bottle, the clear spirit making soft gurgling noises as it flowed into their shot glasses.

Cedrin's thumb played over the ruby Cinanac signet ring on the first finger of his right hand. His father's ring. Riin Cinanac. His true father. As a child, he had thought himself the son of Tarral, a glassmith, then the bastard son of Belin Kaidell, a Suul General. All of it had obscured the truth. He was the heir to the throne of Bulvuran, a once powerful Empire that had controlled all Kelas. Now it was nothing but a loose collection of states under threat from an overwhelming Eathal invasion.

'Here is to a more civilized pace on the road,' said Marken as they lifted their glasses.

'I second that,' said Cedrin. He smiled as he thought of Ellen.

Skye's face brightened. 'Ah. The food.'

Three serving men approached, each with a platter of food. His bodyguards eyed them suspiciously as they crossed the invisible line into their half of the room, but did not stop them.

The first man laid a platter in front of Cedrin and bowed. It was a masterpiece of roasted harena, dripping with savoury sauce, served with cheese and fruit. His stomach rumbled. There was enough on his platter to feed all three of them. 'My Lord. Let me say what an honour it is that you have chosen my humble establishment.'

Cedrin froze. He looked sharply at the man. It was the owner himself. 'What do you mean?'

The man paled. His eyes flicked to the warriors who surrounded the room, each marked with the phoenix. 'It is an honour to serve the Scion of the Cinanac,' he said, bowing again.

Skye cursed under his breath.

The other men quickly laid down their platters, bowed and withdrew.

Cedrin looked across at Kalyth. The lean old warrior was already moving over to them.

'He knows,' said Cedrin. 'They all do.'

Kalyth joined them. 'I should have expected this.'

'That damn fool Osterac,' said Marken, looking across the common room to where the Olcis Suul sat with the other warriors.

Kalyth shook his head. 'No. Kranor's allegiance is well known. Herath is a hot-bed of rumour. Traders live on it. Kranor's men would follow none other than the true Scion, so that part is obvious. Besides – word would have already reached them from Olcis. There is no hiding it. Not anymore.'

The crowd across the room had grown again. Kanis and the warriors standing guard in the centre of the room were forced to retreat a few steps to make space. The buzz of excited conversation grew. Now there was no mistaking it: the brightness in the eyes, the looks in his direction.

'Uros,' hissed Cedrin.

'Hey, this is excellent,' said Skye, tasting the food. 'Eat before it gets cold.'

Cedrin *was* hungry. He had eaten little but dried meat and rock-hard trail bread for more than a week.

He poured himself another glass of bakta and downed it quickly. A pleasant warmth radiated out from his belly and a slow relaxation spread to his limbs.

He reached for the platter.

'Wait,' said Kalyth. Before Cedrin could protest, Kalyth took a slice of meat and ate it quickly, followed by pieces of food from other places on the platter. He paused a moment then nodded.

Cedrin was too stunned to say anything. Kalyth had just tested the food for poison.

He started eating, refusing to consider what he had just seen. As a calvanni, he had prided himself on his independence and had taken great pains to be anonymous. Now . . .

'So how long do we wait in Herath, Kalyth?' asked Marken.

'That depends on how quickly Xyanthius and his men can reach us,' said Kalyth. 'We will need to resupply here as well. Thilil has grown wild and dangerous.'

The three of them ate their meals, and Cedrin relaxed as the noise in the tavern steadily increased. Twice more the line of warriors was forced back.

A richly dressed man, his rotund belly marked with trading guild tattoos, broke away from the crowd and came towards them. He was stopped by the line of warriors. Kanis threatened him with his unsheathed greatscythe, waving him back to the main hearth, but he was insistent.

One of the warriors broke away and walked over to Cedrin. 'He says he needs to speak to you, my Lord.'

Cedrin poured himself another bakta and downed it quickly. *Uros.* 'Send him over.'

The warrior waved for the trader to come forward then took up station behind Cedrin. He watched the man intently as he neared them.

The man bowed and introduced himself. 'Trader in all fine goods, my Lord. There is much I can do for you. The best rates in Herath, be reassured.'

'He is a thief!'

Cedrin looked up to see three more traders stopped by his men. One of them – a thin, short man with a red face – was pointing across the room. 'He will cheat you, my Lord. For honest service look no further than me.'

All four traders began to speak at the top of their voices, trying to outdo each other with combined praise for their esteemed host and vicious derision for each other. Soon others had joined them. Kanis and his men were forced back again. They looked to Kalyth for orders.

The first trader pressed his advantage. He touched Cedrin's sleeve, trying to get his attention. Cedrin snatched his hand back, restraining his instinctive reaction to draw his calv. He heard the snick of a released blade, and the warrior behind him lowered his unsheathed greatscythe between the trader and Cedrin.

The trader took a step back but quickly recovered. 'Perhaps if my Lord will provide me with a list of what you desire? I assure you of the best Herath has to offer.'

'There are things we need, my Lord. I can see these traders tomorrow and see what prices they offer,' said Kalyth.

The trader was outraged. 'You seek to play me off against this rabble?' he said, jerking a thumb back at the other men.

Cedrin narrowed his eyes. Their tattoos revealed them to be traders of equal rank, but from rival guilds. 'Yes. Tomorrow.'

The trader opened his mouth to argue, but Kalyth stood, fixing him with a gaze of silent menace. He turned to the warrior. 'Take this one back. Tell the others to come at noon.'

'Quite,' said the trader. He bowed and moved back to join the others.

The others continued to call out, obviously considering the fact that their rival had reached Cedrin an unfair advantage – and trying to make up for lost ground.

The crowd in the room swelled even more. Now Cedrin and his men occupied only the corner of the room near the stair. Soon they would need to leave. The men and women were here to gawk at the new Scion – or to try their luck like the traders.

The door to the common room opened again, and Cedrin readied himself to get up and leave. The noise in the room dropped. At first, he only saw the two heavy-set bodyguards, massively-muscled men who towered over the crowd. Then, as the crowd parted, Cedrin saw a lithe Suul with dark hair. His richly-woven shirt and trousers shimmered in the lamplight, but even the superb cut and weave of his clothes was overshadowed by the wealth he displayed. A silver glowmetal dangled from his left ear. His wrists were adorned with tinted mought bracers, set with gold and platinum glowmetals. Others hung from his neck in a clashing mix of colours and metals, all but obscuring his tattoos. He stopped at the line of warriors and looked directly at Cedrin.

The tavern grew silent.

Kalyth walked across to the Suul, but the man spoke to Cedrin, easily heard in the quiet without having to raise his voice.

'I am Suul Veltricus Cineth of the House of Herath. Master Trader. Perhaps a word?' His voice was smooth and charismatic, his words precise. Everything about him spoke of refinement.

The House of Herath had never claimed any title to the city. Officially a council of senior traders ruled here. Unofficially, not only did the House of Herath run the city, they *owned* it.

Kalyth looked to Cedrin. He nodded, and Kalyth waved Veltricus through.

The two bodyguards had no visible weapons, but their eyes were hard. Like Veltricus, they sported thick mought bracers on their wrists. Cedrin recognised experienced warriors when he saw them. Each was marked with a distinctive tattoo like a stylised 'N' with an image of a peak behind it.

Veltricus bowed. 'I believe I have the honour of addressing Cedrin Cinanac?' His eyes dropped to the ruby signet ring on Cedrin's hand.

'Yes,' said Kalyth.

Cedrin held up his hand. He could speak for himself.

'My father, head of House Herath, sends you his greetings.' Veltricus paused, searching Cedrin's face, then his tattoos. A flash of strange intensity showed in his dark eyes. A moment later it was gone, replaced by pleasant congeniality. 'Like all Kelas, we mourned Riin's passing and the fall of Bulvuran. Herath rejoices that the Scion is found.'

'Thank you, Suul Cineth,' said Cedrin, conscious of his Athrian dock accent.

'Veltricus, please.'

Cedrin was impressed with the man. Even though he was a Suul, he possessed a quality of real strength and something intangible he could not pin down. He looked no older than Cedrin, but was a Suul through and through. Born to rule.

'How long do you plan to spend in Herath?' asked Veltricus, his voice taking on a hard edge.

'Our stay will be short,' said Cedrin.

26

'We are eager to assist you in any way we can.'

Kalyth caught Cedrin's eye. 'Perhaps Suul Salis Cintor would like to join these discussions?'

The common room of a Herath inn was unlikely to be holy ground, but Salis may be able to read Veltricus despite that. He nodded.

Kalyth waved a warrior towards him, giving him a quickly worded message.

'Join us,' said Cedrin.

Skye and Marken shuffled aside, making room at the table for Veltricus. The man looked out of place beside his friends, like a cut and polished diamond in a bed of gravel. Even so, he seemed perfectly at ease.

'What are your plans after Herath? I only ask so that our House may serve your needs,' said Veltricus.

Cedrin had the uncomfortable feeling he had started a game of karass, except he was playing in the dark and did not know what pieces were on the board. Not only that, Veltricus had made the first move.

'And how can your father help us?' asked Cedrin, trying to rankle him.

Veltricus' eyes narrowed. 'I assure you. I speak for my father.'

Cedrin poured Veltricus a glass of bakta and slid it across the table, waiting for an answer. Putting himself in Veltricus' shoes, he would be keen to see any so-called Scion out of his city. He remembered the riots in Raynor and knew first hand how quickly factions formed – and how quickly the dispossessed and power-hungry could seize on a cause.

'Thank you, Suul Cinanac,' said Veltricus, picking up the glass delicately with his fingertips.

Cedrin paused in shock for a moment. He had spent much of his life resenting the Suul, regarding them as a class of parasites who cared for no one but themselves. He had never been addressed as a Suul before, yet it was true. He *was* a Suul. Even though he did not bare the mark.

Veltricus had seen the reaction. The Herath Suul lifted the glass to his mouth and tilted it. He sighed in appreciative satisfaction, although Cedrin noticed that it returned to the table still full. *Experienced at deception.*

'The House of Herath can help you in many ways. Our services would be invaluable to you throughout Kelas. Our business contacts would ensure your resupply, no matter where you travelled. Even into the wilds of Thilil.' Veltricus' eyes met his, cool and assessing. How could he know their plans to go north?

Kalyth turned to the stair. A moment later, the scent of perfume washed across Cedrin. Salis and Ellen had entered the commons. A ripple of excited conversation swept through the room. For a moment, Cedrin's breath caught in his throat. Ellen was dressed in an exquisite gown of gold, her hair braided back and set with gemstones. A sapphire pendant rested above the swell of her breast. A smile touched the corner of her mouth at his reaction, but was soon gone as she once more became the faultless Suul. Salis wore a fine gown of white, with blue mought bracelets and a diamond necklace.

'Suul Cintros,' said Veltricus, nodding to Ellen. He turned to Salis. 'And . . .'

'Salis Cintor.'

'Of course.' Veltricus nodded in deference, although Cedrin had the feeling no one entered Herath without Veltricus knowing every detail.

Two tables were put together and they all sat. Cedrin had been pondering how much to tell Veltricus. He decided there was no point trying to deceive the Suul. Any plans they made had to involve purchasing supplies and organising logistics for the trip north. Veltricus would soon know from his own people what they planned. Besides, the Suul's concerns must surely centre on his own city. Once they were gone, they would no longer be his problem.

'So. How can the House of Herath aid the Scion?'

'We intend to travel north through Thilil. Ultimately to Exdor,' said Cedrin.

Veltricus paused. Cedrin had taken him off balance with the direct answer. 'The capital Beslin?'

'Almost certainly,' said Cedrin. They had discussed possible routes north over the last few days. There was no other way to approach Ranmyden. To try to make it all the way through the forests of Thilil would be impossible. Much of the way would be unexplored wilderness.

'And your strength?'

'A little over one hundred,' said Cedrin with a wry smile. The full strength of the One Hundred.

'Impressive. Even so, it is fortunate you came to us first before you attempted the old Beslin road,' said Veltricus.

'Bandits?' said Kalyth.

Veltricus shook his head. 'One of the ancient drakons of Asgod-Ki has expired. More than thirty drakon-spawn have crawled from the corpse. They infest the lower ranges of the Mulisar from this point north. Three of our own caravans have been destroyed trying to reach Beslin.'

He and Ellen exchanged a quick glance. Only months ago, Cedrin would have scoffed at the talk of drakons, but their caravan north had been attacked by a big one. Only Ellen's Sorcery had saved him from death.

'Drakon spawn?' asked Skye.

'Yes. They are fast and deadly. The size of big raptors, but they hunt like a pack. At least for now. As they grow, they will begin to tear at each other. Our scouts have a good idea of their territory. For now, the Beslin road is too dangerous.'

'Then how do we get north?' asked Marken.

'There are other ways – less travelled paths through Thilil that will take you to the Myfis Bridge. Once in Exdor, the road is safe.'

'What are you offering?' asked Kalyth.

'Herath will join your expedition with its own caravan. We have been waiting for a strong party moving north to help move precious glowmetals, tints and other wealth to Beslin.'

'And the price?' asked Ellen.

'We will charge a commission on the goods we sell you. As for the rest – we stand to make a good profit if we can reach Beslin. We will provide a company of scouts to guide the combined caravan north at our own expense.'

Cedrin waited but Veltricus seemed content.

'Well. Thank you. We will discuss the offer and get back to you tomorrow,' said Cedrin.

Veltricus rose and smiled. 'Think of it as an alliance. Until tomorrow.'

The Herath Suul turned and exited the inn, the crowd melting before him. Cedrin noticed that the other traders had lost interest in them. The biggest dog in Herath had barked.

Cedrin looked around the table. So much for a quiet meal in an inconspicuous inn.

'What do you think?' Cedrin asked Salis.

'The Earth Essence is weak here, but I think he was telling the truth about the danger. He does need to move those goods to Beslin and stands to profit by it. I did have a sense he is driven by a strong ulterior motive, but what trader isn't?'

'How did he know we were heading north?' asked Cedrin.

Skye poured himself a drink. 'What else is there beyond Herath? We cannot go east – the Eathal are in Tupur. If we wanted to go west, we would have made for the pass at Fulvur and taken the Leyfis road.'

'True.' The noise had risen again. More gawkers had entered the tavern. 'I can see why he would want us out of Herath.'

Kalyth grunted. 'No more public meals, my Lord. I suggest you hire rooms here during your stay for your private court.'

Cedrin opened his mouth to refute him, but he saw Ellen nod slightly. 'Of course.'

His thumb played over the Cinanac signet ring. It seemed even heavier than usual tonight. The bakta and the fatigue finally caught up with him, and he sagged back into his chair.

He felt a warm hand on his arm and looked up to see Ellen smile at him, her eyes lit with mischief. A flame of joy swelled inside him.

'Your rooms are ready, my Lord,' said Ellen. In that moment, he felt he could cope with anything – as long as she was at his side.

Tomorrow could take care of itself.

Chapter Two

Cedrin pushed aside the last of his breakfast and reached for the teapot.

'Allow me, my Lord,' said Osterac.

The tall Olcis Suul had volunteered to act as food taster this morning and had been hovering at his elbow.

'Very well.' Since Osterac had already taken the pot to pour the tea, he could hardly refuse. The warrior took a sip, waited then pushed the cup across to Cedrin. To have a Suul waiting on him was strange to say the least.

Four other warriors of the One Hundred stood guard in the room. Cedrin had come to know them all. Ruus had been a rearguard lieutenant on the caravan that had taken them north from Raynor. He eyed Osterac with mistrust from his position at the stair. None of Kranor's company seemed to get on with the former Olcis Suul. All of them vied for honour in Cedrin's eyes, and they resented his inclusion in the One Hundred. Kanis taunted him continually, but so far it had not got out of hand.

Kalyth had rented out the two top floors of the inn to provide rooms for them and to ensure security. The chambers they sat in were an annex that extended beyond the top floor. They included a private bedroom – which he and Ellen had put to good use – and opened onto the tavern roof, which doubled as a broad balcony. Two of the One Hundred stood guard at the open doors. Outside, in the dim, red light of Uros' first dawn, twelve of his bodyguard were undergoing instruction in the Way of the Scytheman from Vess, a quick-tempered half Meadrel with a compact build and a fearsome scar down the right side of his face. Bovosan had joined them, the hood of his cloak thrown back to reveal the bald and twisted features of a half-Eathal.

A cool breeze came in through the open doors and windows, softly stirring the curtains.

'Shall we get to business, my Lord?' asked Kalyth.

'Yes.' Cedrin looked around the broad polished table, his mind clear for the first time in days.

Raphal, now rested from the journey, had also joined them, along with Salis, Skye and Marken. Ellen, as always, sat by his side. His inner circle. The court of the Scion.

All looked to him.

'Our task is clear,' said Cedrin. 'We must reach the Ranmyden Iris before Raziin and claim the Spear of Carris.'

'To keep it safe from our enemies. Not to use it,' said Kalyth.

It had taken a lot of work to convince Kalyth that it was vital to take the Spear. The old warrior had argued that the Ward, the guardian of the Spear, would never grant the ancient weapon to Raziin, and they should allow it to remain hidden in Ranmyden, even though this would condemn Belin to everlasting enslavement to its magical guardian. Cedrin had experienced the power of the Behemoth first hand. He could not take the chance that the ancient force of evil would not find a way to subvert the will of the Ward. After all, despite the awesome power at its command through the Spear, the magical construct had no true mind of its own. Cedrin could not allow a vicious murderer like Raziin access to so much power, however unlikely that was. He was convinced that as long as he entered the Ranmyden Iris alone, he could safely claim the Spear. That was the other condition that Kalyth had imposed – Raziin had to be nowhere near the Ranmyden Iris when they approached it.

'Yes,' said Cedrin. Until they knew more about it, they all agreed the ancient weapon should not be used.

'We must be clear who our enemies are,' said Kalyth.

Ellen shivered. 'The Behemoth.' She was pale with cold. On her chest, the grieving scar she had cut for her father Myan stood out as a white circle against her flesh.

Cedrin signalled for the doors and windows to be closed

against the chill.

'The Behemoth and Raziin. And in the Olcis Iris the Behemoth declared its allegiance for Raziin. It wants the Northman to have the Spear,' said Kalyth.

'Yes,' said Cedrin. They had been through that night so many times now, and yet still so much was unknown.

Kalyth continued, laying out the facts. 'Raziin, we know. He is a Sorcerer, now fully trained, with perhaps little more than a dozen left of his mercenary company. That threat we can deal with. But what is the Behemoth? What can it do?'

Outside, a wash of bright yellow light announced second dawn.

Raphal cleared his throat. 'I have discussed this at length with Cedrin and Ellen, and with our noble Priestess.' He nodded congenially to Salis, who gave him a warm smile in return.

Beside Cedrin, Ellen shifted uncomfortably in her seat. Like him, she feared the Behemoth. They would be fools not to respect its dark power.

'I believe the Behemoth is a being of Earth-Essence, somehow linked to the Spear itself,' continued Raphal. 'In the Olcis Iris, it slowed the flow of time and invaded both Cedrin's and Raziin's minds.'

'How long has it been there?' asked Skye, reaching for a piece of cheese.

'There is no way of knowing,' said Marken.

Raphal's bushy white eyebrows drew together. 'There were always rumours that the Spear was cursed. Many of the early Emperors came to bad ends.'

Kalyth's face was grim. If he had his way, the Spear would be cast into the sea.

'The best documented case is Tyrellan Cinanac, the sixth Emperor. He was the first to mention the curse,' said Raphal.

'Ahh – the Mad Emperor,' said Marken.

'I see not all the lessons in the Temple went to waste,' said Raphal, giving Marken a wry smile. 'Up until Tyrellan, each Emperor used the Spear to work great feats of Sorcery. He raised the first of the Seven Bridges of Raynor. In the beginning, he was lauded as the greatest Emperor since Carris. Then the deaths began. There were rumours of blood rites. Some even spoke of a return of the Red Feast.

'The first murders were hidden, and none thought to challenge him. Then he went on a killing frenzy, slaying half his courtiers when they refused to address him as Carris.'

'Go on,' said Kalyth gravely.

'Eventually his sons – themselves powerful Sorcerers – seized the Spear. Tyrellan failed quickly after that. On his deathbed, he swore the Spear was cursed. He begged them not to use it.'

'What does this tell us?' asked Kalyth.

'That the Behemoth is old. Very old,' said Salis.

'Perhaps as old as the Spear itself,' said Raphal.

'What can it do? How can it threaten us?' prompted Kalyth. Cedrin realised it must be hard for an old warrior like Kalyth to deal in such intangibles.

'It cannot control the Spear directly. Although it chose Raziin in the Iris, it told him to wait until the Ward had given me the Spear, then seize it from me,' said Cedrin.

'It *does* seek to control the Spear,' said Ellen.

'But through Raziin,' said Salis. 'It Tested you both, and saw him as easier to master.'

Kalyth pushed a map into the centre of the table. 'So. The Spear and the Ward, which has control of Belin Kaidell, are in the Ranmyden Iris. Within a ruined Eathal city you said, Ellen?'

'Yes. Deep underground. There were wild Eathal living there. My teacher Erioth is also a prisoner of the Ward,' said Ellen.

'A Sorcerer?'

'Yes.'

'Can you remember anything else about this Iris?'

Ellen looked across to Cedrin, then took a deep breath. 'There was another being held prisoner by the Ward.'

'Being?' prompted Raphal.

'Yes. A Tahistil,' said Ellen.

Kalyth's fist tightened atop the map. 'A Great Spider?'

Skye laughed and tore a piece of bread in half. 'This just gets better.'

Cedrin had discussed this with Ellen, and they had decided together to tell everyone – despite the fact the Tahistil were considered a myth.

'I don't see the problem. Once Cedrin has the Spear and the Ward ceases to exist, Belin, Erioth and this – Tahistil – will be free – and on our side presumably,' said Marken.

'How can you know that?' snapped Kalyth. 'They may all have their own agenda.'

'Let's just focus on what's important,' said Cedrin. 'The Ward has control of the Spear. It *can* act. And the Ward is our ally. It *wants* to give me the Spear. All we have to do is make sure we reach the Ranmyden Iris before Raziin.'

'And that is the real problem, isn't it? Finding a Temple inside a ruined Eathal city no one has seen in thousands of years,' said Marken.

'That's where I might be able to help,' said Raphal. 'Or, more precisely, Valnis, a brown-robe scholar I knew from Althar. He now lives in Beslin. He has made an extensive study of the ancient Eathal and has even mounted expeditions into the Ranmyden caverns. If anyone knows its location, it will be him.'

'So nothing changes, then,' said Skye, around a mouthful of bread. 'We head to Beslin.'

'As soon as Xyanthius arrives with the One Hundred,' said Kalyth.

'Wouldn't dream of leaving without them,' said Marken dryly. Kalyth scowled at his flippant remark. Marken flashed him a smile.

'Nothing else then?' asked Cedrin.

'Veltricus is coming to meet with us later to discuss the journey north,' said Kalyth.

'Good. Thank you all.'

Kalyth, Raphal and Salis exited down the stairs to their own chambers.

Cedrin walked to the windows and looked up at Riven Peak, now shining in the clear light of Larus. He smelled Ellen's perfume and knew she had come to stand beside him. Skye and Marken were still at the table, swapping jokes. Both of his friends were relaxed. Since rejoining them on the road, Skye had returned to the upbeat, cheerful man Cedrin knew in Athria. Whatever superstitious demons had tormented Skye concerning Cedrin's Sorcery, prompting him to go his own way when they first arrived in Raynor, he had left behind him. Marken was more self-assured than ever, pleased with his new position close to the Suul.

'We really don't know what the Behemoth is capable of,' said Cedrin. 'It invaded my dreams before I even reached the Delta Iris. Inside the Olcis Iris, it took complete control. What happens when I take the Spear, Ellen?'

She looked up into his eyes and smiled. 'Then you become Emperor. Whatever power the Behemoth has, we will find some way to fight it. Together.'

'Like Tyrellan?'

Ellen laid her hand on his bare chest, covering the sixth-degree tattoo with her palm. 'Remember. It rejected you. That means it feared you. You do not have to use the Spear – just take it. Make sure Raziin cannot use it.'

His hands curled into fists. 'I'll do more than that to Raziin. I want to end him once and for all. The bastard almost killed you.'

Her hand moved to his cheek. 'But he didn't.'

Slowly the tension eased out of him.

'We still have a few hours before Veltricus arrives,' said Ellen. Her cheeks flushed red.

Cedrin grinned. 'So we do.'

Arm in arm, they walked through the room to their private chambers. Ruus and another of the One Hundred took station outside their room.

Marken had poured himself a glass of red, and toasted them as they passed.

'You keep the Empire going for me while I'm gone, boys,' said Cedrin.

Skye chuckled. 'No safer hands.'

* * *

Ellen closed her eyes, listening carefully. Nothing. Cedrin had a knack for silent movement, but she had another trick up her sleeve. She channelled the Fire in the Listening Matrix. The distant buzz of the common room below them increased to a roar like pounding surf. The quiet conversations of the guards outside boomed in her ears. *There.* A soft scuff across the polished boards of their chamber. She gripped the piece of fruit tighter in her hand and tilted her shoulder. When she saw the faint shape of a boot heel appear in the rug, she let fly.

The round fruit shot through the air, stopping with a solid *thud*.

'Argh! Not fair.' Cedrin released his hold on the Shadow Matrix, appearing three paces in front of her.

Ellen laughed lightly. Cedrin had picked up all the Matrices with impressive ease, but he was still slow at forming them. His control and manipulation of the forms was still basic.

'Didn't you think of the Barrier Matrix?' said Ellen.

'Well – yes. But trying to hold the Shadow Matrix and form the Barrier all in a split second . . .' He stooped to pick up the fruit. Suddenly his hand shot out and the fruit sped for her stomach.

Ellen opened the Window and channelled the Fire through the Force Matrix. The round fruit stopped dead and bobbed in mid-air.

'It could have just have easily have been a knife. You have to be able to use at least two Matrices at the same time – ideally three.'

Ellen made a slight change to the Force Matrix, and the fruit moved over to Cedrin and circled his head like a miniature moon.

'Show off.' He snatched the fruit out of the air before she could jerk it away. With a laugh, she released it.

Ellen took a pillow from the bed and threw it at him.

Cedrin watched it come, his face creased in concentration. At the last moment, he reached up and grabbed it with his hand. '*Uros!*'

'What happened?' asked Ellen.

'I formed the Barrier Matrix fast enough, but couldn't open the Window,' said Cedrin.

Ellen took the pillow off him and laid it on the bed. 'Enough for one day.'

'What happens if I face Raziin and cannot even reach the Fire?' he asked.

It was a problem. Cedrin had a sharp mind – Ellen had never thought anyone could learn the major Matrices so fast – but he had come to his skills late. His ability to open the Window – the mental gateway to the Fire – was inconsistent. He had to master the basics before she could begin on the Matrix variations or the hundreds of Transformation Matrices. He had to learn to focus his attention in multiple directions and hold Matrices for hours while freeing the rest of his mind.

'It will come. Keep practicing.' Ellen reached up and touched him lightly on the forehead between the eyes, where the Suul mark is placed. On Cedrin, the skin was bare. For much of his life, he believed himself a disinherited bastard. He had grown up rough on the streets of Athria – while she had been a world away – the favoured daughter of the Athrian Sarlord.

He caught her hand and kissed her palm. 'I know. One day.' Convincing him to take a Suul mark was difficult, despite the reality of his high birth.

He walked over to the corner of the room and grabbed his greatscythe. 'I think I need a little training to clear my head.'

Ellen frowned. He was probably right, but she was reluctant to let him go. Time together like this was all too rare. 'You should join the other warriors at devotions in the morning.'

'I get enough practice with Kalyth.'

'Yes – but I'm not talking about that. The Way also includes mental discipline. The meditation might help you reach the Window. It would also inspire morale for the One Hundred to have you with them.' Ellen ran a finger down the taut muscles of his chest, coming to rest on the tattoo of the Way of the Scytheman.

He leant in and kissed her slowly, passionately. Her arms snaked into his open shirt and circled his chest. She loved the smell of him, the feel of his skin. She wanted nothing more than to drag him back to bed.

'I will. Tomorrow.' He broke away, and she let her arms fall.

As they left their private chambers, Ruus and the other One Hundred warrior snapped into rigid attention. The main room was deserted, apart from two other bodyguards. Cedrin and Ellen walked through the open doors and out onto the wide roof-top balcony. The suns were high in the sky, and the city of Herath stretched out around them in a patchwork of tall stone buildings and squat square towers. The whole place had a feeling of solidity, as though it was a natural outgrowth of the Mulisar range itself. Agod-Ki rose above them, a constant presence, awesome despite its shattered peak.

Kalyth was waiting for Cedrin.

Ellen nodded to Kalyth and stopped by the rail to watch them go through their drills and combat training. Some days other warriors of the One Hundred would test Cedrin – in pairs and as multiple attackers – but today Kalyth met him alone.

The last few months had seen a major upheaval in her life. She was still banished from her native Athria, where her brother Torren ruled in her place. She idly twisted her brother's amber-coloured gem-ring around on her finger as she thought of him. It had been a surprising gift, from a man she had misjudged. He had proved both his loyalty to her and his integrity the night he helped her escape Athria. Although that had not stopped him – or her other brother Estle – from criticising her search for the Scion as a fool's quest. Now, against the odds, she had found him.

Together with the Raynor Suul Kranor, his warriors and a small group of loyal followers, they were working to restore the Cinanac line. The Eathal threatened the cities of Raynor and Olcis, fielding huge armies. Despite that, the Warlord would never give up the throne willingly. Through her brother, she could bring pressure to bear from Athria, but it would not be enough.

Somehow Cedrin had to become a power in his own right. Where could he look for allegiance? Raynor was soon to be under siege. The former provinces of the western coast? Culgriv had seized on its independence eagerly after Bulvuran's fall and had cared nothing for the first Eathal attacks on Raynor twenty-seven years ago. Hanis had been loyal, but had paid the price.

Its military strength had been all but destroyed in the fall of Husdoon. Now it was fractured, its ports ruled by upstart warlords little better than pirates. Olcis ruled Tupur, the Temple caring for nothing but its own interests. The Eathal would soon be at their throats. Exdor? A regressive backwater all but closed to the world. Armon? Last remnant of Cioan culture in Kelas, they had always seen themselves as separate. True, their Sarlord Leith Cinnor had come south to fight the Eathal in the first war – but that was a different time. Like her own father, Leith was dead. They were both men from a different age. His own son Raziin Cinnor was their sworn enemy.

Cedrin leapt and spun, narrowly avoiding Kalyth's sustained attack. He feinted forward, giving himself room to manoeuvre.

She had no doubt Cedrin would make a great Emperor. He was brilliant, compassionate and a natural leader. But even if they seized the Spear, what then? Would they return to find Raynor in flames? Kelas ground under the boot of the Eathal? Would that be enough to make the northern provinces unite? Ellen swore in frustration. The Spear of Carris was an awesome weapon. Despite what was said in council, mere possession of it may not be enough. But dare they use it?

Ellen shook her head, pushing aside the thoughts.

She had to believe they had a destiny. Somehow Cedrin would sit on throne of Bulvuran. Together they would unite Kelas and push back Hukum's Eathal armies.

Somehow.

* * *

Raziin sank to the ground, wincing at the pain of the leg wound. The ominous gloom of the ancient Thilil forest engulfed them all, even though the suns were only just past the zenith.

He had thought once he had given Faivel the slip, his path to Ranmyden and the Spear would be revealed to him by Uros. This was the north, after all. Yet the last few days had shown him just how far he was from the familiar forests of Armon. The trees were infested with winged *lamel* during the day and wild Eathal at night. Two of his men had disappeared in the darkness, leaving nothing but blood stains. Now only eight remained.

In his dreams, the Behemoth came to him like a brother. They hunted together, glorying in blood. Those dreams were sweet, like a promise.

The towering form of Merceth loomed over him. 'Orders, my Lord?'

'Post sentries. Scout the area.' The group of Iamel had come on them less than an hour ago, falling from the trees on silent wings, fighting with their sharp beaks and talons. Roughly humanoid, the winged beasts were cunning. While one group distracted them, the others drove away their amelak – and with them the last of their supplies.

The golden-skinned giant bowed and moved away. At least he and Kyal, the most senior of his lieutenants, remained.

He paused to concentrate, channelling the Fire into the Matrix of Form. A golden glow surrounded him. It flashed to brilliance and the pain vanished.

Faivel was a talented Sorcerer. When the Iamel struck, Raziin had hesitated to use the Fire, worried that the Eathal would sense it. He would not baulk again. Uros demanded blood.

Kyal came running back into the clearing and bowed.

'What is it?'

'A deserted logging camp, my Lord. Shelter.'

Raziin sprang to his feet. 'Excellent.'

He followed Kyal and the lead scouts through the narrow forest trail. As they eased into a steady lope, the rain began again, soaking them through. Soon they entered a wide, overgrown clearing. A swift stream ran through it. There were perhaps a dozen buildings, long fallen into disrepair.

'The main building will easily house us all. See what repairs you can make,' said Raziin. 'Then we can get out of this cursed rain.'

As his men busied themselves, Raziin scouted the other deserted buildings himself. Most were wooden structures, crudely made, the doors long fallen off their rotted leather hinges. They contained nothing of use. Beneath them were the foundations of much larger stone structures, long gone. To the east of the camp, beside the stream, he found an ancient temple. The Thilil forest had all but reclaimed it, but it had once been an impressive structure. It had been built in the ancient Cioan style, yet also topped with brick domes that were still intact.

On impulse, he pushed aside the walls of overhanging vegetation and squeezed inside. He channelled the Fire into the Light Matrix. A clear white light flared inside. Small animals and insects fled to the shadows. The walls were carved with scenes of tall men and women, some clearing the forests and planting crops, others battling with the grotesque, over-exaggerated forms of Eathal. Anacian. The newcomers who came to challenge the dominion of the Cioans in Kelas thousands of years ago. Even so, they knew their magic. They would not place a temple like this on anything other than holy ground.

Raziin pushed deeper into the temple chambers, looking for the inner sanctum.

Twice he had to navigate around rock falls. At last he reached the centre of structure. The largest of the domes was above him, capping a circular chamber. Here the walls were carved with scenes from the Yasser Delta far to the south – yet not as it was now – as it was before the Destruction of Carris and the fall of Ciofran-Ac.

The place was dead. Soon the rest of the Anacians would follow. Once he had the Spear, he would sacrifice them all to Uros.

Raziin felt a presence. His senses flared with alarm. The pressure in the air increased, and the chamber flooded with yellow light. It seared into his eyes. Into his mind.

He released his grip on the Light Matrix and channelled the Fire into the Barrier instead. He looked up into the fierce light, ready for anything. Had he triggered some ancient trap?

Movement.

'Who's there!' he demanded.

At first the shape was nothing more than a shadow, then it resolved into the slim form of a woman with golden skin and bronze hair streaked with crimson. His stomach tightened in fear. *The Seer*. He quickly averted his eyes.

42

'What? No greetings, kinsman?' said Marina.

Anger flared in him, but he restrained it. He knew he could not resist Marina's power.

'I went to the Olcis Iris. I did as you asked. I reached first for the power. Yet I have nothing!'

She stepped closer to him, and he felt her seductive power enfold him. He longed to stare up into her face, yet knew that his reward would be pain.

'Patience. Not even I can see all outcomes. The Behemoth chose you, did it not?'

'Yes.' The muscles of his neck bulged with the strain of resisting her.

'Even though the Ward chose the heir of Jykor?'

He remained silent, not wanting to admit that bastard half-Blood Cedrin was Riin Cinanac's son.

'Ranmyden awaits. You must not fail a second time.'

'I will triumph. Uros will give me victory.' Raziin's whole body shook. He sank to his knees, fists clenched as he forced his gaze to the dusty stone.

'With eight warriors? By the time the Scion reaches Ranmyden, he will have a small army at his back.'

'I will take the Spear,' he hissed.

'Look at me.' Her voice swelled with power. In that moment, he understood once more how useless it was to resist her – mistress of both Fire and Earth Essence. He saw the crimson irises, shot with flecks of gold, then he was swimming in an endless sea.

'*No.*'

He was nothing.

Raziin became aware of the space inside him where – something – should reside, yet he found only emptiness. Pain.

'You will turn east towards Apiloth,' commanded Marina. 'Your brother Ralin is there, travelling with a small mounted entourage. Seek his help.'

'He exiled me. He will give me nothing.'

'He will if you renounce your claim to Armon. If you swear it before Uros and all the gods of Cioa.'

'No!'

'Yes. Cedrin is no longer alone. You will need the strength of Armon to challenge him. Do this and you will sit on the Emerald Throne of Bulvuran. I have seen it!'

The blaze of her power became unbearable. *'I will.'*

She released him, and he fell to the stone, drained of energy and will. Just once he wished he could come at Marina beyond the circle of her power. Then he would show the bitch.

The Seer laughed at him.

His strength returned. Even so, he did not look up at her.

'There is an Armon patrol seven leagues north of here. They have *cavon* with them. Use the messenger birds to alert your brother to your arrival.'

The light vanished, plunging him into darkness.

The Seer was gone.

Raziin pushed himself to his feet, dusting off his leather trousers. He casually released the Fire, lighting up the temple.

It could work. His brother revelled in his power as the new Sarlord of Armon. He would do anything to thwart the rebirth of the Bulvuran Empire. Raziin could propose an alliance to destroy Cedrin, the true Scion. With a force of Armon warriors at his back, it would be he who could dictate the terms of the encounter. There were still factions loyal to Raziin in Armon. His brother would eagerly seize the chance to neutralise those factions and consolidate his hold on power. The lives of a few warriors were easily worth that prize.

He grunted with pleasure, deep in his throat.

Although he resented Marina's power, there was no doubt she was sent by the Blood Goddess herself to serve his destiny. He would reach Ranmyden, and once he had taken the Spear from Cedrin, he would destroy the Scion and Ellen Cintros – taking them apart piece by piece. The first offerings to christen his new Cioan Empire.

His brother could keep the Armon throne. He – along with every other leader in Kelas – would bend their knee to him once he had the Spear.

Chapter Three

Daran signed the dispatch and pushed it across his field desk. His aide dusted the ink with sand and shook it off. The Suulqua dribbled a blob of red sealing wax onto the parchment and slid it back across the desk. He pushed his signet ring into the wax.

'Should I add the usual salutations, my Lord?'

'Yes. Yes. Warlord of the Yasser States, Lord of Raynor, defender of the Emerald Throne and so on.' The aide bowed and exited.

Daran reached for a glass of water and drained it. The atmosphere inside his field tent was oppressive, and the oil-lamps did little to dispel the gloom. He cursed his lack of foresight in not bringing the excellent reading glowmetals he had in his private chambers in Raynor. They would be of much more use here than eighty leagues away. He made a mental note to have them sent. Cooling the space would be a simple matter of raising the pavilion walls, but then Hukum's scouts would be able to tell it apart from the numerous decoys placed across the battle camp.

The light inside the tent rose as the Sorcerer Uran entered through the flap.

'Ah. Uran. What news of the attack?' Daran's own two sons led the advance attacks. Both were talented warriors skilled in strategy, and both were eager to show their worth.

'The Yellow Drakon are disciplined. They repulsed the first attacks easily, using heavy shields and stabbing spears.' The Sorcerer dabbed at his face with a cloth. The Cioan had cut his golden hair short for the campaign. He was focussed as always, his silver eyes serious. He sat opposite Daran and poured himself a glass of the tepid water. They had both known each other too long to stand on ceremony.

'Yes. We must find some way of breaking their advance formations. Go on.'

'They have revealed their offensive glowmetal. It releases a directed Force that sweeps across the ground. It played havoc with our cavalry. It's sphere of effect is narrow, thankfully. I would rate it as low power.'

'Excellent, Uran. How is it recharged?'

'Larus Essence. Our Druidin were in a good position to observe their Druids working on the glowmetal to restore its power.'

'Good. Good.' Daran hesitated to ask about his sons. He did not want to appear to favour them. 'And casualties?'

'Minimal. Both your sons are well,' said Uran, smiling. The man knew him too well.

'And the Eathal General?'

'The Sorcerer-Lord who leads the Yellow is well trained, but certainly no more than competent.'

Daran leant back in his chair. Hukum pressed at them with five full Eathal legions – three of them the elite Drakon legions.

'So there is nothing in the Yellow's arsenal that will threaten the Raptor?' Their flying platform, the Raptor, was Uran's brilliant invention. As yet, it was unproven in war.

'No.'

'Excellent.' They needed every advantage they had.

'Hukum is taking no chances. His approach is careful. Methodical. He is consolidating his supply lines and entrenching as he comes.' Uran stopped short of saying what they were both thinking. His true magical strength was still unknown. If his legions reached Raynor . . .

Uran drained his glass and set it down carefully on the table. Then he reached to his belt and drew out a small parchment. Daran's eyes narrowed. From its size he knew it was from a cavon capsule, the tiny tube that messenger birds gripped in their foreclaws. 'News from Herath.'

'Herath?'

'A new Scion has appeared,' said Uran.

'Now?' Daran was incredulous. What idiot pretender would try their luck at Raynor with the Eathal almost at their throats?

'Yes. His name is Cedrin. A former calvanni from Athria.'

'Gods above! What's next? A grocer?'

'It gets worse. Kranor has come out in support. Salis is with this Cedrin as we speak.'

A deep unease settled into the pit of his stomach. Kranor was no fool – far from it. 'This one must be convincing.'

'Yes. And guess who else is with him?'

Daran suppressed a surge of anger. 'No more guessing games, Uran. Tell me.'

'Ellen Cintros. In fact, she appears to be his lover. Not only that. Raphal – the Priest and Moon Druid Ellen rescued – is also with them.' Uran swallowed. 'His supporters are like a who's who of the old guard. Kalyth Orin is leading his warriors.'

'I thought he was dead,' said Daran.

'So did I. Kranor has reformed the One Hundred. Soon this Cedrin will be surrounded by the finest warriors in Kelas – and all completely loyal. Even Osterac has joined him. He delivered the Cinanac ring.'

Daran slammed his fist onto his field desk. He felt the wood crack under his hand. 'Who do we have at Herath?'

'Only informants. But Rehvar is at Olcis, still digging into Osterac's past.' Uran paused.

Rehvar was one of their first Druidin and completely loyal. He was adept with both Sun and Moon Essences and was a master of concealment and deception. He was also Daran's most formidable assassin. 'Dispatch him immediately.'

Uran licked his lips. 'Your orders?'

Daran took a breath and released it slowly. He had not retained his position of power in Raynor by making rash decisions. 'For now he is to only observe and report.'

'It will be done.' Uran rose and turned to leave.

'Uran.'

'Yes, my Lord.'

'Make sure he is close enough to strike.'

Uran bowed and exited.

Osterac! That fool. Daran had warned him. This time there would be no second chances. As for the false-Scion: a calvanni? A street thug?

'Bring me wine!' called Daran. It would soon be time to break camp. They had to be on the move back towards Raynor before nightfall, keeping just ahead of Hukum's advance. By dawn they would have taken position again, ready to test and sting the Eathal. Soon they would have learned enough about the leading Eathal legions to strike back.

One of his servants poured a glass and placed it gently before him. He sipped on the heavy, dry red, letting it slip down his throat and ease his tension.

The Yasser States was falling – piece by piece. Already the harena were gathering to fight over the corpse. Refugees had been flooding to Raynor from North Yasser since Storm Season. He could not afford to let them into overcrowded Raynor, passing them across the Asgod to the Delta province instead. Now a new wave had arrived from southern Tupur, driven before the advancing Eathal. He knew from the reports of his scouts that these men and women were those lucky enough to escape. A far greater number had been taken by the Eathal as slaves. His people were dying, and his cities burned, while the Eathal conquered, revealing a strength not even he and Uran could have guessed at. Their attack on Raynor twenty-seven years ago was nothing more than a feint by comparison. That awesome battle had only been won by chance, inspired strategy and the support of the Armon and Athrian legions – as well as the magical strength of Myan Cintros and Leith Cinnor. Now Ralin Cinnor answered his pleas with silence. Athria, increasingly on the defensive against pirates, offered little more than food and supplies, and the rest of Kelas sat back to watch them fall.

'Short-sighed fools.' He downed the glass and held it out to be refilled. Where did they think the Eathal were going to turn next? Without the might of Raynor standing in their path, the Eathal would take it all.

* * *

Cedrin landed softly in the shadows. He pulled the hood of his cloak down over his face and waited. Soon a dark shape slid out of a window. The figure slipped down the outside wall, moving silently between handholds to drop beside him. He grinned as he recognised Skye's squat shape.

A warrior appeared above. They both froze. Vess. He had taken station on the roof tonight. A moment later he was gone.

Skye waved. Marken exited the same window.

As soon as Marken reached the street, they started to move, weaving between shadows as they left the inn behind them.

When Cedrin judged them far enough away, he stopped in an alleyway and turned to his friends. He gripped arms with Skye and laughed, pounding him on the back, then greeted Marken the same way.

'So you got my message,' said Cedrin. After the last meeting with Veltricus, he had given Skye a message using Brotherhood hand-sign to meet on the street an hour after sunset. Rea, just past full, would not rise for two hours, while Asic's waning crescent would not crest the eastern horizon until the early hours of the morning. A perfect night for calvanni. He had even managed to give the wiley Bovosan the slip. The mysterious minitil was not allowed close to Cedrin by the One Hundred. He now had to content himself with watching his master from a distance.

Skye rolled his eyes. 'Could you have been any more obvious? I'm surprised Kalyth wasn't waiting for us with half the One Hundred.'

'As if Kalyth would know Brotherhood hand-sign,' said Cedrin. 'Slipping you a note would have been worse – like hanging out a sign.'

'He will have a fit if he finds out,' said Marken, his eyes lit with excitement.

'Well. Let's not waste any more time. We need to get back before the shift changes.'

'Where to?' asked Skye.

'Well – we can't exactly go to the docks district,' said Cedrin. For three men who had grown up in the great port city of

Athria, a place with no harbour seemed unnatural.

'Let's just follow our ears,' said Skye.

They moved silently through Herath. Much of the outer city was comprised of warehouses, strangely quiet in the night. Other sections were walled compounds, heavily patrolled. What inns they passed were silent. There was little that was ostentatious about Herath, yet everything was solidly built from the finest materials. The cobbles were even, the streets clean, the gutters well-laid in stone. Far neater than the twisting alleys of Raynor with their uneven cobbles and dirt verges. Perhaps it was different inside the Palastrada, where the Raynor Suul dwelled. He and Marken had never seen that.

Eventually they neared the centre of Herath. Here there was another wall enclosing the private enclave of the House of Herath. The wall itself was constructed of massive blocks of granite and the mought-bound gates were shut. In any other city, this would be the Suul district. Here it was reserved for a single family. Seeing it with his own eyes, Cedrin truly understood the wealth and power of the Cineth.

'No visitors after dark then,' said Marken.

Cedrin frowned. He had never seen a city with such high security. Veltricus and his family, despite presenting themselves as nothing more than traders, ruled Herath with a heavy hand. Justice here was swift and final, the city guard well trained and equipped – and evident everywhere. Veltricus had been more than accommodating in meeting with them – yet not once had he invited them into the Herath stronghold. Kalyth had tried to buy an informant inside the Herath enclave, but their overtures had been rebuffed by even the lowest servants. It appeared many held hereditary positions, and each was marked with the same stylised 'N' tattoo – the sigil of Cineth. There were other related tattoos that appeared to mark levels of initiation into some order, but so far they had not been able to get any information.

There were many secrets in Herath.

They circled the inner city, moving a few streets back from the wall. It was crowded and brightly lit with lamps on tall ornately-cast mought posts. This was the finest district they had seen so far. The houses were small palaces, four to five stories tall, the inns and eating houses luxurious.

'I knew there had to be life somewhere in this dry-docked town,' said Skye.

Marken swept back his hood and shook his golden hair loose. His golden Cioan skin and hair did not draw a single glance. Herath was a trading town, the crowd mixed. Cedrin and Skye kept their hoods down as they moved through the crowd. Ellen had been furious when he told her of his plan to slip away with his friends. She had made him swear he would take no unnecessary risks. It seemed Kalyth's paranoia of assassination had infected her as well. The Scion! He was grateful for the loyalty of Kalyth and Kranor's men, but he was lord of nothing yet. The constant presence of the bodyguards chaffed at him. Then the food tasting! He doubted Daran himself was half as well protected.

They reached a lively tavern on the street north of the Herath enclave wall. The crowd was a mix of traders and off-duty caravan guards, with a few local guardsmen keeping a watchful eye.

Skye and Marken looked across at Cedrin in question.

'As good as any,' he said.

They threw back their cloaks and hoods, showing their tattoos and freeing the leather chest-harnesses where their calvs were sheathed.

They walked up a short flight of steps into the tavern, scanning the tattoos of the men and women with interest, as they in turn were assessed. In Kelas, history and honour were written in ink. Nothing started a bar-fight quicker than refusing to bare your chest.

The crowd was loud and buzzed with talk. All fuelled by drink.

Skye rubbed his palms together in anticipation. 'We have some catching up to do!'

They squeezed into a space by the bar and waited to order. Finally they moved away to find a table armed with a jug of ale and a bottle of fine bakta. Kranor had made the resources of his organisation available to Cedrin. He had never been so flush with coin. Kranor and Salis had investments and property all over Kelas.

'Hey, look there!' said Skye. No sooner had the blond calvanni pointed than he changed direction, heading for a table full of women who had room to spare.

'Ah, Skye . . .' *Trust him to leap in.* If there was space left at a table in a crowded inn there was usually a reason. A good reason. He tried to stop him, but by then it was too late.

'Evening, ladies!' called Skye, setting down a battle of bakta and glasses on the table. Marken followed, just behind him.

It was then that Cedrin noticed the greatscythes that leant against their knees. The women were dressed identically in leather trousers and open shirts styled to just cover the nipples of their breasts, allowing the honour marks to show. Warrior marks. Each had the Way, as well as a stylised phoenix with the number IX worked into it.

A lean, rangy woman stood up and glared at Skye. 'What do you think you are doing?' Her dark hair was tied back in a single tail. As she put her hands on her hips, her shirt opened to reveal small, pointed breasts, the nipples pierced with coloured mought.

'Joining a group of beauties,' said Skye, sitting down.

Marken threw aside his cloak with a flourish, revealing his fine clothes. He gave them a dazzling smile. 'We apologise for the intrusion, ladies. Do you mind if we join you?'

The women looked back to the standing woman. Cedrin had the distinct feeling they were waiting for orders. *The leader then.*

Cedrin took off his cloak and stepped into the light.

'You and your boyfriend can suck my —' When the dark-haired woman saw Cedrin she froze, her mouth open mid-curse. Her eyes flicked down to the phoenix tattoo, then back across to Marken. Both of them had taken Kranor's mark – a fierce phoenix clutching a greatscythe in its talons, both blades extended. Her eyes searched him, looking for weapons. No. A greatscythe. *She knew Kranor's mark.* Cedrin had asked that they leave the field weapons behind tonight. He needed a simple night together as calvanni unburdened by duty.

The woman remained silent as Cedrin stepped up to the

table, balancing the jug of ale. As she looked up at him, a flush of red appeared on her cheeks.

'We don't want any trouble,' said Cedrin. 'Perhaps we should leave you to your drinks?' He tried to get Skye's attention, but the idiot was already pouring glasses of bakta, sliding them across the table to the women with a wink. They sat there untouched, each warrior waiting for a signal from their commander.

The lean woman cleared her throat. 'Maybe I was a little hasty.'

A thickset woman seated beside her frowned. Cedrin blinked. She had the biggest biceps he had seen on a woman. If it came to an arm-wrestle between her and any one of the One Hundred, he would place his coin on her.

'You sure, Spider?' asked the thickset woman.

'Make room there, Jeth,' replied the tall, dark-haired commander, waving her aside.

Cedrin shrugged his shoulders and sat down. At the other end of the table, the female warriors had taken Spider's invitation as a positive signal and had accepted Skye's drinks. The women leant back in their seats, relaxing noticeably.

Cedrin poured himself a cup of beer and passed another to Spider. Closer now, he could see that the phoenix in her tattoo was shedding a single tear. Spider had pierced the skin there, and a diamond glittered from inside the tear. The totem on her left cheek was a simple leaf.

'What brings you to Herath?' asked Cedrin.

Spider's glance slid down across his muscled chest, and she gave him a wry grin. 'No questions, eh?'

'I can drink to that,' he said, raising his glass. At the other end of the table, Skye and Marken's natural charm was drawing out the tense warriors. Whatever duty they were on, they must feel it keenly. If he had to guess, he would say they were some form of bodyguard, their client sleeping in the rooms above the tavern. Perhaps waiting for an audience with the House of Herath. He hoped they were patient.

Spider downed her cup in two swallows and reached across to re-fill it. She was not shy. The muscles of her chest and abdomen rippled as she moved. Her height had at first made her seem lightly muscled, but closer he could see she was lean rather than slight. With her long limbs, he could see how she earned the nickname 'Spider'.

She reached across and ran a calloused palm down his calvanni tattoos. 'What are these?' Her voice was brash and husky. Her fingers traced the marks that showed them as an honoured former path. He was acutely aware of how close her hand was to the handle of his calvs. He leant back and pointed at her phoenix tattoo, giving himself distance. 'One for one. You tell me what that is.'

'Hey. I said no questions,' said Spider, her dark eyes fierce. Beside him, Jeth's hand fell to the haft of her greatscythe. Her eyes lit with anticipation. Uros! These women were jumpy.

He smiled. 'You started it.'

Spider let out a breath. 'You're right.' She turned to Jeth and shook her head slightly. The hand moved away from the greatscythe.

'OK. That's the mark of the Daughters,' said Spider.

Jeth grimaced, clearly not impressed Spider was giving away their secrets.

'Daughters?'

'The Daughters of the Ninth, out of Thanir,' said Spider.

Thanir was city in northern Hanis, one of the few that had not been taken over by the pirate-warlords.

'Formed by the daughters of men who fell at Husdoon with the Hanis Ninth.'

Four of the legions of Bulvuran had been shattered at the fall of Husdoon. The city had once been the eastern jewel of the Bulvuran Empire. The Meadrel horde had wiped it off the map. A blow from which the Empire had never recovered. His father Riin was fleeing Husdoon's fall when he was ambushed and slain.

'Something we have in common then,' said Cedrin.

'What do you mean?' demanded Spider. He should have said nothing.

'My father died after Husdoon – trying to reach Raynor.'

Jeth snorted in derision. 'A coward then. Running. Our folk

died there. Died to the last for the Empire!' Her outburst had drawn attention. Heads turned in their direction.

'Silence,' snapped Spider. A rigid tension went through the group of women. Once more they were ready. He recognised it now. Discipline. These women were elite warriors, from a line of elite warriors. They could be armed in a heartbeat and would kill without the slightest hesitation.

'He was doing his duty,' said Cedrin in a level voice.

Jeth gritted her teeth and glared at him.

Spider gave a discreet hand signal and the women relaxed once more.

Spider's hand swept out. He moved in response, instinctively ready to block an attack or bat her hand away from the handles of his calvs. He stopped when he saw she was only extending her finger. She ground it into the sixth degree on his chest, the sharp nail almost drawing blood.

'Your turn,' said Spider, her dark eyes intense.

'They are Brotherhood marks,' said Cedrin.

'I knew it!' said Jeth. 'Harena-loving assassins.'

'Calvanni,' said Cedrin, challenging them both. He was not about to discuss Brotherhood politics.

'Have a drink and shut up, Jeth,' said Spider.

Spider downed a shot of bakta and laid a hand on his knee. 'Let's arm wrestle for the next question. Winner asks anything.'

Cedrin looked back at Skye and Marken. Both were in animated conversation. 'Very well.'

'You call it, Jeth.'

Feeling slightly ridiculous, he gripped hands with Spider. Her grip was like a band of cast mought.

'Go!'

Cedrin matched her, then slowly pulled his hand down and towards him. There was a real technique to an arm-wrestle, and he had his share in the taverns of Athria. Although she was impressively muscled for a woman, she was no match for his physique. He gradually pushed her closer to the rough wooden table. Then, without warning, she leant across and kissed him on the mouth. Her lips were soft and full. Her tongue darted in between his lips.

He pulled back in surprise, loosing his grip. A moment later, she slammed his hand down on the boards.

The women hooted and laughed, giving cat-calls and whistling. At the other end of the table, Skye and Marken's mouths were open in surprise.

Spider's eyes gleamed in triumph. She touched her lips with a finger. 'Hmmn. You are a sweet boy.'

Cedrin burst out laughing. That's what he got for playing a new game. He had to get out of here before he was eaten alive.

Spider pointed at Kranor's tattoo and the Way of the Scytheman. 'Where is your greatscythe?'

He sobered. 'Back in our rooms.'

She shook her head. 'Your Captain would roast you alive if he caught you without your weapons. Playing truant?'

'Something like that,' said Cedrin.

'Here on a caravan?' asked Spider.

'That's a second question. Want another arm-wrestle?'

Spider's eyes lit up. 'Did you like the kiss?'

Cedrin did not trust himself to speak.

She slid her hand up his thigh, and he felt himself respond. 'If you liked the kiss, you can have more,' she whispered in her husky, seductive voice. 'I have a room upstairs we can use.' Her hand slid further, resting on his groin. He stiffened beneath her teasing fingers.

He pushed aside her hand, fighting against the physical reaction. Only months ago, he would have slid happily into her arms. He liked her passion. The touch of her skin and her lips registered deep in his gut, firing his blood against his will.

'No. Thank you, though. We have to be getting back . . . we have the next shift.' Her face fell with disappointment, then flashed with anger.

'Piss off then. Athrian cocksucker!' Underneath her bravado, Cedrin could see she was genuinely cut. Spider liked him.

Cedrin surged to his feet. The whole encounter had been like a whirlwind to disaster.

'Boys? Maybe we should go, eh?'

The women talking with Skye and Marken seemed disappointed. Despite Skye's carefree manner, he had knack for

56

knowing which way the wind blew. He and Marken bowed and said their goodbyes. The three of them slipped through the crowd and back to the bar.

'Uros. I need a drink.' Cedrin disliked things out of his control, and Spider's brash ways had thrown him.

'What happened?' asked Marken.

'She came on strong. She wanted to bed me.'

'I don't see the problem,' said Skye with a wink.

Cedrin sighed.

'Take it easy. We know you are a committed man now,' said Skye. 'Come on – we still have hours before Rea reaches the summit.'

They talked and swapped jokes, drinking steadily. Gradually Cedrin relaxed.

'Never seen a group of female mercenaries before,' said Skye.

'They weren't. They are some sort of Hanis military unit. Daughters of the Ninth,' said Cedrin.

'I think I have heard of them,' said Marken. 'They were formed as a bodyguard for the wife of the old Governor when he fell with his legion at Husdoon. She took control of Hanis as Sarla after his death.'

'Little good she did them,' said Skye.

Marken shrugged. 'She had a whole Sardom to rule – and no troops to rule it with. Little wonder the warlords took the ports of Swebas and Leygen. Cursed pirates.'

Cedrin downed the last of his drink. 'I think we should be heading back. Kalyth wants to convene the court early tomorrow. Some western contact of Kranor's wants to meet.'

They left the tavern and hurried into the backstreets, quickly leaving the crowded precinct near the inner city wall. Rea had risen, the moonlight clear and bright from a cloudless sky. Faces looked bright in the night and they pulled their cloaks around them, hiding their faces beneath hoods as they slipped through the city. It was a familiar game. In Athria, being found on the streets after dark by the Nightwatch invited question, even arrest. They were all skilled at evasion.

Back at their inn, Cedrin watched them both disappear into the window of their room, then set about the climb himself. He was looking forward to sinking into bed beside Ellen, snatching a few hours of sleep before the pre-dawn devotions of the Way. Just below the lip of the balcony, one of the One Hundred passed above. He leant back against the rough wall, fingers wedged into a gap, weight supported on a tiny lintel stone. When the warrior passed, he levered himself over the wooden rail.

Then he walked casually across the roof.

Vess saw him and reacted instantly. His greatscythe swung up, both blades snapping into place as he closed on him. He stopped short as he recognised his face in the moonlight.

'My Lord. You move quietly. I did not hear you exit the doors.'

'Just getting some air,' said Cedrin, conscious he must smell of tavern smoke and ale.

Vess bowed and moved back to his rounds. Suddenly the whole adventure seemed foolish. There were men who relied on him, men who were willing to lay down their lives for him. His reward to them was deceit. They deserved better.

He touched his mouth, remembering Spider's soft, full lips. The wet warmth of her tongue. Her passion.

Ellen deserved better.

Chapter Four

Ellen adjusted the fall of Cedrin's new, jewelled harness. He still insisted on wearing the twin calvs, even though the best blades in Kelas now protected him. Marken was resplendent in a fine shirt of sky blue silk. Even Skye looked more like a courtier than the down-to-earth calvanni he was. He chatted easily with Salis Cintor, who looked elegant in a gown of creamy silk. *What an unlikely pair they make.*

'It's fine,' said Cedrin.

She smiled up at him, tall and handsome. She'd had a dozen new outfits made for him by Herath tailors. The shirt he wore was of the thinnest weave, yellow and olive with a golden thread that caught the light.

She looked around the room – one final check before the Hanis delegation arrived. They had hired the whole inn for the day, turning the common room into a public court. The first court of the Scion. Her only regret was that Xyanthius and the rest of the One Hundred had not yet arrived.

Kalyth and the warriors of the One Hundred were dressed in freshly laundered clothes, all their gear neatly trimmed, chests oiled to gleam in the lamplight. They stood in two lines, one down each side of the room, and looked fearsome and proud. Osterac stood out in their ranks like a brightly-feathered bird. His outfit rivalled Cedrin's, and he was the very image of a noble Suul. He was unhappy at being placed so far from the dais, but that was a matter for Kalyth. The warriors of the One Hundred took their ranks seriously. Despite being a Suul, Osterac was a newcomer who had yet to prove himself in their eyes. The others had worked their way up through Kranor's ranks over more than a decade of dedication. The first time she met Osterac in Daran's public court, he dismissed her without a thought, his eyes set on cheating his way to the Cinanac throne. Now he was no more than a warrior in her lover's bodyguard and treated her with deference.

'You look stunning,' said Cedrin.

Her heart beat fast. For the first time since Raynor, she had dressed as a Suul in a full court gown of forest green, her hair expertly braided by hired servants. She knew the colour brought out her eyes. She had purchased new jewellery with the hidden wealth she had brought from Athria and revelled in the chance to wear it.

'You look like an Emperor,' she said.

'I will need a few more armies before I can call myself that.' His grey-blue eyes clouded over. He looked drawn, tired from his nocturnal adventure in Herath. She had not slept a moment last night, lying awake waiting for him. Her instinct had been to stop him – even if it meant telling Kalyth – but she did not want to break the trust between them. Her belly fluttered at the memory of their early-morning lovemaking. He had been *very* attentive.

She touched his smooth cheek, her fingers coming to rest where the Suul mark would have been.

'I know. I should have a Suul mark.'

A warmth spread through her at the contact. 'You don't need a Suul mark. You are the noblest man I known.'

He lifted her hand and kissed it. A rare public display for the taciturn former calvanni.

Ruus ran over to them and bowed. Ellen liked the man. Of Anacian stock, he was skilled and intelligent. He had the potential to rise far – perhaps even to Suul.

'The Hanis delegation is approaching, my Lord.'

'Thanks, Ruus.'

Ellen clapped her hands. 'Everybody in place!'

She signalled to the serving men. The tavern owner himself waved back. He had the arrangements in hand. Salis touched Skye lightly on the shoulder in parting and moved up onto the dais.

'You know the only people who aren't where they are supposed to be are us,' said Cedrin with wry grin.

Ellen's eyes swept the room again, and she realised he was right. She had been at this all morning, driven by a restless energy.

They walked back up onto the dais and sat down together on a set of plain chairs. Ellen had tried for something a little more ornate, but that was pushing Cedrin too far.

Cedrin sat in the centre, with her to his right. Kalyth sat to Cedrin's left, Salis beside him.

Vess was the most senior member of the One Hundred present. The short, powerful half-Meadrel stood below the dais on the left, the scar down the right side of his face giving him a fearsome appearance. Marken and Skye stood off to the right, behind the warriors of the One Hundred.

The doors of the common room opened and a young Suul entered, flanked by two lines of warriors. Ellen had to blink twice before she realised the bodyguard that surrounded her were all women – every last one of them. Beside her, Cedrin tensed, his eyes fixed on the approaching delegation. He looked across to Skye and Marken, who seemed shocked. Surely female warriors were not so outrageous?

Ellen returned her gaze to the Suul. At first she thought she was short, then with a jolt of surprise Ellen realised she was little more than a girl. She was pale, thin and doughy-faced, with slightly protruding, light-green eyes. The ink of her totem tattoo – a simple leaf – was so fresh the bruise was still there beneath it. She could be no more than thirteen, perhaps fourteen.

The Suul's bodyguard were dressed immaculately in red leather trousers and shirts of blinding white. Each of the thirty female warriors held a greatscythe upright in their right hand at a precise angle. The effect was impressive. She wondered if they could fight as well as they could drill. Their physiques were certainly peerless.

They stopped some seven paces from the dais. The commander of the bodyguard, a lean, dark-haired woman whose body rippled with taut muscle, stepped forward from her position at the Suul's right.

'My Lord!' said the bodyguard commander, looking at Cedrin directly for the first time. Her eyes widened. There was a moment of silence that stretched overlong. The Suul's brow furrowed, and she gave the female warrior a sideways glance. Another of the bodyguard, a warrior with huge biceps who stood on the Suul's left, looked between her commander and Cedrin, her face ashen. Kalyth frowned. Salis looked between the bodyguard and Cedrin and opened her mouth slightly, as though to say something. Ellen felt the frisson of Earth Essence as Salis applied her gifts.

Cedrin's hands had curled into fists. She longed to touch him, to tell him just to relax, but she forced herself to remain completely still. It was not such a great breach in etiquette. Ellen presented a pleasant countenance.

'My Lord. May I present Thenia Cinlos, daughter of the Sarla of Hend, and Sarqua of the Sardom of Hend.'

'Thank you, Spider,' said the Suul in a high clear voice. *Heir to the Hanis throne.* She came forward a step. Although young, she was self-assured.

'You are most welcome,' said Cedrin, his voice easily filling the room. Ellen felt a chill down her spine. Something happened when Cedrin addressed a crowd. He seemed to grow. To glow. He truly was Riin's son. And he was hers.

'It must have been a tiring journey,' he said, signalling for the refreshments to be brought out.

'Thenia. Lovely to see you again,' said Salis. 'Your mother is well?'

'Yes. Very well. Thank you,' said the young Suul. She smiled warmly at Salis, and it was obvious they shared a bond.

'Kranor and I have been regular visitors in Thanir over the years,' explained Salis. It had been Kranor who had brokered this meeting. He maintained a network of contacts all over Kelas. Supporters of the old regime and others sympathetic to the Cinanac.

The truth was that little remained of the old order in Hanis. Thenia's mother controlled the port-city of Thanir and the farmland between the city and mountains that bordered on Exdor. The rest of the former Hanis province was largely lawless, the major cities controlled by pirate-warlords.

Thenia waved away the offered trays of sweetmeats and drinks.

Both Spider and the other lead warrior of Hanis bodyguard continued to stare at Cedrin with wide eyes. Thenia was oblivious to their reaction. The young Suul was completely at ease.

'What brings you to the court of the Scion, Suul Cinlos?' asked Cedrin.

Thenia walked to the dais and sank to her knees. 'I have come on behalf of my mother to swear allegiance to the Cinanac throne. I pledge Hanis to the cause of the phoenix.'

Kalyth and Ellen exchanged a quick glance. Even Salis was surprised.

Cedrin stepped down from the dais. 'I accept your allegiance. Rise – as a friend of the Scion.'

Ellen, Salis and Kalyth quickly rose and followed him off the dais. The four of them crowded around Thenia.

'Kranor's last dispatch mentioned your plan to travel north, my Lord,' said Thenia.

'Yes. As soon as Xyanthius arrives with the rest of the One Hundred.'

'Then let us join you,' said Thenia, waving at the warriors behind her. 'The Daughters of the Ninth are a formidable force, I assure you.'

Cedrin's brow creased, and he hesitated. No doubt he was trying to digest this new development.

'A welcome offer. Be assured you will be included in our councils,' said Ellen.

'Perhaps you could return later for a more informal dinner in the Scion's private court?' suggested Salis. Cedrin nodded his assent.

'Excellent. We shall return in the hour after dusk,' said Thenia, bowing. 'Until then, my Lord.'

Thenia waved to Spider.

A thrill of excitement shot through Ellen. She leant towards

Cedrin, wrapping her arm around his. The Hanis bodyguard commander met her gaze for a moment, her eyes flashing with a vicious anger. The force of it was like a blow. Then she was gone, marching out of the room with Thenia and the Daughters. *What was that about?*

Kalyth waved Vess over.

'Yes, Captain.'

'Tell the men to relax. Well done, Vess. They looked good.'

'Thank you, sir.'

Excited, Ellen grabbed Cedrin in a hug. 'You did it! Our first sworn allegiance.'

'I can't take credit for that,' he said, turning to Salis. 'Was this Kranor's work?'

Salis shook her head. 'In a way. We have kept contact with Thenia's mother since the fall of Bulvuran. They were among the first we told when you were found. Kranor and I did nothing more than try to arrange a meeting. The rest . . . If I had to guess, I would say it was Thenia's idea.'

'That child?' said Kalyth.

Salis smiled warmly at the old warrior.

'She is heir to a single city. That is a far cry from a Sardom or a province. What army can Hanis field?' said Kalyth.

'Do not underestimate Thenia. She is a very bright child. No. *Young woman.*'

'The ink on her totem is hardly dry,' said Kalyth.

'Just listen to her. She may surprise you,' said Salis.

Skye and Marken walked over to them.

'With your leave, my Lord.' Kalyth bowed and moved away, followed by Salis.

'How about that bodyguard, eh? Bit of a surprise,' said Skye.

'You can say that again,' said Cedrin, dabbing at his brow with a handkerchief.

Skye smacked his lips. 'So when do we get to eat the food?'

'And no point letting all that fine vintage go to waste,' chipped in Marken.

'Isn't it a little early for drinking?' said Cedrin.

Ellen felt giddy with the success. 'Nonsense. Let's celebrate.'

Skye gripped Cedrin's arm. 'Remember the best hangover

cure is a good feed . . .'

'And more drink,' said Skye and Marken together.

Cedrin shook his head and laughed. It was good to hear the sound.

They had much to do. All over Kelas there must be Suul like Thenia, just waiting to join with them. She looked up at Cedrin, her heart swelling with joy. Together they could do it.

* * *

Esmelle paused at the threshold of the Outer Temple, taking a moment to restore her mental focus. The power of Anan-Ac swept through her in a wave of Earth Essence. She had not been back to the mother-Temple since the end of her novitiate, when she shed her old life and took the robes of a full Priestess. She had forgotten the sheer intensity of the power. Now she was here to appear before Kelvoss himself.

'Compose yourself, Priestess. We are not even inside the outer chambers,' said one of the two Priests who were escorting her into Kelvoss' presence.

She turned her gaze on the Priest who had spoken. He was senior aide to Kelvoss, squat and toad-faced, unimpressive despite the magnificent vestments. The other was tall and austere. Esmelle enhanced her senses. Around her, the Unseen leapt into view. The Earth Essence appeared as a gentle golden light suffusing the marble-lined vestibule. It flowed around both senior Priests, not through them. *Neither can sense the flow.* No doubt they considered her sensitivity a weakness.

'Lead on, Worthiness,' said Esmelle.

The summons had come as a surprise. At the end of her training, she and three others had been identified as having a special talent for sensing the flow and nature of Earth Essence. She had been sent to the Temple of the Twins seven leagues west of Anan-Ac. A small temple, yet one of the few that had a magical portal. She had learned the secrets of it from the aging Priestess of the Twins. When the blessed ancient passed from the world, she herself became Chief Priestess. A quiet and simple life. Despite the existence of the portal, the reputation of the Twins had been build on healing. Men and women travelled hundreds of leagues to reach them from the isolated Thilil settlements within the sphere of Anan-Ac.

They entered the Outer Temple, passing through the vast public space. Hundreds of worshippers gathered there, silent clergy moving among them to aid in their devotions. It was dimly lit, the air redolent with fine incense. To her senses, it blazed.

The Earth Essence grew rapidly.

As they approached the Inner Temple, both Priests become aware of it. They weaved the flow into mental shields, protecting their thoughts. Such defensive measures hardly inspired trust.

The Inner Temple was familiar. Here the chosen of Anan-Ac would gather to worship – and to weave magic. It was divided into hundreds of chambers, some for living and study, others for communal worship. The largest of the chambers echoed the design of the Outer Temple, a wide space where all could gather, albeit on a smaller scale.

The Priests led her deeper into the mother-Temple than Esmelle had ever been. The force of the Earth Essence blazed around her. Visions swept across the edges of her sight as fragments of her mind were swept into the future and back on its surging tide. She gasped and steadied herself against a wall. The cool solidity of the dark marble helped her to focus.

'By, Larus. Is she really the best choice for this?' asked the tall Priest.

'Kelvoss has spoken,' replied the squat Priest. 'And awaits us.' The last was spoken for her benefit.

Esmelle tasted the Essence of the mother-temple on her tongue. It filled her. She longed to plumb its depths, to fully come to know it. It was then she understood how her own gifts had flowered. Instead she dimmed her senses.

'I will not falter again,' said Esmelle.

Without a word, they led her on. Twice more she was forced to dull her powers, then finally she too was forced to create a mental barrier against the flow.

They came to a set of carved wooden doors, painted with

gold. Two Temple Guardians stood sentry outside it.

The squat Priest nodded at the guards. They bowed and pushed the doors inward.

The intensity of power increased to a physical pressure. Earth Essence surged around her, battering against her mental shield. They were at the very centre of Anan-Ac. Above them was the central dome of the holy-of-holies, the Inner Sanctum. The circular space was ringed with double doors, all identical to the one that they had just passed through.

A dais had been placed on the gleaming white marble floor, directly below the apex of the dome.

And a throne.

Esmelle drew in a sharp breath. *Kelvoss*.

Kelvoss of Anan-Ac was a big man, his large frame engulfed by rich vestments of red and gold. His face was terribly pale, yet his deep-blue eyes were bright with the Essence, the colour enhanced against his white skin. His lips were thick, a stark ruby red. For a moment she thought they had been smeared with paste, but then realised it was merely the contrast between them and his bloodless countenance.

'Your Eminence,' said Esmelle, prostrating herself.

'Rise,' said Kelvoss. His voice was powerful and charismatic.

Esmelle stood slowly, careful to protect herself against the power battering against her. As she looked up at Kelvoss, she felt a tremor of fear go through her. He let the full power of Anan-Ac flow through him – *without any shield*. Few had even seen Kelvoss, or his predecessors. Once a new leader was selected from the High Priests of Anan-Ac, they abandoned their own name, becoming simply Kelvoss. They never left the Inner Sanctum again.

'What do you require of me, Your Eminence?'

'All in time,' said Kelvoss. Esmelle nodded, her gaze fixed on him. If she had not known better, she would have thought he was in the grip of some illness. His head was huge – out of proportion to even his large frame. She had seen glandular conditions where the body swelled like that. Yet that was impossible here. Any Priest could use the amount of Earth Essence sweeping through this chamber to cure an ailment like that in moments.

'Bring them in,' commanded Kelvoss.

Another of the double doors opened. Esmelle recognised the dark-haired High Priest Dagon immediately. It had been he who had officiated at her own investiture. He had a bulky build and a tangible physical presence and power. He was regarded by many as the most powerful Essence practitioner in Anan-Ac. The two women who followed in his wake were not familiar. They were identical twins, tall and emaciated. Both bald except for wisps of blondish hair. They wore novice robes. Their dull, whitened eyes looked everywhere and nowhere.

Dagon nodded gravely to Esmelle, then bowed to Kelvoss. The two novices stood behind Dagon, unmoving, their postures mirroring each other.

'High Priest Dagon, you will know. The novices are Bles and Ris,' said Kelvoss. 'A gifted pair.'

They stood beside Esmelle. Her head swam for a moment, and she looked sideways at the sisters. She could see them, yet to her enhanced senses – the twins were not there. The space where they stood was simply *empty*. No trace of their power, their essential essence, was revealed to her. Esmelle had never seen such powerful shielding.

Kelvoss shifted forward in his seat.

'The heir of Carris has surfaced,' said Kelvoss, fixing them all with his hypnotic blue eyes. 'He will be desperate to win the Spear. Even now he moves north to the Ranmyden Iris to claim it from the Ward. This is your task: Befriend him. Anan-Ac must stand within his inner circle. We must be close to the Spear.'

'Why should he trust us?' said Dagon.

Kelvoss smiled. Esmelle winced at the sight of his crooked, overlong teeth. She chastised herself for thinking ill of the supreme Priest of Anan-Ac.

'He will have no choice. He will be desperate for aid against the Behemoth. We, alone in Kelas, know *that* beast. Offer him protection. He will not doubt your intentions.'

'You think not?' questioned Dagon.

Kelvoss' eyes narrowed. 'Not with Bles and Ris at your side. Keep them with you always.'

Esmelle was lost. She knew little about the Spear. The Behemoth was known to all the initiates of Anan-Ac. The being was linked with the Temple – a darkness that was continually kept at bay through the efforts of senior practitioners. She had spent many nights as a novice standing with other Priests and Priestesses in the Inner Temple, rebuffing its attempts to breach their defences. Although she was competent in that sort of battle-magic, it was not her forte.

'Your eminence,' said Esmelle. 'What role do I play in this?'

'An essential one. Firstly you must activate the portal of the Twins. The four of you must reach Herath swiftly and join the Scion's entourage before they move north. Then you will need to use your skills to find places of Earth Essence as your travel north. Dagon will have need of the power. There are also key Temples that are linked with us here. These will be made known to you. Use them to communicate.'

Esmelle's heart fell. Just like that she was to leave her Temple, abandoning her sisters and their work of healing to join in some quest of outer-world politics. She steeled herself. She had to trust that Kelvoss – so much closer to the heart of Anan-Ac than her – understood the wider vision.

'As you command.'

* * *

The flare of Earth Essence faded.

Esmelle stepped from a floor mural depicting two twin, trumpet-shaped flowers into an identical room far distant from the one they had departed. This was the sister temple to her own Temple of the Twins. She knew the Priestesses here well, and used the portal to often visit them and pass supplies through from Anan-Ac.

She led Dagon and the twins through the central Temple to the outer chambers. These were old, and in poor repair. From the outside, this Temple looked be nothing more than an ancient shrine on the western edge of the Thilil forest. As far as the Scion was to know, this was their point of origin. Anan-Ac was the greatest of the Anacian Earth Temples. A rival to Ciofran-Ac in the south. Yet its location, its very existence, had been a closely-guarded secret since the time of Carris. Every initiate of Anan-Ac was sworn to protect it on pain of death, each child born within its sphere bound by powerful Essence spells.

Esmelle greeted the Temple Priestess and her sisters warmly. Dagon passed greetings, yet remained aloof, focussed on the task ahead. Bles and Ris hovered near him, speaking only to each other, and then only in hushed whispers.

A line of supplicants snaked away from the steps. Men and women queuing for healing. Like their sister Temple in Anan-Ac, the Priestesses here turned no one away, though many had to wait for weeks to be seen.

'All is in readiness,' said the Priestess, indicating the four amelak tethered outside the Temple.

'Thank you,' said Esmelle, gripping her hands warmly.

The raggedly-dressed supplicants watched them in hopeful silence as they mounted the amelak and cantered down the path from the forest's edge.

The vast Mulisar range filled their view. Nestled into its base was the compact, walled city of Herath. It was no more than three leagues away, and many of the poor supplicants came from there or the small satellite towns around it.

And rising above all, like a brooding giant, was the shattered peak of Asgod-Ki. Esmelle made a circle of protection. Her heart sank as the Earth Essence welling from the small Temple gradually faded with the distance, leaving her without power. A chill of fear went through her at the thought of the Behemoth, and suddenly she felt very alone.

Chapter Five

Cedrin looked out through the windows at the bright, clear day. He considered once more what a strange turn his life had taken. Only months ago, he had dreamed of freedom and independence on the road. Now he was part of something greater than himself, restrained as surely as if he were locked into chains of cast mought. It was the loyalty of those around him that kept him here – and the sacrifices of all who had gone before. It was not enough to protect himself and those he loved. Now all Kelas was his responsibility.

He turned back to Thenia. The young Suul had stood up in her chair, leaning over the polished table to point at a map spread out in the centre. Spider stood behind her at rigid attention. The warrior had not so much as met his eyes again since that strained moment of silence in his court.

They were all seated in the room that opened onto the roof – his private court in Herath. Kalyth, Raphal and Salis had joined them. Skye and Marken had excused themselves on *other business*. He could guess what that would be. Would that he could join them.

'It will help to consolidate the north,' said Thenia. 'Surely you agree?'

'Of course,' said Kalyth. 'So would three Bulvuran Legions appearing out of thin air.'

Thenia blinked. The strange girl was impervious to sarcasm. For a moment it seemed she was considering the possibility that three legions might *actually* appear. She turned back to Cedrin. 'My mother has reformed the Ninth.'

'A thousand men is a long way from a legion,' said Kalyth.

'They are loyal and well trained. With troops from Athria—'

'We cannot speak for Athria,' said Cedrin.

The first dinner with Thenia went smoothly enough, but it soon became apparent she had her own ideas – and insisted on being included in all their councils.

Thenia's green, slightly protruding eyes turned to Ellen in question.

'My brother Torren will already be stretched defending his own trading fleet and providing aid to Raynor,' said Ellen.

Thenia studied the map. 'For every one of the Hanis ports we retake, thousands of Athrian warriors will be freed from guarding against the pirates. Without a base of supply, they will soon collapse.'

She had sketched out an audacious plan to launch attacks on Swebas and Leygen to oust the pirate-warlords. It made good sense, yet she was planning to use forces they simply did not have. Part of her motivation for swearing allegiance was motivated by Ellen's place at his side. She hoped to use Athrian troops in her campaign. He studied the maps, teasing out scenarios.

'A worthy strategy,' said Cedrin. 'However, there are many small ports in Hanis – even in Culgriv – that the pirates could fall back to if their fleet remained intact. They would need to be hit on all fronts, their fleet destroyed or taken in one blow, if they are ever to be crushed. They are simply too mobile to take piecemeal.'

'Every city and port we retake increases our strength,' maintained Thenia.

'Kranor has more than two thousand warriors in Kelas,' said Salis. 'They could be mustered into a single force. Perhaps they should be.'

'A force of mercenaries,' said Kalyth, stating the hard truth.

Although Kranor had a core of elite warriors who believed in the old Empire, most of his men fought for coin. Cedrin should know – he had been one of them.

'A force nonetheless. We have the funds for a sustained campaign – even to hire more warriors,' said Salis.

'Kranor has done more than anyone to make this possible. Although I think this fight will be hard enough without watching our backs. I will not use mercenaries,' said Cedrin. Kalyth grunted in agreement. 'Although bribes would go a long way to weakening the defences of the pirate-warlords.'

'You need a base for your return to power, my Lord. Why not Hanis?' said Thenia.

'Everything you say is worthy of consideration. But for now we need to focus on the journey north. For that we need to stay light and mobile. If we tried to march into Exdor with two thousand men, we would have a war on our hands,' said Cedrin.

'There is another option,' said Salis, resting her pale-grey eyes on his.

'Go on.'

'We could form a new legion. A true Bulvuran Legion sworn to the Phoenix. We could base ourselves at Searn. We have much influence there. Many of Kranor's men would be eager to join. They will surprise you, Cedrin. Let them prove their allegiance.'

The guards at the top of the stair shifted aside, making way for Vess. The scarred warrior walked swiftly across the room and bowed to Cedrin. 'News, my Lord.'

'Tell us.'

'Warlord Daran has engaged the Eathal just south of Talis. He faces five legions,' said Vess.

'Fifty thousand!' said Cedrin.

'And Daran has little more than two,' said Kalyth.

'I thought the Yasser States fielded three legions,' said Thenia.

'The North Yasser Legion – the old Fourth – was all but destroyed one month ago. The Eathal took them without warning,' said Salis. 'The survivors retreated to Raynor.'

Kalyth leaned forward, his dark-blue eyes intent. 'The outcome?'

'Inconclusive.'

'Daran is too experienced to take them head on. He will be testing them,' said Kalyth.

Vess looked to Cedrin. There was more.

'Continue.'

'Lempar has been defeated. There are rumours that the entire Olcis Legion has been destroyed. The Eathal General Yeffrij has crossed the Asgod with four legions. Nothing now stands between the Eathal and Olcis,' said Vess.

'Larus protect us,' said Salis.

Kalyth slammed his fist into the table. 'Destroyed!'

Cedrin's head spun. Only weeks ago they had been in Olcis – the beautiful City of Mirrors – largest city in Kelas. Hundreds of thousands of men and women lived there. Now unprotected. Until recently he could have seen it as the fortune of war and turned the other way. Now that blood would be on his hands.

Thenia cleared her throat. 'You said *rumours*.'

Vess nodded. 'Kranor's agents in Olcis.'

Kalyth cooled noticeably. 'You're right, Thenia. It could mean no more than the Hesguit has lost direct contact with Lempar. We cannot know for sure.'

Vess looked between him and Ellen, clearly hesitant. Cedrin waved for him to continue.

'More news from Olcis. The Hesguit has ratified the edict of the Athrian Temple. Suul Ellen Cintros is now to be taken under edict of Purge if found anywhere on Kelas,' finished Vess.

'Damn fool. His city is about to go up in flames and he still plays magical politics,' said Kalyth.

'It is more than that,' said Ellen, her voice shaken. 'I am Athria. If he did not ratify then my brother Torren could have put pressure on the Athrian Temple to overturn their decree. I would be free to return to Athria and practice Sorcery. What he truly fears is a united Empire styled like Daran's Yasser States – without Temple magic at its heart.'

Ellen trembled with suppressed fury. Cedrin laid a hand on her back in silent support. He would have taken her into his arms if the room had not been full of prying eyes. For a moment he felt Spider's attention on him. He turned, but as always she was staring forward like a statue.

'Thank you, Vess,' said Cedrin, dismissing the warrior, who bowed and exited the room.

One of the reasons they had made for Herath was that the Temple of the Sisters had never gained a foothold here. The whole city was owned and run by traders. Druids took service with individual families, often for life. For centuries, Herath had attracted magical renegades and other cults persecuted by the Temple of the Sisters.

'I think that is enough for today,' said Cedrin.

'What of my proposal?' said Thenia.

Salis and Kalyth watched him expectantly, waiting for his decision. He was once more confronted with the reality of the power at his command and the lives that balanced on his judgement. He had a new respect for his father Riin, and for his Cinanac ancestors. He felt the burden heavily, yet it was his. He *was* the Scion.

'I will consider forming a new Legion at Searn,' he said. 'We will have need of their strength soon.'

Salis and Kalyth exchanged a quick glance.

'My, Lord. Allow me to suggest that you reform the Eleventh,' said Kalyth.

Thenia cocked her head to the side. 'That is the Husdoon Legion. It was destroyed in the fall.'

'Yes. Riin formed it himself to combat the Meadrel hordes. You would honour your father to bring it to life,' replied Kalyth.

Cedrin nodded. 'Very well. A new Eleventh. However I want to make no firm decisions until Xyanthius reaches us. Kranor also must be consulted.'

'I speak for Kranor,' said Salis, her voice firm.

He acknowledged her statement with a nod. 'Thank you all.'

Cedrin rose, and he and Ellen exited the room together for their private apartments. He felt a gaze on the back of his neck, but when he turned, Spider and Thenia had already gone.

Ellen threw herself on the bed. 'Damn that pompous bastard and all his Druids!'

'It was nothing less than we expected from the Hesguit,' said Cedrin, pouring himself a glass of water. The early morning sessions with Kalyth were leaving little scope for drink. He was rising even earlier to practice the meditation of the Way. Once his mind was clear, he would summon and hold the Window, channelling power into the Barrier Matrix while continuing the other mental exercises of the Way. He had experienced mixed success so far, but at the very least it cleared his mind of other worries.

She smiled at him and patted the bed beside her. He put down the glass and kicked off his boots.

He sat beside her and laid a hand gently on the soft skin of her chest, his finger absently tracing the outline of her grief scar. 'We are far from the Temple's influence here – and will only get further away.'

Ellen's cheeks flushed red, and she bit her lower lip. She took his hand and moved it under the neckline of her dress until it cupped her breast. 'Make me forget,' she said, her voice hushed and breathless.

The scent of her perfumed skin filled him. He could not imagine any of this – being the Scion, being at the centre of this new rising power – without her.

'With pleasure.'

* * *

Ellen wandered a strange city.

The streets were deserted. The sky above her was a washed-out blue that merged with the grey margins of the world. She was dressed in a light sleeping shift, but felt neither heat nor cold.

'Hello!' she called.

She stopped at an open courtyard. A small palace backed onto the square. The stone wall was ancient, set with a big window of stained glass. She knew that window. It was part of the Cintros mansion. She looked around her. Some of the buildings were familiar, but they were thrown together wrong, as though someone had tried to rebuild the layout inside the Wall of Sorrows, but mixed it all up.

A low, powerful growl shook the walls around her, sending dust flying. The glass window shivered, but remained intact. The Behemoth was coming. She could hear its breathing, rough and wet, and growing closer. Then it appeared.

It was a massive hound, the size of a war-harena, with a single horn, cracked over part of its length. Its strange, mismatched eyes glowed with hate and lust: one grey-blue, the other gold. She reached for the Fire, but there was nothing. Here there was no Sorcery.

Ellen knew its power. The way those eyes could burn into her, draining her strength.

She backed away, looking for an exit.

Just as she turned to run, the Behemoth roared again. A shockwave raced through the ground ahead of the beast, outpacing her. Before she could react, the ground beneath her collapsed and she fell through the dark into a dusty, underground corridor.

The Labyrinth.

She was beneath the Cintros mansion. In the secret maze that held her family's secrets – where the Athrian Temple of the Iris lay.

Ellen ran. As she turned a corner, she heard the stone floor of the corridor crack under the weight of the Behemoth as it dropped through the opening behind her. She turned left and right, looking for familiar markings, frescos or carvings – anything that could tell her where she was. Everything was familiar but, like the upper world, jumbled into a crazy juxtaposition.

Ellen raced on. Left. Right. Always it was right behind her.

She came to a cross-corridor and paused for an agonising moment, unsure which direction to go. Then down the right corridor she saw a golden glow. It triggered something in her mind, something that slipped away. With nothing else to go on, she raced for it.

The glow shone onto the dusty corridor from an open panel – one of the many concealed doorways of the Labyrinth. She plunged through it, slamming it behind her. Immediately the glow vanished. Ellen lay back against the door, her breath coming fast. Heart hammering.

Outside the door, she heard the breathing of the Behemoth. It sniffed the air. Then came the awful squeal of its horn against the stone panel as it tried to prise it lose. Ellen held her breath.

When it seemed she was about to pass out, the beast moved away.

The glow rose again, revealing a narrow set of winding steps. She followed them, up and up, finally emerging at the summit of a high tower. Her calves and thighs burning, she walked to the stone battlements. As she smelled the sea breeze and looked out across the Sea of Mists, her heart swelled with joy. Here she was free and safe. At the top of the tower was a broad, circular room. Simply furnished, the walls were lined with books in ancient Cioan, Anacian, and even the obscure Myrian script.

A sea-raptor swept into the tower to land on a chair. It fixed her with one of its deep green eyes and spoke.

'Welcome.'

* * *

Ellen woke with a start.

She looked around her in panic. Details began to register. The simple wooden ceiling and the rough furniture, revealed by the dim glow of the oil lamp. The threadbare rugs. Her formal gown, thrown across the chair where it had been hastily removed the night before.

Herath.

Ellen sank back in the bed. Cedrin was snoring softly beside her. Outside the sky was dark. She considered waking Cedrin, but discarded the idea. He would be up soon for his training with Kalyth and he needed the sleep.

Ellen slid out from beneath the warm covers, careful not to disturb him. Naked, she shivered in the chill. She reached for a nightgown and tied it swiftly around her, sliding her feet into fleece-lined slippers. She crept out of the bedroom.

She started when she saw Osterac guarding the chambers outside, Ruus beside him. She still found the apparent devotion of the false-Scion unnerving, but he had served them faultlessly.

'Morning,' she said in a hushed voice.

'Suul Cintros,' they replied together.

Two more warriors guarded the stairs, and two more patrolled the rooftop. Vess had asked for additional men after

Cedrin's nighttime excursion. He had not said anything, but Ellen suspected the man was more difficult to fool than Cedrin imagined. Two of the One Hundred now also patrolled the streets around the tavern.

Ellen opened the double-doors leading onto the rooftop and slipped through the curtains. The sky was clear, the rooftop clearly visible in the light of Rea, directly overhead in its third quarter. Asic's waning crescent had only just crested the horizon. She exchanged greetings with the guards and went to the west rail. A cool gust whispered against her, and she drew the furred collar of the gown closer around her neck. Goose pimples rose on her legs. Her gaze was drawn to the Mulisar range above her, now a wall of deeper dark within the night that blotted out the stars.

The dreams had been worse since they arrived in Herath. They were even more terrifying knowing the Behemoth was real. A dark creature of Essence dedicated to their downfall. Cedrin had also been troubled by them, but was reluctant to discuss it. The worst part was the unknown. What happened if the Behemoth triumphed in the dream realm? Outside of the Iris was it nothing more than a phantom, trying to wear down their spirit before the final encounters, or did it have real power?

The sky began to lighten with the gentle touch of first dawn. Uros would rise first, until Sisters' Blessing, when Larus would take the ascendant. The majestic shape of Asgod-Ki was now outlined against the pre-dawn sky. She heard Cedrin's voice and saw him walk onto the rooftop with Kalyth. Other warriors of the One Hundred – those not on duty – filed into the wide space. Cedrin joined them as they sat in rows, cross-legged in front of Kalyth to begin the meditations of the Way. Bovosan sat behind the group, by now an accepted presence. Ellen smiled as she sensed the Fire rise in Cedrin and the Barrier Matrix fall into place. His dedication was impressive. Despite his frustration, he worked at his control of the Window like a hound at a favourite bone.

Her gaze was drawn back to Asgod-Ki as the tips of the shattered peak began to glow a lurid red, as though dipped in blood. The colour swept down the sides of the peak, reflected off the snow. There was a pause, while the high peak of Asgod-Ki was coloured red and the other Mulisar peaks still lay in shadow. Then inexorably the bloody red leaked downward. Just when it seemed it would overtake the world, Larus crested the horizon, and all was changed. The red dimmed, and slowly the yellow of Larus overtook it.

Ellen was broken out of her reverie by the sound of hoof beats. A large party of men had entered the street below. She heard one of the One Hundred challenge them as they made for the tavern entrance. Alarmed, she darted across the roof and looked down into the street.

Ellen blinked, hardly believing her eyes.

Her Athrian Suulquas, Valdas and Mendor, were here, riding narsiit. Not only that – they had brought her own narsiit from Raynor. Ellen's narsiit lifted her head, sniffing the air. She looked up at Ellen and trumpeted a greeting.

'Valdas! Mendor!' she called.

The two Suulqua looked up to see the Scion's consort leaning over the roof wearing nothing but a nightgown, hair dishevelled from sleep. The warrior of the One Hundred looked up as well, and was just as surprised as her Suulquas to see her there.

'Let them in!' she yelled. She ran across the rooftop to the double-doors and her chambers. Cedrin and the warriors of the One Hundred remained immobile. The ability to block out external distractions was part of the discipline of the Way. Only a specific command from Kalyth would break their devotions.

Ellen had laid out her leathers and travelling boots the night before, ready to do her own martial training while Cedrin worked with Kalyth and the One Hundred. She donned them swiftly, tying her hair back in a rough tail and binding it with a leather thong. She washed her face and looked at herself briefly in the mirror. But for the Suul mark, the young blonde woman who looked back at her showed little resemblance to the girl who had grown to adulthood in the court of Athria. That woman would never have dreamed of being seen outside her chambers in anything but full court attire, and certainly not a nightgown. Ellen chuckled to herself. Valdas and Mendor would just have to get used to it. It was hard to summon concern for breaches in etiquette when the fate of Kelas hung in the balance and the Hesguit had condemned her to death without trial for her public display of Sorcery.

She hurried down the stairs, overtaking two serving women on her way to the common room three stories below. Only the night lamps were lit, wicks trimmed low, and the room was wrapped in gloom. Ellen called across to the owner, who was working at the bar, preparing for the day's custom. 'Can we get some light, please?' He nodded in reply and moved out from behind the bar with a taper. He lit it from the first of the lamps then circled the room, swiftly bringing the others to life.

Her Suulquas stood formally just inside the entrance, flanked by two of the One Hundred. Both had the light skin and hair of the Athria Suul. As the light grew, Ellen could see that their fine trousers and gem-encrusted harnesses were dusty from the road, their faces lined with exhaustion. Valdas was a head taller than the dark-eyed Mendor.

'Come in,' said Ellen. 'The narsiit . . .' She fought the urge to run out and see her own mount.

'Being attended to,' said Valdas quickly, as though to stave off her reprimand. The tall Suulqua had always been the more over-eager of the two young Athrians.

They walked forward with careful poise, each gripping a finely-crafted greatscythe. Hidden in the gloom before, but now revealed by the bright lamps, was Serel, a lady who had come with her from Athria – one of the many she had abandoned when she snuck Raphal out of Raynor and followed Cedrin north. Serel bowed low, with perfect deference, her face set with determination, as though she was ready for anything. Behind her were two young female slaves. Ellen recognised them from Estle's household in Raynor. They were neatly dressed in matching dresses of dull green, skin covered neck to ankle; considerably more than they were wearing in Estle's rooms.

Mendor stepped forward, his dark eyes grave. 'My, Lady,' he said. 'I formally request that we rejoin your entourage.'

Ellen stepped forward and took Mendor's hands. He raised his eyebrows, unused to the informality. 'As far as I am concerned, you never left it. You and Valdas would have been with me since Raynor if my brother Estle had not send you on that mission to get you out of the city.'

Valdas swept forward. One of Cedrin's bodyguard stepped forward, releasing the blades of his greatscythe, but Valdas simply kneeled before her. 'Please, my Lady. Do not leave us behind again. We both swore to serve and protect you.'

'Have no fear of that. Now come – sit down and have something to eat. You must be exhausted. Did you ride all night?'

'If my Lady pleases, I would rather go straight to your rooms and get things in hand,' said Serel. Ellen suppressed her irritation at the veiled implication that all was not already as it should be.

'Very well,' said Ellen. She waved one of the One Hundred across to her. 'This warrior will take you to my chambers.'

Serel bowed and withdrew, the slaves following in her wake.

Ellen led the two Suulquas to a table and the tavern owner sent over one of the serving men with a tray of cooked meats, fresh bread, cheeses and fruits. The two men remained stiffly formal, watching her intently.

'How could you be here? How did you manage to get past the Eathal legions closing on Olcis?'

Valdas eagerly drained a glass of watered juice. 'Thankfully the north road was still open when we passed. Although it was a close thing. We saw some of their jakkund-mounted scouts. Thank Larus they did not pursue us. The amelak Serel and the slaves rode would not have been able to outrun them.'

'The Eathal general Yeffrij is advancing slowly, consolidating his territory,' said Mendor.

'Any sign of Lempar's legion?' asked Ellen.

'Nothing,' said Mendor.

Ellen fought down a wave of trepidation. She and her brother Estle had not left on the best of terms. 'Does Estle know you are here?'

'We left Raynor on his orders. We have been waiting for weeks for word. News that Kranor had sworn to the Scion at Olcis reached Raynor within hours by courier bird. A detailed report followed from one of Estle's agents, which listed those with Cedrin, including you, my Lady. We set out north the next day.

'Estle gave us a list of Athrian contacts to use on the way north. His man at Fulvur already knew you were here in Herath. So here we are.'

Ellen ate some breakfast while she let that sink in. She had to make contact with Estle, and through him her brother Torren in Athria. 'Do you have a contact here in Herath?'

'Yes,' said Mendor.

'Excellent. I will need to give you messages for both Estle and Torren.'

'We have dispatches for you,' said Mendor, handing her a satchel of heavy parchment sealed with the crest of the Athrian consulate in Raynor. The letters inside tumbled as it shifted in her grip. She accepted it gravely, torn between the desire to open it and anxiety over what it might contain.

The implications of her relationship with Cedrin were profound for Athria. Essentially she had forced Torren into allegiance with the rising Scion – at odds with the carefully garnered alliance with Warlord Daran. Her headlong determination to find the Scion and re-birth the old order must seem terribly reckless to both her brothers. Yet at least her success proved it was not the fool's quest they once considered it. Cedrin himself was proof of that.

Although she stood at Cedrin's side, she had been feeling increasingly isolated in the growing court of the Scion. Kalyth, Salis, the One Hundred – they were all sworn to Cedrin. They showed her respect, yet their ultimate loyalty was to him.

First losing her father, then being forced to flee to Raynor had cut her off from her homeland and her family. Having her Suulquas here re-established that link to her brothers and to Athria. Having a lady to wait on her and two body-slaves would also be a relief, saving her having to do it herself or explain the same simple tasks over and over again to unfamiliar servants.

Ellen rose, eager to see her narsiit and get reacquainted. She tucked the satchel into the jacket of her leathers and refastened it. Valdas reddened at the brief flash of neckline.

'What do you command, my Lady?' asked Mendor

'For now – refresh yourself and restore your strength. Then come to my chambers. I will introduce you to Kalyth Orin. You should join with the One Hundred in their training, begin to establish a working relationship with the warriors.'

'As you wish.'

As Ellen moved away from the table, they grew tense, as though concerned they would lose her again in some disappearing trick. She could hardly blame them. The two young nobles had been appointed by Torren to her entourage and had linked their future advancement to her cause. Staying close to her and being seen to provide invaluable service was the key to their eventual advancement to full Suul rank.

Vess was on duty outside the tavern. When he caught sight of her walking to the stables, he sent two of the One Hundred to shadow her. By now she was used to the protective measures.

Her narsiit trumpeted in welcome as she let herself into the stall. The two warriors stayed well back. Her mount nickered happily as Ellen hugged her long, narrow head, running her hands through the soft hair. Skye's narsiit pushed his head out of his stall, watching her with soft, intelligent eyes.

'I missed you,' said Ellen. The bond between a narsiit and rider was formed over long years, the training beginning when the narsiit was little more than a foal.

She took a brush from the stable racks and brushed her narsiit's brightly-coloured coat in long strokes. The narsiit gave a neigh of pleasure. Even the most senior Suul cared for their own mounts whenever they could, regarding the plains-runners more as companions than beasts of burden.

When she had finished, she leaned comfortably against her narsiit and tore open the satchel. There was a letter from Torren, reassuring her of his continued efforts on her behalf with the Athrian Temple and which had detailed updates from the Athrian court. The pirates of the western coast had grown even bolder. Perhaps Thenia was right. Athria needed to deal with them.

Estle's letter was brief. Ellen had left Raynor in defiance of her brother, who had been against her quest for the Scion from the outset. The letter mentioned nothing about that. There were no lengthy remonstrations. It was a succinct note that outlined the Suulquas' mission – to act in support of her – and the prior experience of the slaves. Her ladies had all returned to Athria except Serel, who insisted on being taken with Valdas and Mendor. She was far more determined than Ellen had ever given her credit for. Perhaps, like the two Suulquas, she saw her fortune bound to hers.

Ellen also knew how Estle's mind worked. Any truly important communication would not be by open letter, but through Athrian agents. She tucked the letters into her jacket and patted her narsiit goodbye. The warriors followed her as she left the stable.

The sound of approaching hoof beats filled the air, growing louder as a large party of amelak turned the corner and entered the courtyard. There were seventy warriors, riding beneath Kranor's phoenix standard in neat rows. More amelak followed, laden with supplies. Warriors standing guard duty yelled in greeting.

The rest of the One Hundred had arrived.

Xyanthius rode at their head, flanked by a young Suul who looked about him eagerly.

The old warrior halted his amelak. 'Suul Cintros. Well met.'

'Xyanthius. Good to see you well.'

'Let me introduce Kranor's son, Ranis Cintor. Commander of the One Hundred.'

Ranis swept his right leg across the saddle and slid to the ground in one smooth movement. He bowed and smiled.

'A pleasure, Suul Cintros,' said Ranis.

'Likewise.'

'It seems it's a day of arrivals,' said Ellen. 'If you will excuse me.'

'Of course,' said Xyanthius.

Ellen slipped back into the common room and up the stairs to her chambers. Her two Suulquas were gone when she passed.

She swept into her rooms to find Serel and the two slaves busy cleaning and reorganising.

'A bath. Quickly,' commanded Ellen.

Serel sent one of the slaves to fetch hot water from the tavern boilers.

There would be no time for training now.

'This way, my Lady,' said Serel.

She led Ellen into one of the adjoining rooms, which until now had been unused. All Ellen's things had been shifted in here.

'Even though you and the Lord Scion share a bed, a Suul Lady should always have her own chambers,' said Serel. Her fingers were already deftly releasing the catches on Ellen's leathers. Soon she stood naked. Serel handed her a soft robe.

'And for court?' asked Serel.

'Perhaps the white gown,' said Ellen, feeling the sudden need for formality now that Xyanthius had arrived. The Scion's entourage was growing – and with it the complexity of the alliances.

Serel looked at Ellen for a moment, unsure. 'If I may ask . . . '

'Go on.'

'My Lady shares a bed with the Scion. Have you taken precautions?'

Ellen swallowed. Sorcery could do many things, but control of fertility was not one of them. That was the province of Earth Essence. She had vowed almost daily that she would take Salis aside to ask her for a special Blessing to forestall the seed taking hold, but somehow she had never managed to do it. The stately Suul make her feel so damn awkward. Like a child. Talking to her about this seemed a blow to her own pride somehow. She had such Blessings regularly as a young Suulqua in Athria, planned well in advance, like well-executed business arrangements. Compared to the liaison with her former lover Palsus, her romance with Cedrin had been a chaotic whirlwind. Surely nothing could have happened in these few weeks?

'Have no concern,' said Ellen, unwilling to discuss it with a virtual stranger. She would talk to Salis. Tonight.

Serel looked at her, concerned. 'There are bound to be practitioners in Herath I could talk to . . . '

Ellen shook her head. She did not want to drink some midwives' concoction. She would end up poisoned. Suul did not resort to such crude measures.

'Thank you, but please do not concern yourself.'

A door opened at the other end of the room

'The bath is ready, my Lady,' said one of the slaves.

Ellen walked through the door into the small bath chamber, sinking gratefully into the hot water. The two slaves knelt by the tub, gently washing her skin with sponges and scented soap.

Oh. I have missed this.

Chapter Six

Ellen looked around the court of the Scion.

The common room with its rough wooden floor looked crowded. The walls were lined with the One Hundred and the Daughters. Kranor's son Ranis, looking resplendent in court trousers and worked harness, stood as commander of the One Hundred, Spider as commander of the Daughters. Her own Suulquas stood stiffly to attention in their best gear. Bovosan, once more cloaked and hooded, stood unnoticed at the back of the room.

Rather than a dais, a long table had been set up at one end of the room. Cedrin and Ellen sat in the centre, with Kalyth to Cedrin's left. Xyanthius sat with Salis, talking in low tones. Kranor remained in Raynor to promote Cedrin's interests in the Warlord's court in his new capacity as Scion's Ambassador. Thenia sat with them, accorded a place of honour as the representative of Hanis. Raphal had also joined them. Initially Salis wanted him excluded from their council, uneasy with Raphal's Priestly ability to resist her powers of Testing, but Ellen had argued that his knowledge was vital. Besides, she trusted the old Priest and Druid to act in her and Cedrin's interests, rather than being driven purely by the need to restore the Cinanac line. Cedrin had likewise insisted that his friends Skye and Marken also be seated with them. Marken had outdone himself with a new outfit of red leather, trimmed with fur. The harness beneath the open vest also looked new.

Their plans for a closed council had been rapidly shifted to an open court when they discovered that Veltricus was coming to finalise arrangements for the trip north. A delegation from a minor Earth Essence Temple outside Herath had also asked to see the Scion. Raphal and Salis had both agreed it would be politic to receive them. Virtually all Earth Essence Temples were not aligned with the Temple of the Sisters, so the Hesguit's edict would not affect the formation of any new alliance with them.

They now waited for Veltricus to arrive.

Kalyth and Cedrin had begun their second game of karass, the board set with coins of purple, blue and bluish-green tinted mought – known as rubies, sapphires and emeralds. These were high denomination coins. They were not using the smaller low-value opals and bits. Cedrin swept one of Kalyth's rubies off the board.

The old warrior hissed in frustration and leant forward, increasing his concentration. A ruby would be a week's wages for many crafters. In karass, if you captured a piece, you kept it. It was a form of skilful gambling, and Ellen had never seen anyone more deadly at the game than Cedrin. Kalyth's purse had already suffered.

'Who is that moving mountain, Ranis?' asked Cedrin. He was pointing at one of the new warriors of the One Hundred, a huge warrior who dwarfed all those around him.

Ranis grinned and moved closer to the high table. 'Hard to miss, isn't he? That's Duro. Formerly of Daran's First Legion.'

The big warrior stood out in the ranks of the One Hundred, yet was not the tallest. Another of the new warriors was a startlingly tall Anacian. His height made him look almost slim, although he was himself impressively muscled. He had a specially cast greatscythe almost as long as a spear that matched his odd physique.

'Have you given my proposal further consideration?' asked Thenia.

'Xyanthius has no objections to raising the standard of the Eleventh in Searn. The dispatches were sent yesterday. It will take at least a month to assemble the warriors. Then we will need to see what sort of strength we have,' said Cedrin.

'They will need training. Legions are strange beasts. The fighting style will be completely new to most of Kranor's warriors,' said Kalyth.

'And your plans?' asked Thenia.

Kalyth took one of Cedrin's sapphires. Cedrin immediately responded by taking another of Kalyth's rubies and two emeralds. The old warrior laughed and withdrew to the neutral blue hexagon in the centre of the board. 'That's it for me.' Kalyth removed his remaining coins.

'I told you, Kalyth. The man is not human,' said Marken.

'You should try him at dice,' said Skye with a smug grin.

Cedrin laughed at that. Thenia's pale face remained serious and he sobered. 'I will not make a swift decision. Too much depends on what strength we can muster, and on the strategic situation as it develops. Your ideas have merit, but you must be patient. Consider the matter closed until we reach Beslin. We can reassess the scheme based on more information.'

Thenia said nothing, then her eyes fell on the board. 'Perhaps a game of karass?'

Cedrin's eyes narrowed, and he smiled at the young Suul indulgently. 'Why not?'

Thenia waved Spider to her. A purse of coins passed between the female bodyguard and the Hanis Suul. As Cedrin leaned down to set the board, Spider's gaze swept across to Cedrin, resting on his lean chest then up to his face. Her eyes were intense – hungry. The warrior sensed Ellen's gaze and looked away quickly.

An inexplicable fury overtook Ellen. For a moment she wanted nothing more than to have her scythe in her hands and send a vicious cut at the lean warrior's head. She closed her eyes and took a breath. Come to think of it, that had not been the first time she had noticed the eyes of the Daughters' commander on her lover.

Ellen looked at Cedrin, her heart racing. He was a handsome man. A powerful man. Of course women were going to find him attractive. Of course they would seek to seduce him. Bed him. Her stomach lurched in fear, as though the ground had given way beneath her. Anger flared in its wake. Not while he is at my side, she vowed. She reached across protectively, laying a hand on his thigh. He laid his hand on hers absently as he studied

Thenia's opening move.

'So preparations are complete?' asked Cedrin.

'Yes. Thanks to Veltricus, we have all the provisions we need. Xyanthius and I have already discussed the route with Veltricus' scouts. It will take us deep into the Thilil forests,' said Kalyth.

'At least we will be well equipped,' said Ellen. *And out of reach of the Hesguit.*

'And we will not need to sustain the pace we did on the way north from Olcis.' Cedrin removed two of Thenia's emeralds from the board. She successfully defended one of her rubies and made a temporary withdrawal. Her concentration was total, her eyes dreamy as she hovered over the board.

'So if the preparations are complete, what is Veltricus coming to see us about?'

'Another matter,' said Kalyth. 'He did not elaborate.'

Vess ran to Ranis and bowed, passing a quick message. 'My Lord. Veltricus Cineth.'

Cedrin looked down to board in time to see Thenia remove two of his rubies. He had missed the subtle strategy in the confusion.

'I told you not to underestimate her, my Lord,' said Salis with a smile.

'We will have to finish this later,' said Cedrin. 'I need a chance to win back those rubies.'

'As you say, my Lord,' said Thenia, without emotion. *What a strange young woman.*

Cedrin straightened in his chair, his face composed. He was wearing the new clothes she had made for him and looked the part of the Scion, his face stern and powerful. Her pride swelled, and she reluctantly removed her hand from his knee.

Veltricus entered, his clothes shimmering in the bright lamplight. As before, he was flanked by two heavily muscled bodyguards. They were both tattooed with the sigil of the Cineth, the mark only carried by favoured servants of the House of Herath, as well as other honours.

'Greeting, my Lord Scion,' said Veltricus. The silver glowmetal swinging from his left ear caught the light. Others were set into his wrist-bands or hung from his neck. *The man is wearing a small fortune.*

'You are most welcome, Suul Cineth. I thank you for your assistance, which has been invaluable,' said Cedrin.

'And profitable,' said Veltricus with a tight grin.

'The best deals profit both parties, do they not?' said Cedrin. He had done his share of trading in his former life, buying illicit goods in Raynor for the Athrian black market.

Veltricus' eyes glittered. 'I have news and thought it best to deliver it in person.'

Cedrin nodded for him to continue.

'This caravan to Beslin is a crucial one for House Herath. The threat of the drakon spawn, and the destruction of the prior caravans have meant that some most . . . precious materials have been kept here overlong. The profit for their delivery has likewise been delayed.

'As such, my father and I have decided the Cineth must be represented directly.'

Cedrin tilted his head, his eyes narrowing.

'I will be joining you. In addition to the scouts, I will bring a small group of household guards. Some small strength to add to your already impressive force.'

Cedrin paused before replying. Ellen knew him well enough to know his mind would be working fast.

In Ellen's own mind, the presence of Veltricus could only increase their confidence in the journey north. Herath would not risk its own heir lightly.

'Welcome news, Veltricus. Perhaps a drink to celebrate?' Cedrin signalled to the serving staff, who came forward with trays of refreshments. The Herath Suul accepted with a show of courtesy, but took the merest sip of the offered wine.

Cedrin lifted his own glass to toast. 'To good business.'

Veltricus gave a genuine smile at that. 'Indeed.'

A warrior ran to Ranis to deliver a message. The young Suul then walked swiftly to Cedrin. 'The delegation from the Earth Temple, my Lord.'

'Send them in.'

It would have been better if their business with Veltricus

had been concluded before the arrival of the second delegation. Now there was no avoiding Veltricus' presence at their first meeting. Ellen was relieved that Cedrin did not keep them waiting.

'My apologies, Veltricus. I must receive other visitors. Perhaps you would stay and avail yourself of our hospitality?' said Cedrin.

Ellen was impressed at Cedrin's deft handling of the Herath Suul. She could see that her lover had learned diplomatic skills of his own as a senior calvanni in Athria. He was a natural leader. No wonder the Brotherhood leadership had seen him as such as threat.

'With pleasure, my Lord Scion,' said Veltricus, backing away from the dais to stand near the Daughters. As one of the bodyguards turned, Ellen had the briefest glimpse of two thick-bladed knives with elaborate hooked hilts sheathed at the small of his back, hidden beneath his loose vest. So. *Not unarmed after all.*

Cedrin leant across the table to Salis. 'Veltricus?'

'He is telling the truth about the caravan. It is vital to Herath. There is something else, though.'

'Yes?'

'He is hiding a strong desire. I only caught hints before, yet now I know it. He wants to be close to you. Above all else.'

Ellen considered. The desire itself could imply any number of ulterior motives. 'But why?'

'Could Herath be considering an alliance with us?' asked Cedrin.

If so, their behaviour had been odd. They had kept them isolated from the centre of Herath's powerbase. They had not been invited to the Herath enclave, nor offered better accommodations in the diplomatic quarter. They had been treated as trading partners. Perhaps that was the Cineth way.

'Impossible to say,' said Salis. Her face creased in frustration. 'This location is too weak in Earth Essence for me to tease out a motivation that complex.'

Ellen turned to Raphal, but the old Priest and Druid was lost in his own thoughts. Although skilled with Earth Essence, he had little skill in Testing. For that they had to rely on Salis.

The door opened and the Earth Temple delegation entered.

'Are you ready, Salis?' asked Cedrin.

The Raynor Suul's grey eyes glittered with power. 'Yes. The Essence is weak here – but enough to read intent.'

Cedrin and Ellen both straightened in their chairs and looked down the room at the approaching men and women. They wore simple white robes, trimmed with gold, chests covered as a sign of the Earth mysteries they had been initiated into.

Ellen was surprised to see the leader of the delegation was a Priest. Earth Essence in men was extremely rare. She saw Raphal lean forward, his own interest piqued. The man had a large, bulky build with thick black hair. As he came forward, she could feel the tangible power of his presence. Ellen looked at his forehead, expecting to see a Suul mark, yet there was none. The man carried himself with a certain poise. He certainly looked like no simple Priest. A slim Priestess with reddish-blonde hair walked a step behind him. Her eyes were wide as she looked about the room, clearly anxious. And behind her were the oddest two women Ellen had ever seen: tall and skeletally thin, bald except for wisps of hair. They were identical, and their robes bore an additional swirling design across the chest.

The big Priest led them right up to the table. Ellen blinked as he and the Priestess sank to their knees.

'We have been led here by a Vision,' declared the Priest. His booming voice filled the room. The two twins remained standing. It was only then that Ellen noticed their strangely whitened eyes. Perhaps they were blind. They remained standing, expressions vacuous. Simpletons?

Ellen saw movement in the corner of the room and was surprised to see Bovosan walking straight across the room towards the delegation.

'A vision of what?' asked Cedrin, warily.

'Of danger,' said the Priest, his deep charismatic voice carrying clearly across the room.

Veltricus was rigid with tension, his eyes fixed on the delegation with furious intensity.

Cedrin's eyes flicked to Salis, then back to the Priest.

'Perhaps we should start with introductions?' said Cedrin lightly. There was a sigh of movement around the room as the spell cast by the Priest's dramatic entrance broke.

Bovosan stopped just below the table, next to Ranis. Beneath the hood, Ellen could see the minitil's strange green eyes with their split irises fixed on the delegation. What had gotten into him?

'I am Priest Dagon. This is Priestess Esmelle. Our two novices Bles and Ris. We are from the Temple of the Twins, on the edge of the Thilil forest.' That explained the strange women. Temples often took in the disabled, especially when they had some goddess-blessed trait that echoed the totem or goddess of that particular temple.

'We have come to swear our service to the true Scion of the Cinanac.'

Ellen heard ragged breathing and looked across to see it was Salis. Her face was creased in pain, beads of sweat standing out on her forehead. It was a shock. Ellen had never seen the Suul anything other than composed – one the things that irked her about Salis.

Cedrin was too focussed on Dagon to notice. 'And this Vision?'

Dagon's gaze locked to Cedrin's and his voice lowered. Even so, it lost none of its compelling power. 'Of a Beast. One that has the power to invade the sleeping mind.'

Ellen's stomach flipped. *The Behemoth*. She met Raphal's eyes across the table. The old Priest and Druid was thoughtful. Could this be the aid they needed against the mysterious Essence spirit?

Cedrin leant back in shock. He too had picked up the implication.

'We are here to offer our strength. To shield you from its malign influence,' continued Dagon.

The two twins, who had appeared nothing but vague, turned their heads in unison. Their strange, whitened eyes focused on Salis. The Suul was shivering now, as though wrapped in a fever. Bovosan moved beside her, then turned to face the twins, shielding her with his thickset body. Behind him, Salis let out a long sigh, then collapsed forward onto the table unconscious. The two twins turned away, faces expressionless.

'Mother,' said Ranis. He took a step towards her, then paused, torn between Salis' distress and his duty as commander of the One Hundred.

Cedrin looked to the side, shocked to see Salis' limp body draped across the table.

'If I may?' The Priestess had risen. Her face was creased with concern. 'The Temple of the Twins is above all a healing Temple.'

'Yes. By all means,' said Cedrin. 'Raphal? Can you assist?'

Ellen sucked in a breath, hardly realising she had been holding it. Again Cedrin was thinking on his feet. An accomplished healer himself, Raphal would be able to verify her skill and intent.

Dagon rose. 'My Lord? Will you accept our service?'

Cedrin's thumb played over the ruby signet ring of the Cinanac, turning it on his index finger. His grey-blue eyes fixed on Dagon.

'Gratefully. Although I hope you are equipped for travel. We leave for Beslin at first light tomorrow.'

'Our only wish is to serve,' said Dagon gravely.

Veltricus' face was twisted with fury. He turned stiffly and exited the room without another word.

* * *

Cedrin heard the sounds of the rousing camp. The soft bleating of the amelak at the picket line. The trumpeting of a narsiit as it greeted its rider. The regular breathing of the warriors of both the One Hundred and the Daughters seated around him, greatscythes across their knees, eyes closed as they focussed on their devotions. Not all his warriors were present. Some were on sentry duty, others scouting. None of Veltricus' warriors were with them. The Herath men were not devotees of the Way.

The Fire filled him. The Window lay open, a trickle of power steadily moving through the Barrier Matrix. He swiftly formed the Shield Matrix and directed another stream of the Fire through it. With both Matrices in place, he returned to his devotions. The Way was both a philosophy and a mental discipline. Its meditations were all about purity of consciousness – enhancing and strengthening the power of the senses. In many ways, it was an extension of the traits that had kept him alive on the streets of Athria, and later as a Brotherhood calvanni.

He extended his senses. He tasted the sharp scent of wood smoke. Beyond the camp, the Thilil forest was alive with a rousing chorus of birdlife.

'Pick out one sound,' came Kalyth's voice. 'Focus on it.'

One of the birds sounded different. Deeper. Guttural.

'Know it.'

Cedrin listed to the call, distant, yet distinct. He came to realise there were variations in its melody – pauses, different notes. All at once he knew there was more than one of these birds. They were calling to each other. *Lamel.* Of course. Achieving moments of knowing such as this was one of the objectives of the training; the honing of a special kind of instinct. The winged humanoids had pestered them since they entered the forest, but always attacked in silence. They were out there though, signalling each other.

'Attend,' said Kalyth sharply.

Immediately the warriors sprang to their feet. Cedrin moved with them, swinging his greatscythe up to 'attention' – held vertical in the right hand. His concentration slipped and both Matrices faltered and collapsed.

'Individual training,' said Kalyth.

Cedrin reached for the Window, but it slipped away.

'Ready?' asked Kalyth. That was all the warning Cedrin usually got.

Kalyth's greatscythe shot forward. He blocked instinctively, ready for the counter. The old warrior's blades extended with a snap, shooting out of the ends of the greatscythe and locking into place. Cedrin jerked his head back. One of the blades narrowly missed his face.

'Focus! Remember – a greatscythe's blades are always there,' said Kalyth.

Cedrin pushed away Kalyth's weapon and circled to give

himself room. Still alert, he calmly reached for the Window. This time he had it. He formed the Barrier. The next challenge of his Sorcerer training was to maintain mental control in the midst of combat. It was not easy.

Cedrin sprang at Kalyth. Going on the attack was often the best way of dealing with the old warrior. He extended his blades. Now two sets of deadly lanedd whistled through the air in furious arcs. Block. Counter. Stab forward. Circle.

By the time the suns crested the trees at the edge of the forest clearing, Cedrin was dripping with sweat. As usual, Kalyth was hardly out of breath. Despite his age, his endurance was unnatural.

'Good. Good. Enough for today.' Kalyth clapped Cedrin on the shoulder in a rare display of affection. 'You are almost competent.'

Cedrin gave a short laugh. 'High praise indeed.'

'Rinse off and get some breakfast,' said Kalyth. Cedrin relished these times with Kalyth, when the old warrior dropped the rigid formality.

He walked to the stream and stripped off his shirt and leggings, wading into the cold water. He rubbed his arms and chest briskly, then sank his head under the flow. He threw his head back with a hoot of delight and shook off the water. His numbed skin flushed with a pleasant warmth as the blood returned to it. His head ached from the chill, but his mind sang with a crisp clarity. Other warriors stood in the shallow, fast-flowing stream. Some splashed at themselves, others were shaving. Many of the Daughters were there as well, stripped as naked as the men. They were used to military operations in Hanis and had no shyness when it came to mixing it with warriors.

'Room for another two?' Cedrin jerked around to see Spider and Jeth enter the frigid stream. He had seen them sparring earlier. If Kalyth and Xyanthius had any concerns about the skill of the Daughters, they were soon dispelled on the road from Herath. They were elite – as the bruised egos of many of the One Hundred could attest.

Spider eyed him with a brazen grin, eyes dropping to his

crotch. 'Not so impressive in the morning, eh?'

Cedrin laughed. The cold water had certainly done its work. 'Cruel.'

Jeth stuck out her little finger, wiggling it to emphasise the joke. Spider's lieutenant was bulky everywhere, built like a wrestler. Her breasts were huge, but did not stir him in the least. Spider, by comparison, was lean and sleek, her tanned skin gleaming with sweat. Even her small breasts, the large, pointed nipples pierced with mought, were strangely erotic.

'I'll leave you to it, ladies,' said Cedrin.

'Going so soon?' said Spider, simpering.

'I'm afraid so,' said Cedrin. A hunting party was planned for the morning, and he was eager to get a glimpse of the forests beyond the trail. So far his days had been taken up by long discussions with his inner circle as their party made its slow progress through the wild forest. They barely made twelve leagues a day, forced to stop early to set up camp and forage for provisions to supplement their supplies.

As he passed Spider, her hand flashed out at his rear. He caught her wrist. 'You're incorrigible.'

'Fast hands,' said Jeth under her breath.

Spider twisted out of his grip and shrugged. He watched as Spider and Jeth waded out into the stream. He could not help but admire Spider's toned buttocks. She turned back to him, eyes dropping to his groin. 'Warming up already?'

Cedrin grinned and moved out of the water, dressing swiftly. He had to stay away from that woman.

Vess and Ruus, who had been keeping watch from the bank, took station on either side of him as he walked through the rousing camp.

'Morning, boys.'

'Morning, my Lord,' they responded. He had long given up trying to get them to drop the appellation. The days of simple companionship were gone. He was Cedrin Cinanac. He accepted that. The swirling chaos around him would only grow as the days passed.

Osterac was still training with the other warriors of the One Hundred. There was no doubting the Suul's dedication. He had taken to his new life with a vengeance. He had forged grudging respect among the other warriors with his martial ability. Osterac had been unable to rise higher than the top twenty in the ongoing greatscythe competitions. Unlike the sparring bouts on the caravan north, the Suul was now fighting the best of the best. Still, at the very least he had justified his place in the first thirty. Osterac still stood apart among the warriors though, by virtue of his high birth. It would take some time before they forgave him for once declaring as a false-Scion.

Cedrin passed Veltricus' encampment. The trader's warriors – equipped with square hide shields and stabbing spears – ringed his tent. Beyond the trader-Suul's orderly picket lines was a ragged camp of travellers. Like Veltricus himself, these were all bound for Beslin. They had been waiting in Herath for a well-armed caravan. The House of Herath did not waste any opportunity to make money. The Suul had charged them hefty fees for the privilege of joining him. Some of the travellers had accepted service to pay their way. They stood out from the other men and women in Veltricus' employ by their lack of Cineth marks.

A middle-aged servant walked through Veltricus' picket lines, dropping feed for the amelak. His bronze hair and golden skin marked his Cioan ancestry. Cedrin absently looked at the man's chest, curious to see if he was a southern refugee or from Armon to the north. Cedrin's vision swam. He blinked to clear it. *Too many late nights with Ellen.* The man's tattoos were vague. Indistinct. Faded over time, probably. Certainly nothing he recognised. A pain started in his temple. His attention slipped away and gradually the pain eased.

Cedrin walked through another ring of sentries to where the pavilions of his inner circle had been raised. Half of them were already down, the well-drilled warriors of the One Hundred swiftly disassembling them for loading onto the pack-amelak. His own tent was still up.

He ducked under the entrance. Vess took station outside while Ruus followed him inside.

The interior was sparsely furnished with a small table and chairs. The board was set with an array of breakfast foods. A light curtain blocked off the day area from the small sleeping chamber. Ellen sat eating breakfast with her two Suulquas, her maid Serel standing behind her chair. She was dressed in her leathers, as usual. The taller of the two Suulquas wore rough travelling clothes, stained with dust and sweat.

Cedrin leaned down and gave her a lingering kiss, then broke away. 'Good morning, my Lady.'

'My Lord,' said Ellen, her eyes sparkling. Her two Suulquas echoed the greeting, but with grave formality.

Cedrin sat down. Ruus immediately pulled the platter towards him and set about tasting a small portion of each. The whole routine was quite familiar by now.

He looked down at the small parchment before Ellen and the tightly written characters. 'Dispatches?'

Ruus passed the platter across to Cedrin, who set to it with hunger.

'Yes. The most recent messages from my brother's agent in Herath. Valdas brought them in this morning.' The young Suul's face was flushed with pride at his success.

Narsiit never ceased to impress Cedrin with their speed and agility. Despite being more than seventy leagues from Herath, over rough forest trails, Valdas had managed to reach the city yesterday and return over the same distance the same night. Kalyth told him that the Emperor's Legion – the First – had once boasted narsiit-mounted cavalry units of Suul warriors. Their mobility – and ferocity – was legend.

Ellen glowed with happiness. Since leaving Herath, their dreams had been untroubled. Each night either Dagon or Esmelle stood vigil outside their sleeping chamber, always accompanied by the twin novices. To be free of the nightmares was a blessing. Before the arrival of the Twins delegation, the Behemoth had darkened their nights and filled their minds with thoughts as heavy as millstones.

Salis' strange collapse remained unexplained. Raphal could only attribute it to stress. Esmelle had used her powers to put her into a deep healing sleep. Bovosan had been strangely attentive to her, the enigmatic minitil hardly leaving her side. She had woken the next morning in full health, with no memory of falling ill. Ranis had been overjoyed at his mother's full recovery.

'What does your brother Estle have to say?' asked Cedrin.

'He has discussed Thenia's plan with Torren. As we thought, Torren will not leave Athria vulnerable – especially not since the Brotherhood came so close to taking Regent's Hill. He will not commit any troops.'

'Not while the Masks remains free,' said Cedrin. The Masks were the faceless leaders of the powerful Athrian Brotherhood. All but the Pirate's Mask had escaped to Kelas after their failed attempt at the throne.

'He is willing to commit enough warships to blockade a port for one month,' said Ellen. 'Those ships are already patrolling the Sea of Mists.'

Cedrin took a drink of water, fresh from the forest stream. It was still cold. 'Mnnn. So we are back to taking the western ports piecemeal. While southern Kelas burns.' The thought of the people dying in the south was a continual weight on him.

'Some good news though.'

'Mnn?' The roasted harena was cold, but delicious. His hunger increased as he ripped portions off the bone and gobbled them down. The early morning training had doubled his appetite.

'Torren has asked Estle to approach Daran and open a dialogue about the new Scion.'

'A dialogue?'

'The next step might be recognition of your claim. Can you imagine it?'

'I can't see why Daran would agree to that,' he said. Kalyth had always described Daran as an opportunist.

'Don't forget Kranor. Of all those who supported the old regime, he is the most respected by the Raynor Suul.'

'With the Eathal breathing down their throats? I don't think they will have time for politics,' he said.

Ellen laughed. 'You clearly know nothing about the Suul. When Osterac made his first declaration, there was almost a riot. Any crisis brings opportunity. With the Eathal on the move, the political intrigue will be more intense than ever. '

'We'll see. So are you ready for the hunt?' he asked, abruptly changing topic.

'Of course.'

Both Suulquas grinned. If there was one thing the Suul loved, it was hunting.

Chapter Seven

Cedrin firmed his grip on the spear. He peered through the foliage, waiting. He heard the whoops of Skye, Ellen and her two Suulquas as they drove the prey towards them. Veltricus' scouts certainly knew their trade. They had swiftly located a small herd of forest narsell, tracking them to a small valley some leagues from camp. Those on narsiit were sent upwind, to turn and drive them down through the valley to the waiting hunters.

The first of the narsell appeared, wings spread as it raced. They were a smaller cousin of the plains narsell, with dull green patterns on their pelts. They were certainly no slower. A trap like this was the only way to catch them.

'Now!' called one of the scouts.

Arrows flashed through the air. The narsell squealed in panic, then pain. On either side of the forest trail, hunters sprang up from hiding. Cedrin cast his spear. His target leapt up, using its wings to evade the missile. Another spear caught it as it landed.

In moments, the surviving narsell had fled into the thick undergrowth. Veltricus' scouts dispatched the wounded narsell and set to work with skinning knives. The pelts were valuable and would be taken back to the camp for salting.

Ellen and the others crested the ridge. The narsiit swept down on them, hooves hardly touching the ground. Ellen whooped in delight, her cheeks flushed with the excitement.

'Did I miss it?' said Skye, peering down from his winged mount.

'Yes, Lord Skye,' said Cedrin. 'You missed it.'

Skye shrugged and hung his horn bow back on his saddle. Marken had not joined them, preferring another day riding with Raphal in the main column, discussing the Druid's craft. They would rejoin them all at the new night-camp. The pace of the main column was so woefully slow they would easily overtake it before dark. Veltricus' scouts had led them north-east, so it would merely be a matter of finding a trail west and searching for the telltale path of the big caravan.

'Those will make a tasty meal, my Lord,' said Ranis. The Raynor Suul had remained at Cedrin's side since Herath. Ranis was both leader of the One Hundred and Cedrin's chief aide. To have a Suul at his beck and call still felt odd. The four most senior members of the One Hundred were also with him. Duro – the huge, silent warrior he had first noticed in their court; the unnaturally tall Elthar, a former Priest and master of the Way; the athletic and gregarious Velthius, nephew of Xyanthius, and Vess. The scared half-Meadrel had gratefully relinquished command of the One Hundred on Ranis' arrival. With his classic Anacian looks, Velthius had been a big hit with the Daughters. If camp rumour was any guide, he had already broken a few hearts – and warmed a few beds.

Cedrin watched the swift, economical movements of the scouts as they worked with their knives. Narsell was indeed a prized treat. His stomach rumbled at the thought of the roast meat. 'I can taste it already.'

He heard Elthar mutter a prayer under his breath, his deep voice rumbling in his chest like distant thunder. The man loomed over them all, even in the saddle.

'Mumbling again, Elthar?' said Velthius.

The tall warrior finished his cantation. 'The Gateway stands open.' They all knew what gateway he was taking about. It was the door to the realm of Kallor – lord of death. The philosophy of the Way included a respect for life and advocated a continual preparation for meeting your own end. *To enter the Gateway without regret.* Gloomy thoughts. Then again, Elthar was a sombre man.

'Time to mount up,' said Cedrin.

'Yes, my Lord.' Vess ran back through the undergrowth. He

returned a few moments later, leading their amelak mounts.

Cedrin slipped into the saddle. Veltricus' scouts gathered the hunting spears and packed away the pelts, readying to lift the dressed narsell carcasses onto their pack animals.

There was a flash of movement above them. Then more than twenty lamel dropped from the trees on silent wings. The amelak bleated in fear, rearing back. Cedrin grabbed the reins, trying to get his mount under control.

'Quickly. Grab the meat!' called a scout.

Too late. Most of the lamel were already back in the trees. The chief thieves, meat gripped in the sharp talons of their hind feet, pumped their broad wings to gain height. Lamel dived down to help them, sharing the load. They piped and sang to each other in excitement.

'Curse it!' snapped the lead scout.

Skye, the only one to have reached his weapon in time, shot at one of them with a well-timed arrow. The shaft passed harmlessly through its wing, but startled it. The lamel released its grip on the carcass it was carrying. Others dived to retrieve it, but Skye urged his narsiit towards them, firing from the saddle as he came, his Meadrel blood up. They fled. Skye leaned down in the saddle and swept up the bloody prize, lifting it in triumph.

'Well, at least the day was not a complete waste,' said Ranis.

'It need not be a waste at all,' said the scout. 'They cannot carry the meat far – and lamel do not eat on the wing. If we hurry, we can run them down.'

'Lead on,' said Cedrin.

The scout gave a high whistle. His men leapt for their saddles, leaving the other gear. They led them swiftly along the trail. Every few moments the lead scout would halt the column and listen. Cedrin could hear what he was listening for – the distinctive calls of the lamel as they fled through the forest. Interesting that they stayed as a single group.

Ellen manoeuvred her narsiit next to his mount. Her Suulquas fell back behind them with Ranis, Skye and the four warriors of the One Hundred.

'If you asked me two months ago, I never would have

believed I would be galloping through the Thilil forest chasing lamel,' said Ellen.

Cedrin steered his mount around a tree stump, leaning low over the saddle. Her own mount moved with a delicate grace, dancing casually along the trail, wings only slightly lifted. The narsiit was hardly even warm.

'Whereas I am still chasing dinner,' he quipped.

'Ha!'

The trail crested a rise and led down into a broad hollow. Even though the trail was wider, the forest overhead was taller, denser. They were moving deeper into the forest, further west into Thilil than ever before.

'There!'

They could make out the shape of the lamel moving through the trees above them. The winged thieves were sharing the weight, moving the meat between them. Skye tried another shot, but his arrow was lost in the gloom. Two feathers twirled through the air past them, one green, the other crimson.

'How do the lamel taste, by the way?' asked Skye.

The scouts exchanged a horrified look. 'The meat is taboo.'

The blond calvanni looked across at Cedrin and raised a single eyebrow. 'You would kill them, but leave the meat to rot?'

'Yes.'

'Why?'

'Tradition,' said the lead scout. 'Eating lamel is bad luck.'

'Bad luck for the lamel,' said Skye, with a wink.

The trees towered above them, many of the trunks as broad as wagons. Ahead of them, they could see the lamel on the ground.

'That's it. They have exhausted themselves. They have stopped to feed,' said the lead scout.

They thundered down the trail and swerved off through the forest. The lamel scattered, screeching in outrage, their thick beaks red with blood. They left the meat except for a single carcass, which two of the bigger lamel dragged into the air together.

'Secure those,' said the lead scout to his men. 'We can still get the last one.'

Leaving the scouts to hitch the meat to their amelak, they continued on. The ground flattened out, and ahead Cedrin could hear the sound of running water.

The lead scout pulled up abruptly.

The base of one of the huge trees was carved with an intricate symbol.

'We can go no further,' said the lead scout.

'What is it?' said Cedrin. His amelak was breathing heavily, his leggings soaked with the beast's sweat. Their mounts could not have kept that pace much longer.

'Eathal.'

'Here?' said Skye.

The scout leader looked at Skye in surprise. 'Thilil is full of them. Wild tribes. They defend their territory savagely.'

'But in the forest?'

The scout leader grew impatient. 'Yes. In the forest. They weave domes from living vines and hunt at night. Don't you have forests in the south?'

Skye shrugged. 'Not in Athria.'

'We should cut west, my Lord. Return to the main column,' said Ranis.

Cedrin was intrigued by the wild Eathal, forest-dwellers from a race so often thought of as denizens of the caverns.

'You should return along the trail,' said the lead scout. 'I will join you soon.'

'You are not coming with us?' asked Cedrin.

'I will scout ahead a little to observe them. I can move unseen here. You cannot. The intelligence could be useful.'

'As you say,' said Cedrin. He thought for a moment. 'We will wait for you here. Our mounts need a rest anyway.' He slipped from the saddle.

The lead scout reluctantly agreed. He left his amelak with them and disappeared along the trail, his mottled clothes blending easily with the forest.

'Ranis. Can you take care of the mounts? I would not mind some time alone with Suul Cintros,' said Cedrin with a smile at Ellen.

Ellen dismounted, giving her narsiit a command to stay in

place until she returned.

Cedrin took her hand and led her into the trees. Ranis watched them, clearly unhappy, but acceding to his wishes for privacy. He pulled her behind a tree. She tilted her head up to him. He gave her a quick kiss then reached for the Window. Her eyes widened as he vanished from sight, hidden by the Shadow Matrix.

'I want to follow the scout,' whispered Cedrin.

She opened her mouth to protest then stopped. A moment later she too vanished.

'Along the path. Quickly.'

Cedrin ran along the path. He could hear the regular beat of Ellen's steps behind him, and her breathing. More and more the trees displayed carvings. Perhaps some sort of territorial markers – or warnings.

At first he thought they had lost the scout, but then he appeared up ahead. He walked boldly along the middle of the path, making no attempt to hide. Soon they entered a broad clearing beside a clear river. Two huge domes filled the space. They were living things, woven from vines. They were not recently created either – the vines that comprised their structure were as thick as tree trunks. This settlement had been in place for centuries.

The scout walked straight up to the larger of the domes and yelled out a greeting in a strange language.

'That's Eathal.' Cedrin jumped as Ellen whispered right into his left ear.

Eathal dropped from the trees, shrouded in shaggy outfits of forest green. Others rose from mounds of leaves around the clearing. One Eathal warrior had leapt up less than three paces to their left, carrying a stabbing-spear with a wickedly sharp head of flint. Like all Eathal, they were squat and heavily muscled, ears large in proportion to their bald heads. All had green eyes with slit irises and rows of sharp teeth. Cedrin could not help but think of Bovosan.

The front of the dome parted, and a big Eathal walked out. He was dressed in fine leather trousers and a vest of hide trimmed with fur. He carried twin axes of darkglass, the hafts pushed through his belt on left and right. He walked slowly towards the scout. The Eathal stared at him for a long moment, then he smiled. He embraced the scout, thumping him on the back.

So these are the wild Eathal?

The other warriors – both thal and thel – relaxed. Many slipped back into the dome, while others disappeared into the forest.

'You stay here. I'm getting closer,' whispered Cedrin.

Using all his skill, he closed on the lead scout and the Eathal leader. For a long while, he was disappointed – they kept conversing in the strange, guttural Eathal tongue. Then finally the Eathal switched to Anacian.

'Give my regards to Jakir Cineth. I have been too long from the Veil,' said the Eathal. His Anacian was excellent, the accent as cultured as any Suul.

'I shall, my friend.'

The two of them gripped arms, like warriors. Like brothers. It was then, as the Eathal's vest parted, that Cedrin saw the tattoos on the Eathal's dark skin. They were the sigils of the Cineth. *The same marks as the servants of the House of Herath.*

Then the scout was moving.

Cedrin swiftly retraced his steps.

'Ellen?'

A fist thumped into his arm. 'Don't you ever do that again,' she hissed.

He grinned. He would have never been able to creep up on the scout and the Eathal leader with Ellen at his side – and she knew it. 'Let's run.'

They ran up the path, swerving into the jungle to overtake the scout. The man looked sharply in their direction as they ran past, but he saw nothing and turned away.

They returned to the same tree they had disappeared behind and released the Shadow Matrix. They looked at each other and laughed.

'My Lord,' said Ranis, running around the tree. 'I could not find you.'

'That was precisely the idea, Ranis,' said Cedrin.

The young Suul was fuming. Cedrin clapped him on the shoulder. 'My apologies, Ranis. But even the Scion needs to disappear sometimes.'

Ellen burst out laughing. They walked back to their respective entourages arm-in-arm. He could not wait to return to the camp and tell Ellen what he had learned in private. The House of Herath obviously had some special alliance with these forest Eathal. That explained their ability to take caravans so deep into Thilil. Yet what had the Eathal meant by *Jakir Cineth*?

* * *

Skye brushed the coat of his narsiit with long, even strokes. Around him, the forest had long settled into dusk, and the last glow of Larus was fading in the west, the waxing crescent of Asic hanging low above. As he worked, he chanted softly in the ancient tongue of the Meadrel – a language handed down only through the line of shamans. The words sang in his mind, swimming with a life of their own. Since Raynor, since that strange dream of the Spring, all the things his mother taught him had risen with a new life inside him.

'What is that you're singing?'

Skye turned to see it was the young Priestess of the Twins, Esmelle.

'Just an old song.'

'A song with Power,' said Esmelle. In the early evening, she looked like some apparition, her Priestess' gown catching the light of Rea as it rose full in the east. 'A song of the Earth.'

Skye continued to work in silence, enjoying a sense of peace. Magic no longer frightened him. There was a time when he would have run from Esmelle, terrified of women's mysteries. She moved closer, gliding serenely across the grass to his side.

'You are not like the others,' said Skye.

Esmelle's eyes widened for a moment, as though in fear. Then she was composed once more. 'What do you mean?'

'My mother, Ko-chan, worked at a low temple in Athria. She was a healer – at the end.' He turned to her. '*You* are a healer.'

Her warm brown eyes fixed on his. 'So sure?'

111

'Dagon, and those other creatures. They are something else entirely. What I wonder?'

She took a step away. 'Merely servants.'

'Yes. But of whom?' said Skye.

'Of the Scion. We have sworn it.'

Skye reached out to touch her cheek. The skin was unbelievably soft. 'Vows can be broken – or other vows can be stronger.'

Esmelle flushed red and moved out of reach. Her wide eyes searched his for a moment, then she walked away.

Skye chuckled, running the comb down through his narsiit's coat. Once more he started the chant. The narsiit shivered beneath his hands.

* * *

Faivel leaned forward over the saddle of his jakkund. The long-limbed beasts were fast, but by no means smooth to ride. Balancing on the back of the creature as it jerked along at full pace was now second nature to him.

The forest trail was brightly lit by Rea, the broken light of its full disk stabbing down through the dense foliage. Faivel and his warriors revelled in the night hunt, at last in their element. A jakkund galloped back along the trail and turned, joining their flight along the trail. It was one of the five trackers that Yeffrij had granted him.

'She has their scent,' said the tracker. 'They are close.'

Faivel growled in triumph. At last he had managed to run Raziin to ground. He had feared that he may have lost the mercenary's trail for good after returning to Yeffrij's war camp. Now he knew it had been worth the risk. Yeffrij had granted him one of the handful of trained teremb, the swift, silent hunters of the caverns. Once thought impossible to train, they could track a scent over leagues with savage determination.

'Prepare for combat,' said Faivel. He surprised himself with his eagerness to close with Raziin. He had come a long way from the dedicated scholar who abhorred violence. *Lidu forgive me*. This was no longer some task thrust on him by his father, this was his own personal mission. The whole future of the Eathal depended on it.

Arud and his men drew their long lances, moving in perfect formation. Faivel left his lance in its saddle-sheath. Using the deadly weapon was one skill he had yet to master. Instead he opened the Window, preparing to use his Sorcery.

The trail turned to the right, then down through a gulley.

The ground levelled out and they swept through a clearing with two campfires still burning. One of the trackers had been examining the ground, his jakkund waiting patiently beside him. When he saw the main group approaching, he hauled himself back into the saddle and urged his own mount to match their pace.

'Eight. Perhaps nine,' said the tracker from the saddle.

So few. *Raziin was his.*

The tracker blew his whistle. The high note – beyond human hearing – sounded clearly through the still night. The teremb gave a chilling howl in response, signalling the direction of the quarry. This the prey *would* hear.

'They have left the main trail,' said the teremb handler.

The trackers led them into the jungle. They soon began to climb. Faivel and his men were forced to slow to an ungainly trot and to spread out as the forest grew dense. The ground steepened, and he saw they were climbing up to a long ridge. A jagged basalt peak rose above the forest line, bereft of vegetation. It presented an impenetrable wall, broken only in three places. He used a special variation of the Listening Matrix to sense the land ahead, a ghostly image of the mountain growing in his mind. The first break – far to the west – opened into a pass striking north to the Ranmyden Range. The closest was a dead trail ending in a box canyon. The third, to the east, opened into a narrow pass that turned sharply, leading further east into Thilil. He could not risk losing Raziin again. Not when he was this close.

'Arud. Take thirty riders and sweep around to left. Block the western pass,' commanded Faivel. Raziin would surely head for Ranmyden.

Arud and his warriors shot through the forest, their eyes

reflecting green in the light of Rea.

Faivel led the other warriors straight for the western pass.

The scout signalled with his whistle again. The answering howl came from their right. *East.*

No. Raziin would not head west. He was racing Cedrin Cinanac for the Spear. He *must* head west. The eastern pass would lead him through Thilil to the human city of Apiloth. Far out of his way.

'Signal again,' said Faivel.

The howl came from even further to the east.

'Halt!'

Faivel pointed at one of the trackers. 'Go west. Quickly! Tell Arud to make for the eastern pass.'

Grinding his teeth in fury, Faivel turned his twenty jakkund lancers to the east. He could not believe Raziin had tricked him again. Not that it mattered. His scouts told him the Armon warriors were on foot. They could not outrun jakkund.

Soon the jungle opened out. Faivel squinted in the glare of the moonlight as it reflected off the sheer basalt walls of the pass. There! Less than two hundred paces in front of them. Nine running figures.

'We have them!' The tracker's whistle sounded again. This time a different tone, calling back the teremb. She would continue to run down the prey, attacking with ferocity if not stopped. She had performed her task and was too valuable to risk in close combat.

'Run them down!' commanded Faivel.

Faivel held on tight as the jakkund surged to full pace. The darkglass blades of the lances glittered in the moonlight, pointed down at the prey.

One of the running figures turned. Faivel felt the Fire rise. He swiftly formed the Barrier, then the Shield Matrix, protecting his men. Faivel grinned savagely as he made a special modification to the Shield Matrix that would dull both light and sound. He would not be fooled twice.

A rain of silver missiles appeared, scything at the legs of the mounts. They detonated harmlessly against his Shield. A moment later there was a burst of light, then a sharp detonation like thunder. Raziin had used the trick before in Tupur. The flash of light was disorienting but gone quickly, the thunder muffled to a distant roar by his Matrix. Their line faltered for a moment as the jakkund, with their sensitive hearing, reacted to the attack. They were brought quickly under control.

Now it was his turn.

He sent a razor-sharp disk of Force spinning towards Raziin. The human Sorcerer hastily raised a Shield, deflecting the construct, which cut left and sheared straight through another of the running warriors before embedding itself in the wall of the pass. It vanished, loosing a cascade of rocks that pelted down on Raziin's men.

Every moment the jakkund closed on them.

He was close enough to see Raziin's white face, twisted with impotent fury. The human turned and ran, following his men into the narrow pass. Raziin was in sight and outnumbered, it was only a matter of time. And Arud followed close behind him.

He led the jakkund-mounted warriors into the pass. The formation narrowed, the pass only wide enough for three of them to ride abreast. Faivel slowed his pace, alert for Raziin's tricks. The mercenary was cunning – one of the most savage of Hukum's agents in Kelas until he outlived his usefulness.

The pass twisted to the right, leading into a long straight corridor with towering basalt walls on either side. Less than one hundred paces away, Raziin stood waiting for them, his men behind him. One of his men, a golden giant, towered over the rest.

Faivel swiftly drew on the Fire and put the Shield in place. As he anticipated, Raziin also drew on his power. A moment later, a single bolt of Force flew at them like a battering ram. He strengthened his Shield, already preparing a counter. But the bolt did not strike his Shield. It shot above them, slamming into the side of pass. It shattered the rock. With a groan, a basalt tower tilted and fell. It struck Faivel's Shield harmlessly, fracturing into a hundred smaller pieces.

Faivel countered with another disk of Force, but it was hindered by falling rock as Raziin struck again, then again. Soon a small avalanche had begun, a great mass of rock tumbling down to slam into the pass. When the dust cleared, they stood unharmed, but the passage forward was blocked by a wall of rock.

Faivel waved the tracker forward. The thal scrambled up the fallen rock easily – Eathal were built for climbing – and stood at the top.

'They are running, my Lord.'

Faivel suppressed his frustration. It was nothing but a delaying tactic.

'Get down.' The tracker scrambled to safety.

He channelled as much Fire as he dared into the Force Matrix, pushing at the mass of rock. He managed to slide some of the rock out of the way, levelling the huge pile, yet even with his powers it would take hours to clear a path for the jakkund.

There was still no sign of Huntmaster Arud. He could not wait. He refused to allow Raziin to slip away. They could follow on foot. The lances would be useless in close combat and would have to remain here with the mounts. Thankfully his warriors were also equipped with twin axes of darkglass, the favoured weapons of the Eathal elite. His scouts had only hunting spears and knives.

'The jakkund stay here. The scouts and the teremb can remain here as rearguard. The rest of you with me,' he commanded.

Faivel led his twenty troops over the pile of debris. Together they broke into a steady run. He drew his axes. The weight of the matched weapons felt good in his hands, familiar after hundreds of hours of intensive training.

At last they broke free of the twisting mountain pass onto open hillside. Raziin's men were waiting, exhausted and at the limit of their endurance. Even so, they spread out, extending the twin blades of their greatscythes.

'There is nowhere left to run,' called Faivel in the Eathal tongue.

'Run? From you?' snarled Raziin. He hurled a bolt of Force, but Faivel swept it aside contemptuously. His blood up, he charged for the human Sorcerer. Around him, his warriors plunged into the black-clad mercenaries.

Faivel swung his right axe at Raziin's head, testing the human's defences. A greatscythe blade sliced at his throat. He blocked it with his left axe and circled away. He blocked two more strikes, then feinted in with his right axe. Raziin deflected it with the haft of his greatscythe. Faivel pressed forward, limiting Raziin's movement. Then he chopped straight down with his left axe at the mercenary's head – the very strike the single-headed weapons were designed for. The human warrior managed to block the deadly strike, but the force of the blow drove his blade down. The edge of the darkglass blade sliced deep into Raziin's left cheek. The mercenary growled in rage and kicked out at Faivel's groin.

Faivel blocked the kick with his raised knee, striking down with his right axe. Raziin swung away to give himself the room he needed for the greatscythe, his braided silver hair fanning out as he turned.

'Amelak, my Lord. Human warriors,' called out the scouts from the hill behind him.

Faivel stepped back, letting another of the jakkund warriors take his place against Raziin. A force of more than sixty amelak-mounted troops was galloping up the hill towards them, lead by Suul on narsiit. *Reinforcements.* 'No. *No.*' Even from here he could see the keerhound standard of Armon flying above them. It seemed inconceivable. Raziin was an exile, hated by his own family, reviled by his own people for the murder of his father. Why would Armon come to his rescue?

Faivel's fists tightened around the hafts of his axes. Raziin's warriors had fought skilfully, forming a defensive line on either side of their master, but they faced Eathal of supreme skill. Three of the mercenaries had fallen, leaving only six alive including Raziin. In heartbeats, their whole defence would have collapsed. Yet that was time Faivel did not have. His own men would soon be surrounded by a superior force. A mounted force. The thought that he would lose his own elite jakkund-troops made him burn with fury. He could not permit that, or put his own mission in danger.

'Disengage!' commanded Faivel. 'Retreat to the pass!'

His warriors pulled back, leaving Raziin and his men on the

hillside. The human warriors leaned against their greatscythes in exhaustion, sucking in great gasps of air. Raziin stared back at Faivel in triumph. Blood streamed down his left cheek. One handspan closer and the axe-blow would have killed the renegade.

Faivel glared at Raziin, furious that he was forced to retreat. He turned and ran after his thals. This was too much of a coincidence. Some unseen power had allied itself with Raziin. But why? Who could possibly benefit from seeing such a snake triumph?

* * *

Raziin channelled the Fire into the Matrix of Form. The wound on his cheek knitted closed, as though it had never been. A bad sprain in his left calf also vanished as the muscle repaired.

As the golden nimbus faded, he turned to see his brother Ralin gallop up the hillside with a force of mounted warriors. He dispatched ten of them to pursue the fleeing Eathal and walked his narsiit to Raziin. Two senior aides flanked him, both Suul, also mounted on narsiit.

'I received your message, brother. I warn you. Any deceit in this, and your head will fall. There will be no public trial this time,' said Ralin. Like his father, Ralin had the golden skin and hair of the true Cioan. He and Leith were so alike. Raziin detested them both.

'Brother. I cannot tell you how it has pained me to be exiled from my homeland. Yet it was nothing less than I deserved. I committed a terrible crime, however well motivated my intentions.'

'And now?'

Raziin struggled to seem contrite. The pretence was necessary if he was ever to win his prize. 'Now Armon is threatened.' He paused for dramatic effect. 'The Cinanac heir, a true Scion, is moving north gathering support as he marches. The old guard of Bulvuran are gathering around him like carrion birds. If we do not stand together to destroy this threat, a new Empire will rise. Armon *must* remain independent. Free.

For this I will sacrifice anything.'

The two aides nodded in sympathy with his words. So easily fooled.

'We are the last outpost of Cioa,' said Raziin. 'It is up to us to preserve our culture at all costs.'

His brother's eyes narrowed. 'And for my support in this – venture – you agree to renounce any claim to the Armon throne?'

'I swear it,' said Raziin, with all the grave force he could muster. 'I will destroy Cedrin Cinanac.' *No one will sit on the throne of Bulvuran but me – with the Spear at my command.*

'We shall see. You will return with us to Apiloth. I would have this declaration public.'

'As you say, brother,' said Raziin.

Ralin's warriors brought him and his remaining five warriors amelak mounts. He had lost so many. Yet Merceth and Kyal survived. He would reward them well.

His brother looked down at him from his narsiit, mouth twisted in contempt. 'You will serve, Armon. Or you will die.' His brother turned and galloped away, back straight as a ramrod. Self-righteous prig. *It will be you and the whole of Armon who will kneel, brother. Kneel or die.*

He urged his amelak forward. 'Ralin?'

'Yes.'

'Will Razell be there?' asked Raziin.

'Yes. The whole court must bear witness.'

Raziin suppressed a smile. He so looked forward to seeing his twin sister again. He despised her more than any of them.

Chapter Eight

Ellen laid a hand over her heart to still it.

Asgod-Ki had appeared above the tree line. She had forgotten how it dominated the sky, looming over all. In Herath, it had been a continual presence. Only now did she realise how it had haunted her.

After thirteen days of travel through the isolated forest of Thilil, they had turned west again, towards the Myfis Bridge. Twice they had turned back attacks from bandits, themselves driven away from the road by the drakon swarm. Both attacks had come at night. Each band had met with stiff resistance, retreating swiftly under the ferocious counterattack of their combined forces. The wounded had been swiftly healed by Marken, his Moon Essence skills now considerable after Raphal's continual tutelage. In both cases they had been too far from holy sites for Esmelle or any of the Earth Essence practitioners to assist. Fortunately only a few of their warriors had taken wounds.

Ellen rode at the front of the column with Cedrin and his inner circle, Skye and Marken always close at hand. Dagon and the Twins delegation rode just behind. The senior warriors of the One Hundred flanked them on either side. Osterac, as always, stood out in his finery.

Xyanthius, an old hand at protecting caravans, had organised the guard into three sections. The One Hundred took the vanguard and middle guard, while Thenia and the Daughters comprised the rearguard. The system worked smoothly. Veltricus and his own warriors positioned themselves in the

120

centre, defending their precious goods. The other travellers, all mounted, rode between Veltricus and the rearguard.

The other peaks of Ranmyden became visible as they neared the edge of the forest. Then, all at once, the trees were gone. The twin suns bore down on them, their harsh noon light unbroken by leaf or bough. They came onto the Beslin road just north of Asgod-Ki. It was an imperial highway, set with huge blocks of rectangular stone. Once on the road, the pace increased dramatically. It ran through a broad plain that sloped down to the foothills of the Mulisar Range to the west and the thin ribbon of the Myfis River to the north.

One of Veltricus' scouts raced to the head of the column. His face was drawn, eyes wide. 'The drakon swarm have been this way, my Lord Scion. I found stripped carcasses off the edge of the road.'

The drakon-spawn were the size of raptors when hatched. Who knew how big they had grown already? *Uros.* They had hoped to bypass the threat entirely.

Cedrin turned in the saddle. Ellen felt the Fire flow in him and knew he was enhancing his sight. She was pleased at his casual control. She also formed the Lens. Shapes moved below Agod-Ki, shifting too fast to make out.

'Xyanthius?' asked Cedrin gravely.

It was Xyanthius, once a First Captain in the Legion, who was in charge of the defence of the column.

'I would advise a close watch – and an increase in pace,' said Xyanthius.

Orders were called down the line. The amelak, already tired from the days of travel, bleated in protest as they were pushed again. Her narsiit snorted impatiently. For her mount the pace was still woefully slow. It would do no harm to burn off a bit of her energy. Kalyth ordered the One Hundred to reinforce their guard of Cedrin. The Scion and his entourage were soon surrounded by four ranks of mounted warriors.

'Time to stretch our legs,' said Ellen

'Be careful,' said Cedrin.

'Valdas. Mendor,' called Ellen.

Her two Suulquas left formation and flanked her as she

turned back to the south. Together they let their mounts have their head, flying down the road. The column flashed past on the left, and soon they had left the rearguard behind them. It felt good to move fast. They heard a whoop behind them, and she turned to see Skye close on them on his own narsiit. Although untrained, the former calvanni was an instinctive rider. They pushed the mounts until all four narsiit had their wings fully spread – cooling and lifting them. Ellen felt she was truly flying.

After a few minutes of breakneck speed, they turned and raced back up the road. They quickly overtook the column, racing past Cedrin's entourage and the outriders far in front.

Ellen turned her mount smoothly, followed by the others. Together they galloped back to the column at a more modest pace. Her heart soared with the feeling of freedom.

A cloud moved across the blue sky. Ellen squinted upward. It shifted, then parted, resolving into winged shapes.

'The drakon-spawn,' she whispered as a chill clawed its way down her spine. 'Rejoin the formation. Quickly!'

They closed on the caravan and rejoined the ranks. Veltricus and his senior aides had joined Cedrin in the van. The whole line was moving fast, the amelak breathing harshly in the heat.

'You saw them?' asked Cedrin.

'Yes.' The swarm circled far overhead.

'They are further north than we expected,' said Veltricus. His glowmetal earring swung like a pendulum as he tilted his head to the sky. He swallowed. His Adam's apple bobbed up and down in his neck.

'Should we move into a defensive formation?' asked Kalyth.

'No. We should keep the forward pace. A static formation should be the last resort.' Like the others, Xyanthius watched the swarm, his eyes shaded by his hand from the glare of the suns.

Their narsiit neighed nervously, now restless in the packed ranks.

'Here they come!' called Veltricus' lead scout.

'About turn! Defensive formations!' commanded Xyanthius.

The command was relayed down the line.

Time stretched out. Every breath brought the swarm closer. As they grew in her sight, they resolved from dark shapes to winged creatures, yet like nothing she had seen. Their bodies were long and sleek, their overlong wings narrow and jagged across the trailing edge. Their tails broadened into a wedge, like a kite. They glittered beautifully in the suns. A deadly beauty.

Finally the column halted. The riders drew cavalry scythes or spears and pointed them skyward, surrounding them with a wall of deadly blades. Skye's narsiit whinnied in fear, but he sang to it in a soft chant and it eased. Strangely, the other narsiit also settled. He reached for his bow, but she caught his eye and shook her head.

'Cedrin. Shield,' said Ellen.

Together they channelled the Fire. They joined minds across the Bridge and formed a single Shield Matrix. It formed an unseen dome above them, shielding the front of the column.

The swarm split and streaked past them.

'Force!'

Both she and Cedrin shot bolts of Force at the drakon-spawn. Three of the creatures shrieked as they shattered in the air above them like glass. Green fluid rained down. She saw the Herath men flinch, then straighten as the acid blood vaporised above the Shield and blew away. Veltricus remained unmoved, his face set with stoney determination.

She blinked as she realised the drakon-spawn were transparent, like some sort of sinister glass figurines. The spawn nearest them descended on the shattered carcasses of their birth-mates and fought viciously over the remains. In moments, nothing was left.

The rest of the swarm streaked down the line, darting in to snap at the mounted warriors in the rear of the column, where their Shield did not extend. Men and women screamed in pain as the beasts spat at them, their breath leaving painful burns. Yet the formation held. Everywhere the warriors fought to control their terrified amelak. A small group of travellers, alone on the road, would not have stood a chance.

The swarm circled above them, ready for another strike. The day darkened as a cloud covered the suns. The swarm began to dive, then abruptly they sped away.

'Oh, sweet Larus,' said Marken.

Ellen followed Marken's gaze and saw why the drakon-spawn had fled. Cruising high above them was a fully grown drakon. Black as night. Even flying far above them it looked massive. She used the Lens. Its blunt, armoured head filled her vision, its gaze fixed on her and Cedrin. Ellen's throat constricted. Her lungs burned, but she could not draw a breath. It was the same feeling of menace she had sensed from Asgod-Ki. The sense of a watching presence.

Esmelle came to her side. She whispered a prayer under her breath, and a feeling of peace descended on Ellen. She sucked in a breath, then another. She released her grip on the Fire and sensed Cedrin do the same.

The big drakon sailed by overhead then banked sharply up the distant flank of Asgod-Ki. The last they saw of it, the drakon had disappeared somewhere amidst the shattered peak.

'Let's press on. If we hurry we can cross the Myfis Bridge before dark,' said Xyanthius.

The caravan was restored to order. The burns were small – the size of coins – and swiftly healed by Raphal using the power of Larus.

And they continued north.

* * *

Ellen leaned forward in the saddle as the trading post grew closer, easing her lower back. The town extended all the way from the deep green of the forest's edge to the Myfis Bridge. It was a sprawling settlement, with rough wooden buildings tumbled together like child's toys around muddy streets. A light rain started, and the rutted tracks ran like a maze of streams, the water bright with yellow clay.

'Charming,' said Skye.

'At last I know where to build my summer palace,' said Marken, his eyes lit with amusement.

The Beslin road ran straight through the town's centre, edged with raised stones and gutters. The muddy streets snaked away from it on either side, like ribs from a spine.

Every step north from Asog-Ki had been a blessing. After

their encounter with the drakon-spawn, they had followed the road west around the Mulisar foothills to the Myfis River. From there, the road ran north along the east bank of the Myfis to the trading post. The river ran fast and furious across massive boulders, tumbling with white spray. Not once had she glimpsed a safe place to ford it.

Xyanthius led them along the road to the main square, then halted the column. Market stalls were jammed into the space on either side of the road, overlapping in a jumble of colour. The stall traders called out to them in a babble of voices, but dared not approach the flint-eyed warriors. Ingots of rubber harvested from the forest, fur pelts, harena ivory, minerals for glass making, rare scented woods and animals – even glowmetals – all were offered for sale. Although glowmetals were always rare, those used in magic were rarer still. It was unlikely these possessed any useful qualities, and even if they did, unlocking their secrets was probably a lifetime's work.

Veltricus and his men left the caravan and disappeared into the sprawling mass. Ellen saw two of the Suul's scouts bartering furiously at a stall, trying to get a good price for the narsell pelts.

A crowd began to gather, pointing in excitement at the phoenix standard and watching the narsiit with wide eyes. Word of the Scion had gone ahead of them.

'Stay in formation,' said Xyanthius. His commands were relayed down the column.

Cedrin cocked his head to the side. 'Is that . . . It is. A lamel.' He turned to Xyanthius. 'I won't go far.'

'As you will, my Lord.'

Cedrin led his amelak from the caravan. Intrigued, Ellen followed with her Suulqua. Skye and Marken joined them. Ranis and ten of the One Hundred flanked them on all sides, eyes vigilant. Osterac watched them move away, his face creased with frustration.

The crowd melted away before them.

One of the stallholders selling animals had a large wicker cage set up next to his tables. Inside it was the lamel. Its green and red plumage was filthy. Two festering stumps on its shoulders were all that remained of its wings. It sat slumped at the base of the cage. The talons of its hind feet gripped the wicker bars while it tore at its lank plumage with its right foretalon. A bare and bleeding patch on its chest showed where it had been ripping at itself. The ground in front of the cage was littered with feathers.

Other smaller birds called out from cages. Plump, headless forest birds hung from the front of the stall in rows, slowly dripping blood. Freshly killed.

The lamel opened its beak and issued a plaintive screech. It waited for a moment, head cocked to the side, then gave another cry.

Ellen was immediately reminded of Erioth, her teacher. The Verial were bigger than their lamel cousins, and far more intelligent, but the similarities were striking. The same large eyes and humanoid face, and a broad beak where the mouth and nose would be. The lamel turned its yellow eyes on her and shrieked again, as though it called to her.

The stallholder noted her attention and wacked at the cage with a rough staff. 'Shut up, you filthy thieving animal.' He turned to Ellen. 'I can sell for a good price. Rare to get one in captivity, believe me. Very rare.'

The lamel shrieked at the stallholder, feathers flaring.

'Shut up.' The stallholder slid the staff through the bars and jabbed it into the lamel's ribcage.

'Leave it!' snapped Ellen. The stallholder's face blanched. 'Of course. As my Lady commands.' He licked his lips nervously, eyes on the greatscythes of the One Hundred.

'Better to kill it out of hand,' said Marken. The golden-skinned Druid shivered in disgust. Skye remained thoughtful.

'Without the wings it looks like a skinny child dressed in costume,' said Cedrin.

It was true. Unlike the Verial, who had powerful upper torsos, the lamel were slim. No doubt they were much better flyers. Unaided by magic, the Verial could do little more than glide. Ellen's heart sank at the thought of the lamel sitting in the rank cage. She looked into its yellow eyes, trying to judge its intelligence. Was it nothing more than a beast? Was her reaction purely fantasy?

The crowd grew steadily, blocking the caravan from sight.

The lamel piped at her. A fluting melody.

'It's almost as if they have a form of rudimentary speech. I noticed that in Thilil. The range of calls is impressive,' said Cedrin.

'Perhaps the taboo against eating them is more than just tradition,' said Skye.

All her emotion boiled to release. 'Free it,' she demanded.

The stallholder's face paled with fear. 'But, my Lady. It cost me dearly. I hoped to make a profit. I . . . have three wives. Seven children. Thilil is such a poor place to make a living.'

'Silence,' snapped Ellen. 'You will get your coin. Free it or my men will.' Valdas and Mendor drew cavalry scythes from the sheaths on their saddles and glared down at the man with all the arrogance and ferocity of Suul. The Fire gathered inside her.

The man bowed. He took a small knife from his belt – the lanedd edge chipped along its blade – and slashed through the bindings that held the cage shut. He pulled open the door and hastily backed away.

The lamel looked at the open door and blinked. In one swift movement, it was standing at the opening. The crowd cried out and surged back. The lamel leapt up from the cage then fell sprawling into the mud.

Ellen focussed her mind, forming the Matrix of Form. She had only ever used it on humans, but she could not bear to see this creature without its wings. She reached out, seeking the Key – the essential pattern that formed the physical body. The lamel stood awkwardly on its hindtalons, then sank to the ground. It sat as it had in the cage, reaching to tear at itself once more, its eyes dull.

Ellen's concentration was total. The Matrix of Form wrapped the creature in an unseen sheath. It pervaded its body . . . seeking.

'Ellen?' Beside her, Cedrin sensed her use of the Fire, yet he could have no idea what she was tyring to attempt.

There. She had it. Delicately, she reshaped the Key, itself a Matrix designed to form a coherent structure with the Matrix of

Form. The manipulations were complex, and any mistake would cause an abomination.

A golden light grew around the creature.

The crowd called out in fear and wonder, drawn forward despite themselves.

The light faded.

The lamel looked to left and right, flexing its new wings. The plumage was brilliant green and red with highlights of blue.

The lamel gave a high note and leapt into the air. The stallholder ducked for cover as its talons slashed down at his face, but the move was a feint. It snatched two of the hanging birds in its hind feet and shot over the crowd, flying swiftly to the west. Cedrin and Ellen turned their mounts and pushed through the crowd back to the Beslin road, followed by their entourage. By the time they reached the caravan, the lamel had reached the sanctuary of the trees. She heard its triumphant cry once more, then it was gone.

'My coin! My coin!'

'Stay back if you value your life,' rumbled Elthar. Ellen had not even seen him move. One of his greatscythe blades now hovered a thumb's width from the man's face.

Ellen took a ruby from her purse and threw the purplish-red coin at the man's feet. 'There.'

The man's face split into a grin. He bowed and backed away.

'I have concluded my business here,' said Veltricus. The Herath Suul had joined them in the vanguard with his aides.

'Can we continue the crossing, my Lord?' asked Xyanthius.

'By all means,' said Cedrin. He gave Ellen a puzzled look, and they rejoined the formation.

The ramshackle town ended at the river. Like the road, the Myfis Bridge was a relic of the Empire. Built in four massive spans, the stone arches were supported on a series of rocky islands, levelled in antiquity by Bulvuran engineers. At either end of the bridge rose a four-storey tower, the road passing through a broad archway in the base. They passed beneath the east tower without challenge. Dirty faces peered out at them from the windows above, eyes wide with curiosity. The warriors eyed them carefully, alert for any attack.

'Squatters,' said Veltricus.

At the other end of the bridge, the west tower was manned with soldiers, the archway blocked by a line of scythemen. Ellen prepared the Shield Matrix as she noted the archers on the battlements.

A high-ranking officer came out of the tower, flanked by two lieutenants. Ellen was surprised to see he was dressed in the traditional gear of a Legion Captain. The Tenth, once formed from the provinces of Exdor and Culgriv, was long defunct.

The column halted while Veltricus and his men went ahead to talk with the Bridge Captain. They shared a joke and talked for a few minutes, then the Captain signalled for his men to let them through.

'All routine,' said Veltricus as he rejoined them.

They remained alert though, until they had exited the bridge.

The small town on the other side of the bridge could not have been more different from the trading post. The buildings were stone-built, the narrow streets leading from the Beslin road neatly cobbled.

'Welcome to Exdor,' said Veltricus. The country was open here. Crops and orchards all in neat rows. Amelak and other northern cattle grazed in the fields.

An amelak rider left the western bridge tower, pushing hard and leading two spare mounts. *A Dispatch rider.*

'The Scion has arrived,' observed Kalyth.

'Yes. Word will go ahead of us, there is no preventing it,' said Salis. Ellen could tell she wanted to say more, but remained silent because of Veltricus.

The suns were low in the west. Uros already touched the horizon.

'The Herath compound is on the western edge of the town,' said Veltricus.

'We can take lodgings here,' said Ellen. After watching the strange conversation between his scout and the Eathal leader in the forest, both she and Cedrin had been wary of Veltricus. Neither of them had been able to understand why the Eathal had used such an archaic term of address as *Jakir*. The mythical heroes of ancient times were long passed from the world. The most likely explanation was a mistranslation from Eathal to Anacian of the word 'Lord.'

'Please. I insist. The Herath compound here has been too long vacant. We have room for all. My servants will be eager to serve, you'll see.'

Cedrin turned to Salis, looking for a reading of Veltricus' intent. Ellen waited expectantly. Salis brushed her blonde hair away from her face in a seemingly natural movement. It was a prearranged signal. She could sense no ill-intent.

'We would be pleased to accept your hospitality, Suul Cineth,' said Cedrin.

'It will be nice to have a hot bath, will it not?' said Salis to Ellen. The Suul's light grey eyes glowed with warmth.

'Yes,' replied Ellen. Guilt gnawed away at her. She had still not taken Salis aside to discuss her . . . precautions. Approaching the Twins delegation was out of the question. They were firmly outside the inner circle. She had steeled herself to talk to Salis that last night at Herath, but then the Raynor Suul had fallen ill at court. On the road, the time had never seemed right. Raphal was a dear friend and family confessor, yet for this . . . No.

Tonight. She would ask Salis tonight.

'It's settled then,' said Veltricus.

* * *

Ellen teased at a lock of her honey-blonde hair. Across the room, Salis was deep in conversation with her son, Thenia and Xyanthius, her husband's old confidant.

'Sitting all alone?' She turned at the sound of Skye's voice.

Ellen sat up, adjusting the fall of her gown. It felt strange to be in court attire again after so long on the road. Now that they were in Exdor, soon to be approaching the capital Beslin, she had reluctantly decided to abandon her leathers. It was important the Suul in Exdor were presented the right image of the fledgling court of the Scion.

'Lost in thought,' said Ellen.

The night's celebrations had been welcome by the small court. Veltricus' servants had lived up to his claims, the sprawling compound – designed as a caravanserai – easily accommodated them all. The One Hundred and the Daughters were vigilant as always, but they were all relieved to be free of the dangers of Thilil. Cedrin was talking strategy with Kalyth, while Marken chattered away in Cioan with Raphal. The Twins delegation stood apart as always, as did the silent Bovosan. Cedrin was surrounded by his bodyguard, and she noted that once more Osterac had volunteered to taste his food. He also listened avidly to their conversation. Ellen had never seen anyone more driven by ambition. The Suul's urgent desire to rise in the One Hundred was transparent.

'I remember you from Regent's Hill,' said Skye.

Ellen thought she misheard. 'Regent's Hill, did you say?'

'Yes. I have been waiting to see if you made the connection, but perhaps it was too long ago.'

Ellen's mouth opened in a silent 'O'.

'My father Astor was weaponmaster to Myan. Before his death, we lived in Regent's Hill. You and I played together as young children.'

Ellen lifted her eyebrows. She knew the story. Astor was a Razor in the Athrian Legion. Gifted with all weapons, he soon distinguished himself in the eastern campaigns. Later her father Myan took him as weaponmaster to his court. He was executed for killing a young Suul lord in a duel. It was forbidden for non-Suul to challenge a Lord.

She searched Skye's face, trying to remember a time before her totem at thirteen when all males were removed from her circle. Before the Court training began at eight years. When she had not been surrounded by minders and tutors. There had been a time, when she was one Suul child among many. A brief time of sunshine and play in the cultured gardens of Regent's Hill. The memories were too vague.

'I'm sorry. I cannot remember,' she said.

'No matter,' said Skye. 'You loved hide-and-seek as I remember. And being chased.'

Across the room, Salis rose. She passed a few final words to the small group around her then took her leave. She walked right past her.

Ellen felt light-headed, a flush of sweat appearing under her arms. Her cheeks grew hot.

She looked at Salis as she passed. Yet remained mute. She could not do it. Whether it was pride or fear, she could not tell. Perhaps both. She could not ask the stately Suul for help.

'Are you alright, Ellen?' asked Skye.

She forced a light laugh. 'Of course. Wine and weariness. A fatal combination.'

Ellen pushed herself to her feet and left the room, keeping her poise with sheer determination. Her Suulqua rose to follow, but she waved them back to their seats with a tight smile. Vess and Russ flanked her as she walked to her chambers. Once inside, she fled to her bed and burst into tears. She hugged the pillow to stifle her sobs. The door to her privy chamber opened, and she smelled Serel's cheap perfume.

'Are you alright, my Lady?' She felt such a fool!

Ellen lifted her head from the bed. 'I . . . might need your help after all. With . . . the things we talked about.'

'When we reach Exdor, I will see to it,' said Serel firmly. She laid a soft hand on Ellen's arm. 'Come, my Lady. Let me draw you a bath.'

'Another?'

'Yes.'

She let herself be undressed, her mind growing blank as Serel and the two slaves fussed around her. What would it have been like, she wondered, to have a mother?

* * *

Cedrin stripped off his training shirt and splashed water on his chest and face. The water in the washbowl was tepid, transported with them from the last roadside stop. He was outside his own pavilion in the morning air, surrounded by his senior advisers. All stood except for Raphal, who sat slumped in a canvass chair. The travel had taken its toll on the old Priest and Druid.

Cedrin dabbed himself dry with a towel. Spider, standing guard over Thenia with Jeth, took it from him and laid it on the small table next to the bowl. He had grown used to her presence.

They had reached the outskirts of Beslin in five days, moving swiftly over well-maintained roads. The whole of Exdor was peaceful and heavily patrolled, the countryside untroubled. Under the Cinanac, the whole of Kelas had once been like this. The northern Sardom had been isolated from the worst of the strife by its location and its isolation from the troubled ports of the west coast.

They had made camp the previous night on a plateau that overlooked Beslin. The city was ten times the size of Herath, surrounded by thick walls of grey granite that sloped down to a broad base. Small towns surrounded the city, each set inside a vast network of croplands. Exdor was rich country, once covered by a forest as vast as Thilil, long ago cleared by his own Anacian ancestors.

Veltricus and the other Herath travellers had entered Beslin last night.

'We should approach the Sarlord directly,' said Xyanthius.

'I agree,' said Kalyth. 'Xyanthius and I should enter Beslin as a delegation from the Scion.'

'Why not the Scion himself?' said Cedrin.

'This is not Herath, my Lord. We cannot risk you until we know the politics of the Suul,' said Kalyth. As much as it irked Cedrin to sit outside Beslin and await a result, he agreed. There were simply too many unknowns.

Bypassing the city was also not an option. They needed to resupply and some idea of where to direct their search of Ranmyden. They would also need the permission of the Sarlord. Exdor was a tightly controlled territory. Their advance so far had been on condition they present themselves at the Beslin court.

'I will lead the delegation,' said Salis. 'I know the Exdor Suul. They will need to see one of their own.'

'I thought Kranor's mercenary operations did not operate this far north?' said Cedrin.

'They don't. But I have relatives here. After the fall of Bulvuran, my mother and I were sent to Beslin. We returned to

133

Raynor later, when the Warlord's hold on the city was secure.'

Cedrin was not surprised. The Suul were an exclusive class that only married their own. It was a small world, within the broader circle of the elite. Intermarriage and alliance, maintaining connections between courts, all were bread and meat to the Suul. *And to me.* He had to keep reminding himself he was one of them.

'My son should also come with me to represent the One Hundred.'

Ranis handed Cedrin his harness, which he slipped over his head, then an open shirt of blue silk. It felt soft and cool against his skin.

'My presence is also vital,' said Thenia. 'As Hanis Sarqua I lend credibility to your claims.'

'Agreed.' He had long ceased to think of Thenia as a child. Her mind was a sharp as any of them – in fact sharper. It was her single-minded determination that could be a thorn in his side.

'I will accompany them as well. I need to contact my friend Valnis. His help will be vital on the journey north,' said Raphal. The old Priest's face was drawn, with dark circles under his eyes. Cedrin wanted to see a distinct improvement in his health before he agreed to take him to Ranmyden.

Cedrin's thumb played over the ruby signet ring. 'You should also sound out the response of the local Temple of the Sisters to the Hesguit's edict against Ellen.'

Raphal nodded gravely. 'I will.'

'We are agreed then?' he said, looking around at his advisors, who answered in the affirmative. 'Good luck then. Send word as soon as you have any news.'

Cedrin turned and entered his tent. The main chamber was deserted, although the table had been set with an array of food and drink. All tested of course. All the servants had been sent away, the entrances guarded by the One Hundred and Ellen's own Suulquas. All had instructions to admit no one. They would soon enter Beslin, and he and Ellen were eager to take this last chance for privacy. He picked up a flagon of wine and two glasses and pushed aside the curtain to their bedchamber.

The interior was set with candles. Ellen sat at the small dressing table waiting for him, dressed in a light sleeping shift. One bare leg was draped across the arm of the chair.

Cedrin broke into a grin. He put down the two glasses and poured two measures of wine.

Her foot slid up the outside of his trousers to his groin and rested there.

She took a swallow of wine. 'You seem overdressed, my Lord Scion.' Her eyes were wide and dark, her cheeks flushed.

'Quickly remedied.'

He discarded the harness and shirt he had donned only moments ago, the trousers following them. Ellen threw off her shift and leapt at him. Her legs wrapped around his hips, and her sudden weight sent him sprawling onto the bedding. Then her lips found his.

She tasted of wine, and something sweet. His hands circled her back. Her skin felt impossibly smooth. He wanted to drink her in, like a balm to his lonely past. The kiss filled his mind – the taste of her lips, the wet warmth of her tongue. His calloused fingers swept through her hair. The sensation ignited his desire, and his fingers closed around a fistful of honey-blonde strands. Ellen gasped and he stopped.

He was on top of her, but could not remember how he got there. Her legs were wrapped around his hips. Her skin glowed hot. She growled in frustration and pulled him down. Then he was inside her, and the world fell away. He did not know if it was the training in the Way or the depth of their strengthening bond, but every sensation came alive to him, becoming a world in itself. Every touch and caress, every exquisite movement. Time stretched into a vast landscape of sensation.

Then it ended in a cascade of pleasure. He groaned in ecstasy, and she squirmed beneath him, her breath coming fast and hot across his neck.

'I love you,' she whispered.

Cedrin levered himself up on his muscular arms. 'And I love you, my beautiful Suul.'

He leant down and kissed her red lips, then rolled away. He reached for the glasses. He passed hers across the bed and refilled both.

'To us,' said Cedrin, clinking his glass against hers.

'Forever,' she said. Tears fled down her cheek as she looked up at him, searching his face. Searching.

Chapter Nine

Ellen jerked awake. A hand clamped down on her face, covering her mouth. It was dark, yet she could tell she was in her pavilion bedchamber. She reached for the Fire, but then recognised the rough palm and the masculine scent. *Cedrin.* He saw she was awake and released her.

There was a high tearing sound. Cloth being cut.

Cedrin leant over the bed, drawing both calvs from their sheaths in perfect silence.

Without moving, Ellen formed a Shield Matrix.

Cedrin sprang from the bed. She sensed the Fire. A moment later, brilliant white light flared through the space. Ellen rolled from the bed.

Two assassins were inside, both armed with blowpipes. The explosion of light made them pause for one uncertain moment. Cedrin threw a calv. It took the first in the throat. He jerked and fell, the blowpipe falling from his nerveless fingers. The second swivelled his pipe towards Ellen. *The same weapon that killed Father.* For one horrible moment, she felt utterly exposed, standing naked while the assassin took aim. She tried to form the Force Matrix, but panic overwhelmed her control.

There was a soft concussion as the assanni blew a dart at her. It hit the Shield and dropped.

Elthar and Velthius swept into the room, roaring in fury. One moment the assassin was standing there, the next he fell in bloody pieces. The deadly blades of the two bodyguards sliced into him; head, hands and arms tumbling away in less than a heartbeat. Blood sprayed across the walls of the tent. It splashed

137

over the Shield and drew dark lines across the bedclothes to her left. Ellen cried out in shock.

A horn blew outside. The general alarm.

Ellen let the Shield drop and reached for a nightgown. She wrapped it around her with shaking hands.

'Ellen. Ellen! Are you alright?' said Cedrin.

At first she could not find her voice. 'Y . . . Yes.'

Cedrin slid into his trousers, then stormed out through the rip in the tent.

She had been close to death. A lifetime of training had saved her, enabling her to raise the Shield in a reflex action. Yet if Cedrin had not woken her in time . . .

Esmelle walked into the bedchamber and screamed. The Priestess looked around, eyes wide in disbelief and panic. Her face paled, and she collapsed into a faint. She had been standing vigil in the next chamber, guarding their sleep against the influence of the Behemoth.

Serel and Ellen's body slaves rushed into the chamber to help Ellen.

'I am fine,' said Ellen. 'Help the Priestess.' She followed Cedrin through the ruined wall.

Torches were being lit across the camp. Their pavilion was ringed with the One Hundred. Voiced buzzed in anger. Duro and Vess pushed through the circle, each dragging a bloody corpse. Along with the two from the tent, they were laid in a row below a torch pole.

'Let's see who they are,' said Cedrin. Ellen came to stand beside him. He shook with fury, his knuckles white on the handle of his calv.

Kalyth drew a knife and sliced away their shirts.

Each bore the mark of the teremb. Brotherhood assassins. Yet hired by who?

The One Hundred moved aside. Velthius stalked over to them. Behind him, two of their men dragged another man, who yelled and struggled in their grip. 'The Purge is holy work! You blaspheme to stop me!' His shirt had been ripped away, revealing the marks of a Temple Guardian. Ruus walked behind him, bleeding heavily from a chest wound.

The two warriors pushed the prisoner to his knees before Cedrin.

'The only one captured alive, my Lord,' said Velthius.

The Guardian glared at Ellen. 'Death to all Sorcerers! I do nothing but the holy work of the Purge. Wait. Wait! Let me tell you all why the unclean Sorceress must die!'

Ellen shivered as she met the man's gaze. He truly believed what he said.

'We should question him,' said Kalyth.

Cedrin took a step forward and rammed his calv into the man's heart. The movement was so sudden it stunned them all. Her lover's face was twisted in a terrible fury. In that moment she was afraid of him. The assassin's eyes widened in surprise. Then he slumped forward.

'We need no answers, Kalyth. All assassins die,' said Cedrin. He pulled out his calv and flicked it to shake off the blood.

The One Hundred were silent.

Ruus slumped forward. Duro caught him, lifting him up in his massive arms. 'Easy, brother.'

'I . . . stopped them,' said Ruus.

'Ruus stopped two of the assanni, but the third – the Guardian – took him with a thrown spear,' said Duro.

'Two others made it to the tent,' said Cedrin, his voice low and angry.

Ellen could heal Ruus with the Matrix of Form, but Asic was just off full, standing right overhead. A perfect night for a Moon Druid.

Cedrin also looked up at the moon. 'Get Marken. Everyone else back to your posts!'

The One Hundred reluctantly moved away. She saw Osterac hovering at the edge of the light, his face in shadow. Then he moved with the rest.

Raphal was still in Beslin along with Salis, Thenia, Ranis and Xyanthius. The delegation to the Sarlord had gone well. She and Cedrin and their fledgling court were to present themselves at a formal audience in the morning – now only hours away.

'Velthius and Kalyth. Stay.'

The men filed away. Duro laid Ruus gently on the ground as

Marken ran across the torchlit grass. Duro's eyes narrowed. He bent down to pluck something from Ruus' harness. He held it up to the light. *A dart.*

'The luck of Uros,' said Duro. 'A finger's width to the side, and he would have been killed instantly.'

'Careful with that,' said Ellen.

Duro walked over to the torch pole and held the dart in the flame until it ignited.

'Poison,' said Cedrin. 'No worse way to die.'

Ellen had never seen him like this. She laid a hand on his arm. She of all people could understand his fear. She had watched her own father die after an assassin's dart found him. 'The threat is over.'

Marken knelt beside Ruus and concentrated. The warrior was soon wrapped in the milky glow of Moon Essence. 'A nasty wound.' He laid his hands on Ruus' chest and the milky glow intensified.

When the Moon Essence faded, Ruus lay still.

'Is he well?' said Ellen.

Marken smiled. 'I have sealed the wound and put him in a deep sleep.'

'Take him to his tent, Duro,' said Cedrin, calm now. Ellen sighed with relief.

Kalyth looked between her and Cedrin. 'The Hesguit?'

'Yes. The Templemen have never been short of coin. They must be desperate to hire scum like assanni,' said Cedrin.

Velthius bowed formally, his face twisted in shame. 'I failed you, my Lord. If Ranis —'

Cedrin laid a hand on Velthius' shoulder. 'Let's have no talk of failure. My anger is for the assassins, not you. Ranis left you in command for good reason. The One Hundred responded well. I can ask nothing more than loyalty, and you have all given that.'

'What are your plans, my Lord?' asked Kalyth.

'Plans? This changes nothing. Tomorrow we enter Beslin.'

* * *

Ellen kept her face carefully composed as she and Cedrin advanced across the vast marble floor. The Exdor Sarlord Duras was a spare man, his clothes austere and styled like a warrior. His eyes were unblinking as he watched the Scion and his entourage approach. The man at his left was dressed as a Legion general. The phoenix tattoo styled with an X inside it and the other Imperial honours revealed he had once been a senior commander in the Tenth Legion.

The Sarlord's court was as silent as a tomb. Every face that looked back at them was Suul, the ancestry exclusively Anacian. The fashions bordered on archaic. That and the elaborate court procedures they had just undergone gave the impression of a place locked in the past; following traditions that had passed generations, perhaps centuries ago in the rest of Kelas. Skye had quipped that perhaps they should have left their sense of humour on the east side of the Myfis Bridge. At least he and Marken were on their best behaviour, although their half-Meadrel and Cioan features were drawing disapproving looks from the gallery. What must they think of her slight Myrian frame? *Thank Larus we left Bovosan outside the city.*

Cedrin was dressed in the best of the outfits Ellen had made in Herath. White trousers of dyed leather, and a vivid shirt of green silk woven with gold. He had insisted on wearing both calvs in his jewelled harness. A vein throbbed in her temple as she recalled them in his hands the night before.

They halted before the throne. All of them were here, the One Hundred and the Daughters in their best gear; Salis, Thenia and Ranis resplendent in Suul finery. The Twins delegation followed a modest distance behind, their heads bowed.

'Welcome,' said the Sarlord.

Ellen kept her face carefully composed. Entering Beslin was one of the biggest gambles they had taken yet. Exdor was powerful, and they were surrounded by the full martial strength of city. Cedrin would be a prize for delivery to Daran. What would the Warlord pay to have yet another claimant to the Emerald Throne killed? What would the Hesguit pay for her? The one thing in their favour was that Exdor was notoriously isolationist. They had not formed a single alliance since Riin's death.

'Thank you, my Lord,' said Cedrin. 'Exdor has been welcoming. Your roads are excellent.'

Duras nodded gravely. 'We strive for efficacy in all things.' His gaze fell to Cedrin's right hand. 'I see you wear a ruby signet ring.' He was not kidding. *No preamble at all.* Straight to business.

'The ring of my father,' said Cedrin.

'May we see it?' asked the Sarlord. It was not a request.

Cedrin pulled the ring from his index finger and held it out, his face expressionless. Duras waved to an elderly court functionary. The man come forward and took the ring from Cedrin's fingers. He fitted a jeweller's lens to his eye and examined it closely.

They waited in silence. The Sarlord intent. Time stretched uncomfortably. The Suul of the court were as still as statues. If this were Raynor, they would be chattering like songbirds. Ellen could not help compare the high necklines of the gowns to the open dresses of Raynor, some so daring they showed the breasts.

At last the functionary straightened. He turned to Duras and nodded gravely. Then he returned the ring to Cedrin.

The Sarlord was silent for a moment, searching Cedrin's face.

'We have a holy site within Beslin. A place of great power that has been honoured since our ancestors first arrived here. The Fountain,' said the Sarlord.

'A place of powerful Earth Essence,' said Salis.

'Yes,' said Duras. 'And a place of Testing.' He let his words linger.

The Sarlord leant forward in his throne, overtaken by a new energy.

'If you truly are the Scion, you will not fear it. You will not fear the truth. Do you?!'

Cedrin straightened. As she had seen before, his presence grew. 'I do not,' he said, matching the Sarlord's intensity. His strength was tangible. It seemed that Cedrin was the Lord of the chamber, and not Duras, despite the raised dais. A ripple of movement went through the Suul. *They felt it too.*

'Good,' said the Sarlord, standing. 'Tomorrow you will attend us at the Temple of the Fountain. And there the truth will be known.'

Duras swept from the court, followed by his advisors. Only when he had exited did the buzz of conversation rise from the Exdor Suul.

A Suulqua came to Cedrin and bowed. 'My Lord. Chambers have been prepared. This way please.'

Their carefully organised procession broke up as they followed the Suulqua deeper into the Beslin palace.

'Well. That was . . . brief,' said Skye.

'Just as well. I hate court occasions,' said Marken. 'They play havoc with my dinner engagements.'

* * *

Marken drew on the *se* pipe. He held the sweet smoke in his lungs for a moment and exhaled with a sigh of satisfaction. It was fine se. Spicy on the tongue.

'I don't know how you three can be so relaxed,' said Ellen.

Marken passed the long-stemmed pipe to Skye. It was finely carved from a harena horn.

'No point in worrying,' said Cedrin. 'We have agreed to the Testing. We need not fear the truth. I *am* the Scion.'

'It's not the truth I'm worried about. What if this is some elaborate trick? The Priestesses of the Fountain may have been warned beforehand to declare you false,' said Ellen.

Skye blew a smoke ring. 'You think so little of them?' He passed the pipe to Cedrin, who waved it away. The tall calvanni had been as abstemious as a Temple Druid since he met Kalyth. Marken reached over and took it from Skye. He *was* a Druid, but that was not going to stop him.

'It's not that. I know how much pressure a Sarlord can apply,' said Ellen.

'What would he gain? Why not just take us all as soon as we set foot in Beslin?' said Cedrin.

'Suul politics is just as often about deception as action,' said Ellen. 'What better way to dispose of you and wash his hands of it then have the Fountain Priestesses declare you a liar in front of the whole city of Beslin?'

Marken tapped the ash into a bowl and set the pipe aside. He poured them each a measure of bakta and pushed the glasses across the low table.

'For Larus' sake. Will you two stop talking politics for one second? This is supposed to be a celebration,' said Marken.

The four of them were sitting down to an informal dinner in Cedrin and Ellen's private chambers. Cushions had been set around the table, and the four of them lounged comfortably. Velthius and Elthar guarded the door to the small chamber, their eyes alert. Outside more of the One Hundred stood guard. The warriors had effectively taken control of one wing of the Sarlord's palace.

Ellen was dressed in an informal gown opened at the waist. The fact that she had revealed her breasts – the custom in steamy Kelas between family members – showed how relaxed she had become with him and Skye. At first her Suul facade had been unassailable. Now, despite the fact that neither of them were Suul, everything they had shared together had created a deep bond. It made him remember back to simpler times with his own foster-family, before the death of his step-father Macil.

Marken smiled in irony. Both Cedrin and he *had* been born Suul. In different ways, the fall of Bulvuran had left them dispossessed. But no more.

'To the future,' said Marken. In many ways, Marken had what he always wanted. A place with the Suul. Yet so much more was a stake now.

'The future,' they echoed. The three former calvanni threw down the shots of bakta with the ease of long practice.

Ellen got half way and choked on the clear spirit. She giggled and put the glass down on the table, shaking her head. 'I don't know how you do that.'

Cedrin poured her a glass of the fine red wine that the Sarlord had provided them. 'Here. This is more your style.'

Ellen sipped the wine. Her eyes glowed when she looked up at Cedrin. Marken knew love when he saw it. His tall friend was a lucky man.

She turned to Skye, pointing at his chest. 'I have been meaning to ask you. What is that totem?'

'This fine piece of artwork?' asked Skye, looking down at his chest. He traced the vague shape, a faded mess of blue lines. 'This is a sea-raptor.'

'Ah,' said Ellen, trying to be diplomatic. The sea-raptor was the most common totem in Athria. Skye's totem was little more than a crude sketch. Perhaps it had some distinct shape when it was drawn, now it was beyond recognition.

'You should get it retouched,' said Marken, who never stinted at enhancing his own marks.

'No. It's my history. I will not change it.'

Ellen cleared her throat. 'Why did your father not . . . organise a better one?'

Skye poured himself another shot of bakta and downed it. 'Astor was long dead by then. We were all on the streets. This was all my mother could afford.'

'I'm sorry. I never asked what happened after Astor's . . . passing,' said Ellen.

'Don't be so diplomatic, Ellen. After your father had my father's head removed – we were thrown out of Regent's Hill. We lived on the streets. Eventually my mother took the only work she could. She took the flower.'

Ellen went still, her eyes wide. The story was long familiar to him and Cedrin. Ko-chan worked as a courtesan. Despite her Meadrel blood, she rose to a high position, running a pleasure-house for years until she joined a minor temple as a healer.

'That's awful,' said Ellen.

Skye shrugged. 'It was rough at first, but we had enough to survive. It's all in the past.'

Cedrin cleared his throat. 'So where did Raphal get to?' he asked, changing the topic.

'He found his scholar friend Valnis. The two of them were nattering away like love-birds the last I saw of them, heads deep in parchment.'

'Good. We need some idea of where the Ranmyden Iris is. Otherwise we will never find the Spear.'

Raphal had quickly discovered that the Druidic Temple in

Exdor had hardly changed from the ancient Temple of the Suns and Moons that predated the Temple of the Sisters in southern Kelas. The static traditions of the north had ensured that the Exdor Temple gave little more than a token allegiance to the Hesguit in Olcis. They had refused to ratify the edict against Ellen, an act that essentially declared them independent. It was also a valuable indication of support. The assassins who struck outside Beslin had been acting on the orders of Olcis alone.

'Before you know it, you will be hip-deep in maps,' said Marken. 'Sorting out the grain from the chaff – that will be the problem.'

Marken repacked the se pipe and lit the bowl with a taper. He drew in a lungful of smoke and passed it to Skye. The blond calvanni inhaled briefly then passed the long-stemmed pipe to Ellen. 'Want some?'

Ellen hesitated. 'I've never tried it,' she confessed.

'What? I thought the Suul always had the best parties,' said Marken.

She laughed. 'If they did, they did not invite the Sarlord's daughter.'

She looked over at Cedrin and raised an eyebrow.

'It's a mild stimulant. One won't do you any harm,' said Cedrin.

Ellen put the pipe delicately in her mouth and drew a short breath. She blew out the smoke almost immediately. 'Oh. It's like pepper on the back of your throat.'

She passed the pipe to Cedrin. 'You have to now.'

Cedrin smiled. 'Well, if you insist.' He drew deeply on the pipe.

Both Cedrin's and Ellen's eyes grew dark as the stimulant in the tobacco took effect. They looked at each other with undisguised desire. She wrapped her arms around his neck and gave him a deep kiss. Among other things, se was also an aphrodisiac.

'That's the last sense we'll get out of them,' said Skye.

Marken laughed and shook his head. It was great to see his friends safe and happy. He just hoped tomorrow brought no unwelcome surprises.

* * *

Cedrin let the ceremonial robe slip from his shoulders and walked across the wet flagstones to the Fountain. The Temple was set in the centre of a natural bowl-shaped depression. A broad platform in the centre held both the colonnaded Temple and the Fountain itself, which was set inside a circular pool lined with marble. Once the marble edges of the pool must have shone with perfection, now they were crusted with centuries of mineral deposits. The sides of the broad bowl had been converted into an amphitheatre, now packed with Exdor Suul, all present to witness the Ratification Ceremony. The One Hundred and the Daughters had been forced to wait beyond the sacred precinct, except for Ranis and Cedrin's four senior bodyguards. Osterac had been outraged, demanding a place with the Suul, but the lines were clear. He waited with the others. Salis stood with her son, her eyes alive with the Essence. Cedrin's inner circle was with him. The Twins delegation had not attended, the Priest Dagon concerned their presence might be seen as some attempt to manipulate the result. Only paces away, Sarlord Duras and his senior aides watched Cedrin with merciless eyes. The thinnest of threads separated his success from failure.

A gust of wind circled the amphitheatre, throwing the hot geyser of the Fountain to and fro. An errant breeze sent a splash of the hot water across his face. He smelled the sharp scent of sulphur.

Cedrin stopped a pace away from the senior Fountain Priestess. She was arrayed in vestments of deep red, traced with gold and flanked by two other Priestesses in simple white robes.

'Do you consent to be Tested?' asked the Priestess. Her voice was high and clear, resonating with a compelling power.

'Yes.'

Cedrin felt a pressure against him, as though the air itself had grown heavy. Sound fell away until the gusting wind and the splash of the Fountain were distant things.

'Who are you?' Her voice was hardly above a whisper, and

yet it resounded in his head like the toll of a great mought bell.

'I am Cedrin, son of Riin.' As he said the words, a great weight fell away from him. As though at some deep level he himself had been resisting the truth. Yet this was the truth. Not the son of Tarral. Not the son of Belin Kaidell, his father's old general. Cedrin Cinanac. A force grew inside him, a swelling excitement too great to contain. It swirled around inside his gut then exploded from his tongue. 'I am Cedrin Cinanac!'

'What are you?'

With her words the force grew inside him again.

'A calvanni.' So much of his life had been this. It was a part that could never leave him.

'What are you?'

'A scytheman.' It was true. He was marked with the Way. Kalyth had trained him to be the equal of any of the One Hundred. He knew it.

'*What are you?*' Once more the compelling force took hold of his mind and speech.

'A Sorcerer.' If he truly was going to rebirth the Empire, overturning the Temple of the Sisters and their prohibition against Sorcery was going to be part of his legacy. It might as well start right here, in Beslin. He could see shock on the faces across the amphitheatre, even though all sound was still dampened by the Priestess' power.

'Who are you?'

This time the power of her exhortation was overwhelming.

'*The Scion!!!*' The declaration burst out of him. He felt wetness on his lip and touched it with his hand. His fingers came away bloody. His nose was streaming.

All at once a wall of sound crashed in on him. The Suul around the amphitheatre were on their feet, chanting his name. '*Cedrin. Cedrin.*'

The Exdor Sarlord came forward, his face pale. 'Exdor did not declare for the Warlord Daran because he was not the rightful ruler of Bulvuran. Here in Exdor, we follow the order of Anacian Suul strictly.'

Duras' face set with determination. He took another step then knelt in front of Cedrin. 'I kneel as a Sarlord to rise as an

Imperial Governor.'

Cedrin could hardly believe what he was hearing. Moments ago, death hovered over him. Now Exdor was theirs.

'I swear fealty to you, my Lord. To the Cinanac line, and to the Empire of Bulvuran. I am yours to command,' said Duras.

Cedrin felt the blood on his lip stiffen as it dried in the breeze. 'Rise, Duras. Rise and stand beside me.'

Duras rose to his feet, as grim and serious as ever.

Then Ellen was there. She looked terribly pale, yet the pride in her eyes filled him in a way the Priestess' power never could. She allowed him to believe in himself. He took her hands, and they stared into each other's eyes for a long moment. Cedrin wished he could take her in his arms and kiss her, right there in front of the Fountain, but there would time enough for that later.

'Congratulations, my Lord,' she said.

'Thank you, my Lady.'

Duras and his aides came forward. 'My Lord, there are many items of protocol that must be addressed.'

'Yes.'

'It is inappropriate for the Scion to have men who are not Suul in his inner circle,' said Duras.

Cedrin's heart flared hot, but he controlled his outburst. 'I will decide what counsel I keep.'

Duras' eyes narrowed. 'You misunderstand me. It is you who dictate the membership of your nobility. You have already chosen them. They must all be inducted into the Suul, forthwith.'

Nearby, Skye and Marken exchanged a surprised look.

'We must make sure that you receive your own Suul mark before the Coronation.'

He blinked. 'Coronation?'

'Of course,' said Duras. 'You are the Scion. Yet only the Emperor can rule.'

'I see.' Once more, Cedrin had the feeling of events tumbling out of his control.

'Do not concern yourself, my Lord. My functionaries will have the matter well in hand by tomorrow night,' said Duras.

'Tomorrow?'

'There is no point delaying. The Suul are assembled. The time has come.'

Yes, he supposed. This was Exdor. Any delay would not be . . . efficacious.

Chapter Ten

Ellen waved away the tray. She had been queasy since yesterday and her stomach rebelled at the sight of the rich food. She tore a piece of bread from a loaf and chewed on it. Bile rose in her throat, but she forced herself to finish it and swallow. She drank some watered juice.

'Here, Ellen!' Marken passed her a glass of wine. At the thought of it, she tasted acid in the back of her throat. Nevertheless, she forced a smile and took it gracefully. The new Suul mark stood brightly on his forehead in golden ink. At last Marken had what he always dreamed. He was Suul.

'Thank you.'

The celebrations had started hours ago. The whole floor of Duras' main court had been set with tables. The Suul of Exdor were feasting, toasting their new Emperor at every opportunity. Even Veltricus, whose business interests kept him in Beslin, had somehow procured an invitation. He made a special point of congratulating them, offering a gift of a rare matched pair of glowmetal lamps recharged with sunlight.

It was a moment of triumph for her and Cedrin. After everything they had been through together – Raziin's attacks and the three attempts on her own life – they had not only reached a place of safety, but had been recognised by the Suul. She wished her father Myan could have lived to see it.

She was at the High Table with Cedrin's inner circle, although not beside him. In the rigorous protocol of Exdor, the Emperor's consort ranked lower than an Imperial Governor and his wife – even if she was Suul. Not that it bothered her.

151

Nothing could dampen her spirits tonight.

Duras had announced the restoration of the Tenth Legion to general applause. Exdor's military strength was scattered across the large province, yet a good portion of it had been ordered back to Beslin. The Legion would be under strength, yet it represented another force to support Cedrin's legitimate rule.

Ellen set down the wine and took another sip of the watered juice. Her heart skipped a beat as she looked down the table at Cedrin. With his newly inked Suul mark, he looked every inch the Emperor. This was a true victory. Rulers all over Kelas would now take them seriously as a political force.

She saw Thenia talking avidly with Xyanthius and Kalyth on the other side of the table. No doubt she had already earmarked Exdor's military force for her own purposes. Duras might have something to say about that. Spider stood dutifully behind Thenia's chair. She was watching Cedrin. No mystery there. This was Cedrin's night. All eyes were on the newly declared Emperor.

Another wave of nausea swept through her. She covered her mouth with her hand until it passed and forced herself to eat more of the bread. It was tasteless, but settling.

In truth though, Kelas would not recognise Cedrin as Emperor until he sat on the Emerald Throne in Raynor. That mighty city had long been the heart and soul of Bulvuran.

'My Lady?' Another platter appeared, this one set with spiced amelak, boiled with fruit. The sweet jus dripped from the piled meats like honey. Ellen waved it away.

Salis had remained at the Fountain Temple, where she had served her novitiate years before. Serel had dutifully found a herbal tea that would serve her purpose the very first night they entered Beslin, but Ellen was embarrassed by her inability to approach Salis. Part of the problem was that the Raynor Suul was almost always surrounded by other members of the Scion's entourage.

Ellen stood up and excused herself from the table. She caught Cedrin's eye and waved a goodbye. He gave her an anxious look, and began to follow her, but was soon distracted by another Suul vying for his attention.

Spider watched Ellen go, her eyes defiant. Ellen let a court mask settle over her features and steadily matched Spider's gaze. Eventually the warrior looked away. She would not let the impudent warrior get the better of her, after all *she* was the Suul.

Ellen signalled to her Suulquas. Valdas and Mendor immediately left their places to join her. Ruus and Osterac rose as well, but she waved them back. The fewer who knew about this visit the better.

'I wish to return to the Fountain Temple,' said Ellen, as her two Suulquas approached.

'Yes, my Lady.'

'I think a ride on narsiit might be just the thing,' said Ellen. She had been thick-headed all day, her thoughts strangely muddled. If that was what one lungful of se could do, she was never touching the stuff again. Then again . . . Her cheeks flared hot at the memory of the lovemaking that had followed the informal dinner. She still ached from their vigorous love play. It had been a very late night, despite the fact that she and Cedrin had excused themselves early.

The Suulqua flanked her as she navigated her way through the Beslin palace. They turned into a side corridor and passed a portly palace servant with bronze hair and golden Cioan skin. He was polishing a lamp. There was something about him that piqued her curiosity. For a moment, she was sure she had seen him on the caravan from Herath, perhaps as one of the travellers who had attached themselves to Veltricus. She looked closer at his face, but her eyes blurred. *My fatigue is worse than I thought.*

One odd thing struck her. Why would the race-conscious Exdorians employ a Cioan as a palace servant? Even the women who took away the nightsoil had the classic Anacian olive skin and dark hair. Skye and Marken were embraced only because of their close relationship with Cedrin.

'You there,' said Ellen, stopping in front of the man.

A blinding pain shot through her temple and she bent forward. Valdas gripped her left arm, while Mendor supported her right. She closed her eyes and concentrated on her breathing. The pain eased rapidly.

'I'm fine,' she said, pushing them away.

The corridor in front of her was empty. She looked behind her, but the man was gone.

'Where did the servant go?' she snapped.

'I saw no servant,' said Valdas.

Mendor's eyes creased in concentration. 'There was a man.' He was thoughtful for a moment. 'Nothing memorable about him though. Do we need to take you to a healer, my Lady?'

Ellen shook her head firmly. She would see Salis tonight if it killed her. 'No. As I said: a ride will help.'

They passed a set of palace guards, who bowed formally to Ellen, then exited into the balmy night air. She turned her mind from the servant and felt immediately better. Her stomach was still unsettled, but just being out of the stuffy court atmosphere helped.

In the stables, their narsiit trumpeted a welcome chorus and were warmly greeted in turn by their riders. The intelligent mounts knew they were going for a ride and stood still and composed as Ellen and her men arranged their saddles and riding tack. Once more she silently thanked Estle for sending her men and Serel ahead to Herath. They were a link to Athria and owed their allegiance to her alone. More and more, it was Cedrin who was the focus of the growing court, and it was hard not to feel isolated within the growing chaos.

They set off into the night-shrouded streets of Beslin. The route to the Fountain Temple took them through the Suul district. Here the city was quiet, the neat streets empty except for the occasional Nightguard patrol. The Fountain Temple was on the edge of the Suul district, almost standing as a link between the ordinary citizens and their nobility. They entered from the Suul side along a columned pathway roofed with flowering vines, then through an elaborately carved archway. Here Temple servants took their mounts into one of the many complex outbuildings.

They walked down through the silent amphitheatre to the sacred Fountain. A single lamp had been raised on a post by the circular pool. The geyser splashed up into the air in an unceasing display and the warm yellow light of the lamp glittered in the waters. At night the place was serene. She had no talent for Earth Essence, but as she had at the Temple of Mythar in Raynor, Ellen let the welcome sense of peace settle on her.

Ellen and her Suulquas walked past the Fountain and entered the outer chamber of the colonnaded Temple. Here around thirty worshippers were gathered in the modestly lit interior.

A Temple novice approached them. 'Would you like me to lead you in the devotions, my Lady?'

Ellen set herself to her purpose. 'No. Thank you. I am here to see Salis Cintor.'

The novice bowed slightly. 'Please come this way.' She led them to a small side chamber, sparsely furnished with a small table and chairs and kneelers for prayer.

The door opened and Salis swept in. She was dressed in the vestments of a Priestess. Ellen blinked as the High Priestess entered behind her, flanked by two other Fountain Priestesses.

'Suul Cintros,' said Salis. 'Is all well?'

Ellen immediately realised how it must seem to Salis. She had left Cedrin's celebration feast and sought her out without warning. Of course she would think some drastic event had occurred.

'Yes. I'm sorry. I wanted to see you to discuss a private matter,' said Ellen. She looked across at the High Priestess nervously.

The High Priestess rested her gaze on her. Ellen shivered as she felt the Essence swell around her. Move through her.

'Goddess be praised,' said the High Priestess. She smiled, her face transforming from peaceful to beatific. The other Priestesses took a step forward and the subtle flow strengthened.

'Goddess be praised,' echoed the other Priestesses.

Ellen shook with reaction. All at once her legs gave way.

Mendor caught her and led her to a chair. She could not understand what was happening. There was a strange blossoming inside her, like an eddy within the surging tide of the Priestesses' power. It was unlike anything she had ever experienced. She blinked away tears.

Salis exchanged whispered words with the High Priestess and the other three women withdrew. The Raynor Suul lifted a chair and placed it near Ellen, then smoothly sat down. Every movement the woman made was like that, as though her whole life was one slow, elegant dance.

'What was it you wanted to see me about?' asked Salis.

Ellen swallowed, her mind slowly clearing. She turned to her Suulquas. 'Would you mind waiting in the outer Temple?'

Her Suulquas left the room, passing a young novice on her way into the chamber. The young woman set a glass carafe and a two glasses on the table and left soundlessly. Finally they were alone. Ellen's head was spun from her strange reaction to the Fountain Priestesses.

Ellen took her emotions in hand and pushed ahead. 'I have been meaning to ask you since Herath . . . for a spell of Protection.'

'Protection. Against what?'

Ellen was exasperated. 'Pregnancy. Cedrin and I . . .'

Salis leaned forward and embraced her gently. She stiffened, feeling her heart leap into a sprint. Despite herself, something uncoiled inside her; some knot of sadness. Then the tears flowed. She sagged forward into Salis, sobbing like a child into the collar of her white robe.

Eventually Ellen came back to herself. She leaned back and wiped away her tears. 'I'm sorry.'

Salis shook her head slightly. 'You are safe here. Safe with me.'

Ellen took a deep breath and let it out slowly. 'So. Can you help me?' Her voice sounded small, pleading. Part of her rebelled at her lack of strength, yet another part – a long buried part – longed to surrender, to be enfolded.

'Ellen. I will help you any way I can,' said Salis. 'But you are already with child.'

'*What?!*' Understanding crashed in on her. The strange reaction of the Fountain Priestesses made sense. *Goddess be praised.* They were welcoming new life!

'Already? It's barely been a month!'

Salis' eyes sparkled, and she took Ellen's hands. 'That's all it takes.'

Ellen sank forward and buried her head in her hands. Of

course she wanted children with Cedrin, but not yet. They still had so much to do! The journey to Ranmyden. The quest for the Spear. The restoration of the Cinanac.

She felt Salis' arms around her, then a hand laid gently on her head. 'Be still.' Her words had a strange resonance. Ellen's spiralling thoughts fell away, and soft light filled her mind, chasing away the shadows. Her tears fell in silence.

'Not like this,' said Ellen. Once more, she brushed away her tears. She sat back.

'Life is always a blessing,' said Salis. She reached across and placed a hand on Ellen's womb, closing her eyes for a moment. 'A boy.'

A hopeful joy stirred inside her. 'A boy?' She felt herself smile, thinking how Cedrin would react to the news.

Salis nodded, then reached across to pour Ellen a glass of water. 'Here. This has many beneficial qualities. It will help.'

Ellen reached the glass, surprised to feel that it was warm. The waters of the Fountain. Of course.

'Drink.'

She lifted the glass to her lips and took a swallow. It tasted of sulphur and was thick with salts. As the warm liquid made its way down her throat, Ellen felt the subtle Essence seep through her. She tilted the glass, wincing at the taste as she drained the rest. She needed to think of the child now.

'I never thought I would be a mother at twenty-three,' said Ellen. She had never thought herself as a mother at all. The prospect was frightening.

'Rejoice in it. You carry the Cinanac heir, Ellen. That child will one day sit on the Emerald Throne.'

She thought of the Eathal armies converging on Raynor as they sat quietly at a table in Beslin.

'If the Emerald Throne survives.'

Salis took her hand and squeezed it. 'Faith, Ellen. Look at how much we have already achieved. Cedrin *is* the Emperor.'

'I should return to the palace,' said Ellen.

Salis brushed the hair back from Ellen's face, the touch soft and comforting. An innocent gesture motivated by compassion. 'Pause and take a breath. The world will wait.'

Ellen put the glass on the table. With a shock, she realised the implications of being pregnant. How could she have been so careless! A female Sorcerer could not use her powers if she was pregnant. The risk of Bridging to the child's developing mind was too great. She felt a chill down her spine as she realised she had used the Fire only days ago. She bit her lip. Only the very early stage of the pregnancy had enabled her to avoid damage to her son's nascent mind. She could not take that risk again. For nine months, she would not be able to access the Fire. Cedrin's training was over.

And when they did reach Ranmyden, he would have to face Raziin alone.

* * *

Cedrin waved away the se pipe for the third time. He looked around the room, once more trying to find Ellen. The formal feast had finished hours ago, and he and his inner circle had retired to private chambers to continue the celebrations. Being forced to play host to Duras had been strain enough without Ellen at his side to steer him through the maze of Suul etiquette. Yet now that he had finally managed to rid himself of the Exdor hierarchy, Ellen had vanished.

Thirty of his warriors were stationed around the walls and guarded the entrance under Ranis' watchful eye. The rest of the One Hundred and the Daughters relaxed at the tables. All of them had remained stiffly alert during the formal feast and now welcomed the break. Cedrin was pleased to be able to reward them after the tense weeks on the road from Herath. Both Spider and Jeth were unwinding with the others.

He felt guilty about poor Bovosan. They had concealed the minitil's existence from the Exdor Suul, knowing how they would react to the half-breed. They had smuggled him into the city with the last of their men and installed him in private rooms near the palace. He accepted the necessity, yet it was a poor way to repay someone who had saved his life.

Thenia had little interest in pleasant diversions like drinking and aimless conversation and had retired directly after the formal feast. That had been a relief. She had spent a good portion of the feast outlining the advantages of using Exdor's strength to consolidate his power base in the north – through the restoration of Hanis. The Twins delegation and Xyanthius had also excused themselves.

'The strength of the Eleventh stands at just over three thousand,' said Kalyth. The old warrior was at his side as always, eyes vigilant.

They had spent the last few hours discussing various strategies for the north, but eventually even that line of discussion was exhausted. In the end, there were too many unknowns, and they had too little strength to affect the outcome of the southern war.

'So many? I expected perhaps half of Kranor's men to take to the standard,' said Cedrin. He could not understand why the mercenaries would accept the harsh discipline and reduced pay to support the cause of the Scion.

'Is it really so surprising? Kranor picked his men well. You forget what the phoenix means to these warriors – and to the others who have flocked to Searn to swear service. It represents hope. A better future.'

'By returning to the past?'

'Kelas needs a unifying force to stand against the Eathal. Now that Hukum has shown his true strength, that is understood more than ever before.'

Three thousand men. A force sizeable enough to tip the balance. Perhaps. If used in the right way.

'Who is training them?'

'Kranor has promoted former Legion men to key positions. They are doing the basic training now. Most of the men are already experienced warriors.'

'For mercenary work,' said Cedrin.

Kalyth's eyes narrowed. 'They are tough men. All eager to prove themselves. No more can be asked.'

'They will need an experienced general,' said Cedrin. This would be the first true force he commanded as Emperor. He needed to demonstrate their effectiveness. That required decisive leadership.

'There would be none better than Xyanthius,' said Kalyth.

'Would he accept the command?'

Kalyth smiled. 'He is waiting for it. He and Kranor have been scheming this up since Olcis.'

'And what else?'

'I think the original plan was to take a legion south to Raynor to support your claim. The Eathal attack has changed everything.'

'Mmnn.'

A woman's high laugh cut through the general buzz of conversation. Somehow Skye had managed to find a pair of courtesans. Both were Anacian beauties, immaculately dressed in silk with artfully coifed hair. One of them was laughing at Marken's joke. He and Skye, both with the newly inked Suul marks, were in their element. Both had seated themselves down in the midst of the general revelry. His own Suul mark still stung from the tattooist's needle.

Cedrin had an unwelcome memory of the female assassins in Raynor who had nearly done for both him and Marken at the command of the Brotherhood. They had posed as courtesans. A tremor of anxiety went through him. It was not the poison he feared so much as the loss of control. To die helpless.

Cedrin felt deflated. His recognition as Emperor was a dream he and Ellen shared. For Kelas. For what they could achieve through restoration of the old order. Yet now he sat alone while those around him celebrated. Even his induction into the Suul was hollow without her at his side.

'Kalyth. Did you see where Ellen went?'

'She left with her two Suulquas earlier. I'm not sure where,' said Kalyth. 'Elthar?'

The tall warrior leant across to Kalyth, his solemn eyes alert. He and Duro were standing guard over Cedrin tonight.

'Do you know where Ellen went?'

'No. Although I can make enquiries with the palace. Duras' men keep track of all movements.'

'Please do.'

Cedrin stood up, feeling restless and eager to shake off his gloom. This *should* be a night to celebrate. Ellen would reappear soon, he was sure. He nodded a farewell to Kalyth and made his way down to where Skye and Marken were sitting. The conversation dipped noticeably as he approached flanked by his bodyguards. *The Emperor.*

'Carry on,' said Cedrin, indicating with a smile and wave that he wanted the revelry to continue. The warriors swapped grins and did just that. The Daughters, scattered throughout the room, were the focus of considerable attention. He noticed that Jeth remained at Spider's side. The two seemed inseparable.

Skye and Marken shuffled aside to make room for him. The two courtesans bowed. One them affected a coy smile. 'If my Lord wants company. I could summon another . . . ?'

Skye looked at him and winked. Cedrin smiled. 'Thank you, but no.'

'Whatever my Lord wishes,' said the courtesan in a low, seductive voice.

He found himself responding physically to her. He looked away and pointed at the jug of beer. 'Pass that.'

'Allow me, my Lord.' One of the unobtrusive servants reached across and poured him a glass.

He took an appreciative sip. It was fine beer. Cool on the tongue with nice body.

'Shove aside there.' He looked up to see Spider push into the crowd around him. The warriors moved down, and she sat directly across the table from him. Jeth scowled at Cedrin and sat beside her. What was her problem?

Cedrin drained the glass and another miraculously appeared. He was sick of problems. Of formulating strategies and watching for assassins. He pushed it all out of his head. For this one night, he would let it all go. Tomorrow would be soon enough to reshoulder all the responsibilities that came with his title.

Skye passed him a se pipe. This time he accepted, drawing in the long-familiar sweet, spicy smoke. Immediately his mood lifted. Both drink and se flowed freely tonight. He gratefully joined the repartee, reminded of earlier times in Athria. Although certainly they could never have afforded the fine drink and se-tobacco – and he had always been forced to moderate his intake. There were no bodyguards watching his back in Athria, and the Brotherhood was both vicious and treacherous.

The courtesan who had first spoken to him was soon leaning comfortably against him. Her long slim fingers rested on his thigh. She stirred his blood. There was no denying that. He could have her with a whispered word, as easily as asking for a cup of wine. Across the table, Jeth's eyes swept up the courtesan's torso, resting on her breasts and hips. Cedrin met Jeth's eyes for a moment and the thickset warrior blushed and looked away.

'Hey. Fancy another arm wrestle?' said Spider to him across the table.

'Address the Emperor as "my Lord," Spider,' rumbled Elthar. Cedrin had forgotten the tall mercenary was standing right behind him. He turned to see him and Duro both intent on Spider.

'Apologies . . . my Lord,' said Spider.

His two bodyguards relaxed. He felt a leg brush his under the table and looked at Spider in surprise. She met his gaze defiantly. 'No answer, my Lord?'

Cedrin cleared his throat. He was gratified at the attention, but he did not need anyone but Ellen. Even in Athria, he had never been promiscuous, and then he had been alone. He had always feared the Brotherhood would hurt those he cared for. 'I think my arm-wrestling days are over, Spider.'

The warrior pouted and shrugged. The motion parted her shirt, showing her small, pointed breasts. His eyes dropped to them involuntarily. He looked away, but the se pumped through him, setting his blood on fire. Jeth had followed his gaze. Her face twisted with anger, but she remained silent. The woman certainly was protective of her commander.

Skye pulled the courtesan to his side. She leaned away from Cedrin, removing her hand from where it had been casually resting on his leg. He felt disappointment at the sudden loss of contact. He craved physical sensation and excitement.

Where *was* Ellen?

He turned back to Elthar. 'Any news?'

162

The laconic warrior tilted his head in the direction of the main doors. An Exdor Suulqua had just entered. 'The man returns.'

The Suulqua bowed to Cedrin. 'Suul Cintros left the feast and exited the palace with her two Suulquas. She has not returned.'

Frustration boiled inside him. 'Did she say where she was going?'

The man bowed. 'I regret to say she did not, my Lord.'

'Thank you,' said Cedrin tersely. What had gotten into her? Why would she desert him tonight of all nights? Did he have to set his own guard to following her?

Spider passed him the se pipe and he smoked it in sheer irritation. The se lifted his mood, smoothing away the worry. The lights in the hall brightened, the laughter seeming more infectious than ever before. The pain of his new Suul mark faded to a vague discomfort.

Cedrin grabbed one of the servants as he walked past. 'Get some music in here. Something lively.' The whole Exdor palace was like a tomb.

A troupe of musicians entered soon after, carrying wood and bone flutes, stringed instruments of various sizes and a drum. They set up in the corner and started with a soft lilting melody while servants moved aside tables to make room in front of them. The atmosphere in the room grew more festive. By the time they launched into their third tune – a fast jig – warriors were up and dancing, trying to outdo each other. Even the guards grinned as they watched their comrades cavort across the makeshift dance floor. Osterac led one of the Daughters around the floor, moving with a smooth grace. The warrior was a blonde beauty, almost a match for him in height. Her eyes shone as the Olcis Suul swept her around the floor, his technique faultless. Unless he was mistaken, Osterac would get lucky tonight.

'How about a dance, my Lord?' asked Spider.

Cedrin laughed. 'I don't think the Emperor of Bulvuran should be a figure of fun.'

'Don't you think you should be an example to your men?'

teased Spider.

'That implies I could do something inspiring on the dance floor, which is unlikely.'

Both Skye and Marken led their courtesans up to dance. Marken swung his lady around with practiced ease, having been tutored in dance as a youth. What Skye lacked in finesse, he made up for in sheer enthusiasm.

'What about you, Jeth? Why don't you get up and dance?' asked Cedrin.

Jeth scowled. 'I'm not in the mood . . . my Lord.'

'Yes, Jeth. Why don't you?' said Spider. Her tone was hard as she met her lieutenant's gaze. Jeth bowed her head and got up without a word. She walked straight past the partying men and women and out of the room.

'Hmmn. I guess she really didn't want to,' said Cedrin.

Spider looked up at Cedrin, her eyes wide, her face flushed and intent. 'I want—'

'I think I should call it a night,' said Cedrin. He was pleased that his friends and his loyal bodyguard were taking the opportunity to enjoy themselves. Once they left for Ranmyden, they would need to be more focussed than ever. Yet after the se, he was too restless to sit still any longer. He was also anxious about Ellen and wanted to see if she had returned to their apartments.

Spider's face fell. When Cedrin stood up, she rose as well. 'Me too. I'll . . . accompany you, my Lord.'

'As you will.' Thenia and her Daughters were housed in the same wing of the palace.

Cedrin walked out of the hall, waving to Skye and Marken as he went. He did not begrudge them their fun. His friends were Suul now. That was no light matter. They would soon be burdened with responsibility as the machine that surrounded him grew. They were both intelligent capable men, and he would have need of them.

Spider walked at his side in silence. Elthar and Duro followed a step behind them. Ranis and two other warriors from the One Hundred took station in front of them as he exited the hall. The young Suul was taking no chances after the assassination attempt outside Beslin.

'Jeth seems very devoted to you,' said Cedrin.

'Oh?' Spider had been distracted since they left the hall, as though she was wrestling with something. 'Yes.'

Soon Cedrin was at the door to his apartment.

'Goodnight, then,' he said matter-of-factly.

'I . . . ' Spider looked at Ranis, then Elthar and Duro. 'Can I speak to you privately, my Lord?'

Spider was in a strange mood. It was unusual to see the brash warrior so subdued. She did truly seem to be worried about something.

'Very well.' Cedrin led them both into his apartments. Ranis and the two One Hundred warriors took station outside, while Elthar and Duro entered with them.

'Can you wait here?' he asked Spider.

She nodded mutely.

Cedrin walked through into the inner apartments. 'Ellen?' They were empty. In Ellen's dressing rooms, Serel was reading a book while the two slaves were curled up asleep in a small bed near the fire.

'Have you seen Ellen?'

Serel straightened hastily. 'No, my Lord. Should I look for her?'

'No. She will return soon enough,' said Cedrin. He cursed in frustration, then apologised to Serel. The se pumped through him, making him fractious and short-tempered. He was annoyed with himself for smoking the stimulant tobacco. He had sworn off it months ago.

When he returned to the entrance chamber, Spider was standing pensively. She looked at Elthar and Duro then back at Cedrin. 'Can we speak in *private* . . . my Lord?'

'In here,' said Cedrin, leading her into his own study, which adjoined the entrance chamber.

'We should accompany you, my Lord,' rumbled Elthar.

Cedrin waved them back. 'I'm sure I'm safe from Thenia's own bodyguard, Elthar.'

As he shut the door, he heard the soft rustle of clothing. When he turned, Spider was standing naked. Her chest heaved, her breathing fast.

'What . . . ?'

In two strides, she had him back against the wall. Her lips were on his, thick and soft. Her whole body was hot and slick with sweat. He tried to push her away, but her hands locked around him with desperate strength. The se flooded through him. His whole body was alive to her touch.

He leaned back away from the kiss. 'Spider. Stop.' But he did not want her to stop. His whole body was responding, his leather trousers uncomfortably tight as his member swelled.

Her hands worked across his skin in a fever. 'I've wanted you since that first night. If I have to die for this so be it!' Her deft fingers found his belt, undoing his waistband. His trousers fell to his ankles as her hot palm wrapped around his shaft. He groaned in pleasure.

She sank to her knees, taking him into her mouth.

Cedrin was beyond control now. The pleasure had overtaken him. He threw off his harness and his shirt, then kicked off his boots and trousers, at last standing naked.

His hands ripped at her dark, tangled hair. Spider stood suddenly. She hooked her leg around his and swung him onto the floor. He landed on his back with a thud. Then she was atop him, sliding onto him. Just like that, he was inside her.

Cedrin's whole body came alive. His head flared with bursts of light – a side-effect of the se – and the tide of pleasure surging from his groin was unbelievable.

Spider rode him furiously, ramming down onto him in a fury of desire. Sweat ran off her toned body in rivulets, sparkling in the light. His watched the mought piercings in her nipples flick to and fro. Together they worked towards a climax. As she stiffened, he too found release. She screamed in pure, primal joy, while he could do nothing but gasp in wordless pleasure.

She sagged down onto his chest.

All at once his senses came back to him.

Sweet Larus. What have I done?

The door opened, and Elthar and Duro surged into the room. 'Are you alright, my Lord?'

Cedrin threw Spider off him. She rolled to her feet in an easy motion and stood defiantly with her hands on her hips.

'Yes. Sorry to alarm you. Please close the door,' said Cedrin, climbing to his feet.

The two bodyguards backed out. 'Apologies for the intrusion,' said Duro.

When the door closed, he looked at Spider in astonishment, hardly believing what had happened.

'Would my Lord like to go again?' she said, stepping closer.

To his own amazement, his body responded, no doubt driven by the se. 'No,' he said firmly.

'Are you sure?' Her eyes shone with triumph. His heart sank as he realised this was what she had intended all along. And he had been blind to every signal she sent him. *Fool!*

Cedrin stalked across the room and pulled on his trousers. 'You need to leave. Immediately.'

'So that's it, is it? One quick fuck and out the door?'

He slipped on his harness and shirt, trying to get control of the fury that gripped him. He had allowed this. Through his own stupidity. Once idiotic blunder after another.

'It was a mistake, Spider,' he said, struggling for control. 'One that will not be repeated.'

'Fine! Keep your little Athrian whore then.'

Cedrin felt such a fury his vision went red. There was a calv in his hand before he even realised it. 'Don't you ever speak of Ellen again. Do you understand me?'

Even Spider must have seen something chilling in his eyes. She cursed under her breath and dressed swiftly.

Cedrin sheathed his calv. His head swam as he realised how close he had come to a killing rage. He swore to himself in that moment he would never touch se again.

He walked through into the entrance chamber and waited silently for Spider. She sauntered past him as though nothing was amiss.

He waited until the door closed behind her. 'See that Spider is never admitted to these chambers again.'

Duro and Elthar shared a glance. 'As you command, my Lord,' rumbled Elthar.

Cedrin walked through into the bedchamber. He summoned

a servant and ordered a hot bath to be drawn. Then he once more stripped off his clothes. He poured a large glass of water and drank it down, trying to flush the drugs out of his system. His hands shook with suppressed energy.

A crushing weight of guilt came down on him. At the same time, his body rang with the intensity of his release. The whole experience had been incredibly erotic. Despite his fury with Spider, she still stirred him. That meant nothing now. He would never allow himself alone with her again.

'Uros. *Uros.*'

Why did this have to happen tonight? Of all nights? To celebrate his ascension to the throne of Bulvuran – such as it was – with an action that would do nothing but drive a wedge between him and Ellen?

He took up his greatscythe and worked through a series of forms, burning off energy. By the time the bath was ready, he was soaked in sour sweat, and his arms and shoulders ached from the intense training.

Cedrin sank into the warm waters. He dismissed his servants and scrubbed himself clean. Then he sank under the water, holding his breath, as though the immersion could wipe away his actions. He broke free with a gasp.

There was nothing for it. He would have to tell Ellen first thing tomorrow. Then find some way to make amends.

'Damn!' He hit the water with a fist, sending a wave gushing over the edge of the bath and onto the tiled floor.

And where in Kallor's Cavern *was* Ellen?

Chapter Eleven

Cedrin turned his attention back to Duran's councillor. It was proving almost impossible to focus on the man's lengthy dissertation. The annoying thing was it was a well-considered summary of the structure of Exdor's extensive bureaucracy. He *wanted* to take in the information. There were two problems. The first was that the man's voice was a dreary monotone. The second was that Cedrin had still not had time to talk to Ellen. The whole incident with Spider gnawed at him like a parasite.

Beside him, Skye's head lolled to the side and he began to snore softly. Marken remained attentive through sheer will, the dark circles under his eyes a testament to what that must be costing him. Kalyth and Xyanthius were absent, reviewing the status of the Exdor military. It was telling that Thenia had accompanied them.

He briefly considered giving Skye a jab in the ribs, but discarded the idea. He valued his friend's insights, but did not think he would have too much to add in this arena.

'So in summary . . .' the man continued. Cedrin nodded gravely, at least pretending to give the man his full attention. The summary proved to be almost as long as the first presentation.

Exdor currently comprised Cedrin's whole Empire. In many ways, the centuries-old traditions and institutions that bound it together were the key to ruling it. Duras understood this. Cedrin knew instinctively that any attempt to ride roughshod over the established procedures would not only fail, it could potentially cause major repercussions. The many organisational divisions were called Provincial Houses, in the style of the old Empire. The Exdor Suul were integral to the whole structure, many having hereditary positions within the hierarchy.

Ellen had returned late last night and had gone straight to sleep beside him – while he lay awake for hours in an agony of guilt. Then, this morning, instead of rising early as she usually did, she stayed in bed. He was beginning to worry she was unwell. And that she would learn of events from Serel or others before he had a chance to confess his actions. Spider had not exactly been discreet. The whole act had almost been one of provocation as much as desire.

The councillor bowed and moved back. He gave Skye a sideways look of aggravation, but was too polite to make any comment. He returned to his seat with Duras' other advisors.

Cedrin straightened. 'Thank you for that excellent review. I'm sure I will need to rely on your advice as we move forward. My *counsellors* and I appreciate your efforts.' Skye jerked awake and gave a sleepy smile. At least he had the sense to restrain his humour. The Exdor Suul were a serious lot.

'Do you propose to make any changes to the structure, my Lord?' asked Governor Duras. Not for the first time, Cedrin considered how strange it must be for Duras to have handed over power. As Sarlord, the man had answered to no one. Then again, this was Exdor, where everything had its proper place.

'The reorganisation of the army into a proper Legion may require some changes to its procedures, and to its organisational support. Apart from that, I do not favour any change to the Provincial Houses at this time.'

Duras nodded his understanding. He seemed neither pleased nor disappointed.

'Perhaps we could convene a council of senior representatives from each of the Provincial Houses?' suggested Marken.

'The objective?' asked Duras.

Cedrin grasped Marken's idea immediately. 'Yes. We could gain an immediate insight into the impact of any action on the various Houses by presenting it to such a council.' It was a way of reducing delays and airing any objections.

'It shall be done,' said Duras. 'Now we have another presentation on the Court procedures . . .'

Cedrin stood. 'If we can take an hour's recess? I would like Suul Cintros to be present for that.' Ellen's knowledge of Court mechanics was second to none. Her work with the court scribes in Athria had given her intimate insight into that world.

Duras and his aides bowed and left the room.

'So can we go back to bed now?' asked Skye.

Cedrin nodded. 'Yes, but be back here in an hour. You didn't think the Suul mark came for free, did you?'

'I should have gone with Kalyth. I could have been more help there,' said Skye. He was probably right.

'Thanks for your help, Marken.'

'My pleasure, my Lord,' said Marken, bowing with a flourish.

Cedrin said his goodbyes and exited the chamber, Velthius and Vess one step behind him. Outside, Ranis with Ruus and Osterac also flanked them as he walked rapidly through the palace to his chambers.

With every step, his anxiety grew. His head spun with a sense of disbelief as he remembered the events of last night. He had always prided himself on his control. Yet that had completely deserted him. It made the encounter with Spider even more unreal and distant – almost like a dream. Yet it had been no dream.

At his apartments, two more of the One Hundred stood guard outside. That meant that Ellen was still there. Velthius and Vess entered with him, taking their stations just inside the doors. Ellen was not in the main chamber, and he walked into their rooms alone.

She sat at the window in a soft white gown, her hair loose around her shoulders.

'Ellen,' he said. He felt an intense love for her and was drawn across the room to her side. He laid a hand on her back, feeling her warmth through the soft material. He kissed her gently on the cheek. She looked up at him. Her green eyes were startling, filled with some strange quality he had not seen before.

'I was worried. Have you been alright?' he asked.

171

'A little nauseous,' she said. Then strangely she smiled, as though that was a good thing.

With a sinking fear he realised this was it. He had to tell her now.

'Ellen—'

'I'm with child,' she said. Her face transformed with such joy it broke his heart.

He took a step back, his mind and emotions in turmoil so intense he thought his head would explode. He pressed his palms to his temples.

'You're . . . you're not pleased?' Ellen was stricken. Her eyes moistened with tears.

Cedrin sank to his knees and took her hands. 'No. This is the most excellent news. I could not think of anything I would rather hear.'

'Then what is it?'

He looked up at her. How could he say it? Was it possible without shattering everything they had been? *Larus forgive me.*

'Last night I was with Spider,' said Cedrin. The whole world paused. Even his heart seemed to stop.

At first she was puzzled, as though he had spoken a foreign language. Then her face flashed with anger.

'You had sex with her?'

'Yes. She—'

Ellen snatched her hands out of his grip. She looked at him as though he was a stranger. 'With that *lowborn*?'

'Yes. Forgive me. The se—'

Ellen surged to her feet. 'You could not wait for me for a single night?'

Cedrin climbed to his feet and tried to take her in his arms, but she held up her palms, warding him off.

'No. It was not like that. I would wait for you forever. Let me explain.'

She kept backing away from him until her back was to the window.

'Please,' he pleaded.

She shook her head, her face torn between grief and fury. 'With *her*. Of all people. Do you think so little of me?'

'Of course not,' he pleaded. Cedrin took another step towards her, but her look stopped him.

'Get out.'

'But—'

'*Out!*'

Cedrin backed out of the chamber and closed the door. Velthius and Vess stood on either side of the main door, their faces expressionless. He stood there, at a complete loss. Ellen had been his world, his sanctuary. Where now? What could he do?

He heard something shatter inside their room. Then a resounding crash. Then a moment later there was a high wailing, scarcely human, so full of pain and hurt it turned his heart inside out. This was his doing. Her pain was blood on his hands.

He swung around as the door to the main chamber opened. In swept Kalyth and Xyanthius, with Ranis and Salis close behind them. All were gripped with a sudden urgency.

When they heard the sound, the excitement on Salis' face immediately fled. 'Ellen?'

'Inside,' said Cedrin, sinking back against the smooth marble wall. He felt his legs go weak and feared they may not support him.

Salis slipped into the bedchamber. Ranis led him to the table in the main chamber and poured him a glass of water. 'Drink, my Lord. You look deathly pale.'

Xyanthius and Kalyth sat opposite him and exchanged a concerned look.

'Salis has told us the news,' said Kalyth. 'I guess congratulations are in order.'

Cedrin blinked. *Could this get worse?*

'We must move quickly,' said Xyanthius. 'We have already started arrangements.'

'For what?' asked Cedrin.

'For a wedding, of course. The heir to the Cinanac throne can hardly be born a bastard,' said Kalyth. 'It must be done swiftly, before the pregnancy begins to show.'

The glass tumbled from Cedrin's fingers, and he let his head sink to the table. How could he possibly restore Kelas when he could not even make peace in his own bedroom?

* * *

Ellen kept her features carefully composed as she entered the Temple of the Suns and Moons. Her Suulquas, Mendor and Valdas, walked a step behind her, dressed in formal attire. If he had been alive, their place would have been taken by her father Myan. By rights, her brothers should be standing with her, but the messages announcing her marriage would not even arrive in their hands by the time the ceremony was over. Thousands of Suul packed the Temple, there to witness a historic union.

She had come back from the Fountain Temple so full of hope. The long hours she had spent with Salis had imbued her with a deep sense of peace. She had been ready to embrace her life as a mother, as the life-partner of the man she loved. That the marriage was politically expedient, and necessary, she could rationally accept. Yet inside her, her heart was a stone. The pain of the betrayal had literally been so intense she had shut off her feelings entirely. She was nothing but a facade now. A Suul mannequin performing the motions that were expected of her.

Her future, her love, had ended in her bedroom chamber; in the insane hour following Cedrin's confession. Esmelle had eventually calmed her with a potent Essence spell. Ellen had arrived back from some other place a different person. The fact that Thenia had ordered Spider whipped in punishment was no consolation. She no longer allowed herself to feel anything.

Her entourage reached the top of the broad Temple chamber, where Cedrin and his inner circle waited. Their marriage here was a watershed, showing a tacit acceptance by the Exdor Temple of two leaders who were known Sorcerers. Ellen, by her actions in Athria, and Cedrin, by his own declaration at the Fountain Temple.

The Temple of the Suns and Moons was an ancient structure, with huge, buttressed walls and a vast arched roof. Stained glass filled the high windows, depicting Larus the Lifegiver and Uros the Destroyer, as well as Asic and Rea, the first children of

Larus.

Cedrin looked handsome in his new trousers and shirt. The jewels in his worked harness glittered in the clear light of morning as it filtered through the stained glass. She observed it all objectively, as though from a distance.

She had not seen him since yesterday. All the arrangements for the wedding and the feast had been undertaken through intermediaries. Her clothes and personal items had all been shifted to her own apartment, separate, but adjoining Cedrin's. That made it easier to maintain the detachment she needed to get through this.

A High Druid of Larus stood at the top of the Temple, just below the main altar. He was resplendent in his bright yellow robes and golden vestments. The sigil of Larus hanging about his neck was beautifully cast and tinted a brilliant gold.

Cedrin looked at her with admiration and longing. 'You look beautiful.'

'Thank you. You look handsome, my Lord,' she replied automatically. She looked away and fixed her gaze on the High Druid. His sigil was cast in the classic shape, a large sun in the centre with eight thin triangular rays radiating outward.

Salis indicated for the High Druid to begin. The Raynor Suul stood to Cedrin's left, taking the place of his family, while Mendor and Valdas stood to her right. Serel, who had carried the long trailing train of her dress to the altar, waited behind her.

'Larus. Protector,' invoked the High Druid. 'High Goddess of Life and Fertility, turn your eyes upon us today . . .'

Ellen tuned the words out. She focussed instead on the stained glass windows. They were an excellent example of the early Imperial period. The low windows behind the altar showed depictions of Larus triumphing over Uros and the Demons of Storm Season. Jealous of her sister's children Asic and Rea, Uros banished them to the vault of the night. Uros then consorted with Kallor, Lord of the underworld Llors, and gave birth to the Demons, always seeking to destroy her sister's good works.

'Now take hands in a symbol of your union,' intoned the

High Druid.

Ellen turned and reached out. She took Cedrin's hand in a loose grip and made a pleasant smile. The ranks that thronged the Temple would expect it. This was a show, after all.

From a numb distance, she noted that Cedrin's grey-blue eyes were hollow and sad. He needed to make more of an effort to show happiness, she thought absently.

The High Druid wrapped a ribbon around their clasped hands.

'Be fruitful and happy, and enter the world as man and wife,' said the High Druid, completing the ritual.

Cedrin leant forward as though to kiss her. She remained statue-still. Instead he turned to the crowded Temple.

The hushed silence was broken as a buzz of excited conversations swept through the assembled Suul.

Ellen was now Empress of Bulvuran.

* * *

Once more the main court of Duras had been converted to a banquet hall. This time the degree of formality was greater than ever. As Empress, Ellen now ranked above Governor Duras and his wife and took her seat next to Cedrin.

She had passed the hours in careful conversation, falling back on long years of court training to fill each conversational pause with smooth words and present the correct countenance. She was a great success with Exdor's Suul as they paraded past to pay their respects. They, above all, responded to etiquette.

In the middle of the feast, a Suulqua messenger entered, bringing his dispatch directly to Cedrin. He immediately summoned Kalyth and Xyanthius to their table. The two old warriors bowed and seated themselves.

'News from Kranor's agents in Olcis. Lempar and his legion survive,' said Cedrin. 'They retreated intact across the Asgod after an initial engagement with the Eathal.'

'Intact! I knew Lempar was too clever to meet them head on,' said Kalyth.

'Yeffrij has assaulted Olcis with three legions. Despite

damage to the outer city, they have been turned back. The Hesguit has revealed his magical strength. Defensive glowmetals.'

Xyanthius nodded. 'So Olcis holds. That will keep Yeffrij from joining his forces with Hukum at Raynor.'

'Even more significant. The other Temples of the Sisters in Kelas have refused to give the Hesguit military or magical aid,' said Cedrin. He passed the dispatch to Xyanthius, who scanned the tight script of the cavon-carried message.

'This could signal the end of the Hesguit's hold on the other Druidic Temples,' said Kalyth.

'Yet it says nothing about the politics of those other Temples,' said Ellen. It meant nothing to her if the Athrian Temple of the Sisters refused aid to the Hesguit. Not if they did not overturn their own edict against her.

'That's true,' said Cedrin. 'Still. We must begin somewhere.'

* * *

Ellen was exhausted. The effort of keeping herself composed was beginning to tell. Yet at last the night was finally drawing to a close.

She remained silent as she and Cedrin made a formal procession through the palace to their apartments accompanied by the senior Suul. Ribald jokes and high humour passed between the nobility, already well lubricated from their hours at the feast. Ellen smiled at the appropriate times, while Cedrin remained noticeably withdrawn. Servants followed the procession with trays of drinks and food. One of them caught her eye for a moment. A bronze-haired Cioan man. A pain began in her temple, and she pressed her fingers into the throbbing vein. He was strangely ordinary amongst the fine-featured, beautiful servants of the Exdor Suul. Her eyes blurred as she looked away from him, unable to summon even a casual interest. The night had been hard enough.

The high spirits of the Suul reached a crescendo as they bustled Cedrin and Ellen through the doors of their apartment. The wedding chamber had been lavishly decorated with expensive cloth, which hung in streamers from the ceiling. Flower petals had been scattered across the thick rugs and the wide canopy bed.

Ellen breathed a sigh of relief when the doors closed behind them.

'Serel,' she said, summoning her lady. She held out her arms as Serel set about removing the stiff formal gown.

Cedrin sat in a dressing room chair, watching her in sombre silence.

Finally Ellen stood only in a light sleeping shift. Serel bowed and exited.

'Ellen. Are you alright?' said Cedrin, his eyes filled with concern.

'Of course,' she said.

'I never set out to hurt you. I never sought this out. Never sought *her* out,' said Cedrin.

'What are the actions of an Emperor to me?' said Ellen from behind her court mask. 'Did they not take mistresses when it suited them? Wives by the dozen? As mother of the heir, it was necessary that I wed you. I have fulfilled that duty.'

Ellen walked over to the bed and laid down. Her body was numb. Her mind abuzz with fatigue.

Cedrin stripped off his clothes and slipped under the covers. He reached across and laid a gentle hand on her shoulder. 'Ellen. Forgive me.'

Ellen turned her back to Cedrin. 'Tomorrow I will move back to my own apartments.'

Then, mercifully, she fled from the world.

Chapter Twelve

Daran's narsiit danced beneath him. No doubt his winged mount felt the tension he tried to keep in check. The suns were climbing in the east, their heat already felt by the thousands of Legion warriors assembled on the field below. He had chosen a high vantage today, a small hillock that rose above the undulating terrain. Usually he would avoid such a clear target, but today he needed to see the formations first-hand.

He turned to his senior aides. 'All in readiness?'

'Yes, my Lord,' they chorused. In fact his men had been in place since before dawn.

Daran felt a ripple of fear and his stomach tensed in response. This was it. After months – years – of planning, they were about to roll Kallor's Dice in their first major combat. Around him, the strength of Raynor was in the field. The First and Second Legions. Twenty thousand men ready to fight and die for the Yasser States. If they fell today, there would be nothing to stop Hukum from reaching Raynor. Yet this was only the first of many gambles.

The North Yasser Legion – the old Fourth – had been shattered by Yeffrij in the first weeks of the war. That had been a stunning blow. The battered remnants had fled to Raynor. Their ranks were being refilled, although it would take time to truly restore them. It took years of training and battle-experience to make a Legionnaire. They could simply not be replaced quickly. At least he and Uran had the foresight to reform the old Third when the Eathal first engaged Hend's forces. The Third was a completely new Legion, the warriors as green as new baal. They

179

had never been intended for anything but defence. It was they who now manned the walls of Raynor. Daran would never take them into the field.

Today his forces would face two Eathal legions.

The Yellow Drakon, one of Hukum's elite forces, was advancing with the Silver Legion. Both had been carefully tested in the last few weeks to determine what magical strength they brought to the field. Every Eathal legion was led by a Sorcerer-Lord, so they would have that power to contend with. In addition, each legion also had an offensive glowmetal that could discharge a bolt of directed Force. It had taken time, and lives, to determine exactly what their capabilities were.

Now it was time to reveal Raynor's own magical strength. Each of his Legions was defended by Uran's Druidin. The Sorcerer himself would march with the Second while his apprentice, Nacius Cintar, would support the First. Daran gritted his teeth, once more feeling his frustration at the sheer scale of the power arrayed against him. In total, the Eathal had ten legions in the field – each led by a Sorcerer-Lord. In response, Raynor could muster two Sorcerers, one a newly trained apprentice. He hoped Nacius was up to the task.

All balanced on a thread. A single mistake could ruin them.

Strategy, he reminded himself. It was the strength that could be applied effectively that counted. Hukum's approach to Raynor had been careful and methodical. He always led with two legions, one of his core Drakon legions and another less experienced force under a teremb banner. He always kept his primary Legion, the Black Drakon, in reserve, shielded by two others. Despite continual harassment by Daran's forces, they never even got close to the Black. The glowmetals it protected remained a mystery. He had to rely on second-hand reports from the fall of Hianer, where the walls had been obliterated in less than an hour. Those glowmetals could not reach Raynor.

Yet again, Daran studied the terrain. His scouts had mapped each gully and hill, every valley and plain in exacting detail. For weeks, he had pored over the maps, finally commanding a model to be constructed. He needed every advantage. Somehow he had to do the impossible. He had to stop five Eathal legions and neutralise Hukum's magical strength without losing his own men.

'The Raptor approaches, my Lord,' said one of his aides, pointing to the south-west. Raynor was there, somewhere under the horizon.

A dark shape appeared in the sky.

He felt another thrill of fear. At first it might have been a bird, but it swiftly grew in size. Soon the huge flying platform slipped through the air above them, casting its broad, hexagonal shadow across the assembled troops. At each of the six apexes, a fountain of silver streamed down towards the ground. A line of directed Force kept the platform airborne. Uran's invention, the Raptor was manned by twelve Druidin, each skilled with Larus Essence. With them were scores of archers and other men trained to dispatch flammable missiles through open hatchways in the centre. They had trained in secret for months. So far, the Raptor had only flown at night, manned by Moon Druidin.

Once more he checked the disposition of his forces. The Imperial road ran between two steep hills here. From between the two steep hills, the pass opened out into a broad valley. This was why Daran had chosen this ground for his first major engagement with the Eathal. Any substantial movement of troops from the east had to pass through the valley to reach Raynor – that or splinter into a hundred smaller units. He had gambled that Hukum would not split his forces and so far he had been right.

The First were drawn up in neat lines in the valley below. For months, Daran had been hitting Hukum fast and hard with lightning raids, resisting all attempts by his forces to engage them. Now he offered Hukum's generals a tempting stationary target for their massed legions.

The Second were positioned to the north, spread out in a series of narrow gulleys that ran from the valley to the north-east. As the Eathal approached, they would be hidden from view.

The warriors of the First stood in neat lines. A classic Imperial force. The front lines were spearmen, also equipped with heavy rectangular shields and short scythes. All were well drilled in phalanx formations, trained to use their long spears to deadly effect in the chaotic mass of a pitched battle. Behind them were divisions of archers and javelin throwers. At the flanks were the amelak cavalry, equipped with long scythes designed for use from the saddle. There were scythemen divisions behind the front-line infantry, specialised forces designed to capitalise on any collapse in the enemy formations. Given room to move, scythemen were immensely effective, and had great shock value. They had to be used carefully though. They were easily neutralised when the ranks closed and they ran out of fighting room.

The time was upon them.

The first of the Eathal appeared between the two hills. They quickly broadened their formation as they entered the valley. At the front were three ranks of warriors with short stabbing spears and heavy shields. Behind them, the vast mass of the Eathal were equipped with the small shields and hammers of the Eathal foot soldier.

Daran's hands made fists on the reins as he leaned forward, squinting to see the standard. It was dark, with two silver eyes staring outward.

'The Silver!' said Daran in triumph. *A teremb legion.* Hukum was overconfident. Time and again he led with his less experienced units, allowing them to blood themselves and win honour. Today he would learn to rue it.

'Signal the First to advance.'

One of his aides raised a horn to his lips and blew a short sequence of notes. The call was repeated across the field. The sound of shouted orders filled the air, followed by a great rustling movement as ten thousand men hefted their weapons.

'Blood is spilled this day,' said one of his men.

'Uros will have her fill,' said Daran. 'Let's pray it is Eathal blood she tastes.'

The First advanced, a vast wall of men and armour stretching across the valley. Their booted feet landed in unison, filling the air with a slow, menacing cadence. As commanded, they came forward at one-quarter pace, allowing the Eathal legion time to advance.

The Silver increased their pace, their lines growing ragged. The Eathal general and his men had seen their quarry on the plain before them. Discipline wavered as excitement took hold. Soon the whole of the Eathal legion was out of the pass between the two hills. Daran swallowed as he watched them come – a dark mass of grey flesh and dark leather armour. It was one thing to move wooden tokens on a board and another to see them in the flesh. It had been almost thirty years since he last battled the Eathal to a standstill. Then he was young – and driven by desperation and the need to survive. Was he still that same man?

A dreadful scream filled the air. His narsiit snorted and danced in place.

It was the Screamer, the offensive glowmetal of the Silver. He could see its bulky shape in the middle of the Eathal ranks, tended by Eathal Druids; a twisted mass of red light and silver-grey iron. Thanks to their careful probing of the Eathal forces, they knew that it released a directional bolt of Force the size of a battering ram and emitted a loud, eerie wail. In reality it was a weak weapon, and his men had been well briefed on its effects.

He smiled as he saw the First continue to advance without a single ripple in their formation. The Eathal were using the glowmetal too early, perhaps seeking to unsettle the human warriors.

Behind the Silver, the first division of the Yellow Drakon appeared. These were the true danger. Fully half of these warriors were equipped with stabbing spears and heavy shields, and trained in close-quarter fighting. They had been in the vanguard in Hend when Hianer was destroyed. Daran had grim memories of fighting them as a young general in the first battle for Raynor.

There was a ripple in the air above the Silver. A moment later a series of magical missiles shot across the gap at the First. They detonated harmlessly against a Sorcerous Shield. Daran could not see Nacius from this distance, but knew his strategy. Today his purpose was to neutralise the effectiveness of the Silver's Sorcerer-Lord. The true battle in the valley would be conventional. Seven balls of magical yellow fire streaked from the First towards the Silver across a broad front – delivered from their Druidin. Most exploded against the Sorcerer-Lord's own Shield, yet two slipped past his guard on the left. Eathal warriors bellowed in agony as they were engulfed. The effect on the Eathal lines there was immediate, breaking their formation. A promising lack of discipline.

One third of the Yellow had emerged from the pass. Most of the Eathal remained between the two hills, as did their offensive glowmetal, the Tripper, a wedge-shaped mass of gold and violet light.

'Now!'

Daran's aide lifted the horn. A long, urgent note rang across the field.

With a roar, the Second rushed from concealment. Simultaneously Uran directed a stream of pure Fire at the Eathal warriors of the Yellow as they emerged from the pass. They cried out in pain and fear, staggering back into the other Eathal warriors and compressing the ranks. The Sorcerous attack was swiftly answered. The general of the Yellow sent a scything blade of Force at the warriors of the Second. It struck Uran's shield and was harmlessly deflected away.

Then the phalanxes of the Second hit the Yellow Drakon. The spears flashed back and forth, stabbing into chaos, cleaving forward. There was another series of magical detonations as Uran engaged his foe. A brilliant flash blinded Daran for a moment. It was followed by the roar of flame and a deep boom that swept through the ground.

When his sight cleared, the advance units of the Second had cut through the Yellow's lines outside the pass. As planned, the forward divisions of the Second formed up in tight lines, shields locked, pinning the Eathal in the pass. Their task was simply to keep the main body of the Yellow Drakon locked in place.

The rest of the Second turned and immediately attacked the divisions of the Yellow that had made it through the pass – now cut off from the main body of their Legion. The Second's infantry advanced on two fronts, driving into the isolated Eathal. Meanwhile the Second's cavalry streamed out of the hidden gulleys, striking at the rear of the Silver. On cue, the

First's cavalry spurred forward to join the attack on the flanks.

An eerie scream sounded across the battlefield as the Screamer spoke. A line of cavalry went down, hit with an unseen bolt of Force. Daran cursed. His narsiit reared, eager like he was to join the attack. One of his sons was a cavalry officer with the First. He could not consider that now.

The light dimmed, and Daran felt a hint of coolness. He looked up, and his pulse quickened as the Raptor passed above them, cutting off Larus' heat. Its shadow crept across the lines of the First. Just for a moment they were bathed in the dim red light of Uros, then the second sun was also blocked from sight. The suns returned as the Raptor's shadow moved ahead of it. He saw the Eathal look up and noted the rustling panic in their lines as it moved steadily through the air. Ominous. Unstoppable.

The Raptor took up position above the pass. The bulky shapes of barrels fell from the platform. Each detonated with an explosion of flame as it struck the trapped warriors of the Yellow, unable to manoeuvre inside the pass. They were too far away to see the flights of arrows, but he knew that the archers on the platform would be launching volleys at the Eathal troops below.

'Your plan is working, my Lord,' said his aide.

A bolt of Force shot up towards the Raptor. It did not reach the platform, hitting the Shield maintained by six of the Druidin. Even so, the force was enough to rock the platform alarmingly. Keeping the thing balanced was difficult. The Druidin keeping it in the air were trained as a team, and it had taken months to get the thing off the ground at all.

Across the field, their forces withstood the magical assaults of the Eathal. Inexorably, the First were cutting into the lead elements of the Silver, while Nacius shielded them from the assaults of the Screamer. The Sorcerer-Lord commanding the Silver was kept busy fending off the attacks of the Druidin. The Eathal stood their ground bravely and for a while it seemed they would hold, but the long spears of the Raynor phalanx eventually took too great a toll. The front ranks of the Silver Legion collapsed. Daran's infantry now pushed into the main mass of the Eathal – warriors equipped with small shields and unwieldy hammers. The blades of the first flashed in the light of the suns, swift and deadly.

Daran could feel a fundamental change take place across the battlefield. Where the Eathal had once been secure in their numbers and the belief of their own invincibility, they were now shaken. The First unleashed a terrible vengeance on the Silver, avenging the destruction of Hend and the murdered men and women of Tupur. The First kept their ranks in order, pushing forward with focussed ferocity. Arrows and spears rained down onto the lightly-armed Eathal. Their small shields were a poor defence. *Give me just five Legions like the First and I would wipe the Eathal from the face of Kelas.*

Where the Silver tried to rally their lines, the cavalry of the First and the Second swept in, cutting through the Eathal ranks and leaving scores of dead in their wake. He could hear shouted commands in the Eathal tongue, but the pleas of their captains were in vain. The lines of the Silver broke. In moments, they had become an undisciplined mass, driven before the linked shields of the First. Daran's heart swelled with pride. His men left a bloodied swath of carnage behind them. Any Eathal left alive were slain by the following ranks as they stabbed down with their short scythes.

Daran turned his mount, looking down at the pass. The Raptor had exhausted its load of missiles and withdrawn, flying back to Raynor. The Druidin could not keep the platform afloat indefinitely. They had done their work, preventing the Yellow from breaking out.

The forward elements of the Second stood toe-to-toe with the Yellow at the mouth of the pass, while the rest of the Second were engaged with the forward divisions of the Yellow. Although cut off from their legion, the Eathal warriors had not panicked. They had formed a fighting square, a tight defensive formation, and simply held their ground. Their larger shields were a superior defence against the Second's missiles. They effectively removed the Second from the fight. The Yasser States' warriors could not come to the aid of the First while the Yellow remained behind them.

In the pass, the warriors of the Yellow Drakon had not broken. Here it was not the case of disposing of the front ranks, they were all highly trained and equipped for this type of combat.

With the Raptor gone, the Eathal of the Yellow quickly re-established order.

Daran urged his mount forward as he saw a bulky shape being manoeuvred through the pass to the line of combat. *The Tripper.* It projected a narrow wedge of force two hundred paces wide at about knee height – like an invisible tripwire. In a fast and mobile attack, its effects were easily avoided. But in the pass . . .

Daran spun his mount, seeking out Uran. The Sorcerer was engaged in a battle of magic with the Yellow's Sorcerer-Lord. There was no way of contacting him. Daran watched helpless as the Tripper was placed in position. There was nothing he could do.

'*Uros*' *tits!*' He should have thought of some way to contain the glowmetal. Yet if he had allowed the Tripper to come through, more than half of the Yellow Drakon would have passed into the valley. The chance of them breaking out of his trap and linking with the Silver would have been too great. The Tripper's area of effect began some distance from the glowmetal, allowing it to be used from inside enemy lines.

There was a low thrum in the air, like the release of a great bowstring. A wave passed through his troops in the pass. One moment the Second were standing solid, shields locked, the next they had been knocked flat. The breach was only a couple of hundred paces wide, but in close combat, that was devastating.

With a roar, the Yellow Drakon swept out of the pass. Huge Eathal warriors – each equipped with twin axes of darkglass – leapt into the gap. In that shocked moment of disorientation, they cut deep into the Second's lines. Instinctively the Second pulled back from the pass to reform their lines. It was the respite that the Yellow needed.

The Yellow Drakon advanced into the valley. In moments, they had closed half the distance to their isolated forward elements. Now it was the Second who found themselves trapped. They were caught between the main forces of the Yellow, now pouring out of the pass, and their largely intact forward elements in the fighting square.

Daran held his breath. The next few moments would alter the whole outcome of the battle. He considered sending orders, but then discarded the idea. By the time his commanders received them, the crisis would be passed.

Realising the danger, the General of the Second had pulled back into the valley, allowing all his forces to join together. They had soon linked with the First. Now all the Yasser States' forces were united. 'Thank, Larus,' he said, letting out his breath at last.

The price was that the scattered Silver could escape. With the Second now away from the pass, the bloodied Eathal fled for the safety of their lines, defended by the Yellow Drakon.

His own forces now pushed ahead in a united front. Two virtually intact human Legions facing only the Yellow Drakon. The flash and detonation of magics continued across the lines. Faced now with two Sorcerers and a superior force, the Sorcerer-Lord of the Yellow began an orderly retreat back into the pass. Hundreds of Eathal fell, yet they did not break, their lines smoothly reformed when each warrior fell.

If only the Raptor could return, thought Daran. They could give them even more punishment as they fled back along the narrow defile. Yet it was not to be.

'Congratulations, my Lord. Victory.'

Daran felt a crushing disappointment. He had hoped they would destroy both Legions. As it was, they had perhaps destroyed half the strength of the Silver – around five thousand Eathal – and a little less than one thousand of the Yellow Drakon. Still, they had shattered the illusion of Eathal invincibility. Above all, it was important that the men under his command stay confident.

'Yes. Victory!' said Daran, injecting as much passion into his declaration as he could. 'Our men fight above all expectation.'

The next hour was filled with reports from his commanders. Thousands of their men were wounded and four hundred of his veterans were dead. Light losses compared to the Eathal, yet each legionnaire was a warrior the Yasser States could not afford to lose. Daran gave detailed orders for their continued movement back towards Raynor. Despite the enthusiasm of his aides, they had not achieved nearly enough.

* * *

Daran was poring over a map when Uran finally reported to his field tent. Outside, the sky had long ago darkened into evening.

Uran looked drawn. He had lost weight since the campaign had begun.

'Sit. Sit,' said Daran. He poured his old friend a cup of wine.

Uran sipped it appreciatively. 'A victory.' His hard tone echoed Daran's thoughts. It was a victory, yet not the one they had hoped for.

'Yes,' said Daran. 'The Yellow were even more formidable than I anticipated.'

'Still – they could have led the assault.'

'True,' admitted Daran.

'We captured the Silver's glowmetal. The Screamer. Hukum will be livid,' said Uran.

'That is something. Send it back to Raynor. We will need every defence we have there.' Daran's words hung in the silence. Neither of them wanted to admit the truth. Hukum would reach Raynor.

Uran shook himself and reached into the pouch at his belt. He pulled out three small cavon message capsules.

Daran was instantly alert.

'We have news from Tupur. Lempar drew one of Yeffrij's forward legions into a trap. He almost destroyed it before he withdrew across the Asgod. One of Yeffrij's legions pursued him into the Delta province.'

Daran brightened. 'Clever. With one of Yeffrij's legions guarding his supply lines and another chasing Lempar, he is left with only two full legions to assault Olcis. We should be grateful. Every week that Lempar delays Yeffrij's victory over Olcis is another week Yeffrij cannot come south to link with Hukum.'

Uran looked at the remaining two messages, shuffling them, as though unsure what to speak of first.

'Tell me,' demanded Daran.

'The false-Scion Cedrin has married in Exdor,' said Uran.

'The Cintros woman?'

'Yes,' said Uran bitterly. The Sorcerer himself had hoped to wed Ellen.

He looked up at Daran as though unsure whether to continue. Whatever he saw in Daran's eyes strengthened his resolve.

'Exdor has sworn to Cedrin. He was crowned Emperor five days ago,' said Uran.

Daran was gripped with a sudden fury. *Why would they do that? Exdor has cared nothing for Kelas or Raynor since Riin fell. Why would they do that now?*

The dark circles under Uran's eyes were deeper than ever. He pushed aside two of the messages and held up the third. 'Rehvar travelled with them from Herath. He has placed himself in the Exdor palace and is in place to strike.'

Uran crushed the message in his hand. His silver eyes glinted in the torchlight. 'Give the command. By sunset tomorrow the pretender and the Cintros woman will be dead. Rehvar will not fail.'

Daran leant back on his field chair. His thoughts circled the strange events like unsettled birds.

'It doesn't make *sense*.' Why would a staid backwater like Exdor kneel to a pretender? They had not even acknowledged Daran as Warlord, and he had saved Raynor and the southern provinces from utter destruction.

'Give the command,' urged Uran.

Daran had never hesitated to dispatch assassins before . . . when he felt that his hold on Raynor was threatened. Yet something gave him pause here.

'I want Rehvar to gather more information. I need to know more of Cedrin and events in Beslin. Above all, I need to know why Sarlord Duras would make such a move. I need information.'

Uran's mouth made a hard line. Daran knew what his friend

wanted. Yet how much of that was driven by his rage at Ellen's rejection?

'Let me consider this,' said Daran. His tone was uncompromising. A dismissal.

Uran rose and bowed, exiting the tent.

Only days ago, Daran's eldest son had urged Daran to declare himself Emperor. *'Raynor needs to be defended by an Emperor, Father. You should have taken the title years ago.'*

Yet Daran knew the real reason. He saw it in the ambition in his son's eyes. His son saw *himself* as Emperor.

Daran had never brooked any challenge to his own rule, yet had always stopped short of calling himself Emperor. In the beginning, he too had believed the tale of the Hero of the Last Days. The man who had rescued Riin's newborn and vanished through the Iris. He had investigated every lead, in his heart believing he was preserving the Empire for the son of the man he had sworn to obey. It also served another purpose. The Suul loyalists could not challenge his rule if he stopped short of usurping the Cinanac.

He knew that as long as he lived he could keep the Suul of Raynor in check. Perhaps he could declare himself Emperor and forge a new Empire in the south. Yet would his sons be able to keep the warring fragments together longer than a generation? The thing he feared above all was losing all he had worked so hard to preserve.

Tomorrow he would have to return to Raynor. He dare not leave the warring Suul factions alone too long. His presence was needed there for stability. He would enter the city at the head of his bodyguard and celebrate his victory in the field, however hollow that victory seemed to him.

Chapter Thirteen

Estle Cintros adjusted his outfit, readying himself for the audience with Daran. His yellow hair was loose around his shoulders, following the current fashion. He patted his swelling belly, promising himself, yet again, to cut down on his intake. Thankfully his open shirt was cunningly crafted to minimise the visual impact of his lack of muscle tone.

He turned left and then right, inspecting his profile in the mirror. 'Sister. You were determined to get yourself a Scion, one way or another,' said Estle under his breath. 'But did you have to marry him?' He dabbed on a spot of makeup. Satisfied, he swept out of the Athrian consulate.

Two Athrian scythemen fell into step behind him. Their presence was so familiar he scarcely noticed them.

He suppressed his irritation as he thought over the last message from his brother Torren, Sarlord of Athria. It was all very well for the dour, dutiful Torren to ask for recognition of Ellen's new husband from his comfortable seat three hundred leagues away, but it was *poor Estle* who was the meat in the sandwich. Didn't he and Ellen realise that this overturned decades of policy? That it threatened the very alliance itself?

Not to mention the reaction of Uran. For years the Sorcerer had been Estle's ally at court. Now in one move he would become an adversary. Ellen's rejection of Uran, and her rescue of Raphal from his secure cells in the Eastern Tower, had sent the Sorcerer into a fury. The man would not see sense on the issue. The fact was Ellen and Razell Cinnor were the only two known female Sorcerers in Kelas. And Uran had about as much chance of bedding Razell as a drakon. Uran had been obsessed with siring progeny who could wield the Fire. Ellen had been his ideal breeding mare, and she had the nerve to wreck his plans. Estle himself had tried to broker the whole arrangement, knowing it would cement Athria's alliance with Raynor and bring great rewards from a grateful Uran. Alas.

Estle had regarded Ellen's quest to find the Scion and re-establish the old order as a fool's mission. At best a waste of time chasing shadows . . . at worst a dangerous game that threatened to make the Warlord their enemy. Yet despite everything, Ellen had found her Scion. Whether he was another pretender or the real thing mattered not a whit to him. It was what he represented as a political force, and how the Warlord and Uran reacted that was the crux of the matter. He had to admit a grudging respect for his little sister. She had surprised him, both with her courage and her determination. Perhaps their father's faith in her – she had always been Myan's favourite – had not been misplaced after all.

Estle slowed as he approached the doors to Daran's private court. As usual, the ante-chamber was filled with courtiers and Suul, waiting on the Warlord's pleasure. The room was abuzz with talk of the invincible Warlord's latest victory in the field. Estle had made his own enquiries. The details of the engagement were vague. The captured glowmetal, the Screamer, had been paraded through the city on a cart with bloodied Eathal weapons and armour. You would think it was Hukum's head the way the masses had cheered it. Far from it. The Raptor had followed the procession in the air, Uran's Druidin shooting coloured lights in celebration. The magical platform certainly was impressive. The reality was that the divisions within Raynor yawned wider than ever. The fractious Suul positioned for a change and only the threat of the Eathal kept them in check.

Kranor stood stiffly in a corner, as though standing at attention on a parade ground. Estle gritted his teeth. For years he had deliberately avoided Kranor and his faction of Suul loyalists. Association with them had been akin to political death. Now they were to approach Daran together. On top of that, the man's uncompromising warrior ethic and humourless demeanour irritated him in the extreme. No doubt he and Torren would get along like old friends. *Unlikely allies indeed.*

Kranor's curly black hair had been trimmed short, and the faded Suul mark showed clearly on his fine, angular face. The one-armed man saw Estle immediately, fixing him with his dark eyes, and set out across the room towards him. His patterned grey shirt was pinned neatly at the left shoulder.

'Suul Cintros. Well met,' said Kranor. He seized Estle's arm in a warrior's grip, his hand wrapping around his forearm like a vice.

'Yes. Well met, Kranor,' said Estle. Around the room, there was a noticeable dip in the conversation. Heads turned. Within an hour, every player in the palace would know Athria had changed its stance dramatically. With the news that Ellen Cintros had married the new pretender to the north already common knowledge, perhaps it was not so surprising.

A Suulqua moved to their side and bowed. 'The Warlord is ready for you, my Lords.'

'Lead on,' said Estle. His forearm throbbed with an outline of Kranor's earnest grip. What was it about these warrior types?

The room was familiar to Estle. He had spent many nights here in comfortable companionship with Daran, Uran and their inner circle. He had been secure in the knowledge that Athria stood high in Raynor's good graces. Now he came as a stranger.

Daran's face was stern as he looked down from the raised dais. At his side, Uran looked pale and drawn. Estle could see the strain that the ongoing field campaign had placed on both men.

Estle bowed with a flourish, then straightened. 'Congratulations on your victory, my Lord.'

Daran gave him a tight smile. 'Thank you, Suul Cintros.'

Kranor nodded his head to the Warlord in recognition. Estle was surprised the man could bend that much. It was no secret he regarded Daran as an usurper to the Emerald Throne. The Warlord nodded to Kranor in turn, one warrior to another. Kranor had lost his arm in the battle to save Raynor twenty-seven years ago. The same battle that had seen Daran rise to

Warlord.

'What brings Estle Cintros to the Warlord's throne arm-in-arm with Kranor Zan?' said Uran.

Estle felt his stomach flip. Torren's orders left no room for manoeuvre.

'I present myself as Emperor Cedrin Cinanac's ambassador to the court of the Warlord,' said Kranor in a bluff voice. Estle winced. All the subtleness of a warhammer.

'Together we call for the recognition of Cedrin Cinanac as rightful heir to the Emerald Throne,' said Estle.

'Does Athria ask for this, or the brother of *Ellen Cintros*?' Uran made his sister's name seem like a curse.

Estle's contrary nature immediately flared. 'Athria? Perhaps it has not escaped your notice that Suul Ellen Cintros is now the Empress of Bulvuran?'

'Marriage to one pretender does not make her anything but a fool,' snapped Uran.

'Cedrin is no pretender,' said Kranor, his voice harsh and commanding. Estle could see how the man had risen to command Riin's One Hundred. Even one-armed, the warrior gave off a tangible sense of menace.

'Spurious claims —' began Uran.

'What proof do you offer?' asked the Warlord. Uran silenced himself with difficulty.

'We have two incontrovertible proofs,' said Kranor.

'Please enlighten us,' said the Warlord.

Estle was uncomfortably aware of the scythemen positioned around the room. He had seen more than one unfortunate dragged away from this chamber to the Warlord's cells. He had watched them depart with the casual pity of a man who never dreamed he might one day join them.

'The testimony of Kalyth Orin, lieutenant of Belin Kaidell. He himself received Riin's newborn babe from the arms of Belin and took him to Athria, where he was fostered by Tarral, a warrior of the One Hundred.'

'Nothing could have survived the destruction of the Raynor Iris,' said Uran.

'Belin and the child *did* survive. Belin Kaidell was the Hero of the Last Days,' said Kranor.

'A Hero who vanished like smoke,' said Uran, sneering in derision. 'Perhaps you could explain why this Cedrin appears now? After all this time?'

'Tarral did not know of Cedrin's birth, thinking him a bastard of Belin's,' said Kranor.

'And Kalyth?'

'He had his own pain to bear,' replied Kranor.

'You said *proof*,' said the Warlord.

'Kalyth's testimony was verified by my own wife, Salis Cintor, in a Testing,' said Kranor.

Uran snorted in derision.

Kranor's dark eyes narrowed. 'Have a care, Uran.' The warrior's fingers flexed, as though readying themselves to wrap around Uran's throat. He might just might be quick enough to break the Sorcerer's neck before he drew on the Fire.

Uran's own frayed temper rose.

Fortunately the Warlord intervened. 'Not to impinge on your wife's honour, but you said there were two proofs. The first you offer is Kalyth's testimony. What is the second?'

Kranor turned back to the Warlord. 'The High Priestess of the Fountain Temple of Exdor has verified Cedrin's claims. She has declared him the true son of Riin Cinanac and a Sorcerer of the Old Blood.'

'*A Sorcerer?* More fables. Even a High Priestess can be bribed,' said Uran, blinking rapidly. Beads of sweat glistened on the Sorcerer's forehead.

Kranor gave a tight smile, clearly gratified to have rattled Uran. ' Cedrin Cinanac is a true Scion of Bulvuran. Daran – do you think Duras would be such a fool as to hand Exdor to any pretender who showed up at his door?'

That gave the Warlord pause. 'I had heard nothing of this testing at the Fountain Temple,' said Daran, casting a suspicious gaze at Uran. The Sorcerer licked his lips and looked away.

'I will consider your request and inform you of my decision,' said the Warlord. This whole encounter was a fiasco. As if Daran would even consider recognising some unknown calvanni six hundred leagues away in Beslin.

Estle forced a smile and bowed. 'Athria has another matter. If we could discuss it in private?'

'Certainly.' The Warlord waved at Kranor in dismissal.

Kranor nodded briefly to the Warlord and left the chamber.

'Well?' said Uran.

Estle drew closer and lowered his voice. 'Sarlord Torren has been trying to loosen the hold of the Athrian Temple of the Sisters. This is proving difficult without an alternative for essential magics. Is there any chance we could obtain the services of Raynor's Druidin?'

Daran and Uran exchanged looks. 'At another time, perhaps. Now we need every Druidin we have for the war against the Eathal.'

'Athria could offer substantial discounts on essential food and materials. Perhaps even additional warriors for Raynor's defence,' said Estle. *Curse Torren.* He sends him to the Warlord with a preposterous declaration in support of this new pretender Cedrin, then asks him to beg for favours.

'We will think on it,' said the Warlord.

'We can ask no more, my Lord,' said Estle.

He was relieved when he finally took his leave of Daran's court. As he expected, Kranor was waiting outside.

'Suul Cintros. There are many Suul who are eager to meet you. We have much to discuss,' said Kranor.

'I look forward to it,' said Estle, surprised at the light tone he managed. He knew exactly who these Suul were. They were the same stuffy loyalists he had been avoiding ever since he travelled here from Athria years ago. With a single order, Torren had put him right into a snake pit of deadly politics.

Still, there was no fighting that now. Now it was just a matter of staying alive.

* * *

Hukum held the efreet dispatch up to the light of Rea's full disk. He crushed the message capsule in his left fist as he read Faivel's message. *I never should have trusted him.* Raziin was playing his idiot second son for a fool.

197

When Yeffrij contacted Hukum across the Bridge of Minds with Faivel's requests more than a month ago, he had forced himself to trust his general's instincts. It had seemed inconceivable that now, of all times, the Spear of Carris should resurface. Yet the consequences if it should fall into the hands of Raziin or this alleged Cinanac heir Cedrin were too drastic to contemplate. It seemed worth the risk to let Faivel finish off Raziin then set out on this quest to intercept Cedrin and seize the Spear. Now it was all clear. Raziin had duped them.

Faivel reported that Raziin had turned east, heading to the human city of Apiloth under the protection of his brother, Sarlord Ralin Cinnor. The human had run for sanctuary with his kin. This whole story of striking north to Ranmyden had been nothing but a smokescreen to shield his escape from Faivel's jakkund troops. And Faivel had let him fool them all. The thought that the despised Raziin would escape punishment for the death of his beloved Staraz – his firstborn son – was intolerable.

Hukum watched as another human slave was dragged to the Drakon's Breath. The massive copper glowmetal was roughly pyramidal in shape and squatted with dark menace in its specially constructed cart. The thinnest veins of green light now snaked through the mass of red metal. A pair of acolytes chanted in unison, keeping the glowmetal stable. More was needed though.

Most powerful and dangerous of all his Wallbreakers, the Drakon's Breath was rarely used. Its maintenance was . . . problematic. Fortunately this war provided plenty of feedstock. A second cart was drawn up behind the glowmetal, the interior packed with a miserable press of human slaves. They called out in their brash, overloud human tongue, pleading.

His Kallor Druids dragged the man to the peak of the Drakon's Breath. The human howled in fear. His chief Druid, Isart, hefted a wickedly-sharp knife of darkglass. With a whispered invocation, Isart stabbed down into the man's torso. With four swift incisions, he cut the man's heart from his chest. He crushed the beating mass in his fist, completing the ritual. The lines of green light thinned and vanished.

Hukum sighed in relief as the man's howling finally stopped. 'Isart?'

'Yes, my Lord,' replied the Kallor Druid, his hands glistening dark and wet.

'Rip out their tongues. All that noise is grating.'

'As you wish,' said Isart, bowing. This war would be impossible without the Druids of Kallor. Their skills were essential. They did not come cheaply, however. Fortunately they had their own uses for human slaves and this helped to offset the costs.

Hukum mounted his jakkund and set off through the vast Eathal encampment. His jakkund-mounted bodyguard followed. Everywhere human slaves toiled beneath the lash. They dug pits, collected firewood or undertook any of the thousands of menial tasks required to keep his legions supplied and fed. Most of the humans had already been sent east to the North Yasser, where they would build new Eathal domes or work to restore the vanished forests. It was the lush ecosystems of the upper world that supported the Caverns. The humans had never understood this and had laid waste to them for long enough.

Hukum accepted the salutes of his warriors as his due as he walked his jakkund through the orderly tents of the Black Drakon, his own elite Legion. The Drakon's Breath was only the first of nine great glowmetals carried under the standard of the Black. Six of them were Wallbreakers. Not even the great walls of Raynor would be able withstand these. If his father had taken these glowmetals to Raynor twenty-seven years ago, the human city would now be nothing but a memory. Yet his father, like the Sundars before him, had been conservative, favouring the gradual adsorption of territory, rather than all-out war. His father had always been hesitant to reveal Maht's true strength, still living in the shadow of Carris' Destruction, when the Spear had shattered the world of the Jakir. The Caverns of the Mulisar and Ranmyden, always the arrogant elite of the Eathal world, had been smashed. Only Maht survived, shielded by its defensive glowmetals.

Hukum had taken as much of the magical strength of Maht

on this campaign as he could. Unlike his forebears, he did not fear the humans. Many great glowmetals still remained in Maht, such as The Silence, a Fireseeker that had never reached capacity, even under direct attack by the Spear itself. The size of a small city, it was part of the geography of Maht. Situated between the Upper and Lower Congregations, it effectively made the Lower Congregations invulnerable to Sorcery. Others defeated the attempts of Sorcery to shift them or, like The Silence, were too massive to transport.

The camp of the two hundred Tahistill warriors had been set far downwind. The alliance had been a surprise. The Solatt warrior, Myrn, had emerged from the vast Gimpessu a month ago, offering an alliance between Maht and the Web of Soreth. They too sought the restoration of the forests. Hukum had been gifted with a fine set of crystal blades, crafted by Soreth herself. Hukum had yet to use the Great Spiders in combat, hiding them like his glowmetals and waiting for the moment. The panic in Daran's ranks would be a sight to behold when the spider-warriors were unleashed. He also had another use for them, one crucial to their advance.

He had been livid when he learned of the loss of half the Silver Legion and their Screaming Spear. He was furious with Sorcerer-Lord Zekon, yet should have expected nothing more from the moderate. Why was it that none of his Sorcerer-Lords had the stomach for war? Gestain had led the Yellow to support him, yet instead of driving back Daran's human Legions, they had retreated. Now disgraced, the Silver had been relegated to protecting the flanks of his advance. The Yellow had been retained in his centre, but had lost the honour of advance attack.

Instead Asan would lead the Green Drakon ahead with Blood Legion. This time the Drakon Legion would take the field first. He did not intend to be tricked again by Daran's tactics. Only two human Legions stood between him and Raynor's destruction. The next time Daran's luck would run out.

For the first time that night, Hukum smiled. He had ordered the Warlord to be taken alive.

* * *

Raziin maintained a suitably solemn expression as he knelt before the Armon Suul. He saw many of the war dogs who had supported his failed attempt at the throne, Suul of the old guard that even his father Leith had struggled to keep in check. Men who dreamed of a newborn Cioan Empire. To see them sitting quietly behind his brother Ralin turned his stomach. Unfortunately, being religious types, they would take his oath seriously.

His loyal lieutenants Merceth and Kyal stood with him, their faces implacable. These were men who truly knew his destiny.

'I, Raziin Cinnor, do formally renounce any claim to the throne of Armon, and henceforth abdicate from the line of succession. This I swear before the Gods and Goddesses of Ancient Cioa.'

Ralin gave him a smug smile of triumph. *Keep your Sarlord's throne, brother. Every throne in Kelas will kneel before me once Uros grants me the Spear.*

Raziin looked past Ralin to his twin sister Razell. Skeletally thin, she was dressed in a formal black gown laced up tight to her neck. She could have been a boy for all the curve she showed, even after all these years. Like him, she was also a Cioan albino, her skin and hair silver. That was where the resemblance ended. Where he had been born strong and vital, she was always sickly and weak. His heart beat fast as he anticipated the confrontation with his first, albeit reluctant, lover.

Raziin started to get up from his knees, but Ralin stopped him with a motion of his hand.

'And you swear service the throne of Armon, taking commands from no other,' said Ralin, his eyes narrowed.

Raziin fought to control his fury at this upstart weakling of a brother dictating terms to him, the Chosen of Uros.

'Of course,' he said reasonably. 'I will faithfully serve the throne of Armon.' *By forcing it to kneel.*

'Then rise and enter service,' said Ralin.

A rustling movement went through the assembled Suul, who otherwise gave no other sign of the events they had witnessed.

'Come into my private chambers,' commanded Ralin, turning away from Raziin.

He followed his brother through the crowd to a small chamber that adjoined the banquet hall. Inside, the walls were lined with Ralin's bodyguards. Ralin walked to a desk that was scattered with maps and dispatches. He motioned Raziin to sit opposite.

A side door opened and a thin man in a grey cloak entered. His greying bronze hair marked him as later middle age. Like all of them, he was of the blood of Cioa. None else were tolerated in Armon.

The man bowed to Ralin. He gave Raziin a sly look as he straightened. 'My Lord.' His memory stirred.

'Do you remember Kethis?' asked Ralin.

'Yes. Leith's spymaster,' said Raziin.

'Kethis will accompany you on your journey to Ranmyden. He will carry messenger-cavon to allow regular reports.'

Kethis had a narrow face and a receding chin, which he had tried to offset by growing a carefully manicured goatee. Even with the pointed beard on his chin, he had a weak look. Yet there was no mistaking the intelligence in the man's eyes. Interesting. The spymaster remained standing. *So the man knows his place as well.*

'The latest reports from Beslin indicate this Cedrin is a genuine heir. Exdor has declared for him. He has married Ellen Cintros. Already she is with child,' said Ralin. 'I don't need to tell you what that means.'

'Succession,' said Raziin.

'Yes. And the child will be Old Blood. Both Cedrin Cinanac and Ellen Cintros must be killed. The heir with them. The Bulvuran Empire must stay in the past.'

'Yes,' said Raziin. 'On that we are agreed.'

'Armon will have threat enough without a unified Empire at our doorstep. Our generals are confident we can withstand the Eathal. I am convinced Hukum's ambitions will not lead him this far north. It may be that once Raynor and Olcis are destroyed, he will retreat to his new southern territories. If so, Armon will be positioned to expand into Tupur.'

202

Ralin regarded Raziin for a long moment. 'I have assembled a force of three hundred of Armon's finest, equipped with amelak. They will be placed at your disposal.'

'That should be sufficient,' said Raziin.

Ralin let out a breath. 'Raziin. Serve Armon in this – serve truly – and you will earn a place in my Sardom.'

Raziin felt a surge of triumph but was careful to keep his face neutral. It never ceased to amaze him how men like Ralin were so eager to believe that others were driven by the same fatuous idealism. As if Raziin would ever truly come grovelling to Ralin on some quest for forgiveness and redemption.

'I will serve you in this, brother. You have my word,' said Raziin.

'You are a talented general and are well respected by the Armon military. I can assure you of a high position if you succeed in ending this new Empire.'

'Have no fear of that. Cedrin and Ellen will die.' He had reserved a death of unique torment for Ellen Cintros. Cedrin he would play with, like a palgur toyed with its prey. Then, once the Ward had given the heir the Spear and ceased to exist, Raziin would claim it – and destroy Cedrin Cinanac utterly. As the Seer had foreseen. As Uros had promised.

'Kethis has a list of our stations in Thilil. Each has messenger-cavon. Send reports back to Osellen to update us of your progress,' said Ralin. It was not a request. His brother was giving a command. Despite his hope that Raziin would return to the family fold, he did not trust him. Perhaps he would never trust him. It did not matter to Raziin.

'Thank you for this chance. I will not disappoint you,' said Raziin evenly.

Ralin did not reply. He leant back in his chair and stared at Raziin as though trying to judge his words. His eyes were haunted. Ralin jerked his head towards the door in dismissal.

Raziin stood smoothly and gave his brother a short bow. It cost him nothing. There would be plenty of time after he had the Spear to make Ralin pay.

He passed a gauntlet of bodyguards on his way to the door, each warrior watching him with stony-eyed ferocity. These men knew him better than his brother.

Outside, Merceth and Kyal were waiting for him. They flanked him as he moved through the buzz and chaos of the assembled Suul. He did not waste his time passing pleasantries. He was not here to play politics. The time for that sort of game was over. Eventually he found what he was looking for. Two of his family's old retainers stood stiffly at attention guarding the door to another private chamber that led off from the main banquet hall.

He walked up to the door. Like his brother's bodyguards, these men watched him approach with murder in their eyes. His father Leith had been loved by all. The knowledge had made killing him all the sweeter.

'Is my sister within?'

'Suul Cinnor is resting,' said one of the guards.

'Come now. I'm sure she will make time for her dear brother,' said Raziin. He stepped forward and pounded twice on the door. 'Sister!'

Both guards levelled their scythes, forcing Raziin back a pace. At his sides, Merceth and Kyall lowered their greatscythes, readying to release the blades. Raziin held up a hand to halt them. 'No need for hasty reactions. We are all faithful servants of Armon.'

The door opened. Razell stood in the doorway. Her face was even paler than it had been earlier in the open court. A worm of disgust turned in his guts, although he kept his face pleasant.

'Raziin,' she said. Her voice was rich and melodious. Leith had always praised her singing voice; whenever she managed to disengage from her sickbed long enough to use it.

'Razell. What a pleasure to see you. Perhaps a word in private?' A thrill of excitement raced through him, fuelled by memories of the times he had dominated her. Tormenting Razell had been one of the few pleasures of his dreary childhood. All had reached a culmination in her rape. She had never told Leith, yet had retreated to her sickbed for almost a year. They were thirteen. It was the same year that he killed Lisis, a boy two years his senior whose father was favoured by Leith. And who Raziin had despised. Leith disowned him, banishing him to the frontier. He had not seen Razell since.

'My Lady?' asked one of the retainers.

'I will be fine,' said Razell. She turned and entered the small chamber, walking through a set of open doors onto a marble balcony.

Raziin followed her. A scythe swept down behind him. 'Your men remain out here,' said the guard.

'Of course,' said Raziin, signalling for his warriors to wait outside. 'I'm sure they would love to keep you gentlemen company.'

The guards shut the door behind Raziin as he followed Razell out onto the wide balcony. The provincial mess of Apiloth stretched to the horizon in every direction. A jumbled mass of mostly timber-built three to four storey dwellings. The Apiloth palace, in which they had assembled their court, was the exception. Thilil had been a vassal-state to Armon since the fall of Bulvuran, its Sarlord paying tribute. The fact was Osellen had little use for Thilil's rustic forest settlements or the Anacian slums of its capital. Although Armon was more than pleased to accept its wealth.

'Dear sister,' said Raziin, advancing towards Razell. He anticipated the fear he would see on her face as he closed on her.

'Stay where you are,' she said. Raziin felt the Fire rise in her. He stopped, instinctively matching it.

'Or what? You will call your two little guards? It's too late to go running to Father,' taunted Raziin.

Raziin felt a vice of Force close around him, pinning him in place. Simultaneously, the Final Matrix stabbed at his mind. He swiftly countered with the Barrier. His long subjugation to Hukum had given him plenty of experience in dealing with that type of attack. The gold glowmetal hanging from his neck remained silent. It fed only on specific mental attacks, such as woven Compulsions.

'I know you, brother. I know the pit of rot inside you where a heart should beat. I pleaded with the Council to see you dead, but Ralin's supporters overruled me. With enough proof, I can still sway them.'

She stepped closer, her pale golden eyes the twin of his own.

'What is it you are planning?'

Her Final Matrix drove into his Barrier, like a razor-sharp wedge. He countered the thrust, surprised at her power.

'Yes. Father completed my training before you killed him,' she sang.

Raziin pushed against the Force that wrapped around his body. He widened the Window, using all the Fire he had at his command. His arm moved slowly, reaching a clawed hand up to grip her throat.

Razell saw the hand move, yet remained where she was. When he was only a handspan away from gripping her scrawny white throat, she increased the power of her Force Matrix. Once more he was frozen.

She laughed, her voice high and beautiful. 'I knew it! You got the physical strength, brother. I, the mental.'

Raziin was filled with an impotent rage. Her Final Matrix threatened to sever his Barrier. He abandoned his attempt to break her hold on him; instead he reinforced his mental shield.

'How does it feel? To be helpless?' whispered, Razell. She drew a long, slim blade from her sleeve and rested the point under his chin.

'If Ralin did not need you, I would kill you here,' said Razell. Her hand shook with suppressed emotion.

The pressure of her Final Matrix increased again, but Raziin withstood it. He never imagined that those long years resisting Hukum's mental probes would save him from his weakling sister.

She released him.

Raziin stepped back away from her knife, but not before she cut his chin with a hiss of animal fury.

'When your plan ripens. I will be there to see you get your due,' said Razell. Composed now, she slipped the knife back into her sleeve and faced him as though nothing had happened.

Raziin backed away from her and fled to the door. He threw the door back, slamming it against the wall. The guards were set to rush into the room, but halted in place when they saw Razell walking slowly behind him.

Raziin looked back once, to see her watching him steadily.

His chin stung with the cut. He touched the wound, and his hand came away bloody. His hands curled into fists. He growled and stalked away. Once he had the Spear, there would be no limit to the Fire he could channel. Then all debts would be repaid.

Razell's high laughter followed him through the room.

Chapter Fourteen

Cedrin pulled the map towards him. His inner circle waited while he considered it. The marble-lined chamber, guarded by Ranis and a dozen of the One Hundred, was as quiet as a tomb. Osterac looked smug, having recently earned a place in the top ten with his improved greatscythe skills.

'This is the best we have?' asked Cedrin.

Raphal's bushy eyebrows drew together. 'Valnis transcribed this from works that predate the Bulvuran Empire. We are fortunate to have it.'

'I did not ask if we were fortunate. I asked if this was the best we had.'

Raphal sighed. 'There are others, but none as detailed. That is the best.'

Cedrin gritted his teeth, annoyed with himself for snapping at Raphal. The old Priest and Druid had served them well. He looked across the immaculately polished wooden table at Ellen. As always, she gave him a pleasant smile. Her Suul manners were an invulnerable shield, the distance between them an unbridgeable gulf. To the Exdor court, she was a paragon of Suul virtue, enigmatic and greatly admired. The Emperor's court turned with a will of its own while his bed remained cold and empty.

The scholar Valnis had unearthed the location of the Ranmyden Iris. It was inside an ancient Eathal city, in what he and Raphal had translated as the Hall of Dreams. Cedrin turned the map of the Eathal Ranmyden city around, trying to make sense of it. It was impossible.

'Perhaps the notations will be clearer once we reach the Caverns themselves,' said Raphal.

'Yes,' said Cedrin, abandoning his attempt to follow the chart. 'At least we have a clear path to the Caverns. Valnis' maps and notes will at least get us into the underground complex.'

'While we all agree that seizing the Spear is of paramount importance, events in the wider continent cannot be ignored. Shall we move to addressing the overall situation in Kelas, my Lord?' said Duras.

'Please,' said Cedrin. He sipped on a glass of chilled water. After that night with Spider, he had not let a sip of drink pass his lips.

Thenia leant forward eagerly. Spider, healed from her lashes, stood behind her. She stood like a statue, eyes ahead, face expressionless. The Hanis Suul had stopped short of removing Spider from command of the Daughters. Her continued presence was like a thorn in the heel of his foot.

Kalyth slid a map of Kelas across the table. New coloured highlights showed their latest intelligence. Xyanthius reached across and tapped a point some sixty leagues east of Raynor.

'Daran engaged the Eathal here. He destroyed half of the Silver, then retreated.'

'His own Legions are intact?' asked Cedrin.

'Yes. But essentially it is a delaying action. All indications are that Hukum will reach Raynor with his core legions intact. And his Wallbreakers,' said Xyanthius.

Cedrin remembered the camp of miserable refugees from Hend he had seen when he arrived in Raynor, and the others who had sheltered on the streets during Storm Season. If Raynor fell, the whole south would be an open sore of famine and desperation.

'Let's hope Daran can hold them at Raynor,' said Cedrin.

'Olcis has come under attack from Yeffrij and two Eathal legions. The Hesguit has held them so far with defensive magic, but Yeffrij is driving his forces back,' said Xyanthius.

'The Hesguit will withdraw to the Bulvur Citadel,' said Raphal. 'There are strong glowmetals protecting it.'

'And leave the rest of Olcis to the Eathal?' said Kalyth.

'Why does that not surprise me?' said Ellen.

Hundreds of thousands of men and women, all defenceless. If the Eathal followed the same methods they had used in eastern Tupur and North Yasser they would destroy everything. The humans would be taken as slaves, driven to build the Eathal new dome cities. A lifetime of misery with no hope but the release of death.

'Any reports of Lempar's forces?'

'Details are sketchy. His Legion remains in the northern Delta. He continues to set small ambushes for the Grey Drakon – the Eathal legion dispatched to find him – but avoids a head-on encounter,' said Xyanthius.

'So he survives, yet can do nothing for Olcis,' said Kalyth.

Cedrin stared at the map. He had three forces; the reformed Tenth here in Exdor, around five thousand men, the Eleventh in Searn, at around three thousand and the Hanis Ninth, with a thousand. He had spent many late hours poring over this same map, studying until his eyes ached. He had moved the Eathal and human forces around in his mind's eye, like pieces on a karass board. Yet he could never find the winning move.

'We need to create a powerbase in the north, my Lord,' said Duras. 'Raynor may hold, but Olcis will fall. There will be no stopping it. After building our three Legions to full strength, we could move south and take Olcis from the Eathal. Then consolidate the new position. With the resources of Olcis behind us, we would stand a good chance of driving all the way to Raynor. Daran would have to recognise you,' said Duras.

Xyanthius and Kalyth nodded in agreement. He knew their minds. All three wanted to play the safe course. They saw the advance of the Eathal as a strategic advantage, weakening Daran and the Hesguit, allowing the new Imperial forces to take over the ruined remnants and establish order. But how many had to die so that Bulvuran lived? This order of high-level logic was chilling. As a calvanni, he had risked his life for his own. Now these uncounted thousands *were* his own.

'How long to bring the Legions up to strength?'

'Perhaps a year. Two,' said Xyanthius.

'Retaking the Hanis ports would remove a threat to the

west,' said Thenia. 'With the whole of Hend controlled by my mother's throne, the Ninth would quickly reach its full strength again.' Her eyes were lit with excitement.

That course would see him sit in the north with his forces and watch while the continent went up in flames. While thousands died under the Eathal advance. If this was a game of karass, that would amount to leaving all his pieces in the neutral blue hexagon at the *start* of the game. That was no way to win.

'We will re-establish the old order, my Lord. But it will take time,' said Duras.

Cedrin reached out and tapped Olcis with his index finger. The ruby signet ring glittered in the lamplight. He looked around the table. He could see they were all in agreement. Thenia's watery eyes were fixed on him, anticipating the command that would see Hanis regain its power in the west. He knew what they wanted, yet it was he who was the Emperor here.

'I cannot abandon Olcis. If I am truly Emperor, the whole of Kelas is my responsibility.'

'You owe the Hesguit nothing—' began Duras.

'Silence!'

Cedrin glared at the men and women around the table. Ellen's mouth opened, and just for a moment he saw a break in her facade. Marken and Skye were the only ones who were not surprised. Then again, they had known him longer.

'This is my command,' he said, drawing himself up. 'Xyanthius. You will go to Searn to take command of the Eleventh.'

'Yes, my Lord,' said Xyanthius.

'The Exdor Tenth will move south through Thilil.' He paused for a moment. 'Does Veltricus remain in Beslin?'

'Yes,' said Duras.

'Good. Ask him for the use of his scouts. The man will sell anything for a price,' said Cedrin.

'Your orders, my Lord?' asked Xyanthius.

'Take the Eleventh through the Mulisar pass to Fulvur. Both Legions will link there and advance to Olcis.'

'Who will take overall command, my Lord?' asked

Xyanthius.

'Kranor Zan,' said Cedrin. 'I will recall him from Raynor.' The protocol-conscious Exdorians would find it hard to accept Xyanthius as overall commander. Kranor was a Suul. His connection to the Beslin court would also make it easier for the Tenth commanders to accept his leadership.

The room was silent. Kalyth and Xyanthius were resigned. Duras stricken.

'What of Hanis, my Lord?' asked Thenia.

'You will take Leygen with the Ninth and support from the Athrian fleet,' said Cedrin.

Thenia blinked. 'One thousand men is too few to take the walls of Leygen.'

'Yes. But it will be enough to secure the citadel. The Athrian fleet will land your troops inside the port itself.'

'The Warlord would never allow it,' said Thenia.

'You forget what scum these pirates are,' said Marken. 'The harbourmaster has been bought and paid for.'

'Marken and Skye will join the attack,' said Cedrin. If anyone knew the Brotherhood, it was his two friends. Skye had travelled the two hundred leagues to Leygen and back on his narsiit to broker the arrangements. It had taken a small fortune in bribes to open the doors to Leygen. For the Warlord's traitorous underlings, it was nothing more than another murderous foray for profit. Wealth Cedrin had. Men he did not. 'It will be stealth, not force of arms, that takes Leygen.'

'As you command, my Lord,' said Thenia, acknowledging defeat.

'With both Leygen and Thanir under your mother's control, Swebas alone of the major Hanis ports will elude us,' said Cedrin.

'Why would you do this, my Lord? Sacrifice our troops to save Olcis?' said Duras. 'It is Exdor that has kneeled to you, not Tupur.'

Cedrin could see the Exdor Governor was truly shaken. 'Duras. Why should they kneel to an Emperor who hides in the north? It is up to us to show Kelas what the Empire truly means,' said Cedrin.

'My Lord, if I may.' Cedrin looked up in surprise. It was Osterac. The other bodyguards of the One Hundred looked at the Olcis Suul in sheer vexation. He had broken the code of silence.

'Yes. Go on,' said Cedrin.

'I know the Olcis Suul. They chaff at the control of the Temple. Perhaps the Hesguit will be content to hide in the Bulvur and save his own skin, but the Olcis Suul will not. *They* will fight to save their people.'

'What is it you suggest?' said Cedrin.

Osterac sank to his knees. 'Use me, my Lord. Send me ahead to Olcis. I will begin a coup within the city. By the time your Legions arrive, it will be to a city ready to swear allegiance to *you*. You will gain the whole of Tupur!'

'And what of Lempar?' said Kalyth.

'Lempar is a loyal general of Olcis. If we can depose the Hesguit and raise a Sarlord in his place, Lempar will follow his orders. Your orders,' said Osterac.

'Lempar *will* be desperate to save his city,' said Xyanthius.

'Yes! Give him the chance to link with two Imperial Legions and join with the Olcis Suul – and their personal guards – and the city can be saved.' Osterac's light blue eyes shone bright in his pale face. There was no doubting his zeal.

'It's true,' said Thenia. 'The combined forces may stand a chance against Yeffrij's legions, provided they can fight from a defensive position.'

'The Hesguit will not be deposed so easily,' said Ellen.

'There are many Druids – even High Druids – who would rather fight than cower in the Citadel,' said Raphal.

'Are you forgetting the magic at the Hesguit's command?' said Ellen.

'Druids will march with the Tenth,' said Duras.

'It's true the Hesguit has magic at his command,' said Raphal. 'Yet it is mostly defensive. He may be able to defend the Citadel, but does not have the resources to take control of the whole city – not if the Suul were against him.'

Cedrin was pleased. Even given their initial resistance, they were all ready to follow his commands, despite the risks involved.

'Xyanthius. Stay in contact with Osterac. Your task will be to enter the city with minimal engagement of Yeffrij's forces and link with the defenders,' said Cedrin.

He turned to Osterac, who had risen from his knees, his face flushed with triumph. Cedrin could not fault the man's dedication, yet he still puzzled over what drove him. That did not matter if he got the results he promised.

Cedrin knew the risks he was taking. He knew the gamble and the vast unknowns that could destroy his fledgling Empire. Even so, he could not abandon Kelas to the Eathal. That much he did know.

'Much will depend on you, Osterac. Once the city is under the control of the Suul, you are to seek out Lempar and bring his Legion back to the city. His involvement will be crucial.'

Cedrin turned to Ellen. Her honey-gold hair had been tightly braided back from her face, emphasising her beauty. He looked into her green eyes and felt a longing to be near her once again. For a moment she was his Ellen, then the light went out in her eyes and a wall came down. Her mouth compressed into a thin line and she became Suul Cintros.

* * *

Rehvar knocked five times on the narrow door, using the prearranged pattern. The rough-plank door opened a crack. He could see the fearful face of the innkeeper, all sweat and stubble, through the gap.

'Who's there?'

Rehvar released his hold on the illusion. As the Moon Essence faded, the innkeeper's eyes widened. 'Rehvar.' He made the Circle of Larus and whispered a prayer of protection under his breath. To a weak-minded fool like this one, he would have seemed to appear from nowhere.

'Open the door, idiot,' said Rehvar. The Warlord's agent set a good table, but the man was as thick as a block of stone. If not for the high steeple of his ancient inn, which was perfect for keeping messenger-cavon, Rehvar would never have risked associating himself with him. He could not understand how someone as fearful as the innkeeper, who jumped at every shadow, took the Warlord's coin in the first place. Then again, greed was an underappreciated motivator.

Rehvar slipped through the door and the innkeeper slammed it shut behind him. His contact was immediately more relaxed. As if the warped planks would do anything to keep out Exdor's Nightwatch.

'Any orders?' asked Rehvar.

'No. Nothing,' said the innkeeper.

He turned away, beginning his climb of the narrow, winding stairs to the steeple.

'Would you want somethin' to eat?'

'Yes. I'll be down in half an hour,' said Rehvar.

He gathered the Moon Essence, forming one of the lesser illusions. The innkeeper's attention drifted away, and Rehvar ducked back through a low door into the rooms behind the inn. Rehvar relaxed. He was used to working alone and was secure behind his magical shields. Besides, stupid questions annoyed him. There was nothing more dangerous than a nervous spy who could not shut up.

When he reached the steeple, he was greeted with the familiar sound of chattering cavon, the Kelas cave birds renowned for their homing abilities. Like most birds in Kelas, they had hind and forelegs, as well as wings. The forelegs were dexterous and would carry the message capsule back to the Palanac in Raynor. The hind legs had long, wickedly sharp spikes, which they used to defend themselves against bats. He had more than one scar on his arms and hands from handling the birds over the years. At one time they had tried removing the spikes, but the mortality rate in flight was too high. The cavon needed them for defence.

Rehvar used a focussed touch of Essence to ignite the wicks of the three lamps hanging in the steeple. The birds jostled with each other in excitement, knowing some of them would escape their confinement. Messages were always sent in sets of three, as a contingency against predation – and deliberate sabotage. He prided himself on the fact that not one of his operations had yet been compromised.

He sat at the small desk and opened the drawer. Then he drew out three sheets of thin message parchment, a stylus and ink, and three message capsules. He composed himself. Space was tight on the sheets. The added complexity of the cipher required a careful degree of forethought.

Rehvar sat tapping the stylus on the desk. He had been one of the first Druidin, a refugee from the fall of Althar like so many others. It was that death and destruction that made him realise Raynor had to survive, and the Warlord was the only man capable of holding that melting-pot of Suul factions together. He had become an expert in poisons and the methods of their delivery. He had killed fourteen times for the Warlord and gathered crucial intelligence for more than twenty years. He did not regret one death, and he was proud to say not one of his victims had suffered needlessly. Their deaths were not in vain. The removal of the threats they represented saved hundreds, perhaps thousands of lives.

Rehvar stared at the blank parchment. Now, after all this time, he found himself conflicted. Unlike the other false-Scions, he had not managed to find one bit of evidence that disproved Cedrin's claim. There was no money trail of bribes, no faked documents. The Fountain Priestess appeared above reproach. His own professional cynicism had been worn away.

Not only did Cedrin appear genuine, Rehvar liked him. He treated his men well and truly seemed to care about the fate of Kelas.

'I am just a tool,' he reminded himself. *A weapon in the hands of the great.* Ultimately, he served the Warlord. In that way, it was simple. He need only report what he had found, sticking to the facts. It was up to Daran to decide on Cedrin's fate. Even if the man was the true heir, perhaps Kelas was better served by his death. Who was he to say?

Rehvar would kill him and his wife with regret, yet would not hesitate. His stomach grumbled, reminding him that dinner was waiting. He dipped the stylus into the ink.

Taking a moment to concentrate, he began his message.

* * *

Cedrin made a small variation to the Matrix and sent three arrow-shaped bolts of Force slamming into the brick wall.

'Try five,' said Ellen. 'Fan them out. The broader the front, the harder it will be to shield them.'

Despite the estrangement between them, they still met for an hour a day to work on his Sorcerous skills. They did not perform any sort of Sorcerous combat with each other. Ellen could not so much as open the Window without endangering the child. His son. He lost focus for a moment.

It was lucky that he had such as good memory for the Matrices. Without the Bridge of Minds, there would have been no way for Ellen to have shown him the corrections or introduce any new forms. There was much that he had not learned, but that could wait. Their expedition to the Ranmyden Caverns would head north in six days. In a surprise move, Veltricus had offered the use of his Thilil scouts for nothing in return for a place in the expedition. He was seeking Eathal artefacts and hoped to open up a new source of trade glowmetals from the ruined Ranmyden cities. His men would be a welcome addition to their own strength. Raziin was still out there somewhere. Seeking the Spear. Every man Exdor could spare was heading south to Olcis.

Cedrin had ordered a solid brick wall to be constructed in the exercise yard of the Beslin palace to practice his offensive Matrices. Its surface was scarred and pitted by the daily assaults.

He made an adjustment to the Force Matrix. Five bolts fanned out from his outstretched hands. The central two detonated against the freestanding wall with an explosion of brick dust. The other three had been sent too wide.

'Release. *Quickly*,' said Ellen.

Four warriors of the One Hundred and Ellen's two Suulquas dived to the cobbles. It was not the first time. Cedrin hastily released his hold on the Matrix. The three bolts vanished before they reached his men, but he was not quite quick enough in closing the Window. A gout of raw Fire billowed out from his upper torso. For a moment, it was as though he had turned into a human candle. The yellow and crimson flames flew up above him and vanished with a *whoosh*.

Ellen burst out laughing.

Cedrin turned in surprise. Hope surged through his chest. It was the first time she had broken her grim demeanour since the night, eight days ago, when everything went so wrong.

Ellen turned to him and then came back to herself. She cleared her throat. 'Not so wide.'

'Ellen,' he said.

She looked at the brick wall, her face expressionless, as though she had not heard him.

'Ellen. Give me a chance to make amends.' His body tensed as he awaited her answer, both longing for and dreading the reply.

She looked down at the cobbles, moving a shattered fragment of brick around with the toe of her boot. 'I need time.'

Cedrin let out a breath. 'I can do that. I can wait. Just remember I love you, Ellen. More than anything. I'm sorry.'

She turned to him. A single tear slid down her cheek. 'I'm just not ready . . .'

Ellen wiped away the tear.

This was a breakthrough. Ellen had acted like a stranger, refusing to even acknowledge there was anything wrong. Now, even though the tension was still there, at least she was willing to talk.

'Having someone. Someone who I could . . . hurt. This is all new to me, Ellen. In Athria, I feared how the Brotherhood would use those I loved. I always kept people at a distance. To protect them.'

Her green eyes fixed on his, guarded. At least she was listening.

'I will not hurt you like that again. I vow it.'

The silence stretched out. She continued as though he had not said anything. 'How is your control of multiple Matrices coming along?'

Cedrin blew out a stream of air. 'Good. I can hold two for hours now, sometimes three.'

'And the Window?'

'It has not failed me since before Beslin. The meditations of the Way have helped.'

Ellen considered the wall. 'Shall we test your power?'

Cedrin's eyebrows rose. Ellen's training had always been about control and manipulation.

'I want you to create a single bolt of Force. Direct as much of the Fire as you can into it. I want to see what you can do.'

Cedrin took a deep breath and reached for the Window. He opened it wide, filling himself with the Fire. He let it swell, judging the moment when the raw Fire would begin to escape beyond his control.

'You might want to stand back!' called Ellen. The warriors did not need a second warning. They ran for cover.

Cedrin swiftly formed the Force Matrix and let the whole flow of Fire stream through it. The Force bolt appeared halfway between him and the brick wall. A great silver arrow the size of a tree-trunk, travelling fast. It hit the wall square on. There was a stunning detonation. Cedrin hastily raised his Shield as brick fragments flew across the courtyard ahead of a billowing cloud of dust. They clattered against it in a series of dull thuds.

When the dust cleared, there was nothing left of the wall but a shattered foundation.

Ellen blinked. 'Your power *is* impressive.'

He let the Shield drop. 'Enough for one day?'

'I think so. For one thing, there is nothing left to shoot at,' said Ellen.

Mendor, Valdas and the warriors of the One Hundred cautiously emerged from the doorways around the courtyard.

Ellen's two Suulquas dusted off their fine clothes as they walked across to her.

'Your will, my Lady?' said Mendor.

'You two take a break,' said Ellen. 'You deserve it.' Mendor gave her a wry smile. Valdas remained earnest, always nervous around Ellen.

Elthar and Duro took station in front of Cedrin and Ellen as they entered the palace, while Velthius and Vess followed behind. Ranis was busy making preparations for their journey north.

When they entered their apartments, Ellen hovered uncertainly in the middle of the room.

'Shall we have lunch together?' asked Cedrin quickly.

'Yes. Why not,' said Ellen.

This was also a breakthrough. Ellen had hardly stirred from her apartments except for meetings at court, taking her meals alone unless they were formal events.

Servants came forward with platters of food while they sat in uncomfortable silence. Elthar and Duro were implacable and silent at the door, like unwilling chaperones. He wracked his brains, trying to think of a line of safe conversation. Then he remembered something he was puzzling over late last night.

'Do you think it would be possible to take the Palanac without bloodshed?'

Ellen took a sip of wine, thoughtful for the moment. 'The palace is heavily defended.'

'Yes, but if you could get a force inside it,' said Cedrin.

'By magic?'

'Yes. Didn't you say that Belin escaped through the Iris? What about coming back into the palace the same way?'

'Ah. Uran showed me the Raynor Iris. It's ruptured. Broken,' said Ellen.

Cedrin struggled against disappointment. 'There's no way it could be used?'

'What did Uran say . . .' Ellen frowned. 'Ah. Yes. He said that with the Opening Matrix and enough power it might be possible, but the Opening Matrix was lost.'

'If the Opening Matrix is lost, then how did Belin escape through the Iris? How did the Ward open the Iris in Olcis?'

'Good questions. Perhaps we will have the chance to find out in Ranmyden,' said Ellen.

Cedrin froze. This was the first time that he and Ellen had passed more than a few stilted words of conversation in a week. They had not had a chance to really talk about the journey north. He had just assumed that Ellen would remain here in Beslin, safe in the palace. Not only was she pregnant, she could not defend herself with Sorcery. But now he realised that she was determined to come with him, regardless. He would not be able to challenge her without a stand up argument, and he knew first-hand now determined she could be. It was unlikely he would be able to deter her.

Ellen was watching him. 'What is it?'

He had always believed in picking the right time for his battles. Graveyards were full of the brave and impulsive. Sometimes stepping away from combat took more courage.

'I . . . ah. It's just a pity. If there was some way to strike from inside the palace, we could seize the Raynor court.'

'A bloodless coup?' said Ellen.

'Yes.'

'Daran is too wiley for that. He and Uran would escape. Then there are the Raynor Suul. Just putting them all in the same guarded room guarantees nothing.'

Cedrin chewed on a piece of roasted meat and washed it down with chilled water. 'Then we are back to force of arms.' He sighed. 'I don't want to fight Daran. Too many warriors have died already.'

'If Thenia manages to re-establish order in Hanis, Athria will be free to act. Torren could send forces to link with the other three Legions.'

Cedrin grunted. 'If they are still intact.'

Ellen put down her knife. 'I think your decision was the right one. We were all too busy thinking about keeping power to consider why we have the power in the first place.'

Cedrin leaned back and smiled at her in surprise.

'I'm proud of you,' she said.

He hardly dared to move, scared of breaking the fragile peace they had established. Ellen went quietly back to her meal.

Like a dawning sun, hope rekindled inside him.

* * *

Raziin rode at the head of the column with Merceth and Kyal. The keerhound standard of Armon few proudly above the line of amelak-mounted warriors. Their passage through Thilil had been swift. The size of the force had so far deterred the wild

Eathal. This time he also made sure they were well equipped with nets to protect their camp from the thieving lamel. The first of the winged animals he caught had died slowly under his knives. The exercise in torture had done much to ease his tension and instil a useful degree of fear in his men.

The lamel caught on subsequent nights had been killed swiftly by the Armon troops and left to rot. They followed the taboo against eating the winged humanoids. Raziin himself had long grown out of such foolishness. As a young warrior on the harsh northern frontier of Armon he had learned to eat what he could catch.

Kethis rode just behind Raziin. The man's contacts had already proved useful. At the last Armon outpost – cleverly hidden like many others in the Thilil forest – they had received dispatches from Beslin. Their spies in the Exdor capital had bribed a man supplying Cedrin's northern expedition. The upstart Emperor and his men would be leaving Beslin in three days with around one hundred and fifty warriors. They had taken enough provisions to bypass Hivale, indicating the direct northern route to Ranmyden. At last Raziin could fight on his terms. Not only would he have surprise on his side, he would have an overwhelming superiority in numbers.

Unlike the Armon warriors of his brother, Kethis had not been bothered by his torture of the lamel. This was not surprising in a spymaster, yet Raziin had sensed more – a man of similar appetites. Kethis also had the tattoos of a devotee of the rites of Uros, a popular cult in areas of Armon. Like him, he partook in the Storm Season ceremonies. Another promising point of common ground. Although useless in a fight, a man such as Kethis would be a useful future ally.

A scout appeared from the forest and galloped back to the column. 'There is a small settlement up ahead, my Lord.'

Raziin hissed in irritation. They had deliberately avoided settlements in their travel through the forest to prevent word reaching Beslin of their force. Twice they had swung around small Thilil villages rather than chance a rumour spreading west. Fortunately there had been alternative trails through the dense forest that enabled them to maintain the same heading.

'How much will this delay us?' asked Raziin.

The trail they had been following was wide and well travelled, but ran along the base of a steep ridge.

'We will have to take one of the northern ridge trails. It will be slow going. It will probably cost us a day, perhaps more,' said the scout.

'What about cutting to the south?' asked Merceth.

The scout licked his lips nervously as he replied to Raziin's huge lieutenant. 'Swampland, my Lord. Impassable.'

'How many in this settlement?' asked Raziin.

'Around twenty. Most of the men will be away cutting timber until dusk.'

It was vital he reached Ranmyden first. He would need to send out a wide net of scouts to watch for Cedrin's approach, then choose the right ground for his ambush. He could not afford a day lost for every settlement he passed.

'We will go through it,' said Raziin.

Kyal grinned, the light of anticipation glowing in his golden eyes. Merceth merely nodded, accepting his commands with his usual dour intensity. They both knew his mind.

'If we abandon the need for stealth, we will make better time,' said the Captain of the Armon warriors. One of his brother's men. 'And we will be able to buy provisions from the villages as we go.'

Raziin turned to the Captain. 'Stealth will be more important than ever as we approach the Exdor border.'

'Then . . .' The Captain paled as comprehension dawned. He looked at Merceth and Kyal, then back to Raziin. 'Your orders, my Lord?'

'We go in hard and fast. None are to be left alive. Send the scouts out wide to make sure there are no witnesses,' said Raziin.

'We could make it look like an Eathal attack,' suggested Merceth.

'Eathal use spears and hammers. Our men should leave stab wounds and bludgeon with scythe butts. No slash wounds,' said Kyal. 'Even better if we could leave a few Eathal corpses behind.'

223

'Excellent idea,' said Raziin. 'Send one of the scouts out with fifty men and spare mounts. I want a dozen Eathal prisoners.'

'Thals?' asked the Captain.

'Male or female. It makes no difference,' said Raziin.

The Captain looked at Raziin, as through struggling for words. He blinked rapidly. His knuckles were white where they gripped the reins. Raziin's stomach turned in disgust. Just like his brother. Burdened by sentiment. It was nothing but weakness in a warrior.

'You have your orders, Captain,' said Raziin.

'Yes, my Lord,' said the Captain, in a harsh croak. He turned his mount away to join his men.

'Kyal. Join the attack. Make sure that Captain does what needs doing,' said Raziin.

Kyal grinned savagely and spurred his amelak ahead.

The Armon warriors were equipped with both cavalry scythes and lances. They levelled the lances, the pace increasing as they swept down the track. On either side the walls of greenery raced by. Then all at once the trees fell way and the galloping column emerged into a small clearing. A pitiful collection of houses gathered around a meandering stream. A dozen lines of smoke stabbed skyward from crude mud-brick chimneys, rising up into the still morning air in gentle curves.

A handful of women were washing in the stream, beating their clothes on rocks. Four women and an old man were out in the fields with the few miserable specimens of livestock that the village boasted.

A squad of mounted warriors waded into the stream, surrounding the women. He heard their alarmed voices raised in panic. A warrior stabbed down with his lance, taking a grey-haired woman in the throat. Their terrified screams were quickly silenced. The stream ran bloody as the women's corpses tumbled into the flow.

The women out in the fields ran for the trees while the man ran towards them, brandishing a hoe. A lance took the man in the chest and he disappeared beneath amelak hooves. The mounted warriors quickly overtook the others. One moment they were running, the next they were a tumbled mess of meat and cloth, motionless on the ground, the grass around them splashed with lines of red, like glyphs of death.

Blood for Uros.

At the sound of the screams, a middle-aged woman emerged from a cabin, two young boys clutching to her skirt. Her hands were covered with flour. Her eyes went to the stream, then the fields. She gave a short scream and ran into the cabin. Kyal dismounted and followed her inside. Her panicked pleas soon ended.

Scouts emerged from the trees. With the village perimeter secure, squads of warriors dismounted and walked from house to house until they were all cleared.

The Armon warriors were grim and silent. Most remained mounted, others stood beside their mounts or outside the houses. All watched as their Captain rode to Raziin. Kyal emerged from the log-built hovel, cleaning the blood off his greatscythe haft with a torn section of rough-woven cloth. Raziin's irritation eased. All had gone smoothly enough.

'They are all dead, my Lord,' reported the Captain.

Raziin rode over to the bloodied corpses of three young girls who had been milking an amelak. The beast bleated in confusion, standing beside the overturned pale. All had been killed with stab wounds, as instructed.

'Well done.'

A high wailing began.

'What is that?'

'An . . . an infant,' said the Captain.

'Did I not say to kill everyone?'

'You said no witnesses. The babe will be no threat. The village men will take it when they return.'

'Would the Eathal leave it alive?' asked Raziin.

'I believe they would kill it, my Lord,' rumbled Merceth.

'Then you have your answer,' said Raziin. The sound was highly irritating. If they had to remain for a few hours to stock up on supplies and await the scouts with their Eathal prisoners, it would be insufferable.

'Let me,' said Kyal, turning towards the cabin where the wailing issued from.

'No. Our Captain will see to it. Personally,' said Raziin.

He almost laughed at the play of emotion on the Captain's face. How could this man call himself a warrior? He clearly wanted to defy him, yet struggled against his vow of loyalty – and his fear. Raziin would have no hesitation in destroying him if he gave him cause, and the warrior sensed it.

The Captain dismounted. He drew a calv from his harness and walked to the cabin. A moment later the sound ceased.

'Ahh. Peace at last,' said Raziin.

Chapter Fifteen

Faivel slowed as he entered the village.

The wild Eathal watched him in silence, hands on their stabbing spears and flint axes. The settlement numbered little more than a hundred. Faivel had passed many of the wild Eathal villages in his pursuit of Raziin, but this was the first he had entered. He was forced to. Their supplies were getting perilously low and the jakkund had been pushed too hard for too long. They needed a rest and something richer in their diet than forest forage. The beasts were thoroughbreds and were usually fed the best lungii. The phosphorescent fungi was hard to find in Thilil.

Faivel stopped at the entrance to the woven dome and dismounted. He studied the structure in fascination. The vines were as thick as tree-trunks, speaking of great age, yet still thick with green foliage. Growing something like this would take great Druidic skill. In the Caverns of Maht, only the Liduin Druids had that sort of craft.

The branches at the front of the dome parted and a stocky Eathal emerged. He was dressed in rough leather trousers and furs, two axes of flint in his belt. His upper torso was heavily muscled and marked by a network of fine scars. He studied Faivel and his men. Perhaps weighing the odds. By the deference given to him by the two spear-carrying warriors who flanked him, Faivel judged him to be the leader.

'Strange beasts,' said the stocky thal.

'Jakkund,' said Faivel. 'You have not seen their like before?'

The Eathal shook his head. Faivel was conscious of the

warriors than surrounded him and his men, and the throwing spears that many carried. The arms and equipment that his men carried would represent a fortune to these wild Eathal. Not to mention the jakkund. Yet a force of fifty trained warriors was no small thing.

'What do you want here?' asked the Eathal leader.

'Provisions. Lungii for the jakkund. We can pay you,' said Faivel.

'We have no use for coin,' said the Eathal leader.

Faivel took a ruby from his pouch and held up the gemstone.

The leader's eyes gleamed with avarice as the ruby caught the light. He reached out and Faivel laid the gemstone in his calloused hand. The Eathal stared at it, lost in a dream. After a time, he came back to himself. The ruby disappeared into a pouch at his belt and he motioned to the warriors around the camp to relax.

Faivel sighed in relief as the Eathal warriors melted back into the jungle.

Other thals and thels came forward, unarmed Eathal, fearful of his men. His warriors towered over their squat forest cousins.

'These will take care of your mounts and your warriors. Come. Accept my hospitality.'

The Eathal leader turned to enter the dome. The two spear-wielding guards stayed outside by the entrance. They watched the jakkund with fascination.

Faivel left his mount and equipment and followed the leader, trusting that his Huntmaster would make sure nothing was stolen. Inside, the dome was pleasantly lit with lungii, growing along the underside of the boughs. He blinked, relieved to be out of the uncomfortable glare of the day. As his eyes adjusted, he saw the leathery shapes of bats huddled on one side of the ceiling. A small patch of lungii grew on the ground beneath them. Faivel was instantly homesick for Maht. The whole space was like a miniature cavern, doubling as a communal living area and gathering space.

There were rough stairs cut into the ground, descending to chambers below ground. Faivel followed the leader down a set of muddy flights held in place with rough-cut wooden planks.

As they descended, these become rough stone, worn smooth by centuries of use. Eventually they entered a natural cavern with a low, sloping ceiling, lit with glowplants. The leader ducked under an opening and led him along a narrow passage to a wide chamber. This was also natural but had been smoothed back with some rough attempts at masonry.

In a niche in the wall, set high in a place of honour, was a breastplate of clear glass. Faivel was drawn to it in wonder. It was finely made, cast into a single piece shaped for its original wearer. Faivel ran his fingertips across its smooth surface. Lying below the armour were a pair of darkglass axes. One of them had been shattered into three pieces, but the shards had been reverently laid out together to form the shape of the original blade.

'Aurrilass,' said the Eathal leader.

Faivel could not have been more surprised if the man had shown him a pet drakon. Aurrilass was an ancient form of clearglass that was tougher than mought. The legendary armour of the ancient Cioans. Yet this piece was undeniably crafted for an Eathal – and a powerful one at that.

'My ancestor's,' said the leader.

Faivel drew his hand away and looked around the chamber. There were books here, in both Cioan and the Eathal tongue, as well as ancient vellum scrolls.

'Your ancestor?'

The leader sat at a low table and motioned for Faivel to sit opposite him. 'A Jakir. He fled the fall of Ranmyden like many others.'

'An Eathal Jakir? I thought they were a human legend?'

The leader grunted out a harsh laugh. 'Is that what they teach you in the Caverns? The Jakir were Sorcerers sworn to guard and defend Yos, to advance knowledge and improve the lives of those they served. They were drawn from three races: human, Eathal and Verial. They also had an alliance with the Tahistill and joined with them in many great works.'

'Eathal and human together?' said Faivel. The concept was revolutionary to him. He had long read the human works of scholarship and had been a secret member of the Eathal peace faction along with the Liduin Druids. Yet the idea of actively working with the humans, perhaps forming a partnership, an alliance . . . that was completely new.

The Eathal leader poured a measure of *fush* into two pottery cups and waved for Faivel to drink. Fush was an amber-coloured spirit distilled from special lungii plants.

'Now that we are comfortable, perhaps you can tell me who you are and what you want in Thilil?' said the Eathal.

Faivel took a sip of the fush, which was surprisingly good. The local fruits and spices gave it a unique flavour.

'I am Faivel, son of Hukum.'

'The Sundar's second son.'

Faivel sat back in surprise. The 'wild' Eathal of Thilil were far more sophisticated than he expected. Although cut off from the southern Eathal, they were not isolated from events in the wider world. His scholar's curiosity made him wish he could visit them under different circumstances, study their history and seek out other artefacts like the priceless aurrilass armour.

'Yes. I am seeking a human warrior called Raziin Cinnor. He left Apiloth five days ago, heading west with three hundred human warriors. We tried to follow him, but there were too many Armon outposts for us to track him undetected.'

The leader downed his cup of fush in a single swallow. He put down the cup slowly. 'He has passed to the north of here. His men attacked an Eathal hunting party, killing three and taking nine prisoner.'

'What would he want with Eathal prisoners?'

'We are not sure. He is leaving a blood trail through Thilil that would make Lidu turn her face. The human settlements in his path are being wiped out.'

Faivel drained his cup. 'Yes. That sounds like Raziin. The human is merciless.'

'Why do you seek him?' asked the leader.

Faivel showed his teeth. 'To kill him.'

'Why?'

To prevent him raising the Spear of Carris.

'A blood debt. He was once an agent of my father's. No longer. He killed my brother Staraz. Hukum demands his death.'

The leader refilled their cups. 'The Eathal of Thilil bear no allegiance to Maht, but we will help you. This Raziin is vicious, even for a human.'

'Thank you. We only seek guides through Thilil. You must not engage him directly. Leave him to me,' said Faivel. 'Raziin is a Sorcerer.'

The leader nodded without comment. Once more Faivel was puzzled. He would have expected wild Eathal to be more fearful of Sorcery.

'We will stay out of your way,' said the leader, sipping his fush thoughtfully.

* * *

Daran frowned at the messenger. 'What now?'

'Kranor Zan, my Lord. Ambassador . . . from the north,' said the Suulqua. At least he had the sense not to finish the sentence in Daran's presence. *Ambassador from Emperor Cedrin Cinanac.*

He pushed the map across the field table, eyes blurred from collating field reports. Hukum had reinforced his front with jakkund, which made testing the magical strength of the Green and Blood legions a perilous task.

His war camp was now less than fifty leagues from Raynor, within easy reach of narsiit-mounted Suul who were not averse to risking Eathal patrols. The continual vexation of their visits almost made him wish he had forgone his strategic withdrawal and stayed further east to take on Hukum head-to-head. Others he had sent away, but Kranor was too well-connected with the loyalist Suul to be dismissed.

'Send him in.'

Kranor was tense and alert. His fine angular face gave him a natural look of command. As a young warrior, Daran had once been in awe of the bodyguard commander, and he still had tremendous respect for the man, despite his politics.

'My Lord,' said Kranor, nodding his head.

Daran smiled. 'Kranor Zan. What brings you to my battlefield?'

Kranor's dark, intense eyes settled on him. 'I am here in my official capacity as Ambassador from Emperor Cedrin Cinanac.'

Daran's mouth made a grim line. The scythemen positioned around the room tensed, waiting for his command. He weighed the pros and cons of arresting Kranor. There would never be a better opportunity. Here he was, alone, surrounded by Daran's loyal First.

Kranor took a step forward and handed Daran a small folded parchment.

'And what's this?'

'A letter from Emperor Cedrin Cinanac,' said Kranor.

Daran gritted his teeth in irritation. He should have thrown Kranor in a cell the first time he arrived in his private court as 'ambassador' from this upstart Cedrin, but Estle's presence had complicated things. Besides, Daran had maintained power precisely because he did not act rashly.

The parchment was thin, and he realised it had been carried to Raynor in a cavon-capsule. It had been sealed with a neat circle of red wax. His heart skipped a beat when he saw the Cinanac seal. The last time he had seen a message bearing that seal it had summoned him to Husdoon. He pushed away the memory. *Any fool can use a dead man's ring.*

Daran tore open the letter, expecting some high-handed demand that he turn over the throne. He had read many over the years. Strange that every author had met with an unfortunate demise soon after. The assassin was still in place in Beslin and ready to strike. Uran urged Daran daily to give the command.

Warlord, Daran. You have no cause to trust me. To you I am an unknown. Perhaps a threat. Believe me when I say I am driven to protect the whole of Kelas. The blood of those who died to defend my father Riin, and myself as a babe, demand it.

I have reformed the Eleventh Legion. As you receive this, the Eleventh and the Exdor Tenth are marching south to relieve Olcis. As we engage Yeffrij's legions, this will hopefully take pressure off you in Raynor. If we are victorious, we will march south to add our strength to yours.

I propose that we put aside the issue of Raynor's rulership and form an alliance until the people of Kelas are free from the Eathal threat. To this end, I propose that we join our forces. I do not want a single Legion soldier to shed blood for my ambition.

Cedrin Cinanac

Daran reached for his wine glass, downing it in three gulps. No demands. Instead an offer of alliance. Of support.

'Two Legions?' said Daran, speaking his thoughts out loud in his shock. *Was it possible?*

'Two standards,' said Kranor, his voice deep and harsh. 'Together they will have the strength of a full Legion.'

'And they make for Olcis?'

'The Eleventh has already left Searn. The Tenth marches tomorrow.'

Daran knew better than to question Kranor. The man was impeccably honest.

'I will be joining the Eleventh before they close on Olcis to take overall command,' said Kranor.

Not only did this pretender manage to get Exdor to kneel, he managed to prise Duras' warriors away from him. If Cedrin was assassinated before his Legions reached Olcis, his forces would turn around and march back to the north. If Yeffrij could be held at Olcis . . .

'There is much to consider here,' said Daran. He looked up at Kranor. He and Uran had been fighting this war alone so long, he had forgotten what it felt like to receive any sort of support.

'Thank you, Suul Zan.'

Kranor bowed and withdrew.

* * *

Daran jerked awake at the sound of movement.

He reached for the greatscythe beside his camp-bed, blinking in the dim lamplight to clear his blurred vision.

He saw one of his bodyguards standing three paces away, waiting patiently. *Still in the field.*

'Uran has returned, my Lord.'

'Send him in. Why is it so damn dark in here?'

'Rea has not yet risen, my Lord. Asic's crescent has already set.' So sometime before midnight.

'Heat one of my glowmetals.'

'Yes, my Lord.' The guard walked out into the main chamber of the pavilion and ordered a servant out with one of his glowmetal lamps.

As he sat up, a map and a field report slid off his chest onto the floor. He had not meant to fall asleep, only to rest for a moment.

Daran gathered up the map and the report and put the greatscythe back beside the camp-bed. If he was honest with himself, he knew his greatscythe skills had long fallen away. His great gift had always been strategic warfare. These maps and reports – they were his true weapons.

He poured some water into a bowl and splashed his face. One of his servants offered him a towel and he dried his face, luxuriating in the soft fabric. The faint scent of lemons came to him.

'Have food and wine brought,' commanded the Warlord. The servant bowed in silence and moved away. He moved to his field desk and sat down, swiftly arranging his papers. Tonight was a crucial one. Desperate to test Hukum's leading legions, a joint attack had been undertaken with his cavalry units and the Raptor. A team of Moon Druids had flown the platform under Asic's waxing crescent, starting before sunset when the moon's power began to be felt. Uran himself had manned it. Timing was crucial. They had to be back into safe territory before Asic set, otherwise they would plummet from the sky.

The flap of the tent opened, and the golden-skinned Sorcerer ducked inside.

'Uran. Come. Sit.'

'Why is it so gloomy in here?' asked the Sorcerer as he walked to his accustomed chair across from Daran. He was fiddling with something, turning it in his fingers, but it was too dim to see what it was.

'I had fallen asleep. The servants dimmed it for me.'

The tent opened again and two servants came inside carrying one of his glowmetal lamps. A clear white light issued from it, as though it were a small moon. The egg-shaped glowmetal was fully gold, with only a few strands of violet light showing. They carefully dropped it into a specially made frame of polished wood. The dim tent was transformed into a brightly-lit space with stark shadows.

'An improvement,' said Uran.

In the bright light, Daran could see Uran looked even more drawn and exhausted. No doubt he himself looked no better. Neither of them had managed to get more than three to five hours of snatched sleep a night for months. In the light of the glowmetal lamp, Daran could see what Uran had in his hands. It was a cavon message cylinder. Its seal had been broken.

'Tell me what you discovered.'

Uran dropped the message cylinder onto the table as though it was of no consequence and gave his report.

'The Green Drakon is well defended. Not only do they have well-drilled troops, they have a defensive glowmetal that can resist any Force. They do not have an offensive glowmetal,' said Uran.

Daran nodded. 'A conventional attack then?'

'Yes. And all magical attacks must be heat and fire – no directed Force.'

'The Raptor's oil-casks should do well,' said Daran.

Uran shook his head. 'Their defensive glowmetal stops all falling objects. I have never seen anything like it.'

A servant laid a platter of sliced meats, cheese and fruits on the table. A second servant delivered a tray of drinks.

'Then . . . no missiles at all?'

Uran shook his head. 'No. Not even arrows.'

Daran gritted his teeth. They would need to go head-to-head with them. Conventional warfare. Strategy, luck and courage. 'Kallor's cock,' swore Daran.

'We had more luck with Blood legion. They are another of the new teremb legions. Their glowmetal is offensive. Some sort of magical catapult that creates a crushing blow of Force at a set distance and direction from the glowmetal.'

Daran saw the implications at once. 'And we know its line of effect?'

Uran smiled. 'Yes. We will be able to manoeuvre around it, rendering it ineffective. I have better news though.'

'Mmn?'

'The commander of Blood is a hothead. Twice tonight they broke ranks to pursue our cavalry.'

'And it was not even a full engagement.' Daran's heart leapt with excitement. His failure to crush the Yellow and Silver legions had weighed heavily on him. Perhaps now they could really deal Hukum a blow.

'Excellent work, Uran.' Daran pulled a map across the desk. 'I have the perfect ground for this. Flat terrain, with plenty of room to manoeuvre around the Blood. We will need to bottle up the Green, hold them in place while the Raptor and our other forces rip Blood to shreds.'

Daran looked up to see Uran was unusually sombre. He had not touched the food. The man's clothes hung off him now. His silver eyes dominating his drawn, golden face.

'What is it?'

Uran took up the message capsule and drew out a message. 'Another report from Rehvar.'

Daran's eyes flicked down to dense glyphs. Although he knew the code, he did not have Uran's knack for reading the cipher. 'And?'

'Rehvar stands ready. Cedrin will leave Beslin tomorrow. This is our last chance to end him and Ellen swiftly. Cleanly,' said Uran.

Daran narrowed his eyes. He searched his friend's face. He had known Uran too long not to realise there was more.

'What exactly does the message say?'

'Rehvar has not been able to find any evidence that Cedrin manufactured his claim. The Fountain Priestess is a genuine Truth teller and has not been bribed.'

Daran digested the information. His mind circled it twice before the real implication hit him. 'Is Rehvar saying —'

'He could find no evidence against him. That is all,' said Uran, his voice harsh. 'This changes nothing.'

The Warlord sat back. Stunned. The thought had simply not occurred to him. After all this, could it be true? That Riin's son was actually found? Inexorably the pieces fit together. Kranor, who had never once been taken in by a false Scion, throwing his carefully built wealth and the full resources of his mercenary enterprise behind Cedrin. His wife Salis, a known Truth-teller, verifying Kalyth's testimony. The Exdor Suul – backward, stiff-necked and arrogant – kneeling to a new Emperor when they had never even *acknowledged* the Yasser States.

'Larus save us. Cedrin *is* the Scion,' said Daran.

Uran paled. His hands curled into fists at his sides. 'This changes nothing!'

Daran pulled the stack of papers towards him. He shuffled aside the reports until he found what he was looking for. A thin parchment with the seal of the Cinanac.

'Yes. But this does,' said Daran, sliding the message across the desk.

Uran snatched it up and read it swiftly. 'It cannot be true. Why would he throw away what power he has just to protect Olcis? His own wife is under the Hesguit's edict!' Uran tossed the letter back across the desk.

Daran picked up the letter. He touched the wax seal with its impression of the Cinanac phoenix. He could not believe how close he had come to ordering the death of Riin's son. A chill ran down his spine. *Believe me when I say I am driven to protect the whole of Kelas.*

'Olcis is more than the Temple of the Sisters. Hundreds of thousands of men and women are there. It will be packed with refugees from Tupur with nowhere else to go. The Suul will be desperate. If Cedrin succeeds there, he will win Tupur and depose the Hesguit in one move.'

'Send the order. I beg you,' said Uran. 'The Raynor Suul who support us in the field – the men you yourself groomed and elevated – do not want a return to the old Empire. If we lose their support now, we risk everything.'

The Warlord poured himself a shot of bakta and took it in a single swallow. Uran was right. Daran had faced tremendous opposition from the Raynor Suul when he first took power. To hold onto it he had to break the hold of the loyalists – Suul who saw themselves or one of their chosen Old Blood candidates on the Emerald Throne. To survive, he had formed alliances with those on the margins; minor Suul, rich and powerful merchants, skilled men like Uran who had fled the fall of Althar and South Yasser. He had elevated them all, forming the core of his new court – and getting access to the wealth he needed. The loyalists resented these newcomers. Many saw a return to Empire as a way to reclaim their lost influence and pay back decades of insult. If this was only about holding onto power in Raynor, then he would agree with Uran, but this was about more than that.

'We *already* risk everything. The whole fate of Kelas balances on a knife-edge. If Cedrin can hold Yeffrij at Olcis, we might be able to really win this.'

Uran's face flushed. 'You cannot mean to recognise him?'

The Warlord shook his head. 'No. Merely let him lead his own forces from the north. If he dies now, they will turn back. We need help, Uran. If both Cedrin and Ellen are Sorcerers as the reports claim, they could be a crucial factor in ultimate victory.'

Uran surged to his feet, overcome with emotion.

'*Sit and eat,*' said Daran. 'That's an order.'

Uran sagged back into his chair. Scowling, he picked up a piece of cheese and took a desultory bite. 'I hope you know what you are doing. I guess Cedrin and Ellen can always be taken care of later.'

Daran blinked. Uran knew that Cedrin was the true Scion, yet he still talked of assassination. For the first time, Daran understood the gulf that stood between him and his friend. Daran had always been an idealist. A loyal soldier who had sworn an oath to a young Emperor to serve him and his line faithfully until his death. Uran cared nothing for the old order. The Sorcerer was committed to building something new from the fallen remnants of what had gone before. Somehow Daran had to find the middle ground.

He realised in that moment he longed to relinquish power. He wanted a return to the old Empire, once a cornerstone of his whole being. Yet even if he wanted to return Cedrin to the Emerald Throne, it might not be possible. The most powerful of the new Raynor Suul – including his own sons –would fight against the move. How could Daran fight Uran and his Druidin if his friend turned against him? Would Nacius stay loyal or would he follow his Master? Cedrin may be Riin's son, but that was not enough. Despite his own desires, Daran would never allow Raynor to descend into civil strife.

This new world may have no place for Cedrin Cinanac.

'Forget Cedrin, my friend. He may fall in the north. We must focus on the battles we can fight. Somehow we have to stop Hukum from reaching Raynor with his Wallbreakers.'

Uran grunted. He reached for a wineglass and poured himself a healthy measure. 'I have some new ideas.'

* * *

Ellen fought against a wave of nausea. *Not now, for Larus' sake.* Their company was assembled in the forecourt of the Beslin palace. Governor Duras, his wife and the most senior of the Exdor Suul had gathered to see them off. The make up of the expedition was much like the caravan that had struck north from Herath, including Veltricus and his men, except they were not burdened by the ragged group of travellers. Despite the planned action against Leygen's pirate-Warlord, Thenia had remained in Beslin. The young Suul insisted on remaining close to Cedrin and thought her Daughters would be of more use on the journey north protecting her and Cedrin than joining the action in Hanis.

Raphal, much refreshed by his stay in Beslin, was as eager as an adolescent to begin his great adventure. He nattered away with the scholar Valnis, oblivious to all the chaos around him. They led a third amelak, the poor beast struggling under the weight of books and parchments.

'Are you alright, my Lady?' asked Valdas. The tall Suulqua hovered near her, hand outstretched, uncertain whether he should support her arm or not.

'Yes. Argh—' Ellen vomited onto the cobbles. Her stomach convulsed twice more, and she tasted bile. She spat the foul dregs from her mouth.

'Oh, well. There goes breakfast,' said Ellen. She took an embroidered handkerchief from a pocket inside her leather jacket and wiped her mouth. She tucked the cloth into the waistband of her leather trousers.

Her narsiit nickered in concern, and Ellen reached up to touch her in reassurance. She finished checking her gear and the straps of her saddle for tightness. Ellen took a breath and composed herself. Throwing up had eased her stomach considerably, and she felt light-headed.

The column included all of the One Hundred, led by Ranis and Kalyth. Osterac's place had been taken by one of Kranor's warriors, who had carried dispatches north to Beslin, while the Suul journeyed south to Olcis ahead of the Tenth. They had twice the number of pack amelak than they had taken into Thilil, each loaded with essential supplies, including lamps and torches for the descent into the Ranmyden Caverns. The Priest Dagon, Esmelle and the strange twins Bles and Ris were a familiar presence to them all. They had continued to shield her and Cedrin at night, for which she was grateful. She was not sure she could have coped with the nightmares over the last few weeks. Their presence would be even more vital as they neared the Ranmyden Iris.

Ellen walked to the palace entrance, where Duras and the Exdor Suulvey were talking with Cedrin. Salis Cintor was with them, looking graceful and regal. She smiled at her as she approached. Ellen suppressed her defensive reaction, knowing that Salis had her best interests at heart. Unfortunately Salis had sided with Cedrin. Both of them wanted her to remain in Beslin while Cedrin went north. There was no way she was staying here. Not when Cedrin was at risk. Not when Erioth, her Verial teacher, was a prisoner of the Ward.

Marken and Skye, looking more like Suul every day, stood with Cedrin. Both would be leaving for Thanir today. Her brother Torren's fleet had already arrived there, ready to transport them and the Hanis Ninth into Leygen harbour under cover of night. Other Athrian craft would blockade Swebas, preventing the pirate-Warlord of that port coming to the aid of the Brotherhood ally.

Duras and the other Exdor Suul gave her a bow as she approached. 'Empress.' She could see more than one eyebrow raised at the tight-fitting leather outfit. Although the outfit was comfortable, she would feel more relaxed in it once she was on the road.

'Are you sure you do not want to take a division of warriors from the Tenth?' said Duras.

Cedrin shook his head. 'I want every man we can spare marching south to Olcis. Once we enter the Caverns of Ranmyden, a group that large will only be a liability. And then there is the issue of supply.'

Duras grimaced. They had been over this all before. The Exdor Governor was not happy at the risk Cedrin was taking, although they all agreed that claiming the Spear was vital. Raziin would pose too great a threat should he somehow get his hands on the ancient weapon.

'Take all care, my Lord. You can always fall back to Hivale if you encounter resistance or meet with disaster,' said Duras.

'I will return, Duras. With the Spear,' said Cedrin.

Cedrin said his farewells and moved to the column with Ellen, Marken and Skye. Salis, who was remaining in Beslin as a liaison between her husband Kranor and Duras, remained with the Exdor Suul.

'I wish we were coming with you,' said Skye.

'You will be needed in Leygen. The Brotherhood there may try to double-cross us. You know what to look for,' said Cedrin.

'I, on the other hand, will be more than happy to burn pirate ships to the waterline and see them all hanged while you poke around some dusty ruins,' said Marken in a flippant tone. His golden eyes gleamed, hinting at hidden determination. They all knew of his hatred for pirates.

A gust swirled through the courtyard, picking up a low cloud of dust. A cloth fluttered at her waist, then tore itself free. Marken's hand shot out and grabbed it. It was the embroidered handkerchief she had used to wipe her mouth.

'Yours, I presume?' said Marken, in a charming voice. Then his eyes settled onto the design on the cloth. He froze, partway through passing it to her.

Marken snatched the handkerchief back and stretched it out, looking at the design.

'Where did you get this?' said Marken, his voice soft and breathless.

Ellen looked at the embroidered handkerchief. It took her a while to remember. 'Oh, yes. I got that from Uran's First Consort in Raynor, Ersta.'

'Ersta? Was she Cioan?'

'Yes. She was born a Suul, but Uran freed her from slavery. She said her father was a Suul lord in Althar. That her family was attacked by pirates on the Sea of Mists.'

Marken's jaw dropped. He clutched the cloth in his hand. 'My sister. *Alive.*'

Cedrin and Skye exchanged an amazed look.

Of course. There had been so many similar stories of refugees from the fall of the old Cioan enclave of Althar that Ellen had never made the connection. She stepped forward and gave Marken a hug. 'I am pleased for you. Please keep the handkerchief – although you may want to get it laundered.'

Marken kissed her lips in sheer joy, then held her at arm's length. 'Did she say anything else?'

'Her father remained at Althar to resist the Eathal advance. Her mother and brothers were killed at sea. Your other sisters were also taken by the pirates and sold into slavery. She lost contact with them.'

'Thank you, Ellen. You don't know what this means to me,' said Marken.

Cedrin gripped his friend's shoulder with affection. 'I'm pleased for you. It gives us an even better reason to save Raynor.' He looked between Skye and Marken. 'Good luck in Leygen. You are there to lead, remember. No risks. I want you two to stay alive.'

Skye laughed. 'You two are the ones going north to face Raziin. *You* come back alive.'

* * *

Ellen took a sip of water. It was tepid and tasted brackish, although she knew that was just the resin used to seal the flask. She rested a hand on her stomach, high up under her ribs, wishing yet again the nausea would settle. She imagined what her father would say if he found out she was riding a narsiit over rough country while pregnant. Probably the same things that Salis and Cedrin had said.

They made excellent time out of Beslin. Given the maps provided by Duras and Valnis, they had been able to mark a clear route north to the entrance caverns. In six days they would be entering the vast ruined complex of the ancient Ranmyden Eathal.

'Are you still feeling poorly, Ellen?' Thenia was riding beside her on her narsiit.

'I'm fi—' Ellen's hand rushed to her mouth. *Sisters above.* No one told her about this! She waited until the wave passed. 'Fine.'

'You are a terrible liar, Suul Cintros,' said Thenia, the corners of her mouth lifting in what might have been a smile. Ellen blinked. Did Thenia just make a joke?

Cedrin and she were on speaking terms, and in many ways the friendship had been re-established. She respected him and his inherent nobility, but her passion was gone. Ellen knew she was being unreasonable. Salis and others had urged her to forgive Cedrin and return to his bed, telling her with wry humour of the times their own men had strayed. It helped, but something fragile inside her had been shattered by that infidelity. She told Cedrin she needed time, but the fact was she did not know if she could ever open herself to him again.

When it had come to organising the caravan for the northward journey, Ellen had agreed to form a rearguard with Thenia and the Daughters. It was a way of avoiding the strained silence that often dominated her time with Cedrin. He tried hard, but she could not manage to give anything back. It made her feel petty and weak. Underneath it all was a roiling set of emotions she was not ready to confront. She almost wanted him to take a mistress, or even an official Consort, just to give her some justification for her anger.

At first she thought that the presence of Spider would chaff her, but the woman had been reserved and focussed. She spoke only to give commands to the Daughters, and when she rode her eyes were empty, her face set like stone. Her lieutenant Jeth had taken over most of the organisational tasks, her harsh voice the most often heard of them all.

Ellen reached down to the saddlebag and tore a section of bread off the loaf there. As she bit into it, her stomach heaved. She waited until it passed then began to chew slowly. Mendor and Valdas flanked her. Both Suulquas were more than happy to ride with the Daughters, particularly Valdas, who seemed incapable of keeping his eyes off their toned, lightly-clad torsos. The women themselves were amused and gratified at the attention of two Athrian Suul.

Serel and her two slaves rode behind on amelak. Ellen had done her best to dissuade the lady from following her, but Serel insisted. Secretly, Ellen was relieved. She needed help, and could not ask Thenia or the Daughters.

Dagon, Esmelle and the twin Bles and Ris rode in the centre of the column. They were a strange group. Their appearance at Herath was like the answer to a prayer. Although never accepted to Cedrin's inner circle, they had been an integral part of his new court. It was strange that they had not visited the Fountain Temple while they were in Beslin. The Fountain Priestess had extended the invitation many times. Also strange that Salis had not taken any interest in them, despite the powers of Earth Essence that they shared.

In fact, now that she thought about it, Salis had never offered a single impression or comment about them. That was odd, considering her role at Cedrin's side was to provide insight into hidden motivations. The Raynor Suul still retained no memory of the day they appeared at their court in Herath.

Another wave of nausea rose. Ellen tore another chunk of bread off the loaf in her saddlebag and resolutely set about chewing. It was going to be a long ride to Ranmyden.

Chapter Sixteen

Lempar's heart burned with rage.

Beyond a low line of hills to the north, pillars of smoke rose to the sky, blotting out the suns. Olcis was burning. Less than two days forced march away, thousands of men and women were dying.

He glared at the Hesguit's Suulqua messenger, lost for words.

Lempar had led the Grey Drakon in circles around the Delta province. He had used his knowledge of the terrain well, slicing away at the Eathal legion in lightning attacks. Their scouts had been ambushed, their lead elements decimated. Always he had been careful to avoid the core force, protected by a Sorcerer-Lord and an offensive glowmetal that delivered a turning vortex of Force that obliterated attacking formations.

It had taken him a month and a half to draw the Grey south, while he split his own force, slipping them around the Eathal to reform west of Rybol. The mounted elements of his Legion had cut for freedom last, carving a trail of blood through the Grey's formations. He had carefully positioned himself so he could strike north around the western shore of the Great Lake and enter the city from the west, avoiding Yeffrij's main attacks in the east. Yet now . . .

One of his First Captains, a young Suul, galloped to his side. 'Orders, my Lord? When do we strike for Olcis?'

Lempar crushed the message in his hand. Every one of his seven surviving aides carried a wound. They remained silent and grim.

'The Hesguit has ordered us to stay in the field until the Grey is destroyed. Then we are to cross the Asgod and cut Yeffrij's supply lines and attack from the rear,' said Lempar.

'He is abandoning Olcis to the Eathal?' said the First Captain, his face torn with distress. The Captain's wife and young children were still in the city, as were Lempar's own family. 'What sort of a leader abandons his own people?'

Lempar could understand the Hesguit's logic, but the man had no understanding of what he was asking. Of all the Eathal generals, Yeffrij was the most cautious. His supply lines were guarded by an entire reserve legion, the Twins, one of the new teremb legions. Fresh and ready for battle, and supported by a Sorcerer-Lord. Lempar's Legion had crossed the Asgod once, managing to surprise Yeffrij and slip away, but the Eathal general would not be fooled twice.

Lempar's men had been in the field without support for months now. Their supplies were running low and the men themselves almost at the limit of endurance. If they saw their own city go up and flames – and their wives, children and families die – they would lose heart. If the Hesguit had one particle of sense, he would have followed Lempar's advice and let them back into the city. These same men would fight like the very Demons of Uros to defend their own. Fight and die and take ten Eathal for every one of them.

The Hesguit was asking the impossible, while he remained secure behind the Bulvur's walls, protected by the Temple's Shield glowmetals and the strength of his Druids.

'The Hesguit asks for an answer,' said the Suulqua messenger. His face paled as Lempar met his gaze.

'Tell me, boy. Who remains to defend the Outer City?'

'The Hesguit has withdrawn to the Bulvur,' said the Suulqua.

'We both know where that coward would be,' said the Captain. 'That's not what General Lempar asked you.'

The Suulqua licked his lips, torn between his loyalty to the Hesguit and to his city.

'Suulvey Moren Cinlar has refused the Hesguit's command to withdraw. His men hold most of the Outer City. Three High Moon Druids and a High Larus Druid have joined Moren with their retinues. Most of the Suul remain with him. Moren has opened the garrison and armed every man who seeks to bear arms.'

'And the Bulvur?'

'It has been sealed. We had no choice. Thousands are still arriving in Olcis – fleeing the Eathal in Tupur and the Delta. They would have overwhelmed us,' said the Suulqua.

'What do we do, General?' asked the Captain. His aides looked to him, expressionless. Many had been with him since the Empire fell, when they had called themselves the Seventh. The other Olcis Legion, the Sixth, had fallen at Husdoon. Lempar had been a soldier all his life. Never once had he disobeyed a legitimate order. While the Hesguit was the leader of Tupur, recognised by the Olcis Suul, then the decision was clear. Any other choice made him nothing but another warlord in a continent full of them.

'We obey the Hesguit,' said Lempar.

* * *

Yeffrij watched a burning hulk drift across the Great Lake. Most of the docks were in flames, the fires lit by the city's own citizens. The fishing fleet had been destroyed, preventing its use to flank the defenders.

Olcis had proved a logistical challenge. The Outer Walls had been easily breached, but the sheer size of the city, even the vast population itself, made it hard to manoeuvre. It was not like Hianer, a spacious wooden city easily set to flame. Here many of the buildings were stone. The defenders had pulled back, forming a new front by stretching barricades of debris between the buildings. Every single dwelling was packed with screaming humans, many armed. His warriors had already taken a heavy toll trying to clear them. The human Druids were formidable. If it came to single confrontation, he or Tynan could easily overcome them with Sorcery, but they could not be everywhere. There were dozens of the Druids, attacking night and day. And glass – it was everywhere. Razor sharp shards filled the streets. The human Druids would send it shooting into their ranks with impulses of Force. The wounds were rarely fatal, but they were demoralising.

As usual, Yeffrij responded with a solid methodology. His men were clearing the city one building at the time, with orders to kill all humans. There were simply too many of them to take as slaves. Even the Kallor Druids were overstocked. The bodies were dumped into the lake. This way, his hold on the city was gradually increased, while the defenders were slowly pushed back.

The city itself was set between the steep foothills of the southern Mulisar range and the Great Lake. The ground it occupied was a wedge, narrowing and rising as it went back to the west. The central citadel of the city, the Bulvur, stretched from the foothills of the Mulisar to the lake at the tip of the wedge. It effectively blocked the westward route past the lake. It was this he had to take to truly break the heart of Olcis. First he had to force his way through the city.

He was advancing on two fronts. He pushed back against the defenders in the Outer City across a broad front, driving them back one building at a time. He also advanced along the northern edge of the city, driving like a spear for the Bulvur itself. The reason was two-fold. He wanted to strike at the heart, hoping to break the will of the humans. This would also give him a chance to cut off the defenders in the Outer City, circling them with his troops. Once he achieved that, it was only a matter of time.

A tall spire cracked in the heat of the fire, falling to smash into the streets below.

It was a relief to think that all this – this human plague on the face of Yos – would be wiped away.

Then the Eathal could begin anew.

* * *

Raziin watched as the drakon circled above them.

'We have to run, my Lord!' said the Captain.

The dark shape grew, filling the sky above Ranmyden. It was a black. Oldest and most fearsome of all drakon. Virtually invulnerable, they were rarely seen outside the caverns.

'No. This is an omen.' He had chosen the drakon as his crest, the symbol of his new Cioan Empire. This . . . this was a sign from Uros.

They were camped in a steep valley two leagues north of the south entrance to the Caverns. His strategy had worked, allowing him to reach Ranmyden well ahead of the upstart Emperor. They had cut a bloody path through Thilil, leaving a trail of Eathal corpses in their wake.

The amelak were bleating in panic, some beginning to buck.

'Dismount! Cover the eyes and noses of the mounts with cloth!' commanded the Armon Captain. His brother's commander may be weak, but he knew his business. The amelak were soon in hand.

The two remaining Eathal prisoners, a male and female, looked up at the approaching drakon, too dazed and bloody to react. They were drained from the long captivity and the torture they had endured. The thal had lost an eye, the thel had no hands, the stumps sealed with pitch.

The trussed lamel captured in the nets this morning was more alert; he dragged himself under an overhanging rock. He began to work frantically at his bonds, setting his beak to work on the strands that bound him.

Raziin walked out into the centre of the valley, his heart beating fast with excitement. The Seer had seen his triumph, and here was a sign of his destiny. Merceth and Kyal flanked him. Fearless warriors. Those only truly worthy to stand beside him.

'Lord! Flee!' called the Captain. He was vaguely aware of the cavalry commander leading the men and amelak further into the valley. *Let them run.* The spymaster fled with them.

The drakon saw him. He felt the shock of connection as the force of its gaze fixed on him. The black twisted into a steep dive. There was nothing elegant about its movements. The gills under its wings flared red-hot, and Raziin heard the air roar through them. Its speed increased. The angular, armoured head turned towards him and the jaws opened. The back of its throat glowed with red heat. Its torso swelled as its lungs expanded, the scales rippling with the movement. It was readying to expel its deadly breath, a vaporous exhalation of acid and heat that could dissolve rock and set the insubstantial substance of the upper world to instant flame.

A big drakon caught its prey on the wing, swooping down to seize their prize and carrying it away. This black was preparing to do just that. It was close now. Massive. An incarnation of pure power. The size of a war-galley, it filled the sky above them. Its glowing amber eyes flicked between him and the fleeing column of Armon warriors. Then, abruptly it swung its gaze back to him.

The drakon roared in rage. Its exhalation flared across the slope, setting a broad swath of vegetation to flame. At the last moment it shut its jaws and flared its wings wide, pulling out of the dive and slowing its speed. It extended its claws, which flashed like jewels in the suns, and hit the valley floor less than a hundred paces in front of him. It struck the valley floor with a thunderous *crack*. The detonation echoed off the valley walls, setting birds to panicked flight. It skidded to a halt, using the barbed tips of its wings as well as the razor-sharp talons to steady itself.

He saw rage and hunger in its amber eyes. And an intelligence that had clawed its way from a mindless darkness to cunning sentience. Yet he also saw something else. Another being that had joined Raziin in his dreams of blood. The Behemoth.

Brother.

Chosen heir.

The voices spoke in his mind. He thrilled at the contact. The Behemoth was the true power behind the Spear. It was yet another sign of his victory that the spirit-being had found this way to contact him.

The drakon tensed and shook its head. Massive muscles rippled beneath the armoured scales, twisting in suppressed fury. It opened its mouth, as though to send its breath across them, then it snapped its mouth shut with a sound like a mallet striking a boulder. Its talons ripped through the rock beneath it as they tightened. The beast wanted to destroy them, to sate its hunger. Raziin understood its desire. It was the Behemoth that restrained it.

Come closer. We have a gift for you. This time the voices spoke together.

Raziin came forward alone. He walked so close he could touch the beast. The eyes were huge, multifaceted gems without pupil, and emitted a yellow light. Heat radiated off the black scales. His throat constricted at the acrid odour of acid.

Open your mind to us, brother.

Just for a moment, Raziin hesitated. He had once accepted Hukum as a master, forming the Bridge of Minds. That magical link had become a millstone around his neck for decades, allowing his master to find him anywhere. It had almost cost him his life. If not for the glowmetal pendant he received from the Seer of Ciofran-Ac, he would have perished, led to his demise by Hukum's Compulsions.

We bring you to your destiny.

Yes. What else could this be but another step on the road to his ultimate victory? Now was not the time for doubt. Once he had the Spear, all would become possible.

Raziin looked into the huge, amber orbs and opened his mind. Tendrils of power snaked into him, filling him. Before, in his dreams, he had a distant sense of the connection with the Behemoth. Now that connection strengthened. He could see the drakon on the floor of the valley, Merceth and Kyal, and beside them he could now also see the Behemoth. Its body was like one of the keerhounds of Armon, yet the size of a war-harena. It padded towards him, breath rattling in the huge chest. Its jaws were open, revealing rows of pointed yellow teeth, its black tongue lolling from the side of its mouth. The Behemoth's single horn was bloody and sharp. It fixed him with its strange odd-coloured gaze, one eye grey-blue, the other glowing gold.

See.

The force of its presence was overwhelming. As the pressure grew in his mind, Raziin sank to his knees.

Then the world around him slipped away.

At first he saw the world from above, his vision incredibly sharp despite his height. He was drifting, wings spread to the air. He saw a column of amelak riders below, snaking its way to the Ranmyden entrance caverns. At its head he recognised the upstart, Cedrin. In a moment he understood their numbers and their strength. Ellen Cintros was with them, leading a rearguard. *Earlier today.* From this awesome height, he could study the terrain as never before. He saw the perfect position for his ambush. How he could shape the outcome to his will.

His vision shifted again. He sank into a mist. Thousands of images, shapes and voices raced through his mind. Eventually they cleared.

He had the Spear in his hands. Its forged golden blade radiated pure Fire. It filled him with a wave of intoxicating strength. He was here, in Ranmyden, yet everything was strange.

He stood before the entrance caverns, yet they were not the ragged openings that he had scouted only days ago. These were neatly carved from the native rock in a series of broad arches. Behind him was a small force of men, a mixture of Anacian and Cioan warriors. Beside him was a powerful Cioan man, with hair and eyes of gold.

'Do you think they will kneel, Kaysell?'

The man gave a savage grin. 'I hope they don't, Carris.'

A group approached them from the Cavern entrance. Three Eathal and a man. They were richly dressed, and he could sense the power of the Fire rise in all four.

'Have you come to surrender, Carris? Where is this army of yours?' said one of them, eyeing their bodyguard contemptuously.

He had men positioned around the main exits, with orders to slay all who fled. His main force would enter the Caverns behind him – but not before he destroyed all resistance.

'Is this all the Jakir Ranmyden can muster?' he countered. He felt the power of the Fire surround him and gloried in his own desire to release it.

'You know there are only a handful of us left now,' said the human, a southern Cioan. 'The rest of us fell at Ciofran-Ac. And Asgod-Ki. You . . .' He had met the man once at the Olcis enclave. Arrogant like all the Jakir of Ciofran-Ac, he had sneered at the Anacian provincials and those he called 'the rustic northern Cioans'. It was amusing to watch the play of impotent rage on his face. 'There is not a word for you, Destroyer, that can express my disgust. You are a traitor to everything we stand for.'

'Why are you here, Carris?' asked one of the Eathal Jakir. 'Have you not had your fill of death?'

He could see Eathal and human troops positioning themselves in the shadows beyond the entrance. So, like the others, they would choose to fight.

'I am here to tell you your world is over, Jakir. A new Empire has risen from the enclave of Olcis, named for the ancient citadel of the Anacians. The Bulvuran Empire.

'All you have to do to earn my mercy is to kneel to me.'

Another of the Eathal Jakir stepped forward. He spat at his feet. 'The Jakir do not bow to tyrants, Carris. Or have you forgotten your vows already?'

He smiled as he felt the power of the Fire rise in the four Jakir. Like the others, they were secure in their arrogance. They saw only two Sorcerers and a handful of men.

'Now!' called the Cioan Jakir.

All four Jakir unleashed a torrent of Force. He casually channelled Fire from the Spear into a Shield. The Realm of Fire swirled through his mind, limitless, all of its power open to him without the limitations of a human channel.

He pushed back their attack. First one, then another dropped their Matrices as they realised what awesome power they faced. They would never have the opportunity to learn from their error.

'Like your southern brothers, you will learn the folly of your arrogance,' he said.

Kaysell shouted in glee. 'Destroy them all.' He felt the presence of his brother in his mind, linked for all time at the forging of the Spear. It was not one hand that held the Spear, but two. There was a third, yet he had run in horror at the destruction of Ciofran-Ac. He would never escape them, as long as the Spear survived.

Their plan all along had been the utter destruction of the Eathal. For too long they had hemmed in the growing human population, always protecting the forests that supported their bloated caverns.

Human and Eathal warriors ran from the cavern entrance, screaming their warcries. The Cioan Jakir turned and waved them back. 'No!'

Too late.

He crushed all four Jakir with a form of Force, as casually as brushing lint off his cloak. Their limbs snapped under the sudden weight, the breath driven from them. One of the Eathal made a feeble attempt at an attack. He cracked his skull.

Then he unleashed the Fire.

Kaysell and his men were Shielded from it. They advanced together, eyes bright with the birth of their new future. Flames filled the air. A wall of crimson and yellow. The screams of the warriors were cut off abruptly as their very flesh took flame. The power was glorious!

'The new Empire is born in the flames!' shouted Carris.

'Like a phoenix.'

Yes. *A phoenix.*

As they had in Ciofran-Ac and Asgod-Ki, they unleashed the full power of the Spear. Working in secret over long years, they never would have dreamed of the power they would unlock. They had succeeded beyond their wildest dreams.

The entered the Caverns of Ranmyden. All around them ran screaming figures. They were not flesh and blood, they were the ash of history. The sacrifice that had to be made for the new Empire to rise from the old. Eathal, human, Verial – even the occasional Tahistil – all perished in the conflagration. As he advanced, he destroyed all he saw. Temples, homes, the great Eathal domes. He smashed them. Melted them. Made them tombs for those who had once lived inside them.

Those who escaped and made for the entrance ran straight onto the spears and scythes of his advancing troops. The vast Caverns were one of the three major enclaves of the Jakir, and both he and Kaysell were familiar with the layout. It would take some weeks to clear them all. Their task today was to break the defence and to destroy the hated Jakir, the arrogant leaders of this world who had rejected his ambitions so cruelly. When the work was finished, his troops would loot the Caverns. He needed coin, gems and slaves to build his new Empire.

Five more times he encountered resistance from Jakir and Eathal Sorcerers. He destroyed them all, throwing aside their defensive glowmetals like they were child's toys. To have such power! Eventually he entered the Hall of Dreams, the deepest and most holy precinct in Ranmyden. When the last of the Druids were dead, or had fled for their lives, he rested.

The last of the great enclaves of the Jakir had fallen.

* * *

Raziin gradually came back to himself.

His knees and back ached. Above, the suns hung low in the west. He had been lost in the vision for hours.

He pushed himself to his feet. The drakon remained on the valley floor, its body convulsing against the forced control of the Behemoth. Raziin sensed that its hunger could not be restrained forever. He could understand that lust. That need for blood.

'Fetch the Eathal prisoners and the lamel,' said Raziin.

Merceth and Kyal walked back to their camp.

Raziin drew in a breath of the cool mountain air. The vision sung through his mind. It was Carris himself he had seen. The destruction of Ranmyden. His mind was filled with it. Through those echoed memories he had an intimate knowledge of the whole layout of Ranmyden – and the location of the Hall of Dreams. Vital knowledge if he was to carry out his plan.

The ghostly form of the Behemoth sat on the rocky ground beside the drakon.

'Thank you for your gift of knowledge,' said Raziin.

He felt the satisfaction of the Behemoth through the new bond between them. It remained silent, having achieved its purpose.

His two lieutenants approached, each dragging an Eathal prisoner. The drakon's nose twitched, and its mouth opened slightly. Raziin's skin stung with the heat, and he backed away.

'Where is the lamel?'

'Gone, my Lord.'

Raziin gritted his teeth. He hated the thieving animals. He gathered the Fire and scanned the ridge above. He saw movement and sent a bolt of Force flashing through the air. It smashed into the rock, sending the stubby trees that clung to the face tumbling down. There was a flash of brilliant green as the lamel took flight, swooping over the ridge and away, its tail flaring with highlights of blue and red.

'Bring the Eathal.' He indicated the ground in front of the huge drakon. 'There.' The prisoners were thrown to the ground.

Raziin grinned as he turned to the Behemoth. 'Let our servant feed.'

The ghostly beast leapt to its feet in anticipation. Its roar echoed in Raziin's mind, spurring his arousal.

The drakon shook itself and spread its wings. Raziin and his men backed away as the drakon's huge jaws opened. The Eathal screamed in pain as the hot acid sprayed across them, setting their torn furs aflame. The drakon's head dipped down, seizing the thal's head in its jaws. Blood sprayed as it bit the head from the torso, gulping it down in one swallow. The thel's head followed a moment later. Then the drakon exhaled a single, powerful breath.

Raziin and his men held their hands across their mouths as the acid burned the back of their throats. The corpses dissolved in sizzling flame. Then the drakon's tongue flicked out, lifting the spines from each corpse and crunching them down.

The drakon tilted its head, fixing Raziin with a single, baleful eye. He sensed its hunger, and its intelligence. Only the Behemoth restrained it from completing its feast with *their* heads and spines.

Farewell, brother.

The ghostly image of the Behemoth faded from his sight. The drakon raised its head and roared. The sound reverberated from the sides of the valley with deadly ferocity. Then it turned and ran back up the valley, launching itself at the sheer rock walls and climbing rapidly up the face. Drakons that size needed some significant elevation to get airborne. That was why they ate more and more on the wing as they grew. Raziin watched its massive form climb rapidly up the Ranmyden slopes, its talons and wing-barbs carving up the rock as it dragged itself skyward.

Eventually, the Armon soldiers returned, led by the Captain. They were shaken, and awed that Raziin had survived. He smiled. Kethis' eyes shone with worship.

All was as it should be.

* * *

Ellen looked up along the column. The narrow trail had forced them to stretch out for almost six-hundred paces, riding single file in many places. It zigzagged up the face of a steep, rocky hill. It was the last of the Ranmyden foothills that stood between them and the entrance caverns. Its slopes were rocky and desolate, with only a few stubborn trees and bushes clinging to the slopes. Ranmyden was a remote, uninhabited place, so different from the gentle rolling hills of fertile Exdor to the south.

The northern sky was filled with the high peaks of Ranmyden, even more majestic than the peaks of the Mulisar. They were capped with ice and extended to the east and west as far as the eye could see.

Ellen knew that the Ranmyden range formed an unbroken line across northern Kelas. Many considered it the end of Yos, the beginning of a land of legends and gods. Few knew that the domains of the Verial were hidden beyond it. Ellen and her father had been privy to that knowledge. Her teacher Erioth was from the domains. Her father had never spoken of how Erioth had crossed his path, or what debt lay between them. Or how Erioth had managed to cross the towering Ranmyden range.

Thank Larus that Raphal had managed to secure the help of Valnis. She and Cedrin could have wandered this vast area for months before ever finding the entrance caverns, let alone finding a way through the maze of Eathal ruins to reach the mysterious Hall of Dreams. After six days of hard travel, tonight they would camp outside the entrance caverns. The days in the saddle had been a trial for her. Only the nightly massage from her slaves and the invigorating teas prepared by Serel had kept her going. The nausea was worse than ever, and she had begun to fear for the baby. Even so, her stubbornness would not let her admit that Cedrin and Salis had been right all along.

Ellen watched Cedrin as he neared the crest with Kalyth and Ranis. He rode easily now, a natural in the saddle despite his height. Their pavilion was erected every night by the One Hundred. They shared meals together, and much of the natural rapport had been restored between them, but Cedrin went to his bed alone. Ellen shared another large tent with Thenia. If she was so determined to be with him on this journey, why did she insist on maintaining her isolation? What was she waiting for? She could have easily stayed in Beslin, perhaps confiding in Raphal and Cedrin the true nature of Erioth and her bond to him.

Ellen's senses flared with alarm. Tension gripped her as she sensed something nearby.

Fire.

A pillar of Force slammed into the centre of the column. One minute the riders were calmly guiding their amelak up the trail, the next dirt and fragments of rock were flying everywhere. Men shouted. Amelak shrieked in pain.

Her narsiit gave a high trumpet and flared its wings, ready for battle. Valdas and Mendor drew their cavalry scythes. Ellen reached for the Window and froze. *I cannot use the Fire.*

There were another three detonations as more bolts of Force struck the column. Cedrin and perhaps thirty of the One Hundred had managed to reach the crest. A dozen warriors and a score of amelak were down, laying motionless, bodies ripped apart.

'*Cedrin,*' she called in panic. All her love surged through her in a moment, spurred by the thought of losing him.

She saw him on the ridge. She felt the Fire and knew he had drawn a Shield around those below him. That left many more vulnerable.

Cioan warriors swarmed from the rocks, clad in black leather armour. There were hundreds of them, all armed with scythes. They cut into the centre of the column. Veltricus and his men, outside Cedrin's Shield, fought their way up the slope towards the ridge. The bodyguard of the Herath Suul fought with thick-bladed knives of lanedd, the mought hilts curved up to allow them to catch scythe or spear hafts. The weapons were of little use from amelak, and three fell in the first moments.

'They are behind us as well,' said Spider.

Thenia looked around, counting under her breath. 'Sixty men.' They were closing the trap, advancing cautiously up the trail. 'A well-planned ambush.'

'Which we are inside!' snapped Ellen as she drew her scythe from the saddle.

The breath caught in Ellen's throat as she saw Raziin Cinnor emerge from hiding further up the trail. The last time she had seen him, he had put a calv through her heart. And now she was defenceless.

The warriors of the One Hundred surged at the enemy, cutting deep into their ranks. The side of the hill was transformed into a battleground. Other warriors fought up the hill, trying to reach Cedrin at the crest. Dagon and the Twins delegation had been riding just behind Cedrin, and she saw them reach the top of the ridge and safety.

Raphal and his friend Valnis had lagged behind as usual, and had been riding just in front of the Daughters' rearguard. Ellen saw them sitting on the ground, dazed amid the books and scrolls scattered from their fallen amelak.

She was not the only one who saw them. Two Armon warriors ran at the Druids, faces set with murderous intent.

'Raphal! Look out!'

Ellen spurred her narsiit forward. A moment later, Mendor and Valdas flanked her. Their narsiit skipped across the rugged terrain, nimble and graceful, wings flared wide for balance.

The first warrior turned too late. Ellen's scythe blade took the man's head from his shoulders. As she swept past, her narsiit kicked out with a fore hoof, crushing the chest of the second warrior. Her narsiit reared as she drew rein in front of Raphal and Valnis. Valdas and Mendor swept in beside her.

'Can you walk?' Ellen asked the Druids.

'Bitch!'

Ellen's head jerked around. Her heart went cold as she recognised Raziin's voice.

Raziin stood on the hillside above her. Her skin prickled as he drew on the Fire. For a dreadful moment, she was paralysed with indecision. Her instinct blocked her, a fierce determination to protect her unborn child. And then it was too late.

A blaze of heat and flame shot through the air at them. Raphal raised his hands, directing Larus Essence into a Shield that sprang up in front of her. The wall of flame passed her and Mendor by, but Valdas howled in pain as it engulfed him and his narsiit. His scream ended abruptly, and he toppled from the saddle. His narsiit went wild with pain. The winged mount surged forward, crashing into the ranks of the Armon warriors.

Ellen was stunned. Valdas lay immobile. His face a burnt ruin.

'He is dead, my Lady. We must retreat,' said Mendor.

The Armon forces were overwhelming. Seven warriors of the One Hundred were making a last stand in the centre of the slope, hemmed in on all sides by Armon troops. Kanis' wide half-Meadrel face twisted in fury as he fought back-to-back with Ruus. Some fifty others had reached the ridge, led by Velthius and Elthar. Bovosan was with them, the minitil's hammer red with enemy blood. Meanwhile more than a hundred Armon warriors were coming down the slope towards her and Mendor.

'Raphal,' called Ellen, reaching down an arm. She cried out with the effort of lifting the old Priest and Druid into the saddle behind her. Thankfully he was slight. Mendor had done the same with the more portly Valnis.

Raziin grinned in savage fury, ready to attack her again. Then a bolt of Force as thick as her waist struck him. His Shield flared as he met the attack, but even so it sent him tumbling back into the rocks and out of sight.

Ellen looked up at the crest. She could see Cedrin there.

'We have to go now.' Mendor's voice was shrill with tension.

Her heart tearing, Ellen turned away. She and Mendor flew down the slope, their mounts still nimble despite the additional weight.

Ahead, Spider and the Daughters spurred their amelak down the path at the sixty warriors closing from behind, heedless of the broken ground. One of the women went down as her amelak tripped, but the others did not pause.

'Suul Cintros,' said Thenia, her voice calm. 'I suggest a tactical withdrawal.' Serel and the two slaves watched them in wide-eyed silence.

'Agreed.' She paused only long enough for Raphal and Valnis to be transferred to spare mounts.

'Mendor. With me!' said Ellen.

'Leave the attack to Spider, my Lady. You are too vital to risk,' said Thenia.

Ellen looked down the valley. Spider's warriors were facing twice their numbers. Even with the advantage of their mounted attack, the odds were too tight. Her and Mendor's two narsiit were worth ten men each and would help to break the Armon line. 'No. We are needed.'

Ellen set off down the slope. She ranged out wide on the left flank of the Daughters' line, waving Mendor to take the right. Their mounts would be able to handle ground the amelak would baulk at. She had soon overtaken the Daughters. Ahead of them the advancing men – climbing up the broken ground on foot – faltered in their advance as they saw the wall of mounts descending on them.

Ellen and Mendor drew together in front of the advancing Daughters.

'Cintros!' Ellen screamed out her battlecry.

They cut through the first line of men, then unleashed their narsiit in the midst of the Armon line. The winged mounts danced in fury, hooves and teeth darting at the foe with superhuman speed. The blades of Ellen and Mendor were close behind. Soon more than ten of the enemy were down, and their line had been reduced to a ragged mess. Then the Daughters arrived, their high, ululating battlecries enough to chill the blood. The elite Hanis bodyguard fought with focussed ferocity.

The Armon warriors stood their ground for the long bloody struggle. The last three broke for freedom, but were quickly ridden down. Twelve of the Daughters had fallen. Spider's face was splattered with blood, and her lieutenant Jeth was bleeding from a nasty slash that cut diagonally down her left cheek. Cedrin and the One Hundred were gone, pursued by Raziin and the bulk of the Armon force. Another detachment was working its way down to them.

Thenia, Serel, her slaves and the two Druids arrived with what pack-amelak they could gather. Together they ran south.

They began by retracing their route, but as they crested a rise they saw another thirty Armon warriors riding hard up the slope towards them. With their numbers reduced, and many of the Daughters wounded, there was no question of fighting again. Valnis directed them to the north-west along another narrow mountain trail. They were soon lost amidst the vast, broken landscape.

Ellen sheathed her scythe. Poor Valdas. The lanky Suulqua would never have the glory he dreamed of. He had left Athria seeking a new life, a chance to show his worth, and he had died on a rocky hillside. He had been true to his vows though, and he would be honoured.

The suns had fallen below the western foothills by the time they stopped. Ellen stepped down from the saddle and patted her narsiit, speaking soft words of praise.

Her heart ached as she looked north. What an idiot she had been! What if she never saw Cedrin again? If she had been riding with him, even now they would be together. Her heart was breaking, and all she wanted was for Cedrin to take her in his arms so she could bury her face in his chest and let the pain go.

Tears streaked down her cheeks. They rolled down her chin and she wiped them away, surprised when her hand came away bloody.

'Are you hurt, my Lady?' asked Mendor.

Ellen took a breath, all too aware of the pain in her heart. 'No. It's not my blood.'

Chapter Seventeen

Cedrin stared into the darkness of the caverns, his mind numb with fatigue. The warriors of the One Hundred moved around him at their appointed tasks, silhouettes against the greater dark. Once more, the image of Ellen, alone and exposed at the bottom of the rocky trail, leapt into his mind. He saw her expression of shocked surprise as Raziin readied to destroy her. Then her determination to put herself in danger rather than risk their son. He had saved her then, but he should have done more. He should have been at her side. Gone after her. His last image of Ellen was of her blonde hair flying wild as she hurtled down the slope on her narsiit, scythe held ready beside her.

Despite the ferocity of the One Hundred's defence, Raziin had maintained the advantage. At that point, to advance into his ranks would have been suicidal. Even so, Kalyth and Ranis had to all but physically restrain him. Reluctantly, he had listened to their arguments with the mind of a karass player. Instead of pursuing her, they began a fighting retreat to Ranmyden's huge entrance caverns, his heart tearing inside him at every backward step. Within the gloomy caverns, they found a defensible position and Raziin finally ceased his attacks.

Three warriors of the One Hundred reached them after dark, following their trail. One of them had seen Ellen and the Daughters break through Raziin's rearguard and head to the west, along with Thenia, Mendor and the two Druids. So she was alive. The thought of not being there to defend her, to protect her, ate away at him. He used the discipline of the Way to marshal his thoughts. He had to focus on finding the Spear and getting out of this ancient tomb.

They had made camp inside one of the many tumbled ruins of Ranmyden, in what had once been a large square-built dwelling constructed of rectangular blocks. Only two of the walls were standing and the roof was long gone. They positioned themselves inside where the two remaining walls met. The floor was smooth and level, displaying a high degree of craftsmanship. A small spring ran across the middle of the space. Where it crossed the floor, carrying away the accumulated dirt and dust, beautifully constructed murals had been revealed. The colours were still vibrant, the tiles joined into a seamless whole without as much as a hair's breadth between them.

'Any chance of rain, do you think?' he heard Velthius ask.

Cedrin smiled at the humour.

'Could be clouding over,' replied Duro. Cedrin could just make out the huge warrior's bulk against the far wall. He could not see Kalyth, or the Priest and Priestesses, but they could be anywhere in the darkness. Despite the hardships, he had not heard a single word of complaint from the Twins delegation. Esmelle particularly had been a welcome source of calm. He could sense the Behemoth now, eating away at the edges of his mind, and was more grateful than ever for the protection provided by the Earth-Essence practitioners.

The One Hundred had accepted the loss of their comrades with stoic strength. Death was part of the Way. The fallen had been honoured. Elthar had led the devotions, speaking quietly about their life and achievements. Some of their bodies lay untended on the hillsides of Ranmyden, others – lost since they entered Ranmyden – buried under cairns of stone in the Caverns. The loss of Kanis and Ruus had hit Cedrin the hardest. Ruus had been his friend. A comrade from the time before he was the Scion, and only a newly-inked scytheman. Kanis had been the bane of his life on the caravan north. The man was a mean, vicious bully. Cedrin had eventually defeated him in single combat and cut off part of the man's ear to mark his disgrace. Even so, he had sworn to Cedrin with unrestrained fervour and had died defending him. In some ways, that hit him the hardest. What had he done to deserve devotion like that?

When they first entered the caverns, the luminescent lungii were plentiful. The ceilings of the upper caverns swarmed with bats, their guano giving birth to thick stands of lungii that glowed with blue-green light. It was not enough to truly see – at least for a human – but it helped to outline the terrain. Wild Eathal lived in the upper caverns. They had fled at their approach, disappearing into the darkness with their jakka herds. As Cedrin and his men descended, the ceilings became empty, the lungii increasingly rare until none were seen at all. There was nothing here except the wild teremb that had followed them from the upper caverns. And drakons. The beasts used their hot, rock-dissolving breath to forage in the rock, seeking minerals. They had come across their workings many times now, and had learned to step cautiously across the pools of acid slush left in their abandoned digs.

In the endless dark of the lower caverns, it was easy to lose track of time. He estimated from their dwindling food and water and the number of times they had stopped to snatch sleep that they had been descending into the Ranmyden Caverns for at least three days. Raziin's forces had been as slippery as snakes, striking from the dark, always when they least suspected it. Three times he and Raziin had matched wills, driving at each other with Sorcery. The second time he had tried to break through Raziin's Barrier with the Final Matrix, but had failed. The Northman always played a defensive battle, seeking to neutralise Cedrin while his men carved away at the One Hundred. There were sixty-eight left now. There would be far less if Cedrin had not been able to use the Matrix of Form to heal them. The men were grateful, although they resented the fact that their wounds healed without scars. Veltricus had lost all but three of his bodyguards, while the Herath Suul himself had managed to escape unscathed.

Cedrin brooded on their predicament. Raziin had more than twice their numbers and always used the layout of the Caverns well in his attacks. It was uncanny. Both he and Raziin's forces should be at the same disadvantage, yet somehow the Northman managed to navigate the broken terrain of joined caverns and shattered ruins as though he was born here. Despite his numerical advantage, Raziin never committed to an all-out attack, and he always left Cedrin's men a line of retreat. There could only be one conclusion: they were being herded deeper into Ranmyden. Somehow Raziin knew the layout of these caverns and was driving them towards the Iris. He knew why. Raziin wanted the Spear. The only way to defeat the Ward was to allow it to pass the Spear to Cedrin and wait for it to cease to exist. For now Raziin needed him alive. He wanted Cedrin in the Iris, but with his forces so decimated Raziin could easily overwhelm them when the time came to take the Spear.

'Light a lamp, Elthar,' said Cedrin. They had lost most of their supplies in Raziin's first attack, including many of the torches and casks of lamp-oil. It had meant using only two or three torches as they moved deeper through the ruins.

Bovosan had proved to be an invaluable asset. In the upper caverns, he had regularly returned with freshly killed jakka and edible lungii. There was no live game in the deeper caverns, but he did have the knack for finding the underground springs that trickled through – such as the one in this ancient dwelling. That enabled them to refill their empty water-flasks.

The sheer size of the Ranmyden Caverns was stunning. It had not been a single underground city but many – an entire Eathal nation. Ranmyden could swallow Olcis and Raynor a hundred times over. Perhaps as many as a million Eathal once dwelled here. If the Caverns of Maht were like this, no wonder Hukum was able to field so many legions.

Elthar's sombre face appeared from the dark as a lamp flared to life in his hands. He walked across to Cedrin and handed it to him.

'Thank you, Elthar.'

'A pleasure, my Lord,' rumbled Elthar in his sombre voice.

Cedrin took the map from the pouch at his belt and stretched it out on the stone. He berated himself again for not having the foresight to have carried copies of all the maps on his person. Valnis and all his carefully scribed guides to the Ranmyden Caverns were gone, leaving him with this single cryptic map of the Eathal city with the Hall of Dreams and the Iris at its heart.

That he had the map at all was a lucky coincidence. He had been puzzling over it late the night before Raziin's attack and had tucked it into the pouch at his belt, meaning to return it to Valnis when they reached the entrance caverns.

On the map he could easily recognise the Temple of the Iris in the centre of the Hall of Dreams. Its pentagonal shape and five-fold symmetry was highly distinctive. There were other shapes that could be floor plans, yet nothing in the way of a conventional street layout that joined them into a whole. Cedrin turned the map, trying to get some sense of it. The shapes swam in front of his eyes like some foreign language. He cursed with frustration.

He felt a presence to his left. Bovosan squatted down beside him. Even a sixth-degree calvanni could take notes from Bovosan when it came to silent movement.

'This is where we are heading?' asked Bovosan. His command of Anacian had improved dramatically over the last months. His selective hearing remained though. The minitil was good at avoiding questions.

Cedrin tapped the Iris. 'This is where the Ward is. Where the Spear is. The rest . . . ?'

Bovosan leant over the map. 'It's old, this map.' He stretched out a dark finger and tapped a row of parallel lines on the left hand corner of the map with his claw-like nail. 'This is a . . .' He paused, trying to find the words. 'Sky ladder. No. Ceiling ladder.'

Cedrin drew a sharp breath. It *was* a language. He pointed at the two shapes on either side of the parallel lines. 'What are these?'

'Temples. You can see the columns. Here. And here,' said Bovosan, tapping the parchment.

'Ah!' Now it made sense. Some of the drawings were floor plans, exact representations of places. Yet between them were *symbols*, each indicating the sort of terrain or noting the type of access between the locations.

'So what are these around the Iris?' asked Cedrin, indicating four symbols.

'This one is a small tunnel going deeper. This one is an

overhang of rock, with dwellings beneath it. This is a holy place . . . you would say a Temple square, an open place for worship. This is a sacred well.'

Cedrin imagined the terrain around the Iris, based on Bovosan's description. That was quite a bit of ground. So this map was not really a map at all. Only a type of shorthand, a key to navigation, but not to scale or proportion like a normal chart. Valnis would be in rapture right now to hear Bovosan decipher the symbols. To think the minitil had been hidden away all the time in Beslin when he could have been helping them.

Now at last Cedrin had a way he could use the map.

'These symbols around the margins, can you tell me what they are?' asked Cedrin.

Bovosan started at the top left and worked clockwise around the map. There were thirty-eight symbols around the edges of the city map, twenty-five were describing terrain, four were cardinal points and nine were structures. The buildings were probably ruined, but the terrain should still match. He took in the descriptions hungrily, creating a mental map of the different landforms: knolls of basalt, natural pools, pillars of limestone, arched bridges, stone-cut tunnels . . . even huge glowmetals that had been left in-situ by the city builders for aesthetic reasons. If they came across any of these distinctive features, they would at last be able to navigate their way to the Iris. And he would be able to create some coherent strategy to turn the tables on Raziin.

'*Ahhh!*'

At the shout of pain, the One Hundred were instantly alert.

Ranis and Kalyth ran to Cedrin, Velthius and Duro close behind. They surrounded him in a ring of lanedd. Torches flared to life, bobbing through the dark as warriors rushed to the commotion.

Cedrin went to follow, but Kalyth held him back. 'Let them deal with it, my Lord.'

There was a hiss, then a harsh bark. He heard boots scrape across stone and another shout of pain.

'That's a drakon,' said Cedrin. He opened the Window and channelled the fire into the Light Matrix. He adjusted the shape of the Matrix and a ball of brilliant white appeared high above the cavern.

Five of his men surrounded a green drakon. Vess' arm was red raw with a savage burn, his face twisted in pain. The beast was the size of an amelak, with a grey belly. Of all the predators they had faced in the Caverns, the drakon were the most aggressive. So far they had killed two of the smaller greys and driven back a yellow the size of a war-harena. Dagon was close by, shielding Esmelle and the strange twins with his powerful body. Veltricus was across the far side of the cavern, protected by his three bodyguards. Each of the Suul's men gripped a short shaft-trapping knife in either hand.

'Stand back!' called Cedrin. The warriors ran for cover.

He drew deeply on the Fire and shot a thick spear of Force at the drakon. His aim was improving. It sliced cleanly through the creature's breast, then vanished. Colourless blood sprayed from the gaping wound. It filled the cavern with the scent of acid. The blood sizzled on the stone, eating into it as it boiled to vapour. The green tried to turn, then collapsed.

'Let's move out!' called Ranis.

They had learned the hard way that when a drakon was killed, its cannibalistic brethren would race to fight over the corpse. The last thing they needed was to fight more of them. He had no desire to face a red . . . or a black.

'Bring Vess to me,' said Cedrin.

'His wound is not serious, my Lord. It's vital we move immediately,' said Kalyth. The old warrior had taken a nasty wound to the abdomen in the first engagement with Raziin's men in the caverns and had run for hours as he bled. Only when they were safe did Kalyth admit to the injury. None of the One Hundred were afraid of pain. Cedrin reluctantly accepted his reasoning. He kept the ball of light hovering above the cavern as they struck camp. He folded the map and tucked it into his pouch.

Cedrin let his hold on the Light Matrix go. The light was a blessing, but he was wary of giving Raziin yet another advantage in tracking them, and of attracting drakon. The brilliant light could be seen for leagues in the caverns.

* * *

They picked their way through tumbled masonry and across melted rock that looked like ancient lava flows. Eventually they left the ruins and entered a long tunnel that sloped down. The deeper they went, the more Cedrin worried about the return journey to the surface. Bovosan would be able to guide them out, but whether their supplies would last that long was a real issue. You could not eat drakon. Once their bodies were drained of the acid blood, they cooled into a solid mass of material akin to glass and rock. If this was smashed apart, only their brains and nervous system resembled anything close to normal flesh – and they were poisonous.

The tunnel opened out into a large natural cavern. Kalyth motioned for him to wait while the men scouted ahead.

Cedrin sensed the Fire. He immediately responded with a Barrier and Shield. Dagon and the Twins delegation were nearby, and he included them in his wall of defence.

'We are under attack!' called Cedrin. Raziin at least was predictable. He always led with Sorcery.

A moment later, Cedrin raised the Light Matrix, bringing the cavern into sharp relief. There were three entrances, the one they had entered, the one the Armon warriors were attacking from and another, undefended entrance. *Another line of retreat, left open.* In the bright light, he could see the wide tunnel sloped down. He released a ball of raw Fire down the tunnel. It flashed down the wide opening, illuminating it as it went. *Empty.* There were no troops positioned down there. No second ambush.

'Take the open tunnel!' commanded Cedrin.

The One Hundred fell back, the Twin delegation and Veltricus and his men hustled along with them. Cedrin stayed to defend the retreat, along Kalyth, Ranis, Elthar and Duro. Raziin ran in behind his troops, flanked by Merceth and Kyal. He shot a wide fan of Force bolts, but Cedrin intercepted them all on his Shield. He felt the Final Matrix slam into his Barrier.

Cedrin widened the Window, drawing a Force Matrix. He ground his teeth together as the Fire rushed through him and out through the Matrix.

Seven silver wedges raced for the Armon line, directed not at Raziin, but his troops. As usual Raziin thought of defending no one but himself. The wedges sliced through the first line of warriors and continued through a second before Cedrin was forced to release the Matrix. The Armon attack faltered. Raziin's attack with the Final Matrix fell away. Cedrin and his men had taken down twelve of Raziin's men without a single loss.

'Let's go,' said Cedrin. Together they retreated down the tunnel. Another three silver bolts detonated against Cedrin's Shield. He released the Light Matrix and attacked Raziin with the Final Matrix. His anger and frustration swelled, but he let the emotions pass through him and focussed his mind. The Fire rushed into the attack. For a moment he drove through Raziin's Barrier. He had a glimpse of the Northman's turgid thoughts before his Barrier closed again. Then the distance was too great, and he no longer sensed the Fire from the other Sorcerer. A single image stayed with him from Raziin's mind: sheets of Fire sweeping through a cavern square, reducing a crowd of fleeing Eathal to ash and bone. The glimpse was chilling. It had the clarity of a memory . . . yet that was impossible. Raziin could not have been in Ranmyden thousands of years ago to witness its destruction. Cedrin shivered at the lust-driven mania that lay inside the mind of that madman.

'I don't like this, Cedrin,' said Kalyth. It was a sign of how concerned the old warrior was that he neglected the usual *my Lord*. 'Raziin is still with us.' His eyes were haunted, perhaps by the memories of all the years he had been trapped in Blackthorne tower by the power of the Ward. Years he too had been preyed upon by the Behemoth.

Cedrin nodded. Kalyth had been against Cedrin going to the Ranmyden Iris since Olcis. He had only agreed on the condition that Cedrin would enter the Ranmyden Iris alone – yet here was Raziin, dogging their steps at every turn. It would be the Olcis Iris all over again, when the Behemoth had chosen Raziin, using its insidious influence to freeze Cedrin in place. Under no circumstances could they risk Raziin getting his hands on that weapon.

They had to stay away from the Iris until they were ready. The Ward had a will of its own, as well as the power of the Spear at its command. It could control the mind of anyone it came into contact with.

'You have my word, Kalyth. I will not approach the Ranmyden Iris until Raziin is dealt with. Once we enter the ruined city around the Hall of Dreams, we pick our ground, then turn to attack. It's time Raziin and his men became the hunted.'

Kalyth nodded. 'I'm glad to hear it . . . my Lord.'

* * *

Ellen walked up the hill to Raphal and Valnis. The two Druids were arguing over the map. Again. Mendor walked three paces behind her, taking station as an unofficial bodyguard, greatscythe held loosely in his hand.

'The map clearly indicates a way in,' said Valnis.

Raphal's eyebrows drew together. 'I agree. Perhaps if we were here two thousand years ago we would find it.'

Valnis' face flushed red. 'Look at these markings. They clearly indicate the existing landform. Nothing has changed!'

After cutting north-west, they had swung north. A vast spur of basalt had risen between their path and the main entrance caverns. Valnis claimed the north trail would lead them to another opening on the west flank of Ranmyden, so they continued on. It did, except this entrance was three hundred feet above them, at the top of a sheer cliff. To the far east, just beyond the basalt spur, Ellen could see the top of one of the main openings to the Ranmyden Caverns. In between was an impassable maze of broken ridges.

The suns were low in the west. A dark cloud of bats and nocturnal birds was disgorging from the high opening like a vast swirl of smoke.

They had camped on the side of a low hill nearby. Unlike the southern foothills they had passed through on the way, the slopes of Ranmyden were thickly forested here. They had found a stream, so fresh water was not a problem, but otherwise supplies were low. Most of the pack amelak had been lost in Raziin's attack.

Ellen soon realised she could add nothing to the discussion and walked back down the hill as twilight deepened into night. Mendor followed in silence, not wanting to interrupt her thoughts. They had just finished sparring, Ellen pitting her scythe against Mendor's greatscythe. His skill had improved, but he still relied too much on classic forms. Combat was more fluid that that.

The Daughters had started a fire and set up what tents they had. Amazingly Thenia's tent had made it through the chaos. Other warriors were stationed around the low hill to give warning of attack.

Spider sat at the fire with Jeth at her elbow. Earlier they had undertaken solemn devotions for the sisters they had lost in the hillside fight. Now the mood was more relaxed. They passed around a flask of bakta and talked in low tones about the women who had lost their lives.

Ellen had not wanted to intrude on the rites of the Way, but now she was tired and eager to sit by the fire. Raphal and his scholar friend would have the whole night to argue over the route. If they had not made any progress by morning then they would have no choice but to retrace their path and come at the Caverns from the original route.

One of the Daughters saw her approach and made room for her. Ellen laid her scythe on the ground and shuffled up to the fire. Thenia had already retired to her tent.

One of her slaves approached her. 'Serel is ready for you, my Lady.' There would be a sponge bath waiting for her, but Ellen was not ready for that quite yet. Besides, that brought her one step closer to sleep – and the nightmares. The influence of the Behemoth was stronger than ever in Ranmyden and had returned to her with renewed force. Thankfully she had managed to find the tower of the sea-raptor – her dream haven – or wake, before the Beast found her. Knowing it was a real force made the dreams all the more terrifying.

'Tell her I will be there soon,' said Ellen.

'I'll go in your place, Cintros,' said Spider. Her words were slurred from the bakta. 'I could do with a bed slave.'

Ellen's heart skipped a beat. Her heart flared at the insult, but she bit her tongue, conscious of the grief that would be tearing at Spider. It was the first time the bodyguard commander had broken her silence since Beslin. She decided to ignore the comment.

'I suppose two sets of hands are better than one. Why else would you prefer them to the Emperor's shaft?'

Ellen was too stunned to speak.

'Spider,' hissed Jeth. 'Quiet.'

'Or what? Another whipping? Maybe the Emperor's wife would deign to use her powers on me, eh?'

Ellen pushed herself to her feet. 'Silence!'

Spider threw down the bottle and stood up on the other side of the fire. Jeth tried to drag her back, but Spider slipped out of her grip and gave her lieutenant a stunning backhand that left her nose bloody.

'Going to come off the Suul now?' snapped Spider. 'Go on. You got the guts to use your Sorcery on me?'

Ellen's hand shook. She felt the ground shift under her.

'Mind your tongue, Spider. Or you'll have it cut out,' said Mendor, releasing the blades of his greatscythe.

Spider spat at Mendor's feet. 'Come at me with that, you Athrian ponce, and I'll open you a new one.' She leant down, sweeping up her own weapon. Ellen knew immediately Mendor was outclassed. Spider was lightning fast with natural timing. Ellen had watched her take down every one of the One Hundred who challenged her with contemptuous ease.

This was getting out of hand. The Daughters watched it all unfold. Not one of them moved.

'Stand down, Mendor,' said Ellen.

'But, my —'

'That's an order,' said Ellen.

'You need to get yourself under control, Spider,' said Ellen, trying to keep relaxed.

'Or what? You can let our Sisters die, but now you want me to shut my trap? You don't deserve him. *You gutless whore!*'

Ellen's knuckles whitened where she gripped her scythe. The

woman would have to be punished for her insolence, but now was not the time.

'This is no time to be fighting each other,' said Ellen. Mustering all the Suul dignity she could, she turned and walked away from the fire.

'I know why you don't go to his bed. Now that he knows what a real woman is like, why would he want *you*?'

Ellen's rage flared to a red heat. The boiling sea of emotion she had kept bottled up for so long exploded out of her. With a shriek of rage, she leapt straight across the fire and swept her scythe down at Spider's face. Her heart twisted with hate at the snake who slithered into their bed, poisoning everything.

Spider brought her greatscythe up at the last minute, stunned by the suddenness of the attack. A heartbeat later her blades locked into place and her weapon turned into a deadly blur.

'Get Thenia. Quick. *Quick*.' It was Jeth's panicked voice.

Ellen had no thought for anything but putting a blade into Spider's insolent body. The bodyguard commander was light and fast, but Ellen had been trained by weaponmasters since she was eight years old. Ellen forced her back into the darkness beyond the fire.

Spider dropped back to give herself room. When Ellen advanced, Spider swept a vicious cut at Ellen's legs. She saw it coming and leapt above it, bringing her scythe down in a two-handed cut straight at Spider's head. The warrior lifted the haft of her weapon in a classic block, but the blow had Ellen's full weight behind it. She drove Spider's weapon down, and the warrior had to jerk her head to the side to save her eye as the scythe-blade cut past.

Ellen did not pause for a moment. Lanedd blades flashed and cut. Her whole body was alive with a hot, directed rage. They were surrounded by shouting women. Mendor's face was aghast. He had his greatscythe drawn, yet like the others he dared come nowhere near them. Each strike was neatly turned and countered in a display of supreme skill.

It was not enough. Ellen had never felt a killing rage before, but she felt it now. Spider had threatened everything. She had ripped her and Cedrin apart. Ellen was aware she was screaming, giving vent to a terrible force of emotion.

Spider stumbled. Ellen slipped inside her guard in a moment, slicing along the inside of her forearm. The warrior howled in pain and her greatscythe – in the middle of an attacking arc – flew out of her hands.

Ellen cut straight at Spider's face. The warrior ducked back, managing to save her life, but fell back onto the tangled grass of the hillside. Ellen's blade swept to her throat. A line of blood appeared there. Spider was breathing harshly now, truly afraid. Only the merest pressure would end it.

'Go on,' said Spider. 'Do it.'

Ellen blinked. She came back to herself in a rush. They were surrounded by a circle of shocked onlookers, Mendor and Thenia among them. They were hundreds of paces from the fire. Ellen had no recollection of crossing the ground, only the combat itself.

'You let the others die. That's murder. Just kill me here and have done with it. Why make it a lie?'

'What?'

'You could have saved them,' said Spider. 'I saw what you and Cedrin could do in the practice yard in Beslin. You could have scattered them all.'

'Is that what you think?' Ellen's hand shook with a fatigue. She withdrew it, rather than risk cutting Spider's carotid artery.

'What else?'

'How could you believe I would just let them die if I had a choice? I can't use my powers. Any Fire at all risks the child.' She could not explain the Bridge, but she could make her understand. 'It would destroy his mind.'

Spider's jaw dropped in shock. She rose to her knees. The moment stretched. Ellen had no idea what to say.

'You get everything. You get him. His child,' said Spider.

Ellen met the warrior's dark gaze and realised what she was seeing. Spider had been in love with Cedrin. *Was* in love with him. Her aggression, her insolence, it was a shield. No warrior would rise to her position without strength and integrity, the same qualities Spider saw in Cedrin.

'I had him first,' said Ellen, speaking from the heart.

Spider nodded. 'I always knew I could never truly have him. It did not stop me trying.'

Ellen swapped the scythe to her left hand and reached out to help Spider to her feet. The warrior looked at Ellen's hand and then took it. Spider was heavier than she looked. On her feet, she stood more than a head taller than Ellen. A buzz of talk rippled through the onlookers.

'All he talked about that night was you. Asking where you were. It took two pipes of se to get his blood up and even then I had to just about wrestle him to the ground. If he fell for me the way he has fallen for you I would be the happiest woman on Yos.'

As Ellen looked into Spider's eyes, she saw nothing but a woman who loved the same man. It was not hard to know why – for all the same reasons Ellen loved him: his determination, his nobility, his intensity. In that moment, she and Spider were united by a common understanding.

Valnis and Raphal emerged from the circle and walked to Spider.

'Let me have a look at that wound,' said Valnis. The scholar was not a strong Moon Druid, but with Asic waxing gibbous above them and Rea's waxing crescent still high in the west, he would be well supplied with Essence.

Valnis lifted Spider's arm and clicked his tongue as he examined the long gash. 'Lucky it was not deeper.'

'Are you alright, Ellen?' asked Raphal.

'Fine.' Ellen felt more than that. She felt free for the first time since that morning Cedrin confessed his indiscretion. Now, as though seeing everything through a clear lens for the first time, she realised how cruel she had been. Not intentionally, but cruel nevertheless.

She longed for Cedrin, to be near him. To put her flesh next to his. By now he would be deep in Ranmyden, pursued by Raziin and his small army of Cioan warriors. The pain she had carried was gone, but now it was replaced by the ache of worry. She had to find a way into the Caverns. Somehow she had to lead the Daughters to support him.

Valnis laid his hands on Spider's wound. The milky glow of Moon Essence swam around the bodyguard's arm.

'You know, at one time the Empress had her own bodyguard,' said Spider.

'I thought the One Hundred protected the whole royal family?'

'They do. But once the Empress had her own force of female warriors. That is where the inspiration for the Daughters of the Ninth came from. Thenia's mother is a student of history.'

'What were they called?' asked Ellen.

'The Daughters of the Phoenix,' said Spider. 'I . . .' The tall warrior paused. 'If you ever considered reforming them, I would be honoured to lead them. Provided, of course, Thenia's mother releases me from service to Hanis.'

Ellen's throat was dry. She swallowed. 'I would be honoured.'

Valnis had moved on to Spider's throat, swiftly healing the surface cut. 'There,' he said, standing back.

Spider fixed her gaze on Ellen, her eyes intense. She stepped in and kissed her on both cheeks. When she leant back, tears were running down her cheeks.

'I would be the one who was honoured, my Lady,' said Spider.

Ellen could smell the sweat on Spider's skin. She looked up and down the woman's lean torso, more aware than ever of the strength in her wiry body. Like her, Spider was a master of her weapon. Only luck and fury had given Ellen victory. Both her and her child might be dead right now – condemning Spider to death by execution.

'I've been meaning to ask. Did that hurt?' said Ellen, pointing a finger at Spider's pierced nipples.

Spider laughed. 'Not that much. I have a spare set if you want to try it.'

Ellen choked in surprise. 'I'll keep it in mind.'

Thenia walked to Ellen. 'Suul Cintros?'

'All is well, Thenia. All is well,' said Ellen.

Chapter Eighteen

Daran watched the Green Drakon come.

The mought helmet restricted his vision and the breastplate was tighter than he remembered. He and Uran were together in the ranks, positioned behind the front phalanx. Daran had never lost a field engagement in his long career. His presence stiffened morale and would make the veterans of the First fight harder than ever. He was their luck. Even knowing this, he had been reluctant to risk himself. If he fell, so did the Yasser States.

But today was crucial. There were no tricks today. No hidden traps to spring from the terrain. Today they would be head-to-head with an elite force of equal numbers only thirty leagues from Raynor. They not only had to hold them, they had to push them back. His only advantage was that they were fighting in daylight.

On the hillside above them, his aides were gathered on narsiit. With them was one of his body doubles, decked out in his best court clothes. They would have their own role to play. He prayed silently to Larus they survived.

The view was different from the field. The Green, leading the advance, were a dark line of heavy shields stretched across the valley. Their defensive glowmetal rose from the centre of the advancing mass, a twisted cone of platinum and blue light. He could not see them, but Daran knew from the latest reports that Blood Legion were advancing behind the Green.

Daran's full force was in the field. He and the First took the centre of the field. The First's cavalry were waiting behind, awaiting the command for a crucial manoeuvre. To either flank were the split forces of the Second, and flanking the entire force were the cavalry units of the Second and also the scouts who had made so many lightning attacks on the Eathal to test their defences. His sons were both here with their cavalry units. The eldest waiting behind the First, his youngest on the right flank with his scouts.

He had to stop Hukum from reaching Raynor. Today he was risking all with a single throw of Kallor's Dice.

The air rippled above the Green's ranks. Three fireballs flashed into existence, streaking down at them. Uran stilled as he concentrated. Two exploded on an invisible Shield. Another passed by, until it too was intercepted on the left flank by one of Uran's Druidin, a Larus Druid. The Fire crackled as it flashed and ignited in the air above them.

Daran had positioned his forces in the west of the field. He wanted to draw the Green as far away from Blood as he could. His units would need the additional room to manoeuvre out of reach of Blood's offensive glowmetal.

Bolts of Force shot across the gap, driving into the First and Second. Uran and his Druidin responded with Fire and directed beams of heat. The air above them flashed and flared with detonations. Men cried out in pain as some of the Force bolts slipped through, driving into them like huge spears. Panicked, some of the men threw spears or shot arrows, despite the clear orders to save their shafts. The projectiles arched up into the sky, but when they reached the sky above the Green they halted in mid-air, held by an invisible hand. Even though he was expecting it, it was one of the strangest things Daran had ever seen.

Then the Green were on them. There was a clattering crash as the lines met. The front phalanx of the First gritted their teeth and went to work. Their long spears stabbed forward. Many were turned on the heavy Eathal shields, but many blades found their mark. Daran's guts twisted with fierce excitement as he realised his men could drive through these elite Eathal warriors, could drive them all the way back to Maht! Yet that was not the plan.

Daran counted under his breath. Timing would be crucial.

The First and Second advanced, pushing the Green back ten paces. Then, as expected, the Green rallied, driven forward by their blood-hungry Sorcerer-Lord.

He signalled to the warrior waiting beside him. The man lifted a horn to his lips and gave the signal for retreat. The First were the most highly trained, disciplined warriors in Kelas. They responded smoothly. The whole line of the First drew back, step by measured step. The magical battle continued. The Second on the right flank were taking damage, the Druidin there finding it hard to turn the Sorcerer-Lord's attacks. On the left flank, Nacius was holding well.

Even as the First retreated, the long spears of the phalanx shot out, driving into the advancing Eathal.

On either flank the Second remained in place, changing formation to a defensive square as the First retreated west. To the Green Drakon, it seemed that the human centre was breaking. As the Green drove forward, following the First to the west, the left and right flank contingents of the Second began to pull away to the north and south, opening the gap, letting them come.

Daran gave another signal. The warrior raised his horn and a long, high note sounded. It was repeated across the hills into the distance.

The Raptor lifted from the north-west, cresting the hills there and climbing rapidly into the sky. His men cheered at the sight of the broad, hexagonal platform as it swept to the east. Even in the bright morning light, Daran could see the six fountains of Force that streamed down from each apex. The narsiit force on the hill, and his double, raced to follow it.

Here he was relying on Uran's intelligence about the Sorcerer-Lord who led Blood. He wanted this all to look like a desperate manoeuvre from a commander who was losing his grip on the battle. So far, the Eathal generals had seen the First 'break' and retreat, the Second pulling away to save themselves. In response, the Warlord himself would be seen to attack the Blood legion, supported by the Raptor and the northern contingent of the Second. It was a plausible scenario, an under-strength attack against a superior force. And, he hoped . . .

irresistible bait.

The air was filled with the shouts and curses of his men, and the strange warcries of the Eathal. He chaffed with frustration. He could see nothing but the tight ranks of the First around him. He scanned the hills anxiously, watching for the markers he had placed there yesterday. His palms were sweaty where they gripped his greatscythe. Yet another battle, and he had not so much as extended his blades. His bodyguards, dressed like him in plain legionary armour, surrounded him with their scythes. He longed to strike a blow, to prove to himself he still possessed the courage he once had. Once more he restrained the impulse. There was simply too much at stake.

The Green fought with ferocity. They were tough warriors, many veterans of the first human-Eathal war a generation before. He saw his warriors fall. Others stepped into their place, keeping the line steady as they continued to fall back. His heart surged with pride. A fighting retreat like this was one of the hardest manoeuvres to carry out. Not only because of the physical coordination required, but because the act of retreat itself sapped at a man's courage. Even so they held steady.

Now the two contingents of the Second were out of sight. The outcome of their engagement was now out of his hands.

At last they reached the markers. Daran gave the signal and a series of horn-blasts sounded across the First, repeated through the vast mass of armoured men and the cavalry behind. Ten thousand legionnaires shouted in response, crashing their boots to the ground in perfect time. The Green Drakon crashed into the shields of the phalanx as the First stood their ground. Daran heard the warcries of the First's cavalry as it swept around them, engaging the flanks of the Green for the first time. A shock went through the Eathal lines as the lances of the amelak cavalry stabbed into their unprotected flanks. The Green hastily changed formation on the edges of their force.

'Let's drive through them,' called Daran.

His warriors roared in response. If there was one thing a soldier understood, it was attack. The very act fuelled resolve. Fire flashed above them. Great pillars of Force drove down, many finding their way past their Shields. Men fell, but others ran to their places, lost in a fever of bloodlust.

And the real work of the day began.

Step by step, the First drove into the Green Drakon. The Eathal did not retreat, and the human phalanxes, with their longer spears, were taking a heavy toll. Soon Daran and Uran found themselves only five ranks from the front line, driven ahead as the warriors came forward to fill the gaps. The world was reduced to shouting, pushing men, sweat streaming off their huge forearms as they worked the long spears. Others in the front ranks had lost their spears and were fighting with short scythes. Water boys ran through the chaos, passing skins to the parched warriors. Every hour, the men fighting on the front ranks were rotated back to rest. His most experienced veterans, the Honoured, stood behind him. One thousand of his best. Grim and expectant. He would not use them yet. Not yet.

He could not see the Second engaging the Blood legion, but he knew where the fight was taking place. The Raptor floated half a league to the east, dropping a continual rain of arrows, spears and fire-barrels. Shields flared below it occasionally, but otherwise the flying platform remained unmolested. *Nacius is keeping the Blood's Sorcerer-Lord occupied.*

The ranks in front of Daran opened as three warriors fell at once. A huge Eathal with two axes of darkglass leapt through the gap. Without thinking, Daran twisted the release on his greatscythe and leapt at the warrior. He ducked under one axe and took the second on the half of his greatscythe. The force of the blow almost drove him to his knees. He countered, the greatscythe coming alive in his hands. For those furious moments, all thought fell away. There was no Raynor. No strategy. No future. Only combat and fury.

An axe slipped past his guard, slamming into his breastplate with a *crack*. It pushed him back a pace. The tough mought did not shatter. He countered instinctively, sweeping the blade of his greatscythe in from the right. The lanedd sliced through the Eathal's throat as though it was air. The grey-skinned warrior staggered back in shock, then toppled.

Daran came back to himself in a rush. The whole exchange had probably lasted less than a minute. Men swarmed around him. His bodyguard. They hustled him back.

The First cheered. *'The Warlord! The Warlord!'*

'Uros' tits, Daran. What were you thinking?' said Uran. The Sorcerer's eyes were wide, his robes drenched in sweat and covered in dust as he continued to match wills with the Eathal Sorcerer-Lord.

'It was not like I had a choice,' said Daran. He was invigorated by the combat. His fatigue and worry had vanished, replaced by a sublime clarity. He had missed this.

For the third time, his front line rotated back. Daran felt the change come through his men. They were driving into the Green Drakon in sheer fury. The tide had turned. They – and Daran himself – began to smell victory.

He looked up at the markers on the hills and grinned. The Green's own stubborn resistance had played into his hands. If they had retreated, they would have been able to link with Blood legion. Instead the more inexperienced teremb legion was standing alone. By now the other contingent of the Second and the Legion's cavalry would have hit the Blood legion from the south. While Nacius pinned down the Sorcerer-Lord, and his men manoeuvred away from the point of effect of Blood's offensive glowmetal, the Eathal legion would be attacked from three directions: from the north, the south and from the air. If their formations broke – as he hoped they would – it would become a rout.

The big defensive glowmetal in the centre of the Green was closer than ever now. Daran took a skin from a runner and slaked his parched throat. The wait this morning – standing in formation since before dawn – had been interminable. Yet now time was streaming past. He could see his Captains readying for the fourth rotation on the front ranks. The suns were high in the sky. The Larus Druids on the Raptor would be at peak strength.

'Send in the Honoured,' commanded Daran.

The front ranks halted their attack, switching to a defensive formation. In a carefully choreographed movement, the Honoured came forward to take their place. Each rank peeled away and moved back, replaced by the Honoured across the line. Finally the front line fell back through them, and the

Honoured faced the Green Drakon.

Now the Green Drakon, exhausted from four hours of fighting, faced his best. Tough warriors who were fresh and ready to prove themselves. They set to work with directed fury, the long phalanx spears like an extension of their arms. Eathal fell across the line and the First advanced.

The Green had now been pushed back to the position of their glowmetal. He could see Eathal warriors hastily pulling it back into the new centre of their reduced force. The Sorcerer-Lord sat astride a jakkund, surrounded by a small mounted guard. He was beside the cart that held the platinum glowmetal, his grey face bathed in its blue light.

'I see you,' hissed Uran.

Uran's face twisted into a mask of intense concentration. Immediately the Sorcerous attacks on the First stopped. The Sorcerer-Lord's arms went rigid at his side, and his slitted green eyes fixed on Uran. The Druidin hurled their attacks at the Green, and they went unblocked. Eathal howled as balls of fire and streams of heat seared into them. Their front ranks opened and the First drove in. The Eathal reserve – shock troops equipped with axes of darkglass – rushed forward to fill the gap. They were fearsome, but without shields they made easy prey for the long phalanx spears of the Honoured. Daran's heart beat fast. It was coming.

He turned to Uran, tyring to understand what was happening, but his friend was locked into some unseen contest with the Eathal Sorcerer. The glowmetal disappeared into the centre of the Eathal force, but the Sorcerer-Lord remained rigid, the raised muscles of his shoulders tensed.

Daran heard Uran's teeth grind against each other. Twin streamers of blood ran from his nose. 'Yes,' he hissed.

The Eathal Sorcerer cried out, clutching his head. He howled in pain, his clawed hands tearing at the skin of his face and bald head. Then he froze. The green eyes went dull and the Eathal Sorcerer tumbled from his jakkund to the ground. Dead.

Uran staggered, and Daran rushed to support him.

Then all at once the First was moving forward. The Green Drakon, their reserves now slain, had collapsed. The Sorcerer-

Lord's mounted bodyguard loaded his body onto his mount and fled the field.

'Stay in formation!' commanded Daran.

The Honoured steadied the line as the First's cavalry raced ahead to cut off the Green's retreat. With no formations to stop them, the First cut through the remaining two thousand Eathal without mercy. Their orders were clear. Leave none alive.

They passed the defensive glowmetal. The jakka team were dead in their traces, the wagon itself destroyed. Daran growled in anger. The huge glowmetal would be too heavy to shift without a wagon and team of draft-beasts. The fleeing Eathal had sabotaged it to prevent them carrying it from the field. They had learned from the loss of the Silver's glowmetal. Perhaps it could be loaded onto the Raptor.

With the Green broken, Daran took his bodyguards and a hundred of the First and climbed the nearest hill. His breath came fast and ragged as he waited for that first glimpse that would tell him everything.

He reached the crest.

His knees almost buckled with relief. The Blood legion had collapsed. The two contingents of the Second had linked to the east, cutting off their escape. The whole field was a scattered mass of combats as groups of isolated Eathal fought for their lives. The Raptor, its load of missiles and fire-barrels long exhausted, had dropped low above the field. Bolts of Force shot from the sides of the hexagonal platform, striking into the knots of Eathal below. The Blood legion's glowmetal had been abandoned, its smashed cart surrounded by thousands of Eathal dead.

The Blood's Sorcerer-Lord fought on with a small force of jakkund, the standard of the Blood legion – a striking teremb bringing down a jakka - flying above them. He could see the flash and detonation of Sorcery as the jakkund force drove at the Second from the north. Their attacks were turned. *Nacius survived.* Daran's aides, forming the small force of narsiit, were also still on the field, darting in and out to deliver swift, precise strikes against the surviving formations.

He had done it. He had destroyed both Eathal legions.

If I can hold the Eathal here, I can save Raynor. Even as he thought it, the cold wash of reality struck him. The Yellow Drakon still remained intact, and the Black Drakon – Hukum's own elite legion – its powerful array of glowmetals as yet untested.

He saw movement in the east – a force of jakkund racing hard. Behind them was an advancing line of Eathal.

'There. Can you see the standard?'

One of his bodyguards, known for his good vision, squinted into the distance. 'Standards, my Lord. The Yellow and Silver.'

Daran's heart tore with rage. They must have been waiting in reserve, all this time. His men had been fighting for almost five hours. He had lost perhaps three thousand men. A second major engagement – once more on equal terms – was risking disaster.

Only the bodyguards of the Sorcerer-Lords had jakkund. All at once, Daran saw what was unfolding. The leaders of the Yellow and Silver had come ahead of their forces. Soon Nacius would face not one, but three Sorcerers.

'Send a message to Uran. The Lords of the Yellow and Silver approach. Nacius needs support. Run!' One of the warriors darted away.

The Sorcerer-Lords joined with the leader of the Blood legion, all three turning to engage Nacius. A deluge of Fire and Force fell on the Second, pounding into the ranks around Nacius. The apprentice's shield flared again and again as the Eathal Sorcerers pounded into him. There was no way Uran could reach him in time.

He could not lose Nacius. *Not now.*

The Raptor disengaged and rose, turning ponderously to meet the new attack.

'No.' The word was torn from his throat. The Raptor's Druidin were no match for three Sorcerer-Lords. Yet there was no one else to come to Nacius' aid.

The First had finished their methodical destruction of the Green Drakon. They now advanced across the field to the Second, ready to join forces and complete the destruction of Blood Legion. A single amelak rider raced from the lines of the First towards Nacius, weaving through the isolated combats.

Uran.

Bolts of Force shot down at the Sorcerer-Lords from the Raptor. They struck a Shield high above the field, detonating with flashes of bright white light.

Two lines of silver Force swept out towards the Raptor. There was a brief flash of a Shield raised by the Druidin, but the lines swept on, fixing themselves onto one edge of the platform.

Daran took an involuntary step forward. His hand ached at the intensity of his grip on his greatscythe. There was a furious magical exchange, a flash of green and yellow, then another of brilliant white. Fire and bolts of Force continued to shoot across from the ranks of the Second. Nacius still lived. Above the Second, the platform was still tethered by the two lines of Force. The lines shortened, and the massive platform began to tilt. There was another furious exchange of Force and fire, then the Raptor flipped. Hundreds of small, dark shapes tumbled from the deck. *Men.*

Daran held his breath.

One moment the Raptor remained airborne, the next it plummeted to the ground. The crash shook the earth. A vast cloud of dust and broken timber rose above the valley. When it cleared, the ranks of the Second were in disarray. Fighting above them, the Raptor had fallen onto their forward ranks.

Undeterred, the First had now reached the Second. The ranks were re-established and the bloody work of destroying the remnants of the Blood legion continued at a renewed pace.

Daran could not see Uran, but the magical combat had resumed with increased fury. Daran guessed that both Uran and the Druidin of the First had reached Nacius to support him.

His hopes were confirmed soon after when the three Sorcerer-Lords fled the field with their jakkund-mounted bodyguards.

'Congratulations, my Lord. Another victory,' said the leader of his bodyguard.

'Yes. Uros has feasted today,' said the Warlord.

The destruction of the Raptor was a terrible blow. He had lost hundreds of his best archers and spear-throwers, along with a dozen of the most powerful Larus and Uros Druidin they could field. And still Hukum's forces ground onward. If they had been able to rest and consolidate, perhaps take Green and Blood's glowmetals from the field and use them against their former owners, then they would have had a chance to stop the Black Drakon from reaching Raynor.

Only a single day, and he would have entrenched. He could have beaten back the Yellow and the decimated Silver and stood his ground, daring Hukum to show his true strength. That was impossible now.

On the field he watched, dispassionate, as the last of the Eathal warriors were slain.

'Give the signal to retreat to the night camp,' said Daran. As always, he had prepared a fortified position behind him. He would need it tonight.

Daran slung his greatscythe across his back. His hands curled into fists as his two bloodied Legions retreated to the west. The Eathal glowmetals lay abandoned on the field, treasures of incalculable worth, left for the enemy to retake.

As the suns sank to the horizon, the Yellow and the Silver marched onto the field, reclaiming their dead. They stopped their advance, wary of extending themselves too far past their own lines. Daran's cavalry loved nothing better than to strike at them from the rear in swift night attacks. The Eathal knew better than to give him the chance.

Daran gave a grim smile. He had taught them that much.

* * *

Cedrin whistled in awe as the vast cavern opened up before him. Despite the tremendous depth, the ground ahead was outlined in ghostly shades of blue-green. Lungii. They smelled the distinctive, acrid tang of guano and heard the bats on the ceiling overhead.

At their last rest stop, he had sat down with Bovosan and gone through the chart of the Eathal city methodically, getting the minitil to identify each of the many symbols. Cedrin had been amazed to discover that one of them denoted a *skyshaft*. It was an ancient volcanic vent that led right up through the mountain to the surface. Given that, it was not too hard to imagine that this isolated cavern would be wild and productive, like those in the upper regions of Ranmyden.

'This is it, Kalyth. We are close,' said Cedrin.

The old warrior passed the word. The warriors of the One Hundred knew what was at stake. They would be particularly alert now.

Bovosan held up his hand. Kalyth signalled to the men, and the word was quickly passed to halt.

There was the sound of falling rocks off to the left, then he saw a fleeting shadow outlined against the lungii.

'Eathal. A tribe lives here,' said Bovosan.

Cedrin frowned. That was one complication he had not foreseen. He had assumed the ancient city, so far below the rest of ruined Ranmyden, would have been long abandoned.

'Let's continue,' whispered Cedrin. Their plan was to establish a defensible base on the edge of the city and learn the terrain thoroughly. They had to assume Raziin and his men would already be here, or nearby. The ancient map should enable them to lay a few surprises of their own for the Northman, or at least come at Raziin on equal terms. One thing was for sure, he was done running from that vicious bastard.

They entered an open area, free from broken and melted stone. Their booted feet whispered across smooth stone as they crossed the flat ground. He heard a snort in the darkness and the sound of hooves as a group of animals moved away.

'Jakka,' said Bovosan.

In front of them, a shape grew out of the gloom – a tall finger of stone, outlined with lungii plants. Something about the shape tugged at his memory. *Yes.* He signalled for his men to stop and drew out the map, waving Duro closer with one of the two torches.

The shape of that finger of stone was echoed in one of the symbols on the margins of the map. One of the knolls of basalt that Bovosan had identified.

Immediately he knew where they were. They were entering the city from the south-west. If he was right, they would soon encounter a series of natural pools. A Temple with a square layout would be to the north. That would make an ideal base, particularly if it was still largely intact. Already Cedrin could see that the degree of damage in this isolated city was far less than in other areas of Ranmyden.

'Move forward. Stay alert,' said Cedrin.

The warriors of the One Hundred crept ahead, flanking him on all sides. Dagon and the Twins delegation walked just behind.

'It's strong here,' whispered Esmelle.

'Shh. Do not speak of it. And do not say its name,' said Dagon. 'We are also strong here, in this holy place.'

Cedrin knew exactly what they were talking about. The Behemoth. He had felt its strength growing, a formless presence in his dreams despite the Essence shields of Dagon and his delegation. Their powers varied depending on location. Last time he slept, they had been unable to find holy ground. In his dreams, he had run through a torn, dead landscape, the Behemoth's rank breath always on his neck.

Bles and Ris came to stand on either side of him as they crossed the open ground. He felt a pressure he had not been aware of ease from the edge of his mind.

Cedrin felt a gaze on him. He looked behind, straight at Veltricus. It was too dark to see the man's eyes in the dim torchlight, but he saw him turn away. The Suul was always watching the Twins delegation, yet kept his distance from the Earth Essence practitioners. It was strange, considering they both hailed from Herath. The One Hundred welcomed their presence and frequently asked for Blessings, or healing from Esmelle or Dagon. Did Veltricus mistrust magic, or did he fear what they would see within him?

If it was true that Ranmyden had been laid waste in the Destruction of Carris, Cedrin was both awed and overcome with guilt. It was hard to believe his own ancestor could have been responsible for such a vast swath of ruin. He remembered that image from Raziin's mind and shivered. Surely it was a myth. He had no doubt Carris Cinanac was some breed of Warlord – what Empire was not born in blood – but to carry out something like this?

291

The ground sloped down. The flagged area ended, and they entered a wide road that snaked around the basalt knoll. Cedrin took in a sharp breath as the floor of the cavern spread out ahead. He could see three dark shapes carved from the faint blue-green luminescence. The pools. Lungii grew on the ground around them, but not on the water's surface, leaving an area of dark.

They turned to the left and found their way blocked by a tumbled mass of rock. He and his warriors picked their way over the debris and down the other side. Cedrin heard the telltale trickle of water. Soon they were at the rocky bank of the pools. They snaked past them, surprising another herd of jakka, perhaps even the same herd. He caught a glimpse of a harness on one of the beasts as it fled. Not wild jakka, but domestic. They had not seen another Eathal. The first had no doubt warned of their approach and the rest had probably fled. He hoped they had run. He could not fight Raziin and a tribe of wild Eathal.

Soon the cavern roof to the north, which had been outlined above them with scattered lungii like a star-strewn sky, darkened. Some structure blocked the light. The light of the torches soon revealed wide steps, leading up to a temple forecourt. They carefully circled the building. It was built with solid columns and square lintels, in the ancient style. Two of the columns had fallen, and all but two of the seven huge crossbeams across the roof had followed them to the ground. The roof had been baked tile, and some of it remained intact. As he hoped, the foundations were square, matching the map. At last he understood where they were.

Fifty of the One Hundred scouted the interior of the temple while the others – less than twenty now – formed a defensive ring around Cedrin. The scouting party returned soon after. All was clear. They had found a secure series of rooms under the surviving roof. They all moved inside, grateful for the concealing shelter.

'This is good ground,' said Dagon. 'Holy ground. We will be able to defend you here.'

'Good,' said Cedrin. He would be glad of an uninterrupted

night's sleep, but he had more in mind than sitting in an old temple for his own safety.

Cedrin spread the map on the ground. Elthar lit a lamp and placed it beside the parchment.

'We are here,' said Cedrin, indicating the building at the edge of the map. 'Kalyth, take Bovosan out with the first group. I want detailed reports. If you see Raziin or his men, do not engage them. Not yet.'

Kalyth gave a grim smile. 'I understand.'

'Start finding good positions to post lookouts. I want runners and spotters all over the cavern.'

Cedrin stared at the map, mentally sketching in all the details he had discovered as they entered the city. He tapped the temple where they were sitting, then traced his hand to the centre of the map, to the Hall of Dreams and the Temple of the Iris.

One way or another, it was all going to end here.

* * *

Belin maintained his concentration through pure will.

He sat cross-legged in his Temple chambers. At the back of his mind, the Ward's insistent presence pushed against his Barrier. The magical construct had no true consciousness, merely the shadow of one. Emperor Jykor created it to defend the Spear and seek an Old Blood Scion of the Cinanac line adept at Sorcery. The Ward could control living beings through direct mental control, and through powerful Compulsions. With the Spear of Carris at its command, it had access to awesome power. Yet for all that, it was predictable.

When the Ward slumbered, Belin had been able to gradually win back control of his body and senses. For long years, he had been a prisoner in Ranmyden, dwelling with the Eathal servants of the Ward in the darkness of the Hall of Dreams. The first years in this dank cavern were a trial of isolation that had almost driven him to madness. Gradually he had learned the tricks of Sorcery that the Ward employed, such as enhancing sight. Gradually, he convinced the Ward to allow him freedom of movement, and he learned the tongue of the Eathal servants. He even managed to construct a rudimentary greatscythe from a lungii spike and flint knives. Years had passed. Then, Erioth and his ally from the webs of the south had arrived to take the Spear. The Ward had defeated them in moments.

He had long been aware that a complex work of Sorcery was at work on his body, keeping him in perfect health. His old battle scars had vanished, the ache in his old wounds fading as the healed bones re-knit themselves.

The Ward had inherited the knowledge of Jykor and the dead Emperor's arrogance. Its spies had reported the approach of both Cedrin and Raziin, and yet it did nothing, confident in the supreme power at its command. And there was its weakness and their danger. The Ward could not sense the presence of the Behemoth. No amount of argument had been able to convince the Ward that Raziin – chosen by the Behemoth in the Olcis Iris to wield the Spear – was a threat. To Belin, as a military strategist, this was frustrating in the extreme. The Ward had the power to destroy Raziin utterly, but would only respond to a direct threat.

Over the long years, Belin had fought his own battles with the Behemoth, both in nightmare and while awake. His will had proven enough of a weapon to keep it from poisoning his mind. The same could not be said for most of the Ward's Eathal servants in the Hall of Dreams. The Ward controlled them through its Compulsions, yet they seethed beneath this leash, corrupted over time by the insidious influence of the Behemoth. They watched and waited, longing for their chance to serve the Beast.

Belin heard soft footsteps approach and opened his eyes. A thel he knew ducked through the doorway to his room.

'Hungry, Belin?' she asked in the Eathal tongue, offering a bowl of gruel and a flask of water. A Liduin Druid among her own people, the thel was one of the few who had resisted the Behemoth's influence. Belin had learned the Eathal tongue from her. Her kindness had enabled him to survive in this dark prison, and he had come to think of her as a friend.

He pushed himself up from the stone floor and took the bowl

and flask. The Spear of Carris, as always, was strapped across his back. The Ward insisted it be in contact with his body at all times. At the moment, the weapon slumbered. Only a soft golden radiance issued from its forged blade. It was an unnatural thing this blade – metal without light. An abomination that had no place in the world.

'Yes. Thank you.' He had long grown accustomed to the food of the cavern-dwelling Eathal. Belin had been a soldier all his life and had no objection to simple fare.

He ate quickly and passed the bowl and empty flask back to her. She bowed and withdrew. Like all the others, she had learned to tell when he, and not the Ward, was preeminent.

Belin emerged from the ancient Temple and walked through the Hall of Dreams. Despite its name, it was not a hall at all. It was the central part of the cavern city where scores of temples had been constructed around a large open plaza. The Temple the Ward had chosen as their base of operations was small, but well constructed. It had been built under an overhanging curtain of basalt and was one of the few intact structures in Ranmyden. The Temple of the Iris was on the other side of the Hall of Dreams.

With his enhanced sight, Belin could see the Verial Erioth and the bulky Tahistil across the square, near the sacred well. Like him, they were kept supplied in food and drink by the Eathal servants of the Ward, but were prisoners of the Ward's will. Erioth sat at one of the unbroken stone benches that ringed the well's thermal spring, while the Tahistil squatted at his side. As he drew closer, he could see steam rise from the waters in swirling eddies. His skin prickled with the heat. Belin had been able to overcome his instinctive fear of the Great Spider only with difficulty. The being was the size of a small wagon, with razor-sharp mandibles as thick and long as his arms. Its multifaceted eyes were devoid of expression and reflected a thousand miniature Spears.

'Greetings,' said Belin.

They rose as he approached. Erioth's large eyes – set above the beak – swivelled towards him.

'Have no fear. The Ward slumbers,' said Belin. He adjusted

the fall of the Spear across his back.

'And yet it watches,' hissed the Tahistil.

Belin grimaced. It was true. And because of this, because he was the Ward's unwilling vessel, Erioth and the Tahistil had never trusted him. Through the Ward, he knew the Great Spider's true name, yet this was unpronounceable. The being had not offered him any other.

'The Cinanac heir approaches. The son of Riin,' said Belin.

Erioth's wings lifted slightly. 'So it ends.'

'And when the Ward ceases to exist, its hold on your power will end,' said Belin.

'There is more,' said the Tahistil in his sibilant voice.

'Yes,' said Belin. 'Raziin. The son of Leith Cinnor is also in the cavern.'

'To contest the Spear,' said the Tahistil.

'And he has already been chosen by the Behemoth,' said Erioth.

'He must not be allowed to take it,' said Belin. Although he knew what a danger the Behemoth represented, he believed a strong enough man could use the Spear and stay true to his own will. He had served the Cinanac Emperors all his life. In this, he and the Ward were in complete accord. Cedrin must have the Spear.

'Why should we help you? Place the Spear in the hands of another Carris? Look around you, Belin. This is what that weapon wrought,' said Erioth, gesturing with his delicate, long-fingered hands at the empty ruins of a once great Eathal city.

Belin knew where they stood. He also knew they would fight to prevent anyone from taking the Spear. Perhaps, if it came to it, he could somehow use them as allies against Raziin.

An Eathal scout padded across the plaza to them. The young thal bowed.

'Ward. An Eathal force is moving into the Hall of Dreams.'

Belin had time only to grunt in surprise as the Ward pushed through his Barrier and took control. The circle of golden light expanded around him as the flow of Fire the Ward drew from the Spear increased. Erioth's wingtips quivered with tension. The Tahistil's huge body lowered to the ground, its head raised.

They both backed away. The Ward had already dismissed them as inconsequential.

'Numbers?' The voice issued from Belin's throat, but it was high and thin, and oddly devoid of expression.

'Forty. Perhaps fifty. They ride strange beasts. Like jakka, but longer of limb.'

Belin was a passive witness to all this. He sensed some movement in the Ward's mind. It was like watching the cogs of a strange machine through a curtain of gauze. Some of the Ward's thoughts made sense to him, others were an unknowable function of its magical construction.

'Let them come,' said the Ward.

Chapter Nineteen

Osterac pushed the amelak to its limits. He was close now. Twice he had been challenged by Legion outriders and forced to show the official seal on the orders he carried. Orders that would recall Lempar's Legion to Olcis. Everything depended on how the old general chose to react.

Osterac's uncle, Suulvey Moren Cinlar, had been surprised to see him. He had been even more surprised to hear of the two Imperial Legions being led south to Olcis' aid. The seeds of the coup had been already in place. Moren and many of the Suul had already defied the Hesguit's orders to withdraw to the Bulvur and fought on in the city. Outright rebellion had been something they had not yet considered, not with the Eathal already in the Outer City. Even so, they had been easy enough to sway with the promise of military support. In one stroke, he gave them a way to recall Lempar to the city and ensure Cedrin's Legions came to their aid.

Osterac had always been the leader of the Suul wards of the Hesguit. Like him, they were always eager for advancement within the ranks of the Suul. Convincing a few of the Suulqua to open the gates to the Bulvur with the promise of elevation to full Suul had been easy. The fighting had been brief and bloody. The glowmetals the Hesguit had prepared to defend the Citadel had been positioned to wreak havoc on major forces approaching its walls. The surprise attack – with hand-to-hand combat – had taken the defenders by surprise. The Hesguit's Druids and Templemen, facing Moon Druids at the time of their strength, broke and ran. The coup had not been completely successful, yet enough of Olcis was now in their control for Moren to declare himself Sarlord.

Osterac winced as the gash on his left forearm opened. The Druids had offered him healing before he left Olcis, but he insisted that this wound and the other on his right side be merely bandaged. It was all about credibility. He needed to sell this. If there was one thing an old warrior like Lempar understood, it was blood and sacrifice.

Osterac topped a rise. Below, he saw the disciplined lines of the Olcis Legion snaking east towards the Asgod. At the front, he saw the narsiit of the senior officers.

'At last.'

His exhausted mount slowed as he overtook the marching men. Amelak had a reputation for sturdy endurance, but since he left Olcis yesterday he left three spent mounts in his wake. His own narsiit was stabled in Raynor, lost to him after he fled the Warlord's court. He had been a fool to take it south. He knew that now. At the time, after a lifetime groomed to play the part of the Scion, he had been unable to conceive of anything that would keep him from the Emerald Throne. Instead he had been fooled. Captured. Tortured. Betrayed by the High Druids. That experience had been a rough awakening.

Now he knew he could not trust his fate to anyone but himself.

When he saw Lempar amid the knot of senior army officers and aides, a flame of excitement lit inside him. If he succeeded here, he would earn a place in Cedrin's inner circle. And he would be that much closer to realising his true ambition.

Osterac pushed his mount into one last gallop, reining it in before Lempar. Blood had begun to leak through the bandages on his left arm. *Excellent.*

Osterac drew himself up. 'General. An urgent dispatch from Olcis.'

Lempar's eyes narrowed, and he walked his narsiit forward. His eyes took in the two wounds, both obviously recent, and the new tattoos he had earned in service to Cedrin.

'Osterac Resius?'

'Yes, my Lord.' Osterac took the message from his pouch and

handed to it Lempar.

'You joined Cedrin in the north. What are you doing back in Olcis?'

'I could not abandon Olcis. Emperor Cedrin gave me leave to return and fight.'

And to hand Olcis to him.

Lempar gave him a level stare at the reference to the Emperor, yet said nothing. He cracked open the seal with a deft twist. As he read, his eyes widened.

'Moren Cinlar had declared himself Sarlord of Olcis,' said Lempar aloud to his aides. 'He orders that we return to the city.'

'Does Suulvey Cinlar have the authority?' asked a First Captain.

'Sarlord Cinlar,' corrected Osterac gravely.

'What of the Hesguit?' asked Lempar.

'The Hesguit and his Templemen and Guardians have retreated to the inner keep of the Citadel. Moren holds the rest of the Bulvur.' The outer section of the Bulvur was where the bureaucratic apparatus of Olcis was housed and where the many Suul and Suulqua that kept Tupur administered lived and worked. A system unchanged since the Empire. 'We discovered another ring of defensive glowmetals and other traps. The Hesguit and his followers have been impossible to shift. They have fresh water from natural springs and stockpiles of food. Yet they are trapped.'

'So the rebellion has ended in a stalemate,' said Lempar.

'Not so. Moren has most of the Druids and all the Suul behind him. He controls and defends the city. That duty alone makes him Sarlord, does it not?

'The glowmetals captured from the Hesguit have been moved out into the city. Moren has forced back Yeffrij's legions and created a new defensive line to defend the people.'

'Thank the Sisters,' said one of Lempar's First Captains.

'It was a day of bloody revenge on the Eathal,' said Osterac, his voice thick with gravity. He had ensured that he was always in the thick of the fighting. It was important that he was seen as a loyal son of Olcis.

Lempar nodded in solidarity. This was always the way to

appeal to a man like him. The General's gaze shifted to the horizon.

Sweat ran down Osterac's back under the heat of the suns. A raptor circled overhead. The rattle of armour and weapons and the tramp of marching feet were the only sounds as Lempar considered.

'Turn the men around. We return to Olcis,' said Lempar.

Osterac suppressed his surge of triumph.

'Have those wounds seen to, Resius,' said Lempar. 'Then you may join my entourage.'

'Yes, General.'

Shouted orders filled the air as he turned his weary mount in search of the Legion Druids. Across the long line, thousands of men stopped, then turned, marching back the way they had come.

He smiled. He was one step closer to the Emerald Throne. There was much to be done, but the day would arrive when only one person remained in his way.

Cedrin himself.

* * *

Faivel and his warriors had truly been in their element since entering Ranmyden. The warriors of the Thilil Eathal had led them swiftly through the green tangle of the forest to the ancient cavern entrance, but had refused to enter Ranmyden, leaving them to track Raziin alone. It hardly mattered. Here the teremb had come into her own, racing through the maze of melted ruins, shattered buildings and empty tunnels as she tracked the human Sorcerer and his men. The jakkund had also been more settled since they left the upper world.

Faivel had read extensively on the fallen Eathal realms, both Ranmyden and Mulisar. The ancient descriptions were of wondrous places of learning and civilisation. He knew Ranmyden far exceeded Maht in population, but seeing it firsthand was humbling. At the time of the Destruction, Maht must have seemed little more than a rustic backwater, at best a distant corner of the Eathal world. That very insignificance had saved it, allowing his ancestors to prepare for Carris' arrival. They had used the natural glowmetal defences of Maht well.

He understood why the Thilil Eathal did not enter Ranmyden. It was a dead place – the vast corpse of a fallen giant. The Eathal who lived in the ruins were tribal. Simple creatures who hid from their approach, fearing all outsiders – even their own kind. They were also few in number. The destruction of the great forests that once covered Exdor had gutted the cavern ecosystems. Now the few productive caverns were right up at the surface level, supported only by the remnants of vegetation that clung to the Ranmyden foothills. The exception was the deep cavern Faivel and his warriors found themselves in now. Here the walls and cavern floor glowed with lungii.

They knew from the sign and corpses left in Raziin's wake that both the Northman's force and that of the Cinanac heir were here in this cavern. As luck would have it, the two groups had been tearing at each other since entering Ranmyden. Together they would have comprised a formidable force. One beyond their ability to face. It seemed Cedrin and he shared a common enemy in Raziin.

'How are our supplies holding up, Arud?'

'The last of the jakka is gone, but we have plenty of fresh water,' said the Huntmaster. 'This cavern will supply plenty of meat.' In finding edible prey, their teremb had proved her worth ten times over.

'Good. Good,' said Faivel. They were well rested and had gained strength. Being here beneath the earth again had restored both the endurance and morale of his elite troops.

He had to take the Spear. That was his task. He had to seize it before either human Sorcerer could claim it. He would still complete his father's mission if he could, but killing Raziin no longer seemed important.

Faivel and his warriors advanced in silence, moving steadily down into the centre of the cavern. The scale of the destruction was less here, this deep place saved from its ferocity for some reason.

One of his lead scouts approached, his jakkund leaping

adroitly between piles of ancient masonry with little more than a whispered sound of movement. Behind him came the teremb, the muscles in the lean beast rippling as it smoothly swept over the terrain. Its handler followed, face flushed with success.

'Raziin and his men are camped below a great overhang of rock, my Lord. Perhaps one hundred and eighty warriors.' More than three times their number.

'Any other sign?' asked Arud.

'The local Eathal have noted our approach. They keep their distance. We saw another human, but he fled before we could identify him.'

'Did he make for Raziin's camp?'

'No, my Lord.' So Cedrin was also here, but cautious. He could use that to his advantage. In attack, all the advantages would be with his Eathal.

Another scout approached, his jakkund racing over the broken ground with little care for stealth. Faivel's harsh words of reproach died on his tongue as heard his report.

'My Lord. I have seen the Spear,' said the scout.

Faivel's heart leapt into a sprint. 'Tell me!'

'Deep inside the cavern is a wide plaza. There is another group of Eathal there. All bow to a human warrior who bears a spear with a glowing blade of golden metal. There is a bird-being there, larger than a lamel and capable of speech. One of the Great Spiders is also with them.'

A Tahistil. His father had recently made an alliance with the Web of Soreth in the Gimpessu jungle to the south. They had provided Tahistil warriors for their campaign against Raynor. To find one in this remote cavern was more than surprising. Although strange to find these creatures here, it was the bearer of the Spear and the Eathal who served him that concerned Faivel.

'How many Eathal are with the bearer?'

'There are around forty. Yet only twelve of these are warriors. They are armed with spears, but do not carry shields.'

Faivel closed his fist in triumph. Neither Raziin nor Cedrin had advanced to take the Spear. At last the odds were playing into his favour. If he could strike swiftly; he could win the powerful artefact for himself. Then he would turn to face both groups of human warriors with the power of the Spear of Carris at his command.

'Arud. Prepare the warriors.'

The Huntmaster's face split into a savage grin. 'With pleasure, my Lord.'

Along the line behind Faivel, his warriors secured their gear and levelled their long lances. Fifty of Maht's best, ready to fight in their element. The local Eathal warriors would break and flee rather than face them, Faivel was sure. The sight of them bearing down on them would inspire nothing but terror. The key would be to subdue the human bearer of the Spear before the magical artefact could be brought to bear against them. Faivel cleared his mind and opened the Window. He raised the Barrier then readied both the Matrix of Binding and the Final Matrix. In the first moments, he would hit the bearer with twin assaults. He would freeze the man in place while driving into his mind with the Final Matrix. Before he could counter, Faivel and his men would be on him.

The teremb and her handler and most of the scouts moved to the rear of the column. The scout who had found the Spear remained at his side, leading their advance with clear, concise instructions.

The jakkund troops advanced at a swift, ground-eating lope. The mounts were built and trained for exactly this type of terrain. Soon they had left the upper margins of the cavern and entered the main part of the ruined city. The great, shadowed walls of fallen temples grew around them amid the fallen heaps of lesser structures. Tumbled rock and dressed stone had been melted together as they fell, then cooled into bizarre shapes, like weird sculptures. It was a maze of ragged paths, each more like a natural canyon than a city street. Yet this place did not possess the same empty quality as the rest of Ranmyden. There was something else here.

Faivel saw movement on the roof of a broken temple. A local Eathal ducked out of sight. His scout and Arud had both noted the movement.

'A lookout,' said the scout.

'They know we are coming,' said Arud. 'We cannot count on the element of surprise any longer.'

Faivel absorbed the information. Part of him urged caution. In any other situation, he would have hung back and observed his quarry before committing to an attack. He could not afford that now. Not with so much at stake. He had to take the Spear before the humans. The fate of Maht now rested on him alone.

'The odds are still with us,' said Faivel.

Arud grunted in agreement. After all the leagues spent chasing Raziin, the Huntmaster and his men were eager to close on an enemy they understood. Even forewarned, twelve warriors were no match for even five jakkund lancers, let alone fifty. The one enemy who concerned Faivel was the bearer of the Spear. The outcome of this combat would hinge on his Sorcerous skills.

'Make straight for the Spear-bearer. Take him swiftly,' said Faivel.

'Yes, my Lord.'

The ruined heaps of buildings fell away and he and his troops emerged onto the wide plaza his scout had described. Up ahead, a ragged line of Eathal warriors had drawn up in front of a single man. Faivel's face stretched into a grin. The ground was perfect for his jakkund lancers. Off to the side of the plaza, he saw the shadowed forms of the Tahistil and another feathered figure. He dismissed them. The golden glow issuing from the Spear on the bearer's back intensified.

Faivel's heart burned with determination. 'Attack speed!'

Arud passed the command. Faivel hung on tight as the jakkund leapt into its jerky full-paced gait.

Time raced. One moment the defenders and his men watched each other across the dusty stone, the next the lines closed. The local Eathal did not run. They yelled harsh warcries and rushed to the attack with berserk fury. It was enough to slow their advance a few moments, but nothing more. All twelve defenders fell, cut down by the darkglass blades of the jakkund lancers.

Faivel drew heavily on the Fire. He unleashed the Matrix of Binding. He felt a surge of triumph as it gripped the human

305

warrior. A moment later, he unleashed his attack with the Final Matrix, pushing into the man's mind. For a moment, he felt it give way, then he struck a Barrier of such power it sent shockwaves of pain through his mind.

Faivel gasped. His grip on the Binding Matrix slipped. He tried to counter but never got the chance. His Barrier was ripped aside. His mouth opened in a soundless scream. Faivel's vision went red as streamers of pain swept through his head. His vision dimmed to black. He channelled everything he had into re-establishing his Barrier, but it was like chaff against the wind. Tendrils of blue stabbed into his mind, searching. His jakkund leapt. The skin of his fingers ripped as he lost his grip and slammed into the cold stone. A new pain flared in his shoulder like a savage sun. He teetered on the edge of consciousness. The power he had faced had been beyond anything he had known.

He felt the Fire rise. There was a detonation, then a stream of flame. Eathal warriors and jakkund cried in pain. Faivel's mind was filled with blue. He saw the shape as it came. His guts turned to water as he recognised it. *A Compulsion.*

Slowly his sight returned.

His shoulder screamed with pain. *Broken.* He looked up to see the Tahistil and the feathered being above him. He blinked. There was no mistaking the Verial now. He recognised it from ancient manuscripts. All credible sources had listed them as extinct.

'An ill-advised attack,' hissed the Tahistil in the Eathal tongue.

Faivel rolled onto his good side and pushed himself up to a sitting position. The plaza was littered with the crushed and burned corpses of his jakkund troops. Numb with shock, he counted them. Thirty-seven, including two scouts. He could not see the teremb or her handler. The rest had fled.

Beside him lay the body of Arud. The Huntmaster's powerful chest had been crushed like a lungii pod.

'No,' he moaned. It could not have ended like this.

The Spear-bearer was walking through ranks of his fallen Eathal warriors. The old man bent down and laid his hand on a still form. The fallen warrior was encased in a sheath of gold. A moment later he rose, whole, to join five others. The Matrix of Form.

'Do you want me to heal your shoulder?' asked the Verial in the Eathal tongue.

He turned and met the Verial's large, pale eyes. 'I can heal myself.'

Faivel reached for the Fire and found the Window as close as ever. He used the Matrix of Form to re-knit his shoulder. As the pain faded, he rose to his feet.

'So. Another Sorcerer trapped in the Ward's net,' said the Verial. 'I am Erioth.'

'You may call me Malann,' said the Tahistil.

'I . . . am Faivel. Second son of Hukum,' he said. 'Trapped?'

Verial's wings quivered. 'You are a guest of the Ward. You may use your powers, but the Compulsion will prevent you from leaving the plaza or working against the Ward. You are also bound to follow its commands.'

Faivel's head swam. After all this. After all the leagues spent chasing Raziin, working to save his people from the re-emergence of the Spear. This was how it ended.

'What now?' said Faivel.

'Now we wait. Both the Cinanac heir and his contender Raziin approach. It will end soon,' said Erioth.

The golden radiance issuing from the Spear dimmed. Around them, the more subdued light of the lungii plants grew to dominance again.

Faivel tensed as the Spear-bearer approached them.

As he drew closer, Faivel studied the powerful figure. He appeared to be an old human male, yet he moved with confidence and strength. He in turn looked Faivel over.

'I am sorry for your warriors,' said the Spear-bearer. This must be the Ward the Verial and Tahistil had spoken of.

'Why should the Ward care?' said Faivel bitterly, uncaring if he provoked the Spear's guardian.

The man smiled ruefully. 'The Ward does not care. Yet I am not the Ward. I am Belin.'

Faivel looked between Belin and the other two beings. 'I don't understand.'

The man laid a warm hand on his shoulder. 'There is much to explain. And little time.'

* * *

Ellen's neck ached as she looked up at the sheer cliff, searching for any sign of a path. The Daughters were spread out across the base, searching for an entrance. The scholar Valnis meandered past them, carrying a huge map. Every few paces he would look between the parchment and the rock wall, his face intent. He had been doing much the same thing for two days.

'This is hopeless. We should have turned back and retraced our steps days ago,' said Raphal.

Ellen rubbed her neck, trying to ease the stiff muscles. 'It's too late for that. Cedrin's trail is too cold. If Valnis is right, this shaft will take us straight to the Hall of Dreams.'

She felt her gorge rise and slid off the saddle. A moment later, her breakfast was lying on the ground. She swallowed the bitter taste of bile.

Raphal dismounted, hobbling his mount. He walked to her side. 'Anything I can do?'

'Argh,' she moaned in frustration, waving him away. She rinsed her mouth and spat. She had long given up trying to keep anything down in the morning, or battling the strange fog that filled her mind. At least the nausea eased once she had given way to the urge to empty her stomach.

She sat on the sparse grass and lay back, exhausted.

Far above them was the wide opening they had seen when they first arrived here. A yawning mouth where a swarm of bats emerged each evening and returned at dawn the next day. If they could fly with them, they would be in the Hall of Dreams by now. Raphal walked over to Valnis. Soon the two of them were bickering like an old married couple.

At the thought of Cedrin, she suppressed a feeling of panic. There was no point obsessing over unknowns. If only there was some way to come to his aid. Raziin had more than double his numbers. The thought of that murderous mercenary taking the Spear chilled her blood. With that sort of power, the Northman would undo everything they had fought for. A new terror would be unleashed in Kelas and their reborn Empire would die in its infancy.

Ellen laid a protective hand on her belly. Their child would be the heir. *My son.* A sheen of sweat broke out on her forehead. She took a cloth from her belt and dabbed at it.

A flash of movement above her drew her attention. There were many birds here in the Ranmyden foothills, but there was something odd about this one. It took her a while to realise why it seemed so odd. It was big, almost human sized. *A lamel.* She sat up, intent on the creature. It had found itself a perch high up on the cliff, near the wide opening. She gasped as it leapt off the ledge, its brilliant green wings flaring as it soared smoothly away from the grey basalt. It circled above her, gliding in wide circles as it dropped in height. As it drew closer, she could see red feathers under its wing, with highlights of blue in its tail.

Two of the Daughters had seen it and spurred their amelak towards her, waving their arms. They had all grown wary of the clever beasts on their way through Thilil.

Ellen leapt to her feet. 'No. Let it come!'

The two Daughters looked at each other in surprise, then ceased their efforts to ward off the lamel. Ellen felt foolish for a moment, then her intuition reasserted itself. There was something familiar about this creature.

Soon it circled directly over her. Its huge eyes were fixed on her with keen interest. Now she was even more certain. This was the lamel she had healed in the outpost at the Myfis Bridge. It sang to her. A swift series of notes. It was trying to tell her something, but its speech was meaningless to her.

She thought of using the Final Matrix to touch its mind, such as it was, but banished the thought instantly. She would not risk her son, not for anything.

Ellen turned to the two Daughters. 'Back away. I want to see if it will land.'

They followed her command without question.

The lamel eyed them warily for a moment then abruptly dropped down to the grass beside her. Ellen's heart thumped. She looked at the wickedly sharp beak and talons of its foreclaws and swallowed.

It sang to her and tilted its head to the side, as though waiting for a reply.

'We need to get up there,' said Ellen, pointing up at the huge cavern opening hundreds of feet above them.

It followed her arm, looking up at the high opening. The lamel blinked, its second eye membrane partially covering its big yellow eyes.

Ellen yelped as the lamel leapt into the air. The fast movement had startled her. It worked its wings, slowly gaining height, then it shot away. A moment later, it had dropped out of sight below a nearby hill.

'So much for that idea,' she whispered under her breath.

The two Daughters came over to her, bemused. Then Mendor arrived on his narsiit.

'I saw the lamel. Are you alright?' asked the Suulqua.

'Yes, Mendor. Fine.'

She walked back to her narsiit and pulled herself up into the saddle. Now that the nausea had eased, she felt light-headed, but her mind was clear.

Her narsiit danced to the side abruptly. A green shape darted past, fluting a melodious call. The lamel circled overhead then headed north-west. It stopped at the crest of a hill and circled, calling to her.

'Ha! I *was* right. Come on,' said Ellen.

The lamel was trying to show them something. If not for the years spent with Erioth, she might have missed it. The lamel was not a Verial, but it was still communicating with her.

She urged her narsiit up the slope. As soon as the lamel saw her following, it swept back to its north-west course. Mendor followed, as did the two Daughters. The Ranmyden foothills here were a continuous series of hills and valleys that could have hidden a legion. As soon as they crested the hill, their view of the base of the cliff and the others was cut off.

Twice more the lamel circled at the crest of hills, waiting for them to catch up. Finally they topped a rise to see a large flat valley with low grasses below them. It was dotted with pools. A faint trail of smoke rose from the surface of each, to be churned away to nothing by the wind. No. Not smoke. *Steam.*

'Thermal springs,' said Mendor.

There was something odd about the pools. As they set off down the slope into the valley, Ellen realised what it was. Each was either neatly square or rectangular.

When they reached the bottom of the slope and set out into the valley itself, Ellen realised why the grass was so short here. It was growing on a thin layer of soil that covered vast stone foundations. Soon she could see tumbled columns and other masonry, covered with soil and grass like the rest of the valley. When they passed the first of the pools, her suspicions were confirmed. It was stone-lined, yet so ancient that its sides were covered by soil and grass.

The lamel led them to the centre of the valley, where there was a break in the ground. At first it looked like a landslip or crevasse, perhaps following an earthquake. As they drew closer, she saw that it was way too regular in shape. The lamel climbed up into the sky, then dove down, straight at the opening. She gasped as the lamel shot into the hole and disappeared.

Mendor cursed. 'Where does that leave us?'

Ellen galloped over to the opening. Closer, she could see that it was a broad set of steps, wide enough to take thirty warriors riding abreast. It disappeared into darkness.

'Uros!' said Ellen. She turned her narsiit away from Mendor to give her room to think. She circled to the south-east. The rest of the Daughters, Valnis and Raphal were below the crest. She could still see the tall cliff and the opening. Ellen was watching the high cavern when a green shape shot from its dark mouth. It spun in the air and turned into a dive. The skin prickled on the back of her neck.

'Look!' called Ellen.

The shape grew until there was no longer any doubt. *It was the lamel.* Somehow it had come from this valley into the high cavern. It flashed past overhead, calling triumphantly. It circled once more then disappeared to the south.

She smiled, reassured her instincts were right. 'I consider the debt repaid,' she said softly.

'Beg pardon, my Lady?'

'Nothing, Mendor. Let's get back to the others. We have to tell them we have found the path.'

* * *

Ellen descended the steps into the valley entrance. She shivered as the cool dark closed around her.

'Torches,' she said. Two Daughters worked briskly with firestarter glowmetals. Four oil-soaked torches leapt into life. The shadows drew back to reveal a wide, well-made tunnel that cut directly south-east.

'Let's move,' said Ellen. Many side passages led off the main tunnel, but she ignored these. They were all narrow. The lamel had *flown* through here.

Her elation at finding the way into Ranmyden had waned quickly once she outlined her plans to Thenia. The stubborn young Suul had argued at length about the risk to Ellen in Ranmyden, proposing that she should go in Ellen's stead to support Cedrin since Ellen could not use her Sorcery. She wanted Ellen to return to Beslin, guarded like some prize breeding livestock by the Daughters. The young woman's ponderous logic was annoying in the extreme. Especially when she was right. Ellen had flatly refused to be swayed. Finally Thenia relented. Instead, she ordered all but two of the Daughters to follow and protect Ellen, while Thenia herself elected to return to Beslin to gather another force. She intended to return in strength to provide aid to them or oppose Raziin should he emerge victorious. They took as many supplies as they could carry on their backs, while a stockpile had been buried at the campsite as a backup. The rest would be taken south with Thenia and their string of empty mounts. There was no place for their narsiit or amelak in the caverns of Ranmyden. Serel and her two slaves travelled south with them.

The broad tunnel ended at the base of a steep circular stair cut from the native rock. They eagerly began the ascent. Valnis was soon puffing with exertion. Raphal fared little better. Some half an hour later, calves burning, they emerged onto a ledge inside the huge cavern opening. *We made it.*

The view was magnificent. The Ranmyden range and its foothills stretched out to the west, the peaks lost in snow and cloud.

Three ancient altars had been carved from the rock here. Closer to the edge of the platform were twelve columns, the roof that supported the small shrine long collapsed and rotted away. Valnis ran to the altars. He brushed off the dust and examined the carved glyphs, tracing each with a finger. 'Wondrous.'

'Very interesting, I'm sure. But what about finding the path to the Hall of Dreams?' asked Raphal.

'What do you think I am doing?' snapped Valnis.

Indignant, the scholar drew out the same large parchment that he had been scrutinising since they entered the foothills.

'This is the first of the Temples. There is a sacred path here. A pilgrim's walk called the Breath of the Mother. I should have seen it before. It began at the valley, in a precinct of Temples that once existed there. Of course! I mistranslated. Not "Place of Beginnings," the "Place of Births!"'

'So where now, Valnis?' said Ellen, trying to focus the scholar.

Valnis cleared his throat. He held up his map, studied it for a moment then looked down the dark tunnel behind them. 'There should be a series of Temples, all along the Breath of the Mother – a stair that descends all the way to the Hall of Dreams.'

'Come. There is no time to lose,' said Spider.

They walked into the dark opening, careful not to slip on the ancient layer of bat guano. They found a wide path that climbed to the right side of the wide tunnel opening. It took them deep into the mountain, then sloped downward. The gloom of Ranmyden swallowed them. The tunnel was a steep chute, cutting down straight to the heart of the mountain range. Ellen could see why the ancient Eathal had thought it sacred. Soon the rock around them became crowded with the strange, luminescent plant life of the caverns.

An hour later, they came to another temple. It was intact, but deserted.

'Carris never walked here,' said Valnis in wonder. The old scholar was torn that he could not stop to examine their finds in more detail.

'On our return journey, I promise you,' said Ellen.

He nodded in resignation, and they continued downward. The hours weighed on them, but Ellen refused to give in to her fatigue. Like her, Spider and the Daughters were tight-lipped with determination. They had been kept out of this fight for too long. Raphal and Valnis were in a fever of excitement, drawn forward by each new discovery, and the promise of reaching the Hall of Dreams and the Temple of the Iris.

They had passed the eleventh Temple along the steep stair when the path levelled. It seemed they had been walking forever. Her legs burned, her mouth parched from lack of water. The darkness and silence had combined to put her into a trance as they plodded on.

Then the walls and ceiling of the tunnel, a heavy weight on her shoulders for so long, lifted away. They opened out into a vast space sprinkled with the lights of thousands of individual lungii plants. Ellen gasped in wonder. Her stomach fluttered with the sense of how alien this was. As though they had entered another world.

'Extinguish the torches,' hissed Spider.

They felt their way through the darkness, creeping along a wide ledge.

There was a whispered command to stop, then Spider's voice in her ear. 'Come.'

Spider's calloused hand closed on her arm and drew her forward. Raphal and Valnis shuffled along with her.

'This is the edge,' whispered Spider.

She looked down. Below, there was a wide open square. She could see a man walking across that open space. Her stomach clenched as she recognised him. It was Belin. No. *The Ward*. On his back, the Spear of Carris shed a golden glow that illuminated the stone for a dozen paces around him. She searched the darkness, looking for Erioth, but she could make nothing else out. There were other shadowed figures down there, but they were impossible to see. She gritted her teeth in frustration at not being able to use the Fire.

'Now what?' asked Spider.

Ellen looked into the darkness below. 'Raphal. Is there any way to see more?'

'This is a powerful place,' said Raphal. 'The Earth Essence has been growing stronger since we entered the tunnel.'

Raphal laid a hand on her brow and whispered under his breath. Her vision shifted. What had been dark was now outlined in golden light. She could see many figures on the square below. She bit her lip as she recognised Erioth beside a Great Spider. *Just as I saw it that night in Searn.* There were Eathal there as well. She was about to ask Raphal what he could see when a large group of men emerged from the darkness on the other side of the Hall of Dreams. They were warriors, equipped with greatscythes.

She gripped Raphal's arm as she recognised the man who led them.

Cedrin.

Chapter Twenty

Daran walked the walls under light of the moons. Rea was high overhead in its first quarter, while Asic dawned full on the eastern horizon. He kept his back straight, his head high. Dressed in his simple warrior's gear and plain mought armour, he was a living symbol. The undefeated Warlord. Uran walked at his side, his bodyguard and aides following. Trebuchets, catapults and ballistae lined the walls, all pointing east. Dotted between them were their four offensive glowmetals – one of them captured from the Eathal. Raynor once boasted dozens. Over the centuries, they had been taken to Olcis by the Temple.

'Give a cheer for the Warlord, lads!' called a Second Captain as he passed.

A thunderous cheer echoed across the parapet. Daran lifted his hands and smiled, accepting their accolades. Fresh from their victories on the field, the morale of his men was high. Up on the massive walls of Raynor, it was easy to believe that nothing could touch you. They would need all their courage before the night was through.

'The Tickler is ready, my Lord!' called the Razor manning one of the glowmetals. The warrior patted the twisted bulk of gold and violet light. Like their other defensive glowmetals, it was set into a specially designed carriage, allowing them to turn it and adjust its elevation. Nacius stood by it, ready to use his Fire to recharge it. The young Sorcerer had grown taller over the last year. His nervous manner was gone, replaced by a quiet dignity. He had been tested in combat and shown himself courageous and resourceful. Daran nodded a greeting, and

Nacius bowed in response.

He led his entourage up to the top of a wall tower in the centre of the eastern wall. The position would give him an excellent view of the battle as it unfolded and was strategically positioned near his most powerful offensive glowmetals. His signalmen were already here, ready to relay his commands across the city with a series of horn blasts. There was no question of him taking to the field with his men tonight. The defence of the city was too complex an undertaking to tie himself to a single aspect of the combat. Tonight he had to focus on strategy alone.

Daran walked to edge of the wall and leant against a merlon, looking out through the crenel. Across the eastern horizon, a dark mass moved towards them under the moons. Any human force would glitter with the light of torches and lamps as they advanced, but not this one. The Eathal were in their element, the light of the moons like noonday sunshine to their cavern-dweller's eyes. If only Raynor had an offensive glowmetal that released light. *That* would be an effective weapon.

Below the walls, the Outer City stretched all the way to the Asgod River. This was his first defensive line. The forward command post was at the Suul docks on the western bank, which was protected by its own garrison wall. Across the river, the sprawling Docks District was deserted. The ships that usually lined the quays had sailed to Athria or ports further north along the western coast of Kelas. Even though the Docks were the beating heart of Raynor commerce, they were indefensible. They had been destroyed before, and rebuilt. He was young then and energetic, ready to restore Raynor's greatness. His heart burned with frustration. If they survived this siege, he would have to start again in Raynor. He ground his teeth together. He at least intended to profit from their destruction. He had ordered his men to clear wide paths through the mostly wooden structures of the Docks District, but to leave others intact. He intended it to look as though he had begun to clear the area, but ran out of time. The paths he left would serve a dual purpose. They would bring the advancing Eathal into the line-of-fire of his weapons and put them into the heart of a firetrap. Then, if they managed to cross the river, another surprise waited for them. The floating city – hundreds of hulks that were usually moored near the joining of the Yasser and Asgod – had been ferried up the Asgod and set in the middle of the river. Each was a tinderbox waiting to ignite.

Seven drawbridges arched high over the Asgod, joining Raynor and the Outer City with the Docks District on the eastern bank. Vast and elegant, their pale mought blocks glowed under the moonlight. Three had their central spans neatly drawn up. On another, fires still burned on the remnants of the heavy wooden beams that had replaced the original drawbridge. The other three had long fallen into disrepair. Whole sections would tumble away without warning. Even so, they had been used, travellers paying a low price for the trip across the Asgod, braving the wooden rails that spanned the gaps. Daran had ordered their central spans destroyed. It had pained him to see those ancient blocks tumble into the river below, but he could not allow the Eathal easy passage.

Despite his best efforts, Hukum was here. All his strategy, the months of careful probing attacks and his intricately planned field engagements had failed to stop the Sundar. Three Eathal legions advanced to face them, the Yellow Drakon, the Silver and the Black Drakon – Hukum's own legion. He had never managed to test the strength of the Black, or gain any knowledge of the Wallbreakers, the massive glowmetals that Hukum carried with him. Daran's success had always relied on knowing his enemy. It was no accident he had never been defeated in the field. Because of his meticulous preparations, the outcome of his engagements were almost certain before the first spear was cast. Now, for the first time, he faced an enemy of unknown strength.

Daran looked up into the sky and grimaced. The loss of the Raptor had been a hard blow. He and Uran had counted on being able to harass the Eathal as they approached, and during the siege.

Uran joined him. 'So it begins.'

Daran turned to his friend. Uran was better rested than he had seen him in months. These few days in Raynor had done much to restore him. He would need that strength. 'We have equal forces, at least conventionally. And we have Raynor's walls.'

'If not for the Wallbreakers and the Sorcerer-Lords, we could laugh at the threat,' said Uran.

Everything would depend on their ability to neutralise Hukum's magical attacks. If they could do that, they would have a chance. Ideally, Daran would have left a Legion in the field to break Hukum's supply lines and harass him from the rear, but he had been forced to bring all his forces across the Asgod. He had to assume the Eathal would eventually win the western bank. At best, this would become a drawn-out siege. Then their own supply would be an issue.

The wealthier population of the Outer City had been harder to shift than the Docks dwellers. Most had left for the cities of the Delta province, but many others remained, stubbornly defending their houses. They would come to rue their decision. He had sent the remnants of the shattered Fourth Legion west with the refugees with orders to take in new recruits from the Delta province. His wife, his sons and the Raynor cavalry were with them. Should Raynor fall, they would be the last line of defence. His eldest son would take the title of Warlord of the Yasser States should he fall here. Sisters' help him if it came to that.

There were no more preparations to undertake, no more strategies. Now history would unfold.

Uran leaned forward against the parapet. From his intent expression, Daran guessed he was using Sorcery to enhance his sight.

'What do you see?' asked Daran.

Uran's hand gripped the merlon as he leant forward. 'He is leading with them.' His voice was harsh with tension.

The Wallbreakers.

Daran waved to one of his aides. 'The lenstube.'

He put the tiny lens to his eye and looked out through the instrument. The cunning combination of lenses was a recent innovation of a Raynor glassmith and was useful in the field. The contraption suffered from limitations though. Magically enhanced sight could compensate for lack of light, the lenstube could not. Sometimes it was worth it though, just to be able to see things with his own eyes.

Daran hissed with frustration. He could see Hukum's advancing force and a line of vague-coloured shapes in the midst of Eathal line, but little more.

Daran put down the lenstube and turned to the Sorcerer. 'Tell me what you see.'

The Sorcerer's lips moved soundlessly. 'Nine,' he said finally.

Daran's heart skipped a beat. They had sacrificed hundreds of men just to discover what the offensive glowmetals of the lead Eathal legions had been capable of. For all that, they only knew the nature of the glowmetals of the Blood, Yellow Drakon and Green Drakon legions. Three glowmetals.

'So six new glowmetals. Three of these we know of already?' asked Daran.

Uran shook is head. 'No. These are all new. The others must be in reserve, behind Hukum's forces.'

Daran restrained his urge to rail at the Sorcerer. He needed to appear calm in front of his men. 'Give me your report.'

Uran nodded. 'The Black is leading in the centre. Yellow and Silver on the left and right flanks. Hukum has most of his glowmetals in the van.'

Daran considered this. Usually the glowmetals were positioned in the centre, where they could be defended. That meant they were offensive, and that Hukum meant to use them at the outset.

'The two glowmetals at the fore are iron and silver. Five are arrayed behind them, the largest of them copper. One glowmetal is positioned inside the main body of the force . . . Silver and green. Zinc. Another is being held back at the rear. Strange. A variegated metal with a bright yellow light . . . Ah. Arsenic.'

Daran lifted the lenstube. He could make out some of the colours. The van of Hukum's Black had reached the eastern edge of the Docks District. His shoulders tensed as he waited to see if Hukum would advance down the wide alleys he had prepared. The dark mass of the approaching Eathal halted at the edge of the Docks District. They stood in neat rows under the light of the moons, displaying an infuriating degree of discipline.

'They have stopped,' said Uran.

Daran's hands shook, making his magnified vision jerk. He rested his elbows on the crenel.

Light blossomed. There was a crackling discharge that snapped through the air like a whip. A moment later, a sheet of blue flame hundreds of paces wide cut through the Docks District. Then came another, and another.

'It's the iron glowmetal,' said Uran.

The sound of crashing timber and masonry reached them from across the river. Buildings collapsed across the riverfront, cut to the ground by the iron glowmetal.

'He is clearing his own path,' said the General of the Third. It had been the task of his men to prepare the trap in the Docks. It was the Third, the newest recruits, who manned the walls. The First and Second, his only true fighting men, waited in reserve with their Generals.

'This is what must have happened to Hianer,' said one of Daran's aides, his voice hushed with awe. The fallen capital of Hend had been constructed of wood. Its fall to the Eathal legions had been brief and bloody.

After a time, the iron glowmetal ceased its scything attack. A loud crash echoed from the walls as a new attack began. Debris flew out across the river. Some heavy beams and pieces of brick even reached the Outer City.

'It's the silver glowmetal. A ram of Force,' said Uran.

They had come across offensive Force glowmetals before, yet nothing like this. This was more powerful than anything they could have conceived of. Vast tunnels were punched through the already tumbled buildings, shooting the debris out into the Asgod. Holes were punched through the hulls of the anchored hulks. They bobbed and jerked like toys, then settled into the water. Daran's fists clenched. The brick and stone sank out of sight and the smaller pieces of wood were swept away by the flow. The river soon became choked with heavy beams and whole sections of shattered warehouses. The attacks of the glowmetal were being carefully aimed so that the debris was all pushed to the same part of the Asgod. His stomach sank with the realisation of what Hukum was doing.

'Should I give the signal to fire the Docks, my Lord?' asked his senior aide. The plan had been for a Moon Druid in the Suul docks to set the fire that would engulf the Docks in a massive conflagration of pitch, oil and wood. Yet Hukum's forces remained outside the District, making the move meaningless. But if he did not trigger the flames soon, there would be nothing left to burn. Perhaps it would at least delay Hukum. Either way, he had to act fast.

'Give the signal,' commanded Daran. A horn rang out a series of short and long blasts. Another horn repeated the signal in the Outer City below the wall, then another at the Suul docks.

Daran bit his lip in frustration as the Eathal glowmetal continued to punch paths through the Docks. Even though he had planned to sacrifice it, to see the whole district levelled so easily was disturbing. So far only two of the nine new Eathal glowmetals had spoken.

Three balls of green fire arched up from the Suul docks. Precisely aimed bolts that struck the pitch-soaked buildings on either side of the prepared alleys. The wooden warehouses and ramshackle buildings leapt into flame. Hidden ditches in the alleys, filled with fire oil, roared to life. Walls of fire raged above the whole Docks District. The angry yellow flames belched dark, oily smoke.

'Perhaps that will win us an hour or two,' said Daran.

Men cheered from the walls. Daran forced a smile and turned to wave at them. It felt good to have taken some sort of action against the invader.

Then came another pulse of Force from the glowmetal. It sent a burning wall of debris flying out across the river. The heavier brick and stone sank almost immediately, but the burning wood reached the opposite bank. Daran felt his stomach flip as he realised what he had done. One hulk that had not sunk leapt into flame in the middle of the river.

The pounding continued without a pause. Soon flames had taken root on the eastern bank, and the Outer City began to burn. The attack on the Docks District was relentless. An hour later, the flames on the eastern bank had died down to almost nothing. There was nothing left to burn in that empty wasteland. The fires in the Outer City spread slowly through the mostly stone structures. Daran thought he had been prepared to see his city in flames. He was wrong. The sight tore at him.

The Asgod boiled around the rubble, topping both its eastern and western banks. Great heaps of material broke the surface of the river like stepping-stones.

'By the Sisters. He means to bridge it,' said one his aides. Daran had hoped for a day – perhaps two – while Hukum moved his forces across the river. He would not get that.

Asic was high overhead by the time the destruction of the Docks District was complete. Now Hukum came forward through the smoking ruins with his entire force.

At last Hukum was coming into range of Daran's weapons. He intended to make it count. Another hour passed in tense silence while the three Eathal legions arrayed themselves across the ruins of the western bank. Even if Hukum completed his bridge, he would still be vulnerable to their attacks for hours while he struggled to bring his massive force across the Asgod. Daran had arranged the glowmetals and weaponry on Raynor's walls to concentrate their fire on the Docks District and the Outer City to the east. Hukum was advancing directly into his strongest position. Forward elements of Hukum's force, indistinct in the gloom, were descending to the river bank where the debris from the Docks had created a rough ford.

Daran lowered the lenstube. 'Signal the forward command to start their bombardment.'

Horns rang out across the city as the command was relayed.

Daran watched in eager expectation as a series of dark shapes took flight from the walls of the Suul docks. The trebuchets and catapults there unloaded a deadly rain of stone. The missiles arced high over the river then halted in midair. An unseen barrier flared to blue brilliance for a moment, then the missiles tumbled back into the river.

Daran lifted the lenstube, almost dislodging the lenses in his haste. He watched another volley arc across the river, this time striking at a point to the south. Once more they hit the unseen Shield. The barrier was huge. A sphere of Force that covered an area thousands of paces wide. As he watched, a third volley struck at a point to the north. Only one missile found its mark, hitting the edge of the Yellow Drakon's lines.

'*What is it?*' Daran heard the tremor in his own voice.

'It's a defensive glowmetal. Covering their whole attacking force.'

'Force only?' snapped Daran.

Uran paused to concentrate for a moment. 'I've commanded Nacius to unleash the Tickler.' Daran knew that Uran could communicate mentally with his apprentice over any distance.

A jagged fork of yellow lightning stabbed across the river from the wall below the tower. It passed through the Shield and hit the ranks of the Black. Around thirty Eathal were engulfed in its white flame.

'Unleash all the glowmetals,' commanded Daran. Horns rang out.

Firebolt, a silver glowmetal positioned to the north along the wall, belched out a purple and green comet of ghostly fire. It arced into the air then settled slowly down onto the ranks of the Black. A chorus of hideous screams echoed across the water.

Then Hurler and the captured Screaming Spear discharged. Hurler's projectile – a titanic mought block – hit the Eathal Shield with a high note and discharge of blue light. It tumbled towards the river, hitting the Shield twice more on its way down. The bolt of Force from Screaming Spear – released with the loud, eerie wailing that gave the glowmetal its name – hit the Shield with a nothing more than a ripple of blue light.

A whirlwind of panic ripped through Daran's mind. They had spent weeks setting up the war machines, carefully training the crews and calibrating their aim so that they would deliver the maximum damage to Hukum's forces on the western bank. Now, in one moment, his whole strategy had been overturned. Daran's aides watched him, waiting for orders. He bent his mind to the problem with sheer force of will.

'Turn all the missile weapons including Hurler. Concentrate their fire on the Outer City between us and the river. We will have to hit them as they cross,' commanded Daran.

His aides paused for a moment. They all knew how hard it was to turn the huge weapons. Orders were given nonetheless and runners dispatched.

'See how well defended the Eathal glowmetals are,' commanded Daran.

The Tickler and Firebolt unleashed their fire on the forward glowmetals across the river. The Tickler's lightning and the ghostly fire of the Firebolt both met Sorcerous Shields.

'I thought as much,' said Uran.

'Keep the Tickler and Firebolt focussed on the forward elements of the Black,' said Daran. 'Contest the crossing.'

'What about Screaming Spear, my Lord?'

'Move Screaming Spear to the inside of the main gates,' said Daran. His aides looked at each other but said nothing. Daran was as much as telling them the gates would be breached before dawn.

'General. Time for you to rejoin the Third,' said Daran. The General nodded and left the tower for the battlements.

Daran's heart was pumping hard. His head was ready to burst apart with the pressure inside his skull.

He heard the shouts of a crane crew to the south and watched as the beam of the machine moved slowly to a halt above Screaming Spear. Ropes dropped and the crew moved into action. The walls swarmed with activity as the men of the Third worked to turn the war machines. Their aim would be poor, but each missile delivered into Hukum's packed ranks should count. They would have a narrow window.

'What is that down by the river?' asked one of his First Captains.

Daran focussed his lenstube with a twist. Dark shapes leapt from the eastern bank. They sprang between the heaps of debris, leaping all the way to the western bank and back again. He could see missiles from the Suul docks arcing down into the river, but the enemy was moving too fast.

'I can't make it out. Uran?'

The Sorcerer stared open-mouthed at the river.

'Uran!'

'Apologies, my Lord. I . . . thought them a legend. Tahistil. Hundreds of them. They are weaving a bridge across the river.'

Tahistil. Great Spiders. The world tilted. Everything was slipping out of his control.

'What are they doing?'

'They are building a bridge between the piles of debris, weaving with spider-silk. I have read of web bridges in antiquity. One spanned the Yasser near the Narrows – before Carris.'

'Can they burn?' demanded Daran.

'Y . . . yes. They should,' said Uran.

They were lit by the Tickler's discharge as it spoke again, stabbing its fire deep into the ranks of the Black. Firebolt followed a moment later, colouring the faces of his men in ghastly green. For a moment he considered using Tickler and Firebolt against the spiders, then dismissed the idea. They were moving too fast. The glowmetals would do more damage in the Eathal's packed ranks.

'Tell the forward command post to switch to fire missiles. Burn that bridge.'

'Yes, my Lord.' Horns echoed. Daran was conscious of the silence on the walls. There was no cheering now.

Soon barrels of burning pitch and clay mortars, filled with fire oil, dropped onto the Eathal bridge. Some missiles fell out of sight into the river, others hit the newly-woven web and immediately burned through it to the river. Only the missiles that struck the piles of debris themselves burst into sustained flame.

'Uran. Keep watch on the glowmetal in the centre of the Black. Tell me if it gets closer to the river,' said Daran. 'Send missile fire at the edges of the Eathal Shield. We need to know where it is at all times. Fire around it.'

Perhaps one third of the woven bridge was on fire. There was enough light that Daran could see the huge forms of the Tahistil for himself. They were big. He could understand why Uran had hesitated. The instinctive fear they produced was difficult to overcome.

'Tell all the ballistae crews to concentrate their fire on the

Tahistil,' said Daran. The giant crossbows would have more luck with the fast moving targets.

The flames in the Outer City were spreading. His one consolation was that they would hinder Hukum's advance.

The ballistae crews swung into action. Dark shafts shot at the web bridge. At first they slipped past into the water below. Then one of the Great Spiders was impaled, tumbling into the Asgod. Men cheered across the walls, but more subdued than before.

Daran considered his options. Sooner or later Hukum would get his forces across the water. If his defensive glowmetal stayed in the centre of the Black, then half his legion would be outside of its influence before he could bring it over the Asgod. That was the time to strike hard. The repositioned trebuchets and catapults would not be enough.

'Send a command to the Generals of the First and Second. Tell them to get the Legions ready for an assault outside the eastern gates.'

'Yes, my Lord,' said his aide, passing the command.

He was in uncharted territory here. In a conventional siege, he would never risk his men outside the safety of the walls, but in a conventional siege he would be able to continually assault his foe from the walls. Once Hukum crossed with his full force, his defensive glowmetal would make him invulnerable to anything but Sorcerous attacks. He had seen the power of that glowmetal that levelled the Docks District. Even the huge mought-reinforced gates of Raynor would not stand against it for long. His worst fears were being realised. Hukum would be inside the city within hours.

'My Lord. A new glowmetal is coming forward,' said Uran.

Daran swivelled his lenstube.

'Tin. Do you see it? Silver metal and white light,' said Uran.

Like all the others it was a monster, on its own specially designed wagon drawn by a team of twenty jakka. Two Sorcerer-Lords channelled Force into the bulky glowmetal. Daran's stomach tensed as the bands of white light rapidly contracted. The thing was absorbing power. They continued to work it as it came forward to the eastern bank. Slowly it turned.

Then it was in position.

A silver comet of directed Force streaked across the river. It hit the Suul docks with a thunderous concussion. Dust blew up from the bank below them and a tremor passed through the battlements. When the dust cleared, a large section of the Suul docks – perhaps seventy paces wide – was gone. Three war machines lay in the rubble, nothing but tangled debris. Fire leapt up from the fallen mess, burning inside the forward command post. Their attack on the web bridge continued despite the damage.

Uran gathered his power and shot a bolt of Force across the river at the tin glowmetal. The magical missile disappeared into the bulk of the glowmetal as though nothing had happened. The golden-skinned Sorcerer cursed and let loose a bolt of Fire instead. It flared out across the river, roaring uselessly against the combined Shield of the two Sorcerers. The bands of white light thinned again as the glowmetal absorbed their power.

Another silver comet shot across the water. It slammed into another section of Suul docks, right were the war machines hurled fire at the web bridge.

'Stop it! Use the other glowmetals,' commanded Daran.

The Tickler and Firebolt were directed at the tin glowmetal. Their attacks met the Sorcerous Shield. A pain stabbed into Daran's left temple as he watched the Eathal glowmetal prepare for another attack. He was powerless to stop it.

Once more the Suul docks were hit. There was a groan of grinding stone. A whole section of the river wall gave way. It tumbled down into the Asgod. No more missiles arced across the river at the web bridge. They had been silenced. The fire that had started after the first strike now roared higher as it found their stocks of fire missiles. Men ran for their lives. A moment later a stunning explosion lit the darkness. A mushroom of cloud and flame billowed above the ruined docks. The sudden light lit the banks, showing a scene of utter devastation.

Daran turned his lenstube towards the river. The Tahistil had repaired all the damage to the web bridge. All the fires were out. As he watched, the platform grew thicker, covering the river like a grey blanket, strung high above the flow. The Tahistil had used the piles of rubble as anchors. He had seen enough. He lowered the lenstube and turned to Uran.

'It's time. You will need to join the First and Second to shield them as they meet Hukum's forces. Take all the Druidin you can muster. This will be our one chance. Remain with the Legions.'

They gripped forearms, Uran laying his other hand atop Daran's. 'We will make them pay for every step.'

Uran bowed formally and left the tower.

Daran swallowed, his throat dry. He had been forced to watch for hours while all his careful preparations had been rendered useless by Hukum's glowmetals. He longed to *do* something, yet nothing remained but to watch his men die.

He turned to the east and strengthened his resolve.

'Tell the First and Second to take position in the Outer City. They are to remain under cover until I give the command.'

The Tickler and Firebolt continued to discharge. They had accounted for perhaps two or three hundred Eathal dead while twenty-five thousand waited to cross.

The ballistae crews continued their attacks on the Tahistil. Many of the giant spiders had fallen, but the rest continued to work on strengthening the bridge. It might seem a waste of the precious ballistae bolts now that the bridge was already built, but he did not want those spiders free to attack his lines. They would cause panic.

Daran cursed in frustration as the Black marched down to the riverbank and swarmed across the web bridge. The Tahistil had created a wide crossing. The Eathal moved across in ranks two hundred wide.

'Shall I signal the First and Second to attack, my Lord?' asked an aide. The man should have known better than to pre-empt his commands, but Daran could forgive him. He felt the tension himself, the urge to attack, but the moment had to be right.

'Not yet. If we bring the troops forward before the Black reach the bank we will come under attack from Hukum's glowmetals,' said Daran.

'Of course,' said the aide, chastened.

The Black began their march up from the bank into the Outer City. Daran let out a breath he had not been aware that he was holding. They were now in direct line-of-sight of Hukum's offensive glowmetals. The Sundar could not attack Raynor's forces without first going through his own.

'Signal the attack. Close quarters.'

Horns echoed. The warcries of the First and Second filled the night as they surged through the Outer City. The lines met with a crash of shields. The air above the two forces lit with Sorcerous Fire and the silver flash of Shields.

Daran leant forward, eyes wide as he waited for the initial outcome. He laughed out loud as he saw Uran and his Druidin were holding the attacks of the Sorcerer Lords. At last a fight on equal terms.

He swung the lenstube across the Outer City. Almost half the Black were across. Now was the time.

'Begin the bombardment,' commanded Daran. 'Tell the crews to concentrate their fire on the western side of the bridge.'

The Tickler and Firebolt continued their attacks on the eastern bank. Daran ground his teeth together as he searched the lines. Where are you Hukum?

The Hurler tossed a huge block of stone over the Outer City. The stone dropped right into the centre of the web bridge, ripping through the woven platform as though it was tissue. Hundreds of Eathal tumbled into the dark water below as the platform rippled. Tahistil scuttled forward to repair the damage.

Fire barrels and boulders flew from the eastern wall, dropping down onto the packed ranks of the Black as they struggled up from the western bank.

'Yes!' Daran pounded the stone of the merlon with his closed fist.

The Hurler released again, sending a block of red mought arcing down towards the bridge. This time there was a discharge of blue as it struck the Shield of Hukum's defensive glowmetal. Even though he had been expecting it, Daran's heart tore with disappointment. More than half the Black had crossed now, and the defensive glowmetal was being drawn inexorably closer to the eastern bank. Soon they would be across. The ballistae crews turned their fire onto the western bank, realising the Tahistil were now protected by the Shield.

'Signal the First and Second to push forward!' commanded

Daran. He had to stop the glowmetals from crossing. The only way to do that was to push the Eathal warriors back to the river, choking the bridge.

Horn blasts echoed across Raynor. Men cheered as they recognised the signal to advance.

The First and Second pushed into the Black with redoubled fury. The Eathal line retreated, then strengthened again. Incredibly, they held his forces. These were the Eathal elite. The Sundar's own legion. Even the spears of the phalanx could not break them. The Eathal dead were dragged into the side streets of the outer city and others took their place. The very nature of the city was working against him. On an open field he would have been able to contain the Eathal, here the maze of alleyways, streets and squares was giving the Eathal too many options.

The rain of missiles continued. The Black were taking heavy damage. Even so, time was running out.

Daran watched, powerless, as the defensive glowmetal crossed the web bridge and reached the western bank. Then came the Wallbreakers. Only the arsenic glowmetal remained behind, well at the rear of the Eathal forces on the eastern bank. Its size indicted substantial power, yet Hukum had left it behind.

It was noticeable now. More and more of their missiles were hitting the Shield. So far, they fell back onto the ranks of the Black, but soon they would be dropping down onto the First and Second.

Daran looked back across the river. The Yellow and Silver were preparing to cross now. *Unprotected by Hukum's Shield.*

'Tell the Hurler to fire across the bank. Aim high,' said Daran. An aide ran down the steps to relay the message.

A block of stone arced over the Asgod. It sailed over the Black and dropped down on the eastern bank, straight into the massed ranks of the Yellow Drakon.

'Send runners to turn the war machines back towards the eastern bank,' commanded Daran.

The bombardment of the Outer City ceased as the machines turned.

Below, the Black and the Raynor Legions were head to head.

Losses were high on both sides. The Wallbreakers had crossed the Asgod and the teams of jakka were pulling them up the bank. The ranks of the Black parted to let them through. At the front, he saw the tin glowmetal with its distinctive white light. Its powerful Force bolt would destroy his troops.

'Signal the retreat. Get them back inside the gates.' The men on the walls watched in silence as the First and Second retreated in good order.

The Hurler cast again, the huge projectile crushing a group of jakkund cavalry waiting at the rear of the Silver. Riderless jakkund ran in panic.

'Start the bombardment of the eastern bank as soon as the machines come to bear,' said Daran.

Daran did not need the lenstube now. The Black and the forward elements of the Yellow swarmed through the Outer City. His heart hammered as he watched the inexorable progress of the Wallbreakers through the Eathal ranks.

Once the fighting was inside the city, he would fall back to the first defensive line he had created inside the walls. He realised then he had never truly expected to use it. Had he truly thought he could win this? When did he begin to believe his own legend?

The trebuchets and catapults loosed their loads. Back on their original alignment, they were even more accurate. He watched in grim satisfaction as the rearguards of the Yellow and the Silver legion took heavy damage. One strike hit the Yellow's standard-bearer, provoking a chorus of cheers from the trebuchet crew. A lucky hit. They had perhaps quarter of an hour before the last of the Eathal crossed the Asgod and his wall-mounted war machines were effectively removed from the fight. The Tickler and Firebolt continued their attacks on the Black, but the Wallbreakers and the defensive glowmetals were protected by Sorcerous Shields as before.

The Eathal now had command of the Outer City.

The warriors of the Black – protected by Hukum's defensive glowmetal – stood in neat rows as the Wallbreakers were halted in front of Raynor's eastern gate.

Daran looked up to see Asic high in the sky. He would never

have believed Hukum could have come so far so quickly.

He expected the tin glowmetal that had loosed such devastating Force bolts against the Suul docks to attack the gates, but instead a new glowmetal was brought forward. It was a copper glowmetal – a rough pyramid of red metal with hardly a wisp of green light showing. It was already fully charged. As it came forward, he saw it was surrounded by Eathal Druids in dark cloaks, dragging a naked man between them. Their strange, low chant rose through the air. The men on the walls watched in silence as the glowmetal was stopped at the gate and a bruised and bloodied man was dragged to the top of the glowmetal. A blade cut into his chest. As they watched, the last of the green light disappeared from the huge glowmetal. The dark-robed Eathal Druids ran back the way they had come.

Commands were barked out on the harsh Eathal tongue and the front ranks of the Black drew smoothly back. The jakka hitched to the glowmetal's wagon bellowed in panic as they were abandoned.

Larus! Even as he saw the danger, it was too late.

'Get the men away from the gate. Get them back!'

A vibration came through the stone beneath his feet. His teeth ached, and a sharp pain stabbed into both his ears.

The air filled with screams. Men on the battlements above the gate, and behind it, howled in agony. They dropped to the ground. Others ran in panic, blood streaming from their ears and nose.

Daran's vision blurred as the vibration reached a crescendo. The jakka screamed in pain then grew silent, falling dead in their traces. His stomach twisted in nausea, and he staggered forward against the merlon.

As he watched, the mought bracing on the towering eastern gate just *dissolved*. It fell like dust. The walls around the gate began to sag. At first he though the foundations had been undermined, but then the whole gatehouse structure disintegrated. Where a proud wall had stood – huge mought blocks of tough ceramic – was a circular pile of sand swirling with red tint. The wooden gate stood for a long moment, unsupported, then fell back inside the city. A tremor passed through the tower beneath Daran, then a low grinding noise as the blocks ground against each other. He heard the distinctive wailing of the Screaming Spear, but he could see nothing.

'The tower is no longer safe, my Lord,' said his senior aide.

'Fall back,' commanded Daran. 'Get everyone off the east wall and back to the first defensive line.' Horns blew, repeating the same command over and over. Men ran. It seemed he was the only one not in motion, but he had to see Hukum's next move.

Another Wallbreaker was brought forward. He paused for long enough to see it was an iron glowmetal that had not been used before. The earth shook as a tremor raced through the stone. The ground shook beneath the fallen eastern gate – an earthquake – yet focussed only in that area. The walls to either side tumbled to the ground, widening the gap, while the huge pile of sand flattened out.

The tower tilted dangerously. The merlon in front of him tumbled away into space. He fell forward and for a long moment hung over the long drop. A hand grabbed his belt and drew him back. One of his commanders had saved him.

'We must get off the tower, my Lord.'

Daran pushed himself into motion. He and his aides joined a mad rush of men from the Third, all trying to get off the walls. Nacius joined them. Behind were the Moon Druidin who had been manning the Firebolt. Both glowmetals were lost to them.

A section of wall to the south lifted up off the ground then dropped with slamming detonation. It teetered for a moment then tumbled to the ground, the big mought blocks crushing the houses inside and outside the walls. The Shaker spoke again, and another section of wall fell – this time into the Outer City.

A silver comet of Force shot through the gaping hole in the wall. It slammed into the running men as they raced for the safety of the barricade that had been raised behind the eastern gate. The tall wooden barriers had seemed substantial when they were erected, now they looked like matchwood. The Screaming Spear had been positioned inside the gates as he commanded, but it and its crew now lay under the fallen main gate. Useless. The glowmetal must have discharged when the crew were crushed, its Force absorbed by the fallen door.

Daran scrambled over the barrier with the rest of the men. The night was filled with terrified faces. Razors and Captains shouted orders while all was chaos. He saw Uran with the General of the First.

'Nacius. Go and join Uran. You must stand with the Legions.'

'Yes, my Lord.'

Daran had to take control.

'To the secondary command post!' This was located on the top of a five-storey stone building with a good view of the eastern gate. When he and his aides reached the top, they ran to the side of the roof. Daran realised he had lost the lenstube in the mad rush, but he had a good view nonetheless. The barricades were manned by all his remaining troops – the First, Second and Third. A wall of men. Uran, Nacius and the surviving Druidin were with them.

A gap of more than seven hundred paces had been opened up in the eastern wall. Through it marched the Black. At their sides were the surviving Tahistil, armed with large shields and long, glittering blades of gemstone.

'Missiles!'

Archers and spearmen loosed across the line. The missiles struck the Shield of Hukum's defensive glowmetal and fell to the ground in a useless clatter.

'Hold,' commanded Daran. That Shield could not protect the Eathal forever. Once the fighting spread into the city, it would be impossible to cover the whole force.

The ranks of the Black drew back. His heart sank as a new glowmetal was dragged forward. This was platinum, the shiny metal traced with threads of bright blue. Once more two Sorcerer-Lords worked to charge it, pouring lightning into the glowmetal from their outstretched hands. Daran tensed as the lines of blue light dwindled. The very power of Hukum's glowmetals was a potential weakness. Each required the dedicated attention of one or two Sorcerer-Lords to operate, which meant that they could not all be brought to bear at once. A small mercy, and not a fact he could currently exploit.

The Sorcerer-Lords ceased their lightning. A tongue of red heat licked out from the glowmetal. It halted at Uran and Nacius' Sorcerous Shield for a moment, then broke through, engulfing a broad swath of the barrier. The wooden barricade leapt into flame. Men screamed as they burned. Uran and Nacius were not strong enough to stand against it.

'No! *No!*' Daran slammed his fist into the roof's parapet again and again, until his flesh was torn and bloody. Despite Hukum's glowmetals, he had managed to carve away at the Black during its advance, almost halving the legions numbers. The Yellow had taken damage, and the Silver was less than half its original numbers now. His own men outnumbered them! Yet once again Hukum's glowmetals had defeated him. There was no way they could hold here. Not faced with those glowmetals. The only way to take away Hukum's advantage was to spread the combat. He had to let the Sundar advance into the city.

Daran's eyes blurred with tears of frustration. They could not stand against the Eathal. Not like this.

'Retreat,' he said, his voice little more than a harsh whisper. He watched as the two Sorcerer-Lords directed lightning back into the glowmetal for another attack.

'My Lord?'

He cleared his throat. 'Retreat!'

Daran's hand throbbed with pain, but that was nothing to the helpless rage he felt as another section of Raynor's walls tumbled. Hukum was destroying them section by section. He meant to wipe the city from the face of Kelas.

His last line of defence was at the Palastrada itself. The Suul district was protected by its own walls. Then within that was the Palanac – the palace of the Cinanac. In between, he had set up a network of traps and blocked streets that would make the advancing Eathal pay for every step. He would break the Legions up into squads and hit the Eathal in the streets. Hit them and run. Then hit them again. The tight streets and towering buildings would force the Eathal troops to stretch out. It would also neutralise the effectiveness of their glowmetals, which would always triumph in head-to-head encounters.

Uran and the senior Legion commanders would rendezvous

with him and his aides in one of the manor houses on the Palardos, the street that ran around the outside of the Palastrada. There they would plan their last defence.

As his men retreated, the Black advanced. The terrified population of Raynor watched in shock as they came. Flames from the burning barrier leapt from house to house. Panicked men and women rushed from their houses, straight into the path of the Eathal. They were cut down without mercy.

Daran tried to close his ears to the screams, but he could not. For the first time, he realised that they would lose this. They had hit Hukum with their best and been crushed. It was no longer about Raynor; it was about survival. He had to open the western gate and get as many people out of Raynor as he could. Perhaps send the Third with them while he and Uran and his remaining Legions kept Hukum pinned here.

He ran with the rest, while around them Raynor fell.

Chapter Twenty-One

Cedrin tensed at the whispered sound of movement. The curtain that served as a makeshift door to the chamber flicked aside. Beside him, Ranis and Kalyth looked up from the map as Bovosan entered the temple chamber flanked by Duro and Elthar. The minitil was enigmatic as usual. Cedrin tried to restrain his impatience as he waited for his report. The strange twins Bles and Ris stood unnoticed in the corner of the chamber. Vess and another of the One Hundred stood guard duty behind him.

'The local Eathal have agreed to join the attack,' said Bovosan.

'How many warriors?' asked Cedrin.

'Around fifty with light shields, axes and stabbing spears,' said Bovosan.

Kalyth scowled. He had made his objections fairly clear to this unusual alliance, but Cedrin was determined to use every advantage he had against Raziin. Over the last few days, his men had carefully scouted the cavern. They found Raziin and his men camped beneath an arched bridge to the north of the Hall of Dreams where an underground river plunged down into the earth in a spectacular waterfall. It was a choice spot and had been the village of the local Eathal, but Raziin had driven them out ruthlessly, leaving many of them dead.

Raziin had the knack of making enemies everywhere he went. It occurred to Cedrin that this was a weakness he could exploit. The northern Sorcerer still had more than twice their numbers. Surprise could help to even the odds, but it might not

338

be enough. If he could win the local Eathal to his cause, it could tip the balance.

Veltricus entered the temple chamber with another of the One Hundred who had been scouting the cavern. They bowed to Cedrin.

'News from the Hall of Dreams,' said Veltricus.

Cedrin took in a sharp breath. He had given orders for his men to only watch the Hall of Dreams from a distance. He had no intention of getting anywhere near the Iris until the threat of Raziin had been dealt with. 'Go on.'

Veltricus waved for the scout to give his report.

'There has been a battle there, my Lord. A force of around fifty mounted Eathal attacked the Ward. They were scattered with Sorcerous fire, and their leader was captured. He remains there with the bird-being and the Great Spider.'

'Mounted?' said Cedrin.

'Jakkund cavalry,' said Bovosan, showing rare surprise. 'Only the Maht Junta have them.'

Veltricus spoke up. 'Our other scouts report that an Eathal force entered the cavern from the south, riding beasts like long-legged jakka, and with a trained teremb. It has to be the same force. They must have made directly for the Hall of Dreams.'

'How did Eathal from the Caverns of Maht end up here? Right now?' asked Ranis.

'Are you sure about the teremb?' asked Kalyth.

'That's the report. I have no reason to doubt it,' said Veltricus.

'Teremb can be trained as trackers,' said Bovosan.

'So they followed us here,' said Ranis.

'Or they followed Raziin,' said Kalyth.

'As long as they do not stand between us and Raziin, we can eliminate them from the coming battle,' said Cedrin. 'Veltricus, search for the survivors of the Eathal force. I need to know where they are before we press the attack on Raziin.'

'Yes, my Lord,' said Veltricus. He bowed and exited with the scout.

Cedrin looked back at the map. Raziin and his men were camped close to the Hall of Dreams. Attacking him would mean going closer to the Temple of the Iris than he had been since Olcis. Since they had been here in the cavern, he had felt the influence of the Behemoth growing. Once he seized the Spear, the presence of the Twins Delegation would be even more vital to keep the darkness in the Spear at bay.

He shared a simple meal of dried rations and water with Kalyth, Ranis and Bovosan. They ate in tense silence. Much depended on the upcoming attack, and it was difficult to make small talk. The minitil also made the other two nervous. Although Bovosan had saved his life in Olcis, the One Hundred found it hard to trust the half-Eathal.

Finally Veltricus returned.

Cedrin got to his feet. 'You found them?'

'Yes. Around twelve of them, many wounded. They are camped to the south, well away from the Hall of Dreams.'

'No others?'

'None.'

Cedrin picked up his greatscythe. The same one given to him by his foster-father Tarral.

'Ranis. Kalyth. Gather the men.'

* * *

Cedrin waited in the darkness.

Above them, the roof of the cavern was scattered with bright patches of lungii, all growing in the mist from the waterfall. The luminescent plants also grew from every surface on the arched bridge, outlining it in ghostly shades of blue and green. The One Hundred crowded around him. The whole party was here. Veltricus and his three hulking bodyguards would join the attack, while the Priests and Priestesses of Twins Delegation would hold back at a safe distance.

Raziin and his Armon warriors had secured their camp well. A rough barricade stretched between the stone huts, and sentries had been posted around the perimeter. On the other side of the camp, a large copper glowmetal – threaded with green light – protruded from the ground. It looked to be a natural feature and was one of the many indicated on the map.

Its muted light provided little illumination.

Much would depend on Bovosan and the Eathal warriors. They had two tasks to perform. The first was to take out the sentries. Here he was relying on the natural stealth of the Eathal cave-dwellers and their knowledge of the small village. The second was to provide a distraction. He had also asked them to join the combat once they attacked. They probably would, although he expected them to break and run at Raziin's first counterattack.

Cedrin started as Bovosan appeared from the gloom.

'The sentries are down,' said the minitil. Eight less warriors to deal with.

Cedrin touched Kalyth on the shoulder and together they led the men through the dark to the edge of the village. *It will be soon.*

They heard the strange, muted calls of the jakka as the herd approached. *Here comes the distraction.* As the sound of the hoof beats grew, they slipped over the edge of the rough barricade at the other side of the village. Cedrin took the lead. He opened the Window, ready to pay back the deaths the One Hundred had suffered over the long dark days in these caverns. He had to enter combat focussed on victory. To achieve it here – against the odds – he had to hit the enemy as hard as he could without thought of mercy.

Alerted by the sound of the jakka herd, Armon warriors streamed from the huts to the front of the village. They stood in loose ranks, tensed, but with their attention forward, unaware the sentries were down. Raziin and his lieutenants emerged from a large central hut and pushed through the crowd of warriors.

The One Hundred crept forward. They spread out in a long line with Kalyth and Ranis commanding the left and right wings. Cedrin himself took the centre, leading the core of the force with Veltricus and his three bodyguards. The Herath Suul extended the blades of his greatscythe. He had already shown his skills in the many brief combats in the caverns. Although no master, he could hold his own.

The One Hundred advanced until they were no more than

five paces from the Armon line. Only the darkness of the caverns could make that possible – that and the distraction provided by the jakka. His men were positioned a pace and half apart, perfect for greatscythe combat. Kalyth and Ranis would sweep into the sides of Raziin's force like the points of twin horns. It was time.

Cedrin drew heavily on the Fire. He raised the Barrier, then channelled everything else into a Force Matrix. He shot a wide fan of Force bolts at the crowd of Armon warriors. Five warriors dropped, another howling as the deadly bolt drove through his shoulder. Cedrin shot twice more, then raised a Shield.

Raziin turned to face him. 'You!'

'Attack!' bellowed Cedrin.

His men roared their battlecries and ripped into the loose Armon ranks. Many of the enemy warriors were still foggy from sleep. The deadly lanedd blades cut at exposed throats, arms and legs, slicing through armour and flesh. The Armon warriors wielded cavalry scythes, but were out of their element on foot and in single combat. They fell across the line.

Bovosan, usually in the thick of the fight, hovered on the edge. He defended himself, but did nothing more. Cedrin had no time to ponder his strange behaviour.

A cavalry Captain cut at his head with a scythe. Cedrin blocked and countered without thought. His left blade sliced through the man's throat. Blood sprayed across Cedrin's cheek. He was already turning to meet the scythe of the man behind him. All the training with Kalyth had drilled instinctive reactions into him. His greatscythe moved as though it had a will of its own, while he floated through the combat, his mind serene. This was the Way.

The Herath Suul was hard-pressed, two Armon warriors attacking from his left and right. One of his bodyguards ran in. An Armon scythe cut at his head. The bodyguard swept up a thick knife, trapping the shaft in the hooked hilt. The second knife punched though the Northman's armour into his heart. The bodyguard stiffened in pain as another Northman stabbed him from behind. With his two blades trapped, he could do nothing. He sank to his knees in a pool of blood. Veltricus dispatched his opponent with a quick jab to the throat and stepped back. His two other bodyguards shielded him.

Their attack had been devastating. They had more than halved the numbers of the Armon force. At last they pressed the attack, instead of running from an ambush. Little more than eighty enemy warriors faced seventy men under his command. The odds were even at last.

Cedrin stepped back from the front line. Duro and Velthius, fighting on either side of him, came together to plug the gap. Now he needed all his concentration for his Sorcery. The Barrier was already in place. He prepared his Shield and the Final Matrix. Raziin would now seek to attack with Fire and Force. He did not intend to give him the chance. It was time to attack!

Raziin and his lieutenants ran to the centre of the enemy line. They shouted commands in Cioan. The Armon line fell back and grew more compact. Now Raziin's own warriors had to draw back together in response, and they had less fighting room to use their greatscythes. The One Hundred were the elite. The Armon warriors were not equipped or trained for this type of head-to-head combat. Northern warriors fell up and down the line. Their shrieks of pain and fear rose in counterpoint to his own warriors' triumphant battlecries.

Cedrin drew heavily on the Fire and stabbed at Raziin with the Final Matrix. The Northman's head snapped towards him, his eyes lit like pale moons. Cedrin slammed into the Sorcerer's Barrier, his heart flaring with determination. He did not have to breach it, only occupy Raziin while the rest of the combat played itself out. Then Raziin hit him with the Final Matrix. The world around him contracted to a tunnel. It was a contest of sheer will and power. All the mental training had prepared him well. His focus was razor-sharp. The Window yawned wide. Fire raged through him, transformed as it fled through the two Matrices. He gripped that power like a glassmaker, shaping it to his will in the heat of his purpose. Ellen. Kelas. The lives of thousands of men and women hinged on his victory. Raziin had to fall. He had to meet his end here, so Cedrin could raise the Spear without fear of the Behemoth's dark agenda.

Under the command of Merceth and Kyal, the Armon

warriors rallied. The most skilful and experienced warriors now remained, and the One Hundred began to fall. Yet they had forgotten the jakka. From the midst of the strange bleating animals rose the Eathal warriors. They struck in silence, stabbing into the rear of the Armon warriors. The unexpected attack sent a shockwave through the enemy ranks. The northern warriors turned, fearing an attack from the rear – only to find a blade of the One Hundred cutting their flesh.

Cedrin felt the tide of battle turn. For the first time, they outnumbered the enemy. The northern warriors were now being hit from all sides. Their fearsome leader Raziin had done nothing to turn the tide, standing rigid and unresponsive in the middle of their force.

Cedrin intensified his attack. He could sense Raziin's Barrier weakening, while Raziin's attack was becoming less focussed.

Then the Armon warriors broke. One moment they were standing toe-to-toe, the next they dissolved into chaos. The One Hundred gave a rousing shout and surged forward. This was the type of work they were made for. They cut deep into the ranks of the Armon warriors, their blades slicing too fast to follow. Other northern warriors ran into the darkness, only to meet the spears of the Eathal. Some tried to throw down their weapons, but there was no mercy. His warriors had lost too many, had been surprised too many times in the darkness of the caverns. This was revenge. Justice.

Raziin broke off his attack and retreated with a small force of men. Cedrin and his men pursued. Raziin attacked his warriors with bolts of Force. Cedrin was forced to deflect these on his Shield. The Northmen kept attacking, forcing him to abandon the Final Matrix. Raziin sent raw Fire at his men. Cedrin deflected it off into the darkness. It no longer mattered. He had to do nothing now but contain Raziin. Once his men were down, Raziin would follow. He intended the murdering butcher to fall under his own blade, to pay for what he had done to Ellen.

The Eathal warriors surprised him. Even though they were lightly armoured they hammered into the Armon warriors, some fighting on with grievous wounds. They battled for their homes and to avenge the death of their own. The One Hundred were inspired, fighting back-to-back in the general melee. This was the type of open combat that favoured the greatscythe. They wreaked a terrible carnage on the collapsed Northman ranks, their lanedd blades slicing through the leather armour with ease.

Raziin and a small circle of warriors retreated to the edge of the chasm where the waterfall plunged into the darkness. The surviving One Hundred pushed forward, surrounding them. The chests of the warriors heaved with exhaustion, their faces splattered with blood but lit with the exhilaration of victory. The northern warriors stood with their weapons raised, grim and ready to fight on. The golden giant Merceth stood at Raziin's right. Kyal, another of Raziin's mercenaries, at his left. Cedrin recognised them as Raziin's chief lieutenants, men who had been at his side in Athria.

Cedrin weaved through the One Hundred until he stood in the middle of the two forces. He met Raziin's pale eyes. At the sight of the vicious murderer, his heart burned with rage. He suppressed it. This was about more than revenge. 'This is where you meet your end,' said Cedrin.

The Northman Sorcerer snorted in contempt. 'You know nothing.'

Raziin spoke rapidly to his two lieutenants in Cioan. They and Raziin's remaining men backed away to the edge of the chasm, leaving Raziin to stand alone.

Raziin waved Cedrin forward. 'Come and kill me if you can, Anacian.'

Cedrin could feel it. He knew he had the strength to overcome Raziin. The last time he faced him at the Olcis Temple of the Iris, he defeated him blade to blade. It was only the Sorcery that had allowed Raziin to triumph. Now he was his master in both.

Bovosan pushed his way through the ranks of the One Hundred. The minitil stepped between them, shielding Raziin.

'No,' said the minitil.

Raziin laughed. 'The Seer's servant speaks. See what I mean, Anacian? You have no idea what forces are at work.'

'Bovosan. Get out of the way,' said Cedrin.

The minitil looked back at Cedrin with his strange, green eyes, his face impassive. Behind him, Raziin backed to the edge of the chasm, a shadowed figure in the darkness. One minute he was there, the next he stepped off into the raging flow. His men jumped after him.

'No!' yelled Cedrin. He ran to the edge, but there was no sign of Raziin. Nothing but darkness and the roaring echo of falling water.

Kalyth stepped up to the edge. 'He's gone. No one could survive that fall.'

'Raziin is no ordinary man,' hissed Cedrin.

'It's over,' said Kalyth.

'Uros!' Cedrin felt cheated. He did not want it to end like this. He had wanted to face Raziin. To prevail in their final, lethal contest. Now that had been taken from him. Could Raziin truly be dead?

Cedrin turned to Bovosan. 'Why? *Why?*' After all he had suffered at the hands of Raziin, why would Bovosan act like this? The minitil had been there in Olcis when Raziin drove his calv right through Ellen's heart, leaving her dead on the stone.

Raziin had called him *the Seer's servant*.

'Who is the Seer?' demanded Cedrin. Had the minitil served another all this time? Then why protect him with such devotion on their journey north? The Window burned in his thoughts, the Fire inside him longing to be released in furious vengeance. He could not trust himself to deal with Bovosan now.

'Take his weapons and bind him,' he commanded. Two of the One Hundred came forward warily. Bovosan let them take his shield and hammer without resistance.

'I will have an answer,' said Cedrin. He met those enigmatic green eyes and brought every ounce of will and command to bear against the minitil.

Bovosan looked down at the stone.

Cedrin hissed and waved for the two warriors to take him away.

Veltricus emerged from the ranks, his two surviving bodyguards with him. He walked towards Cedrin, his face set with determination. Cedrin sensed the Suul was about to confront him. The two bodyguards wore the bracers and glowmetal pendants of their fallen comrade. Cedrin had noticed the custom. The Suul himself also wore pieces from his men who fell on the journey north.

The Twins delegation emerged from the dark.

Veltricus stopped. His brow furrowed as he watched Dagon, Esmelle and the twins take their place behind Cedrin. The Suul cursed under his breath and turned back the way he came, whatever he had intended to say left unsaid.

Cedrin sighed. Veltricus was not his concern, and neither was Bovosan. The Spear was. Now that nothing remained between him and the Temple of the Iris, it was time to go and claim it.

* * *

A gush of spray leapt from the prow of the doubled-masted merchantman as she plowed through the swell. The salt mist stung Marken's face. He narrowed his eyes, looking through the balmy night at the lights of the Leygen citadel on the cliff above them. Their small fleet of wide-bellied trader-galleys had rounded the headland, sailing from the inhospitable and rocky shores to the east. They had waited for three nights for favourable winds. Everything depended on timing, and they needed a stiff wind to get their eight ships to quay and disembark the six-hundred warriors of the Hanis Ninth before the alert was given. As promised, the Brotherhood men on the Leygen watchtowers – ancient stone structures built on small rocky islands in the bay – had let them pass without lighting their beacons. The harbourmaster had assured them that the patrolling galleys had been ordered west to Searn, to observe the Athrian fleet at their blockade. *The bribe to the Leygen Warlord's harbourmaster had bought that much at least.*

To the north, Leygen was surrounded by an inland wall that was kept well manned with the Warlord's men. The former pirate relied on his considerable seaborne strength to protect the harbour. A native of the small city, the Brotherhood pirate had achieved here what Jorrel had attempted in Athria, deposing the

Suul rulers and taking the city for his own.

Marken shifted his grip on the rigging and the coarse rope tore at his hands, already raw from salt. The Leygen docks formed a compact stone crescent along the shore that ran from the base of the citadel cliff to the jagged islands that formed the western extent of the small bay. Seven trading vessels were tied up close to the citadel and the small city at the base of the cliff. The inns and taverns that fronted the docks there were alive with light and movement. The short section of quay near the ships flickered with torchlight. Marken tilted his head as he heard the faint strains of music on the wind. Below, Hanis warriors manned ballistae that had been mounted along the sides of the grain-trader. What magical strength the Hanis Sarla could lend them was concentrated here on the lead ship. The seven dark-robed figures stood at the prow, watching as the docks drew closer. Moon Druids, all of them. Marken looked up at the full disk of Asic above, Rea waxing gibbous behind it. *Moon Essence, here at my command.*

Pain flared in Marken's palm as his grip tightened on the rope. He could not believe that no alarm had been raised from the shore. The Pirate's harbourmaster would control the men out in the bay, but the shore would be a different matter. Each of the ships tied up on the quay would have lookouts on watch, as would the citadel. Under the moonlight, their fleet would be easily visible to their trained eyes. Marken expected resistance as the defenders realised they were being attacked from the sea.

The cliff loomed to starboard. The islands to the west were nothing but an ominous smudge of darkness. And ahead was Leygen itself. Here was his chance to strike a blow against the pirates that had grown like a disease in western Kelas. All was going according to plan, yet an uneasiness gnawed at his guts. Skye and his men had been put ashore yesterday, in a small cove to the east. Their mission would be vital. Timing was everything. That and deception. Everything depended on drawing the Warlord's men away from the inland wall. Marken's attack would achieve that – but the blood price would be high.

The captain turned the wheel and the ship ran before the

wind, cutting through the choppy water to the ill-lit and deserted western section of the docks. As they neared the quay, sailors – already in the rigging – hoisted up the canvass and their speed dropped away.

Marken lowered himself down to the deck. It had been many years since he had climbed the rigging of his foster-father's ships as a young trader's apprentice. Compared to the easy agility of the Athrian sailors, he looked stiff and slow. The scythe-staff strapped across his back did not help either. He walked across the deck to the prow, where the Ninth General, Clonnodus, stood with his Captains. The squat General bowed in deference as he approached.

'My Lord,' said Clonnodus evenly. Marken was still getting used to the honorific, and the golden Suul mark that accompanied it.

Like Xyanthius, Clonnodus was a warrior of the old Empire. He was short and powerful, his head bald except for tufts of silver above his ears. It gave his bluff, scarred face an even fiercer demeanour. 'Do we proceed as planned?'

'Yes, General,' replied Marken. 'As planned.'

Clonnodus turned to watch the quay draw closer. Marken looked up at the citadel. *Goddess defend us.*

Sailors dropped fenders and the ship glided gently up to the stone. They leapt across the gap and held up their hands. Lines were thrown ashore and the ship made fast. There was a bustle of movement as planks, muffled with cloth, were laid out and they began to disembark. A Razor led a squad of men across the plank and formed a shield wall, their movements neat and precise. The Ninth might be only a shadow of its old Empire strength, but they were elite warriors. Tasked with rebuilding the shattered legion in the wake of the Empire's fall and the destruction of Husdoon, Clonnodus had refused to lower his strict standards.

The Ninth General led his officers off the ship, followed by legionnaires equipped with shields and short, stabbing scythes. As planned, the lightly-armoured sailors formed ranks of spearmen. They would use their long weapons to stab at the enemy from behind the front ranks. Marken paced up and down the deck, making a last inspection of the warriors stationed at the ballistae, then approached the Moon Druids. Each wore a simple cast mought pendant of the twin moons Asic and Rea.

'It's time, brothers,' said Marken to the senior Druid, a laconic man with a trimmed, dark beard and brooding eyes, who nodded once in reply. 'Blood will be shed this night. I know that is an anathema to those devoted to healing, but it is for the good of Kelas.'

The Druids remained silent. They knew what was required of them.

'Follow me.' Marken disembarked, leading the Druids through the assembling ranks of legionnaires to the centre of the formation, where Clonnodus stood with his officers.

Marked watched as one-by-one, their other vessels approached the quay and tied up. It was too late to change their plans now. Despite all their efforts, there was a loud din of stamping feet, rattling weapons and a buzz of low talk. The warehouses that lined the quay were dark and deserted. A scrawny harborside dog raised its head from a pile of refuse to watch them, then returned to its search.

He scanned the eastern side of the docks and the citadel far above. *Still no alarm.* The uneasiness in the pit of stomach grew.

Marken saw movement out on the water. For a moment he thought it was one of their own vessels, lagging behind the others, but with a shock he realised all eight transports had already tied up. He took an involuntary step forward as the sleek shape of a war galley slid into the harbour entrance, followed by another, and another, each outlined in ghostly moonlight. *The fleet of the Leygen Warlord.*

A signal lamp lit up on the lead galley. The doors to the warehouses were thrown open, flooding light onto the cobbled quay. Torches flared to life in the narrow lanes between. Hundreds of men spilled from each open door and alleyway. The music stopped, and with a roar a ragged crowd advanced from the tavern, bristling with weapons, blocking their path to the citadel. Every Brotherhood warrior at the Warlord's command had gathered here to close the trap. Judging by the numbers – more than a thousand – the Swebas Warlord had lent part of his strength as well.

Marken knew the harbourmaster could never be trusted. Betrayal was the only coin these murderous scum dealt in. The harbourmaster had taken their money and reported straight back to his pirate master. Even so, Marken had never expected the Warlord's war galleys to return tonight – and with them close to five hundred fighting men. His determination hardened. These were the same pirate scum who slew his family on the Sea of Mists. Their plan could still be salvaged. He lifted the scythe-staff off his back and pressed the release stud. The blade shot into place with a lethal *snick*.

Marken turned to watch the Warlord's war galleys as they swept towards their helpless ships, oars rising and falling on the moonlit waters. Their jagged mought rams rose from the surface with each stroke. The speed of the galleys increased as they entered the calmer waters of the small bay. He could see them all clearly now. There were eleven of them. Three hung back, then turned smartly, defending the bay. The other eight slid smoothly towards the quay where their own ships were tied up. Their ships would be defenceless against the rams. The Warlord could sink them easily, but he did not.

As he had hoped, the Warlord could not pass up the chance to add eight Athrian traders to his fleet. They gradually cut back their speed, holding station some four boat-lengths out from the quay. Not enough sea room for them to get to full ramming speed, even if they decided to attack.

A signal light flared on the citadel tower. Marken drew a sharp breath, watching in suspense at it grew. He gritted his teeth at the sight of the tall, yellow flame.

Commands were screamed down the ragged fighting line of Brotherhood men.

'Shields!' commanded Clonnodus.

The warriors of the Hanis Ninth lifted their rectangular, mought-braced shields, locking them in place along the front lines and overhead. The Athrian sailors ducked beneath the makeshift roof. A rain of short crossbow quarrels, darts and arrows whistled down. They hit the shields with a series of dull concussions, but nothing penetrated the dense rebin wood.

Clonnodus signalled. One of his lieutenants raised a torch and waved it back and forward. Big lanterns were uncovered across the decks of their ships, lighting the working crews of the ballistae. The weapons were drawn and ready. Huge bolts shot across the space, arching over the linked shields of the Hanis Ninth into the Brotherhood's packed ranks. There were shrieks of pain and surprise as the Warlord's men were impaled by the deadly projectiles. One of the long bolts skewered through a lithe Brotherhood man and into the bulky torso of the man behind him, taking both to the cobbles. If the Warlord's men had attacked, they would have come inside the range of the weapons. The ballistae's field of fire was blocked by the packed ranks of the Hanis Ninth, but their lack of training and central command worked against them. They backed up to the alleys and warehouses – right into the deadly range of the ballistae. There was some sporadic missile fire in retaliation, but their attack had died away. Some groups within the Warlord's force broke and melted away into the darkness. The Brotherhood warriors were used to working in small groups of two or three, always with surprise on their side. This type of head-to-head battle was foreign to them. The Brotherhood was also a many-headed beast. In the assembled force would be thieves and smugglers, and calvanni more used to keeping the peace in brothels and taverns than open warfare. The Brotherhood leaders barked out commands, but nothing could induce those men to close with the Ninth, even though they outnumbered them two to one.

The ballistae kept up a steady rate of fire. Out on the bay, signals flashed between the Warlord's ships. The eight war-galleys surged into motion. The ballistae stationed on the bay-facing side of their ships now began firing, but moving targets were hard to hit in the dark. The war-galleys soon came alongside their own ships. Grapnels were thrown and the Warlord's crews clambered onto the vessels. The three ships left to guard the bay entrance turned towards shore. The ballistae crews on their ships would resist the boarders, but would be quickly overwhelmed. There was no point surrendering their lives for a few minutes respite.

'Send runners. Tell the men on the ships to join the force on the quay,' commanded Marken. The crews had orders to cut the ballistae springs before they abandoned their weapons, disabling them.

'Yes, my lord,' replied one of Clonnodus' Second Captains, a young Hanis Suulqua.

The Ninth General turned to Marken for orders. He had been given overall command of the Ninth, and he felt the responsibility keenly. Warriors like Clonnodus had extensive knowledge of warfare and more experience in combat than he could ever hope for. From the look of tension on the old warrior's face, he longed to take the fight to the Brotherhood, but they could not afford to get pinned down here. If they were caught between two Brotherhood forces, they might never reach the citadel. That was the key to everything.

The men from the ships ran to the quay. The last man from each trader threw the plank down into the harbour behind them. It would do little to stop the Warlord's men, but every delay counted.

'We have lost the ballistae and will have more men behind us once the Warlord lands his pirate force. We have to retreat now,' said Marken.

'As you command,' replied Clonnodus. Orders were relayed with swift economy, and the formation changed to a fighting square. The Ninth began a slow march up the quay to the base of the citadel cliff. From there, they would have to climb up a steep, winding road to the citadel gates. In all, less than a third of a league, but they would have to fight for every step.

Marken turned to the Moon-Druids. 'Spread yourselves across the lines and use Shields to turn the missile fire.'

'We cannot Shield them all,' said the senior Druid in a low rumble.

'I understand. Do what you can,' said Marken.

The Druids hurried through the lines. With the Moon Essence so strong, their Shields would be highly effective – and they would need to be. Now that the Ninth had begun their fighting retreat, the men on the outside of the lines had to use their shields to turn attacks from the Brotherhood, leaving them exposed from above.

Realising that the ballistae had stopped firing, the Warlord's men surged forward. The Brotherhood warriors had seen scores of their number slain from a distance and could do nothing. Now they hit the Hanis lines with an enraged ferocity. The lines buckled under their assault, but the Legion Razors barked out commands and the veterans pushed back. Their force was soon surrounded by a vicious swarm of men wielding clubs, scythes and spears – even greatscythes. Most would be expert calvanni, yet knife-fighting skills counted for little against the line of Hanis shields. The Athrian sailors lowered their spears. Lanedd tips bristled beyond the shield wall. They rested the spears on the shoulders of the legionnaires as they picked their targets, then stabbed forward with both hands.

Marken gathered the Moon Essence and waited, ready to deploy a magical Shield, yet all he could do was watch. Few of the missiles reached so far inside the square. Most of the Brotherhood men were now committed to an all-out attack. He could not even use the Moon Essence to strike out with a blow of Force – there were too many Hanis warriors in the way. All he could do was watch as the Brotherhood warriors threw themselves again and again at their shield wall. Despite their expertise, Hanis legionnaires began to fall. Some were dragged from the front lines by mobs of shouting Brotherhood warriors, others fell to lucky strikes. The Warlord's men were brave and determined. This was their home ground, and they were fighting for their own survival.

Marken looked back along the quay. They had covered less than half the distance along the wide crescent of the shoreline. Marken's heart twisted as he saw the Warlord's men scramble across the Athrian traders and leap to the quay. These were hardened raiders, used to fighting in close quarters. They would be bitter opponents. Added to the numbers already on the docks, the Warlord's men would outnumber them three to one. They had to get off the wide open space of the docks and onto the steep, narrow citadel road, where their shields and discipline would give them the advantage.

'Clonnodus! We must move faster,' said Marken, pointing

down the docks at the approaching pirate mob.

'I see them,' said the old General. 'Yet if we move any faster we will lose our formation. And we have too few men to split our force.'

Marken thought rapidly. He could not fail here. Could not fail Cedrin. 'Give me a hundred men. I will take the Druids and hold them.'

'No, my Lord. You must remain safe,' said Clonnodus.

Marken's heart hardened. 'You have your orders.'

'Very well.' Clonnodus passed the orders to one of his First Captains, who would command the contingent. The Captain followed Marken as he wove through the ranks to the rear of their force. On the way, he gathered all the Moon Druids to him. A lump grew in his throat as he realised what he was attempting. He tried to swallow, but his mouth was too dry. This was a desperate gamble. One that could see every last one of them torn apart.

Marken turned to the Captain. 'Form a line across the docks. Block them off!'

'Our ranks will be no more than two deep. They will push right through us,' said the Captain.

'Do it.'

The Captain gave the command. Even though the Ninth warriors were disciplined, they looked at each other nervously as the pirates sprinted up the quay towards them. Regardless, they spread out in a long line from the water's edge to an empty warehouse. The retreating Ninth drew away from them, moving along the dock front in the direction of the citadel. The Brotherhood followed them.

'Hit them with Force. Everything you've got! Keep them at bay!' Marken called to the Druids.

As the pirates approached, their ranks broke up into a ragged line. A group of about thirty – all brandishing spiked clubs and short-scythes – drew away from the others. Pirate captains and their mates eager to show the others how it was done.

'Now!' screamed Marken.

He drew heavily on the Moon Essence and released it as a

single bolt of Force. By chance, he and the other seven Moon Druids all targeted the leading group. Their attack struck them with enough Force to shatter bone. They were smashed off their feet and hurled back into the main body of attackers like missiles of flesh and bone, their screams full of pain and terror. The whole advancing force staggered to a halt. *Yes!*

He could see that some of the Druids were shocked at the damage they had caused. Moon Druids were expert healers, usually weak in offensive combat.

'These bastards want to cut out your heart. Keep hitting them!' called Marken to the Druids.

Shouts and angry commands rang out through the pirate lines, rousing their battle fury. The pirates screamed out their defiance and ran forward. This time there was no halting them.

Marken and the other Druids hit the approaching force again. This time their Force-bolts hit different targets. He soon realised that only the senior Moon Druid and one other matched his own power. The others delivered less than a quarter of their Force, doing more to trip and throw men off their feet than crush them outright. They had time for two more attacks before the lines closed.

Now the veteran warriors of the Ninth were hard-pressed. The Captain was right. There was no way such a thin line of defenders could hold back the advancing horde. Within the first few seconds, the line broke in two places. Marken used a bolt of Force to push back the pirates at the first, then sealed the breach with a Shield of Essence while the Ninth closed the gap. At the other gap, the pirates howled with glee as they cut at the unprotected backs of the Ninth warriors trying to hold the line. The Captain managed to re-establish the line by retreating his men ten paces.

'Use Shields to plug the line!' called Marken.

They held the onslaught, but the losses were high. Soon only a single line of defenders was stretched across the quay, with small knots of warriors in reserve. The pirates had suffered losses too and were slower to come forward, the bravest and strongest already dead and cooling on the ground.

'We cannot hold them any longer,' said the Captain.

Marken looked back up the quay. His heart leapt as he saw Clonnodus and the Ninth pass the tavern. Now they were less than a hundred paces from the base of the cliff. In his relief, he relaxed his Shield.

'We can start a retreat,' said Marken.

'Ye—' A crossbow bolt sliced through the Captain's neck, cutting off his reply. A spray of blood splashed across Marken's face. His eyes stung with it. He blinked in shock.

The attackers roared in fury and surged forward. The line broke, and there was chaos. One skinny Druid let out a shrill scream as he was battered to the ground. Warriors of the Ninth went down under the howling mob. Others formed fighting circles, back-to-back, trying to defend themselves.

A screaming pirate ran at Marken, short-scythe raised above him, his lips drawn back over a jagged line of blackened teeth. He cut at Marken's head. Marken side-stepped and slashed into the pirate's lower torso. His attacker's scream of fury turned to a wail of pain and he staggered to his knees, tripping on his own guts.

It had turned into a massacre.

'The alleyway!' called Marken, accelerating into a sprint.

The surviving Ninth warriors fled to a narrow lane between two warehouses. Marken stopped in the mouth of the alley and shot bolts of Force back at the pursuing pirates. It was enough to slow them and give the others a chance. Three Moon Druids joined him there, the senior Druid among them. Less than thirty of the one hundred warriors reached the alley. Scores of men had died violent deaths at his command. For a moment, the horror of it turned in his stomach and he felt balanced on the high edge of some mountain, a dark abyss yawning to either side. He felt something drop onto his neck and reached to touch it. Blood. More was flooding from a shallow cut across his left cheek. He had not even felt it. He could spare no time to heal it now.

Faced with attacking the narrow, defended alley, the pirates soon lost heart. They left them and ran to join with the other force harrying the Ninth, further up towards the citadel. Marken walked out onto the quay and watched them go. He saw the tight disciplined lines of the Hanis Ninth on the narrow citadel road. High above, the citadel signal fire now burned with a vivid green flame. *Skye's signal!* He laughed in relief and triumph. It had been enough! Despite everything – the harbourmaster's betrayal, the arrival of the Warlord's fleet – they would win.

The whole fleet of the Leygen Warlord was tied up alongside their own ships, empty of men.

He turned to his surviving legionnaires. 'Who's in command?'

The warriors looked at each other.

A thickset, scarred Razor stepped forward. 'I guess that be me, my Lord.'

'Take the remaining men and the Druids. I want you to board the warlord's galleys. Set them adrift and burn them. Then return to our ships and defend them,' ordered Marken.

The Razor smiled, showing a cracked tooth. 'With pleasure.' His forehead creased with concern. 'What about you, my Lord?'

'I will rejoin the Ninth.'

The Razor looked between Marken and the citadel road, where hundreds of Brotherhood warriors swarmed the Ninth's shields. Any single man trying to get close to those lines would have to run a murderous gauntlet. Even so, the Razor replied simply, 'As you command, my Lord.'

Marken turned to the senior Druid. 'Search for survivors on the way to the ships. Heal those you can.'

'Yes, my Lord,' replied the Druid.

As the Razor mustered his men, Marken hefted his scythe and ran up the harborside, staying to the warehouse shadows. Some Brotherhood men remained, but were further towards the edge of the quay and too busy looting the dead to pay attention to a single man running through the gloom.

He slowed as he reached the tavern. Here a crowd of old men and dockside whores watched as the Warlord's force pursued the Ninth up the citadel road. As he passed the brightly lit tavern, two men with clubs moved out to block his path. Their Brotherhood tattoos marked them as second degrees.

'Oi! Look at this. A bloody Suul,' said one, pointing with his club. 'The Warlord'd love to have a chat wi' him.' His mouth split in a nasty grin.

Marken drew on the Essence and smashed them both off their feet with a bolt of Force. They hit the cobbles hard. The speaker's head lay askew on his broken neck. The other man twitched once, then lay still.

'Sorcerer!' screamed a whore. The others drew back in fear. *Let them think what they will.*

He had to reach Clonnodus and the only way was right through the Brotherhood. He soon reached the citadel road. At first there was no alarm as he pushed through the tail end of the force. There were plenty of Brotherhood men content to stay on the fringes, who hung back to avoid blood and risk. They were only too happy to let him through. When the alarm was raised, Marken was ready.

The steep road had been carved from the side of the cliff, and was open on one side. Marken stuck to the edge, a perilous drop opening out beside him. He surrounded himself with a Shield and pushed forward. The men ahead of him, already close to the deadly drop, either drew back or were forced, screaming, to their deaths. Others he met with crushing bolts of Force.

The journey became a blur of leering faces leeched of colour by the moonlight and the stink of unwashed bodies pressed too close. Blades stabbed at him from the dark, while others sought to club him from his feet. His hair was soon damp with sweat, his own ragged breathing harsh in his ears. A concerted effort would have seen him off the cliff, but he kept moving forward, leaving them off balance.

Finally, he broke through.

The Ninth were drawn up in front of the citadel. The legionnaires were exhausted: lungs heaving, covered in blood and sweat. Three hundred and fifty legionnaires now remained of the six hundred who had marched to the docks less than an hour past. He ran for the line of shields. For a tense moment it seemed they would not open for him, but then a command was given and he was safe. He dropped his Shield with a sigh of relief. Only his fierce concentration and the purity of the night's Moon Essence had enabled him to pass through the attackers in one piece. He pushed through the spear-wielding sailors to Clonnodus.

'My Lord,' said Clonnodus, with a cool reserve. Marken had saved himself, but he was acutely aware that most of the warriors Clonnodus had lent him were dead.

'Perhaps a third of the one hundred remains,' said Marken. 'I have sent them to secure the ships.'

Clonnodus turned away without comment.

The moons were still high. The whole of Leygen and the small bay spread out below them. Marken saw a glimmer of light out on the bay near the docks, then another, and another. The Razor had succeeded. The Warlord's ships were burning.

A Brotherhood man emerged from the ranks of the Warlord's men, flanked by two lieutenants bearing torches. By his tattoos he was a sixth-degree – a Mouthpiece – a leader of the Brotherhood.

'Where now, eh? You've nowhere to run.' The sixth-degree's lips drew back from his teeth in a savage smile. He stabbed his old scythe at them, as though to punctuate his words.

'How right you are.' Skye appeared on the walls behind them. The gates opened and four hundred Ninth legionnaires marched out to swell Clonnodus' ranks.

The sixth-degree looked up and blinked. He lowered his scythe. 'Who in Uros' name are you – and where's the bloody Warlord!' he called up to the blond Suul.

'Right here!' Skye lifted the severed head of the Leygen Warlord and tossed it through the air. It landed at the feet of the sixth-degree with a soft thud. He had been a big man, in life, and there was a rather surprised expression on his big, tattooed face.

Marken grinned up at Skye, who grinned back. The Warlord had ordered every single warrior at his command down to the dockside to spring his trap. While the Leygen's defenders were drawn away from the inland wall to the harbour, Skye's force had scaled the wall under cover of darkness and taken the citadel by stealth. When the Warlord's stronghold was in their hands, Skye had thrown a special tint into the citadel signal fire to turn its flame green.

'Orders, my Lord?' Clonnodus was not smiling, and there was a glint in his eyes that chilled Marken.

'We advance,' said Marken. 'By dawn I want every last pirate in Leygen dead.' It was not enough to avenge the deaths of his mother, infant brother and sisters on the Sea of Mists, but it was a start.

The commands rang out. The shields of the Ninth came together with a thud. The warriors levelled their scythes and spears and moved forward in perfect time.

The Leygen Brotherhood ran.

And died.

Chapter Twenty-Two

Cedrin enhanced his sight with an adjustment to the Lens Matrix. The Hall of Dreams transformed from a dim expanse to a broad plaza, bordered by the high columns of ancient temples. The Temple of the Iris was distinctive with its five-fold symmetry. It was built on a raised pentagonal dais, a set of marble stairs rising from the plaza to the Temple level at each of the five apexes. Next to it, Eathal warriors stood in silent attendance to a thickset man with silvered hair. His upper body was powerfully muscled, with thick forearms and huge biceps. Cedrin's stomach tensed at the realisation of who this was. The man who he had once thought his father. Belin Kaidell. A man who had risked his life to save him as a child, taking him through the Raynor Iris to the Delta province.

'It's time to claim the Spear,' said Cedrin.

He set out across the dusty flagstones, flanked by Kalyth and Ranis. Dagon, Esmelle and the twins walked behind him, shielding him from the influence of the Behemoth. Fifty-seven of the One Hundred followed, with Veltricus and his two surviving bodyguards. The Matrix of Form had brought many back from the brink of death, but another eleven had passed through the gates of Kallor's realm, never to return. It was time to take his birthright. Time to find Ellen and return to Beslin.

Bovosan had been questioned by all of them, but refused to say a word about his inexplicable defence of the Northman Sorcerer. Cedrin could not forget the devotion the minitil had once shown him, or the fact that he had saved his life in Olcis. Even so, Bovosan had forfeited his place of trust at his side. He walked at the rear, bereft of weapons.

'Perhaps some light, my Lord?' asked Kalyth.

'Of course.' Cedrin channelled the Fire into the Light matrix and a ball of light blossomed high above the Hall of Dreams. A Sorcerer did not have the ability to enhance the sight of others as a Priestess or Druid might.

'*Belin*,' whispered Kalyth under his breath.

'*The* Belin,' said Ranis in awe.

'The Ward,' said Cedrin in a cold voice. 'Until I claim the Spear of Carris.'

He saw movement at the other side of the Hall. Figures moved near a circular opening in the plaza, surrounded by low stone benches. Steam rose from the well, hinting at a hot spring there. He saw the Tahistil first, the Great Spider's body low to the ground, as though it was trying to become less visible in the bright light. The winged humanoid that stood beside it had to be Erioth, Ellen's teacher. There was also an Eathal. All prisoners of the Ward. This last must be the leader of the Maht jakkund cavalry that had recently attacked the Ward. His identity remained a mystery, as was the reason he had followed them here. There would be time enough for that later.

Cedrin made directly for the Ward.

As he drew closer, he could see the blue lights that danced in Belin's eyes. He was possessed by the Ward, his face cold and expressionless. The golden Spear slung across his back shimmered with power.

'At last. The Scion of the Cinanac comes to claim the Spear,' said the Ward in a high, thin voice.

They met less than ten paces from the Temple of the Iris. The ancient structure was identical in its construction to the one in Olcis. The solid mass of it loomed over them.

The light issuing from the Spear dimmed. When Cedrin looked closer, he saw that a dark shape was forming. The Ward remained oblivious to it.

'The Behemoth rises,' said Dagon, the Priest's deep voice rumbling in his chest. The hairs on the back of Cedrin's neck rose as the Priest and Priestesses joined their power and began a low chant. A golden sheath formed around the Spear. The indistinct form struggled inside it. Cedrin saw a brief image of the cracked horn, then the flash of a single golden eye, before both dissolved. The dark shape pulsed and writhed against its golden bonds like a living thing.

'The Beast has been contained, my Lord,' said Dagon.

Cedrin swallowed, remembering the Behemoth's soul-sapping touch in the Olcis Iris.

Blue light flickered over Belin's features. Another face appeared. The angular visage of Emperor Jykor, Cedrin's own grandfather, who had constructed the Ward to guard the Spear.

'Come, grandson. Take the Spear and lead the Empire to greatness once more. I am pleased Riin could at least sire a child of the Old Blood.'

Cedrin resisted the urge to raise the Barrier. Against the Ward, such a gesture would be useless. With Dagon and the Twins Delegation here to contain the Behemoth, it was a simple matter of surrendering to the Ward, allowing it to confirm his identity and grant him the weapon.

As he approached, two tendrils of blue swept out from the Ward like thin, reaching arms. The shock forced him to stillness. He felt their powerful, yet clumsy presence in his mind as they searched through his memories, confirming his identity. Through the blue curtain, he saw the Tahistil, the feathered Erioth and the captured Eathal hurry across the space towards them. His throat tightened at the sinuous movement of the Great Spider. The One Hundred moved out in formation, blocking the advance of the strange prisoners of the Ward. Veltricus and his men came forward to stand behind the Twins Delegation.

The two tendrils withdrew, and his vision returned to normal. Erioth stopped three paces from Cedrin's men.

'Are you the Cinanac heir?' called Erioth in smooth Anacian. The resemblance to the more bestial Lamel made the cultured speech surprising. Cedrin had to remind himself he was dealing with a representative of a completely different race – and a Sorcerer.

'I am Cedrin Cinanac. Here to claim the Spear of Carris as my birthright,' he said, his voice hard with the knowledge of all he and his men had sacrificed.

'The Spear is cursed. It should never be raised again. If you deny it now, the Ward will never yield it to another. Do not take it!'

He met Erioth's large silver eyes, trying to read the true intentions of the birdlike being.

'I must take it,' said Cedrin. He could not risk it falling into the hands of another. If he was ever to defeat the Eathal and help restore the Empire, he would have need of its power. They had sacrificed too much already. The lives of the fallen had to count for something.

'I am Faivel, of the Maht Eathal,' called out the Eathal, in rough Anacian. 'Listen to us! Look around you. Look at the Destruction. Do you want to become another Carris? How much death do you want on your hands?'

The power of the Spear grew. Soon the golden radiance outshone even the ball of light hovering above them.

The Ward held up his hand in command. 'Do not interfere. And remain silent.' All three of the prisoners stiffened as though an invisible noose had been tightened around their necks.

'Come forward,' said the Ward, beckoning him.

As Cedrin walked towards the Ward, his skin tingled with the intensity of the power emanating from the Spear. The dark roiling mass of the Behemoth swirled above the Ward's back, trapped in a prison of Earth Essence.

His instinct warned him back.

Despite everything, he knew in that moment he did not want to be linked to the Spear. Or allow the poison of the Behemoth into his mind. Then the power of the Ward wrapped itself around him, and he no longer had a choice. Cedrin was drawn forward until the ghostly face of the Emperor Jykor filled his vision. The Ward reached behind it and lifted the Spear from its back. It reversed the artefact and offered it to him, and Cedrin took it without question. The wooden shaft was cold against his palm. The radiance of the blade was blinding. It seared his eyes as a Bridge of Minds formed between him and the Ward.

Grandson. Receive my knowledge. Use it well.

The cavern, the tense crowd around Temple of the Iris, all were lost from sight amid a flood of images and thoughts. His

Light Matrix collapsed as fragments of a different life raced through his mind's eye. Images of the court splendour of Raynor. Faces he did not recognise. Knowledge of Sorcery. The ancient secrets of the Cinanac Emperors, passed down from Emperor to heir in unbroken line from the time of Carris. Jykor's son Riin – Cedrin's father – had never displayed any talent for Sorcery. He had broken the chain. Jykor, already under siege from a powerful Temple of the Sisters, had created the Ward to house his knowledge and protect the Spear of Carris. Part of his grandfather's mind now filled his own. There was too much there to understand at once, yet he knew all could be brought forward to be examined later and each memory would come to him with a crystal clarity undimmed by time.

Slowly the Hall of Dreams resolved around him. Foreign memories and thoughts raced through his mind. Matrices formed. Strategies came to him, along with memories of ancient battles.

He held the Spear of Carris. Its blade dimmed as the flow of power fell away. The ghostly mask of Jykor was gone from Belin's face, as were the blue lights in his eyes. The old general staggered back and sank to his knees. He groaned in pain and held his head between his hands.

Cedrin heard the sound of running feet and looked up to see the Hall of Dreams in chaos. The Eathal warriors who had served the Ward ran from the broad square. Its three prisoners, like Belin, were in obvious pain. Some artefact of the passing of the Ward.

Cedrin lifted the Spear in wonder. He had but to touch it with his mind and the whole Realm of Fire opened to him. Jykor's knowledge showed him that there was now no limit to the amount of power he could channel. The Cinanac Emperors had developed a new series of Matrices that could be activated only with this immense store of power. Sorcery that could achieve miracles – or destroy on a vast scale. He also knew the danger to his own mind. Such power could not be contained. One mistake would see him reduced to ash. It would take him time to learn to use it safely.

He could sense the Behemoth, and knew it was held back by

the shields of Essence that Dagon and his delegation had raised against it. He had done it! Relief swept through him, and he thrust the Spear above his head in triumph.

'All hail the Emperor!' called Kalyth.

The One Hundred sank to their knees, and the members of the Twins delegation bowed low.

Yet Veltricus and his two bodyguards did not kneel.

The Herath Suul walked slowly to Cedrin, his face as hard as granite. Cedrin's eyes widened as he felt Fire rise inside the Herath Suul. He had time only to raise a Shield as a crushing vice of Force surrounded him. He responded with the Force Matrix. Seven unfamiliar Matrices rose into Cedrin's mind. Panic threatened, but he pushed it away along with the unbidden knowledge. He opened his mind to the Spear, allowing its power to flow through him. There was a rush of Fire, and he brushed aside Veltricus' construct with ridiculous ease. But then the very force of the flow destroyed his Matrix. Unchannelled Fire threatened to destroy him. He hastily closed himself to the Spear.

The two bodyguards ran forward, thick-bladed knives with hooked hilts in either hand. Cedrin responded with a wall of Force that should have sent them both flying across the flagstones. Instead, glowmetals set into their heavy mought bracers rippled and began an eerie wail. He increased the power of his attack. The two men slowed, but kept advancing.

Once more, Cedrin thought to use the Spear. A memory overtook him. For a moment he was Jykor, filled with power as he channelled the full force the Spear through a foreign Matrix. He let the memory flow away and restored his focus.

Veltricus attacked again, once more with his Force vice. Cedrin shrugged it off, using his own powers. He opened himself to the Spear and attacked Veltricus with a streaming comet of heat that should have charred him to the bone in an instant. Instead one of the glowmetals hanging from his chest shrieked as it absorbed the power.

The One Hundred rushed forward, but met a wall of Force that sealed them from him and Veltricus. The Herath Suul had erected a Shield. Erioth, the Tahistil and the Eathal had recovered and watched the unexpected contest in tense silence. Bovosan circled, his face intent.

Before Cedrin could try a new attack, the two bodyguards closed on him. If he had been wielding his greatscythe, both would have fallen in a breath, but his weapon was slung across his back. Instead he held the Spear. He swung it to the left. The huge warrior swayed and trapped the shaft of the Spear with both knives. Cedrin kicked out. His boot met solid muscle. Then the second warrior was on him, his powerful hands trying to peel away his grip on the Spear. He gritted his teeth in frustration. With all the power of the Spear at his command, he was reduced to a wrestling match. Matrices and strategies raced through his head, the knowledge of Jykor, rising in a rush. He knew the answer was there, but there was too much to focus on. He channelled Force again, using his own Window, but the power was absorbed by the glowmetals on the bodyguards' wrists. He increased the flow. The wailing stopped and the bands of light rapidly dwindled. Soon his power would overcome the capacity of the glowmetals.

Then he was out of time.

A muscle tore in his bicep and Cedrin heard his finger bone snap as the ancient weapon was wrenched from his grip. He staggered back, then watched in disbelief as the bodyguard threw the Spear to Veltricus.

The Herath Suul drew himself up. Cedrin looked at the glowmetals the man wore with new eyes. Now he realised that what he took to be an ostentatious display of wealth was a carefully assembled array of magical protections. This had been planned from the beginning.

'I am Veltricus Cineth, sworn Jakir of the line of Nyssus.' He held up the Spear. 'This weapon is an abomination. The Jakir cannot allow it to destroy Yos a second time.'

What he and Ellen had overheard in the Thilil forest had been no quirk of translation. As incredible as it seemed, Veltricus considered himself a Jakir, one of the ancient guardians of Yos. To Cedrin, he was merely another player in this game. He knew nothing of the Jakir. What he did know was that he could not allow some unknown faction to wield that amount of power.

Erioth came forward, halting at Veltricus' Shield. 'How can this be? The Jakir fell at the Destruction.'

'Remnants remain.'

A silent exchange passed between the Tahistil and Erioth. 'We stand with you, Veltricus. We journeyed here to see an end to the threat of the Spear.'

Faivel's ears quivered with tension, but he remained silent, spellbound by the confrontation.

Kalyth and the One Hundred circled the magical barrier, cursing in fury. 'What do you want us to do?' called Kalyth.

Cedrin held up his hand, telling Kalyth to wait. 'What do you intend to do with the Spear, Jakir?'

'Find some way to destroy it,' said Veltricus.

Dagon pushed through the One Hundred. 'How do you propose to counter the Behemoth? Or do you think a Jakir is too pure to be ensnared by its coils?'

Veltricus' eyes narrowed. 'I do not answer to you, Priest. Perhaps I should ask what Anan-Ac wants with the Spear? Or do you think that snake-pit of a Temple is a fitting home for such tainted power?'

Cedrin looked between Veltricus and Dagon. *Anan-Ac?* More mysteries. Right now he had to trust what he knew. Dagon and his delegation had done nothing but shield him and Ellen from the power of the Behemoth since they arrived in Herath.

The big Priest grew in stature. He signalled Esmelle and the twins Bles and Ris to join him. His eyes glittered with strange highlights. When he spoke, his voice was now sibilant with the power at his command. 'Do you forget where you stand, Jakir? Where are the glowmetals that deflect *our* power?' The Herath Suul looked up at the Temple of the Iris then back to Dagon.

'Find out,' challenged Veltricus.

Dagon and Esmelle raised their hands. A flame of Earth Essence sprang up around them. Their power rushed through Veltricus' Shield as if it was not there. Veltricus swung the Spear towards them. A fountain of Fire cascaded from the golden blade then collapsed. The Suul's jaw dropped in surprise. *Veltricus had discovered how the power of the Spear destroys a normal*

Matrix. He lowered the Spear and hastily countered the wall of Earth Essence with his own power. The Fire swept around the Essence. The warriors of the One Hundred scrambled to safety as the Fire roared past. The wall of Essence continued to expand. Despite the power of the Spear, the Essence soon reached Veltricus. One of the glowmetals on his neck squirmed, shooting streamers of purple light into the cavern. The bands of vivid green light on the glowmetal began to rapidly thin.

Veltricus would soon be overwhelmed, and Cedrin readied his own power. He swiftly drew the Matrix of Form, healing his bicep and the broken finger bone.

The Tahistil sprang forward. 'You will find Veltricus has an ally that matches your power!'

A nimbus of Essence appeared around the spider. The magic rushed forward and wrapped around Veltricus, halting the power of Esmelle and Dagon. Light flashed as the walls of Earth Essence met. Small stars flashed into existence and burst with a sizzle.

Dagon glowered. His dark hair stood out around his big face like a mane. 'Bles. Ris.'

The twins stepped forward. They turned slowly towards the Tahistil, the sickly whitened eyes coming into focus on the Great Spider. Cedrin shivered. He would not want those strange eyes to come to rest on him. This had happened once before. Moments before Salis had collapsed in Herath. Why had he not remembered that before? Even as he had the thought, it slipped from his grasp.

The Tahistil hissed. The flame of Earth Essence issuing from the Great Spider moved from Veltricus to meet the new threat. It extended across the cavern to wrap itself around the twins. Inside that long flame, streamers of white appeared, stabbing from each twin's eyes into the Tahistil's insectoid head.

Cedrin's breath caught in his throat at the smell of burning flesh. The Tahistil growled in pain, but the contest continued. The flesh of each twin began to glow, as though they were twin lamps, lit from within. The last wisps of hair fell away from their bald scalps.

Veltricus unleashed his power. Waves of heat and Force

descended on Esmelle and Dagon, battering them. Esmelle cried out in pain. Sweat beaded the big Priest's forehead. Their tide of Essence continued on to wrap itself around the Herath Suul. A darkness grew from the Spear. A form that Cedrin had come to dread. The strange, mismatched eyes, and the cracked, bloodied horn of the Behemoth.

Belin, standing some ten paces behind Veltricus, climbed to his feet.

'Cedrin! The Eathal. The Behemoth now has control of them,' called the old general in a deep voice.

Cedrin's gaze swept the cavern. The Eathal who had run before had now returned. They ran directly for the Temple of the Iris. He saw another figure as well – Bovosan, creeping through the shadows at the base of the Iris' dais.

There was a high, inhuman shriek. The Tahistil burst into flame. The air was filled with an acrid, burning stench as the Great Spider jerked and danced in pain. Then its cries of agony ceased, and it flipped limply onto its back.

The light inside the twins extinguished. Their heads drooped, then each collapsed, dissolving into themselves as though their inner essence had been burned away. Soon nothing remained but two sacks of skin, puddling on the flagstones amid their tumbled robes.

Veltricus cried out. His two bodyguards were thrown across the Hall of Dreams as though they were made of paper. Veltricus' Shield collapsed. The Suul was pushed flat to the flagstones by a crushing weight of Earth Essence and the Spear flew from his hands. His eyes rolled back in his head and he lay unconscious. The ancient artefact skittered across the stone, the golden blade now dull.

A dark figure darted forward and snatched up the weapon. Bovosan.

Cedrin ran to the minitil and held out his hand.

'Give it me,' said Cedrin.

The minitil grimaced, then backed away to the Temple of the Iris. A chill ran down Cedrin's spine as he realised Bovosan did not intend to give him the weapon. What had Raziin called him? *The Seer's servant.*

Cedrin's gaze swept the Hall. His hands tightened into fists as he saw Raziin and his men run from the shadows towards the Temple of the Iris. He should have known. From the very start, the Northman had possessed an uncanny knowledge of the caverns. He should have suspected he knew some way to escape the trap by the waterfall. Some hidden exit down in the dark chasm below. The Eathal now surrounded Raziin and his lieutenants, a small army provided by the Behemoth to its chosen Spear-wielder. There were around fourteen thal warriors, but there were another twenty thel as well, armed with spears and knives. Their eyes gleamed with a dark fury that was all too familiar to him. The Behemoth had taken their minds.

Bovosan slipped back towards Raziin. With a sick certainty everything now made sense. The minitil *had* protected him in Olcis, but only to keep him away from the Iris. Bovosan had always served another master, one who wanted Raziin to have the Spear of Carris.

'No, Bovosan! You cannot let Raziin have that power.'

The minitil's bright green eyes were resigned as he neared Raziin.

Kalyth ran to his side, followed by the One Hundred.

'Dagon!' called Cedrin in warning.

Dagon and Esmelle turned the combined power of the Earth Essence onto Bovosan. The minitil staggered to a halt halfway between Cedrin and Raziin. He slumped into the wall of the Iris dais, between two of the sets of stairs up to the Temple platform. He fought to turn, but was held in place.

Raziin and his combined force of Eathal and human warriors ran for the Temple of the Iris, trying to get to Bovosan.

'Come on!' called Cedrin. 'We need to head them off.'

Kalyth and the One Hundred responded. Although unarmed, Belin had joined them, running beside him and Kalyth. Yes! Cedrin knew he would reach Bovosan first.

Then Erioth and Faivel unleashed their combined powers of Sorcery on Dagon and Esmelle. The area between the two sets of stairs blazed as the power of the Verial and Eathal Sorcerers met the dome of Earth Essence that pinned the minitil in place. Cedrin looked between the two groups. They were locked in magical combat, neither getting an edge on the other. *Erioth's Shield had somehow held back the Earth Essence.* A variation of the Matrix that he was not aware of.

Cedrin and his men backed away, held back from Bovosan by the intensity of the magical maelstrom. He cursed in frustration. He had to leave the two former prisoners of the Ward to Dagon and Esmelle. Raziin and his small army of Eathal and Northmen arrived. They faced each other at the base of the Temple of the Iris, with Bovosan unreachable between them.

Cedrin let out a long, slow breath. It seemed he and Raziin would have their final battle after all.

Behind Raziin, a small group of Eathal broke away and ran up the stairs into the Temple of the Iris. One of them was carrying a silver glowmetal, the others held dried lungii stalks and bundles wrapped in greasy paper.

'It's the activation glowmetal I used to escape Raynor,' said Belin. 'They mean to open the Iris. All they need is a fire. Those are packets of lug - lungii seed resin. It burns with an intense flame.'

So that was how Raziin planned to escape. Once more the knowledge of the Behemoth had come to Raziin's aid.

'They have to win the Spear first.' Cedrin measured the odds. Raziin had roughly equal numbers, but the core of his force numbered no more than twelve – the rest were Eathal, many thels, controlled by the Behemoth. No doubt they would fight with berserk fury, but they would fall quickly to the One Hundred.

Inside the Iris, a fire flared to life. The flames eagerly consumed the lungii and lug. In the midst of the fire, the bands on the silver glowmetal began to writhe and shift. The Iris itself is nothing more than a gateway, he reminded himself. *Focus.*

As long as Dagon and Esmelle kept Bovosan contained, keeping the Spear from Raziin, victory would be theirs.

'Engage Raziin's forces. This time I want none to escape,' said Cedrin. He had come too far to fail now.

'Yes, my Lord,' said Kalyth. 'Elthar. Duro. Take ten men and circle around them. I want them under pressure from all sides.'

The tall warrior and the huge Duro ran to Raziin's left flank, going wide around the Eathal. They were under pressure almost immediately, a dozen crazed Eathal surging at them with their strange warcries.

Cedrin focussed on Raziin, blanking out the magical battle centred on Bovosan and the threat of the Behemoth. He opened the Window, establishing the Barrier and readying a Shield. He knew Raziin's tricks now. He slowly lifted the greatscythe from his back and locked the two blades into place with a twist. He embraced the Way. He heard the fast breathing of the warriors behind him, saw the wisps of steam from the well dance across the Hall of Dreams, lit by discharges of Essence and Fire and the radiance of the Spear.

He turned to Belin, who was still standing at his side, unarmed.

'Belin. Perhaps you better fall back,' said Cedrin.

'And miss this fight? No. There will be plenty of weapons to be had soon enough. Eh, Kalyth?'

Kalyth grinned and the years fell away from his usually grim face. 'Yes, General.'

Cedrin led the attack. On either flank, the One Hundred followed at a jog, each intent on the enemy. As for the prior attack, they had spread into a long, loose line, the blades of their greatscythes extended and ready for combat.

Raziin hit him with the Final Matrix. Cedrin held the attack easily. Then the lines met. The air was filled with a confusion of shouts and cries as the One Hundred clashed with the Eathal. Cedrin increased his pace.

The Northman realised only at the last minute that Cedrin did not intend to battle him with Fire and brought up his greatscythe to block.

A roar of pure fury escaped Cedrin as he swung his greatscythe at Raziin. The first blade was deflected and his second followed it in a lateral slice at Raziin's neck. His arm shuddered with the impact as Raziin took the blow on the haft of his greatscythe.

The combat around them fell away. Their weapons moved like living things. Blades sliced and cut, each movement

374

countered in a blur. Cedrin had better technique, but Raziin's reflexes and attacks were battle-trained. The Northman's attacks were brutal and effective. Raziin feinted in at his midsection, only to counterswing at his leg. Only a hasty sidestep prevented him being hamstrung by the razor-sharp blade. Cedrin countered with a swing at Raziin's face. The Northman blocked his blade. Instead of attacking with a counterswing, Cedrin used his weight to drive the blade at his face like a spear. Their two blades squealed against each other as he pushed in. Raziin tried to break away, but did not move aside fast enough. Cedrin's blade opened up a wide gash on Raziin's neck.

The Northman cried out in astonished surprise and disengaged. Cedrin's heart flared with a savage determination. That chink in the savage warrior's confidence was the beginning of the end. Raziin lashed out with Fire and Force, but Cedrin shrugged both off easily with neat manipulation of the Shield Matrix.

'Afraid?' taunted Cedrin.

'Of you?' sneered Raziin in response. His eyes narrowed in calculation and Cedrin readied himself to attack.

Cedrin blinked as the light in the cavern intensified. He stepped back a pace to give himself room and flicked his gaze to the battle of magic. The two walls of opposing magic had grown in size. Magical flames and bursts of light flashed into existence above the immense front. Belin had found himself a greatscythe and fought back-to-back with Kalyth, the ground around them littered with dead. Elthar and Duro had cut through Raziin's lines from the rear to link with the rest of the One Hundred. They now surrounded less than a dozen of Raziin's men, including the golden giant Merceth and Raziin's lieutenant Kyal. They were moments away from complete victory.

There was a flash of blinding violet light. Cedrin strengthened his Shield and backed away, trying to clear his vision. Light remained, but now it issued only from the Spear of Carris. His heart sank as he saw Dagon and Esmelle slump prostrate to the stone. He looked to the other side of the cavern. Erioth was on his knees, exhausted. Faivel supported him. Veltricus' two bodyguards were carrying the unconscious Suul across the Hall of Dreams away from the conflict.

The battle had ended inconclusively, yet now Bovosan was free. He rose to his feet and started to run to Raziin.

The minitil was not the only thing that was unleashed. Without the power of Dagon or Esmelle to contain it, the Behemoth rose from the Spear and took form. The huge Beast ran beside Bovosan. It had no physical form, yet it wielded the Essence. It slammed the warriors of the One Hundred from its path as it ran to Raziin. Others who tried to cut them off were also thrown aside.

Raziin tried to back towards his men, but Cedrin circled to cut him off.

'No. I don't think so,' said Cedrin. He could not use the Spear if he could not reach it.

A new light lit the Hall of Dreams. The Iris was coming to life. His breath grew tight as he sensed its song at the edge of his hearing. Soon a whirlpool of light turned inside the Temple's fivefold symmetry. *Raziin must not escape with the Spear.*

Cedrin heard a rousing chorus Eathal warcries. *Uros!*

Hundreds of Eathal emerged from the darkness. Some of them were the tribal warriors who had fought against Raziin less than a hour ago, yet now they rushed to his aid, their eyes dark with the taint of the Behemoth. The power of the Beast had been unleashed here in this cavern, where it had been prisoner for half a lifetime. It had three decades to work its insidious will on these cavern dwellers.

The One Hundred had battled hard, but not even they could survive odds like this. Not with the horned Behemoth on Raziin's side like a rabid war-harena.

Cedrin watched Bovosan and the Behemoth run across the Hall of Dreams, unwilling to accept defeat. Then just before the Beast and the minitil reached Raziin's lines, two nets of finely woven yellow light appeared in the air. One dropped onto Bovosan, while the other draped the running Behemoth. Both drew tight.

Bovosan shrieked and tripped to the floor less than ten paces away, the Spear caught against his body. The Behemoth roared and slashed at the magical fibres with its horn. The net parted, yet reformed in an instant. The net around the Behemoth shrank. Waves of darkness curled off its body as the ropes of Essence cut into its form. Its body grew less substantial as it was forced into a ball of swirling black. The eyes, with their mismatched gaze, glared from the prison. Two thirds of the Eathal were loosed from the Behemoth's influence and retreated back into the dark, but more than fifty remained. The Beast fought back, and the net contracted no further.

Cedrin lifted his head in disbelief as he heard a familiar ululating warcry.

'The Daughters!' called Ranis.

Ellen and Spider ran into the Hall of Dreams, leading the Daughters. Behind them was Raphal, his face grim with concentration as he channelled the power of the Hall to contain the Behemoth and trap Bovosan. The dark-haired Suulqua Mendor ran at Ellen's side, his face fierce as he watched for any threat to his Lady.

The Eathal ran at the One Hundred, who now found themselves fighting on two fronts. Yet the Eathal in turn found themself under pressure from both front and rear as the Daughters hit them.

Raziin looked back at him once, then ran for Bovosan. Cedrin surged into motion, a step behind.

'No!' Before he could stop him, the Northman had wrapped his hand around the shaft of the Spear where it protruded from the magical net.

Chapter Twenty-Three

Daran watched the flames rise higher in the east. As for the Outer City, the houses inside the walls were slow to burn.

'How close are they?' he asked the commander of the First. The man had been the most senior of the Legion's First Captains. Their General had fallen less than an hour ago in one of the many street battles.

'Less than three hundred paces from the corner,' said the First commander.

Hukum's single-minded advance had one benefit. It allowed Daran to open the western gates. The walls were abandoned as the Third marched west ahead of the panicked masses to link with the Fourth. The huge population of Raynor choked the roads into the Delta and jammed the gates. It was simply not possible to get them all out. Hundreds of thousands remained in the poor quarters. Looters and mobs ran rampant.

Daran stood on the Palardos, before the opened gates of the Palastrada. He saw no point closing them against the Eathal advance. The last two hours had been an exhausting trial of blood and flame. The fires had grown, his men had fallen while he stood in silent fury. He knew he should have retreated with the Third and taken the Suulvey with him, but he refused to let his men die alone. He also refused to leave his city while thousands waited to escape.

The Palardos was crowded with Suul. Many had fled with the Third, but many more remained. Hundreds stood in loose groups defended by their bodyguards. A score of others had donned ancient armour and mounted their narsiit. The winged beasts danced impatiently and lifted their noses to the wind, scenting blood. The intelligent mounts called to each other and stamped their frustration. Daran had refused to let himself be cornered inside the palace like some caged animal. If he was going to die, it was right here, with his men.

As he had hoped, Hukum did not bring his Shield glowmetal into the city. The Sundar remained inside the eastern gate. He had used the Wallbreakers to clear a wide square and had made camp there under the protection of the Shield glowmetal. That did not mean contesting the Eathal advance had been easy.

The Silver and Black had joined forces and had marched directly for the Palastrada determined to rip the heart from the city. Even without the Shield glowmetal, their magical strength was formidable. They carried both glowmetals used to cut down and level the Docks District. Their effect on any formation was devastating. They also carried the platinum glowmetal that had burned the barricade at the eastern gate. Its intense tongue of flame melted mought and stone, and even set rebin wood alight. His defensive barricades were useless.

His men had fought hard. Squads of volunteers had remained behind the advancing Eathal lines, hitting the flanks of the Silver and Black and selling their lives dearly. Yet it was not enough. The Black were elite troops, and they fought with ferocity in the darkened streets.

Meanwhile elements of the Yellow and a Sorcerer-Lord escorted three of the Wallbreakers around the Raynor. All used varieties of Force. The regular detonation and rumble of the Wallbreakers sent tremors through the cobbles beneath their feet. They had been at work continuously for hours, methodically demolishing Raynor's walls. They were almost at the south gate. One quarter of the once impregnable walls had fallen. The copper glowmetal that had turned the eastern gates to sand had not been used again.

His heart burned at the arrogance of Hukum. The Sundar did not even deign to lead the last attack against him, leaving it to his subordinates. That lack of respect for Raynor's power chaffed at him like a bloody splinter under his skin.

Daran could hear the clatter and shouts of battle draw closer.

He had ordered Uran and Nacius to drive a wedge between the glowmetals and the bulk of the Eathal forces, to deprive them of the weapons before the final confrontation. He saw the squads from the Second run around the corner in retreat. A scything blade of blue shot past the corner, cutting half of them down. Daran's knuckles whitened on the haft of his greatscythe as he watched the survivors run for the streets. His remaining men were hidden in the streets that ran onto the Palardos. He intended to draw the Black and Silver right to him, and give his men a chance to cut into their flanks as the magical attack was directed forward.

His men came into view, the Legionnaires had their shields locked, retreating before the advancing Eathal lines. A broad ram of Force shot at the lines. A Shield flared, deflecting the blow above the retreating men. *Nacius and Uran lived.* Windows exploded in the upper storeys of a mansion behind them. Glass rained onto the street amid bricks and other masonry torn loose from the facade.

Magical fire arced above the lines from their Druidin but was intercepted in turn by the enemy's Shields.

'Fall back!' called Daran.

He could not leave himself or the Suul in full view of the advancing Eathal forces. He would leave the gates open, hiding his forces behind the flimsy walls of the Palastrada. He needed to draw them inside and get into close quarters, break their lines.

Daran ran back inside the gates and up the stairs to the Palastrada wall. As planned, Uran and Nacius, leading around a thousand Legionnaires, continued to retreat to the open gates. Hopefully they would draw the Eathal force with them. If they continued to lead with their three glowmetals then all the hidden warriors in the streets beyond the Palardos would be able to drive into their exposed flanks without fear of magical attack. It was his last roll of the dice. Nothing more remained after this.

He saw the standards of the Black Drakon and Silver Teremb legions draw closer. Two Sorcerer-Lords on jakkund rode behind the lead glowmetals. He studied them, hoping that he might get to face Hukum, but was disappointed. There were too few jakkund bodyguard. The Sundar remained at the eastern gate. His stomach tightened as he saw more than fifty Tahistil marched with them. The hairy backs of the huge spiders overtopped the heads of the Eathal, the legs eerily smooth in their movements.

The Scythe glowmetal struck out, only partially deflected by Uran and Nacius' Shield. A score of men were sliced in two. Daran's temples pounded and his vision blurred. The ram glowmetal slammed into their Shield again. Men were driven back off their feet and the lines grew ragged. The platinum glowmetal was tilted up. Daran ducked as a tongue of heat lashed out at the Palastrada. The wave of heat passed overhead to hit the Palanac. He smelled burning hair and realised it was his own. The mought tiles cracked on the palace and the wooden internals leapt into flame. He licked his lips. If the palace was set to flame, there would be no retreat. They would be caught between the gates and the flames at their rear.

'Come on. Come!' shouted Daran, willing the advancing Eathal into his trap.

The pace of Uran and Nacius' retreat increased, opening a gap between them and the Eathal. They were two-thirds of the way back from the corner where he had first sighted them to the Palastrada gates. The Black and Silver marched on at a deliberate pace. The three Eathal glowmetals spoke again. This time all three attacks were directed up at the Palastrada. The Scythe cut through a tall spire. He held his breath as it tumbled back onto the palace, crashing into the roof of the Great Hall and smashing through the vast glass ceiling. The ram punched holes through the walls. Beams groaned. Flames rose higher as the platinum glowmetal sent another stream of heat into the palace.

'Curse you, Kallor. *Let them come.*' Time seemed to slow as Daran measured the distance between the advancing Eathal and the gates.

The wall shook beneath him as a bolt of Force hit it, driving blocks all the way through it like missiles. He heard screams behind him and saw the courtyard behind the wall was littered with the bloody bodies of fallen Suul. Narsiit trumpeted in fury.

A Suulvey yelled a warcry and raced out through the gates on his narsiit. He manoeuvred around the rear of Uran's retreating men and raced straight for the Eathal van. There was a roar of Fire as a Sorcerer-Lord's attack swept past him. Then he was at the lines. The narsiit leapt high, coming down amidst the crew of the platinum glowmetal. The narsiit spun, leapt and bit, driving the Eathal back in bloody disarray. The Suul's cavalry scythe took a heavy toll, slaying both Eathal warriors and the jakka who drew the glowmetal's wagon. Then an Eathal bearing twin axes of dark glass leapt up onto the narsiit. His first blade took the Suul in the ribcage and both tumbled to the ground. The glowmetal's wagon shuddered to a stop as the narsiit went wild, killing all who came within striking distance. Then it was down. It gave one last high whinny, then was silent.

The Black and Silver came on, yet the toll had been so high amidst the platinum glowmetal's crew that the huge artefact stayed where it was. The advancing Eathal lines flowed around it.

His men had finally reached the gates. He ran down to the courtyard. His feet twisted on the narrow steps and he stumbled into the wall, cracking his knee against the stone. For a long moment, he was stunned with pain. His body was an empty shell, like a corpse drained of blood. Too much tension. Too many nights without sleep.

Hands pulled him upright. 'My Lord. Are you wounded?'

He pushed his aides away and continued on. Two gaping holes had been punched in the wall and the battlements tilted at a dangerous angle. They could collapse at any moment.

'Uran! Uran!' He pushed through the lines of his retreating men.

The golden-skinned Sorcerer was covered with soot and dried blood. At his side, Nacius was like an emaciated ghost, his violet eyes glowing in his pale face with the residue of channelled power.

'You live, my friend.'

'Yes. Still,' said Uran, forcing a smile.

Daran gripped Uran's forearm with something akin to desperation. This was the end. Raynor. The Yasser States. The rebirth of the Empire he had once sworn to serve. It had been a beautiful dream. Now the time of the Eathal was here. Every victory he had ever won would mean nothing now. He would be remembered as the man who lost Raynor to Hukum.

Daran released the grip and turned to peer out through he gates. As he hoped, the Black and Silver led with their glowmetals. His heart leapt as he saw contingents of the First and Second charge into the flanks of the Eathal. He laughed as he saw the orderly lines of the Eathal dissolve into a grand melee.

'Uros! Finally. At least I lived to see the lines of the Black broken,' said Daran.

'Now?' said Uran.

'Yes,' said Daran. At last he could let all worry go. He would meet the Eathal head-to-head and pay the debt with his own blood. No duty – no god – could demand any more of him.

The Warlord nodded to his aides. A trumpet was raised and a command rang out across the palace courtyard. There was no answering trumpet, not here. They were all that remained. The last defence of Raynor.

The retreating Legionnaires split smoothly into two flanks. The left, led by Nacius, swept around behind the left side of the gates. Uran and Daran fell back with the right flank to the other side of the gate. Behind each of the left and right flanks were the Suul, both mounted and on foot.

The courtyard behind the gate was left open. Inviting.

Daran began to laugh. He tried to still it, but the tension had become too much. The night was surreal around him.

'A good time to die, lads!' he called.

The answering shout was like thunder.

A scything blade of blue shot through the gates, followed by bolt of Force that demolished the rear wall of the courtyard. Men at the rear of the left flank screamed in fear and pain as they were swallowed by falling masonry.

The lead elements of the Black and Silver issued their warcries and stormed through the gate. They had left the glowmetals outside, but that no longer mattered. They were now blocked by Eathal troops. Useless. The two Sorcerer-Lords passed through the gates, their jakkund bodyguards alert for any threat.

Fire roared out from both flanks. The Sorcerer-Lords were caught off guard by twin attacks from Uran and Nacius. Eathal howled in pain as they were engulfed.

'Attack!' roared Daran.

Daran's left and right flanks drove into the Eathal. The Black and Silver continued to advance, pushing into the backs of their lead warriors. Soon the courtyard was jammed. A shoving match where strength and ferocity counted for as much as skill. Amidst it all, the narsiit trumpeted in fury. The mounts danced through the Eathal ranks, hooves striking out with crushing force.

Magical Shields flared silver. Fire and flame roared in the air. Tahistil bounded above the packed ranks, springing lightly from shoulder and head to land behind them. One fell on a narsiit. It gripped it with its pincers, driving a crystal blade into the narsiit's side. The rider stabbed the Great Spider through its insectoid head and it convulsed, dragging the mount down with it. Both were lost in the confusion of battle.

Daran was wedged in between his aides. His greatscythe was pinned against him, useless in the press. He drew a calv, but need not have bothered. None of the Eathal could reach him. He cursed in frustration.

One of the Great Spiders sprang into the air behind them. Uran spun and raised a hand. A stream of heat crackled over their heads, engulfing the beast in a sheath of flame. It fell back down into the chaos of the courtyard with a high-pitched shriek. Others fought with shield and blade. Yet for all their speed and fearsome aspect, they were vulnerable across most of their large bodies. The long spears of the phalanx soon impaled them, and the short scythes cut at their vulnerable limbs.

Opposite he could see Nacius was rigid, his violet eyes locked onto one of the Sorcerer-Lords. The Eathal's jewelled armour was worked with the standard of the Blood legion. It was the hothead. The one who had led his own legion to destruction west of Raynor. He too was motionless. Beneath him, his jakkund jerked and tossed its head. One of the Sorcerer-

Lord's bodyguards grabbed the bridle to steady the beast. The human and Eathal Sorcerers were locked into mental combat. The fight on the left flank was blade-to-blade now, a welcome respite while the two Sorcerers squared off.

Daran measured the distance. *Yes!*

He looked to the front of the right flank. 'Crescent Razor!'

The Legionnaire looked back, surprised at being addressed directly by the Warlord. 'The Sorcerer-Lord!' yelled Daran, motioning with his hands in a thrusting motion.

A grin spread on the Razor's face. He motioned to two of his men. Two of them guided the front of the long spear as the Razor prepared to drive an all-out thrust. The spears were usually used in a stabbing movement where they would strike and be withdrawn. Now they would extend the long spear far beyond hope of retrieval. With a shout, the Razor drove the heavy weapon over the heads of the Eathal. A surprised Eathal bodyguard jerked back as the big lanedd blade slipped past his face. He cried out in despair as he saw the weapon drive through the back of his Lord. The Eathal Sorcerer howled in pain, then toppled from his jakkund mount.

'One for the First, my Lord!' called the Razor. The men surrounding them roared in response.

The second Sorcerer-Lord found himself beset. Uran, Nacius and the surviving Druidin drove at him with a storm of Fire and Force. Jakkund screamed as the Sorcerer-Lord's bodyguard was engulfed. He gave orders in the Eathal tongue and abruptly the pressure lessened on the line.

The Eathal were retreating.

'Follow them!' commanded the Warlord. His Legionnaires and surviving Suul roared in response and cut into the retreating Eathal, climbing over the fallen to get at them.

Uran was at his side. 'They have three glowmetals, but each requires a Sorcerer to charge it. If we can bring down the last Sorcerer-Lord, we will have them.'

Daran saw it immediately. He gave swift orders and a phalanx formed in wedge formation, driving forward at the glowmetals. He advanced with Uran and Nacius as they kept up the attack on the Sorcerer-Lord.

Outside the gates, he now had time to judge the effectiveness of the whole strategy. His heart sank as he saw that the Black and Silver had restored their lines. The flanking attacks from the contingents of First and Second had been driven back. His men continued the attack, but faced a stationary line of Eathal with large, linked shields. And sitting defended in the middle of the Eathal formation were the three huge glowmetals.

The phalanx drove forward into the front ranks of the Eathal, trying to cut off the Sorcerer-Lord. Yet even the combined attacks from Uran and Nacius did not penetrate the Eathal Sorcerer's Shield. His jakkund bodyguard fought with smooth precision, using their lances to deadly effect on his infantry. The phalanx attack slowed then stopped, halted by the forward elements of the Black. The Sorcerer-Lord reached his lines and went straight to the platinum glowmetal.

Their gambit had failed.

'Back inside the gates!' commanded Daran. He turned to one of his aides. 'Tell the contingents on the streets outside to fall back to the western gate.' Two runners were sent. There may be a chance to use them again, but he doubted it. He needed to get his remaining men out of the city now, into the Delta province.

He looked down at his greatscythe. He had not even had a chance to release the blades. His aides hustled him back towards the Palastrada. His Legionnaires and the remaining Suul retreated back into the courtyard and his men shut the gates. There were little more than two thousand of them left now. Outside, the combined forces of the Silver and Black numbered almost eight thousand. And they retained their offensive glowmetals.

Daran walked to one of the gaping holes in the wall and looked out. The Eathal Sorcerer-Lord stood immobile in front of the big platinum glowmetal. Lightning crackled from his outstretched hands. The blue bands of light that snaked through the glowmetal shrank to silver metal as it absorbed energy.

Uran stood at his side. 'So. He means to burn us out.'

Daran nodded. 'There will be no frontal attack now. He is too cautious.'

They covered their eyes as a tongue of intense heat wrapped

itself around the mought-reinforced gates. They exploded into flame. Men and narsiit were forced back to the palace entrance. The gates collapsed to ash, the mought puddling on the cobbles, hissing as it met the pools of blood there. The acrid smell of burning flesh caught in his throat.

'My Lord.' His aide tried to get his attention, but he was entranced, as though hypnotised by his own oncoming death. He watched the Sorcerer-Lord channel lightning into the glowmetal once more. The next burst would incinerate living flesh. He clenched his fist. The pain in his hand helped to clear his head.

'Back into the palace!' commanded Daran.

Suul streamed back through the palace entrance. The hot breath of the glowmetal came again. This time it was met by the combined Shields of Nacius and Uran. The intense heat roared around the edges of the Shield, cracking stone and setting bodies to flame as though they were tallow.

Daran looked behind him. Part of the palace was already in flames. With the glowmetals at his command, the Sorcerer-Lord could demolish the Palastrada and the Palanac at will. There was nothing left to counter him. The Yellow Drakon – almost a full Eathal Legion – remained, along with its Sorcerer-Lord, Hukum and the other Wallbreakers. Daran had one comfort left – the longer he pinned the Eathal forces here, the more time he gave the Third to get to safety. For the people of Raynor – his people – to escape.

Almost all his men were inside the palace itself now. Only Uran, Nacius and his forward guard remained. Above all else, the palace of the Cinanac was huge. The Great Hall was large enough a space for a pitched battle.

He looked up at the Eastern Tower, which was on the other side of the palace. The summit of the Tower glowed with a wavering golden light. It should not be affected by fire yet. If it was, it meant they would be retreating into a firetrap.

'We have to get inside, my Lord. Out of direct line-of-sight,' said Uran. He laid his hand on Daran's arm, as though to draw him away.

'Uran. The Tower,' said the Warlord. 'Is it in flames?'

Uran looked up at the Eastern Tower. His face grew still, the familiar look of concentration that betrayed his use of Sorcery.

Another wave of heat hit the courtyard. Nacius Shielded the remaining men, Uran and himself.

'No. Not flames. That . . . it can't be. The Face is ruptured.' The golden-skinned Sorcerer's jaw grew slack.

'What is it, Uran?'

'The Iris. The Gateway has opened.'

* * *

Cedrin closed on Raziin.

Raziin cursed as his hand slipped from the shaft of the Spear. Closer now, Cedrin could see that the ancient wood was covered by a fine sheath of Earth Essence. Only Raphal could release it.

Cedrin's greatscythe cut at the Northman's head. Raziin dodged away, circling onto the other side of the trapped Bovosan. His anger surged as he realised Raziin was on the run.

'Uros!' called Raziin.

Cedrin was unprepared as Raziin used a surge of Force to leap the fallen minitil.

Raziin cut down at Cedrin as he dropped, his blow aided by Force. Cedrin cut the Northman twice, opening long gashes in his leather armour, but Raziin was possessed. He fought with a new savagery. He did not attack Cedrin directly with Sorcery, but used the Force to reinforce the power of his attacks. This was a level of finesse with the Force Matrix that Cedrin had never achieved. The attack was so concentrated, so primal, he had no time to gather his own magical attack. He had the Shield in place, but none of the Force was specifically directed at him so it was useless.

He blocked a cut to his neck. His elbow joint flared painfully at the shock of contact. An instant later, Raziin sliced up at his groin. He spun away and caught the blade, but his position was awkward. He heard a high-pitched *crack*. Shards of lanedd burst through the air. He cried out as a splinter lodged in his thigh. His right blade was gone.

Raziin's face was a rigid mask of hate, looming closer. He cleared his mind, opening himself to the Way. Another attack came at him from the left. Time slowed. He blocked with the haft of his greatscythe, using the Force Matrix to aid it. Raziin rocked back, off balance.

Cedrin let his left hand slip off his greatscythe and slipped the haft under Raziin's extended weapon, then re-established his grip. He stepped in and pulled Raziin's greatscythe haft against his body, pinning it. The Northman's face was now less than a handspan away from his. Cedrin felt the Fire rise and guessed Raziin was going to use the Force to push him away. He countered, using the Force Matrix to trap his weapon. Raziin shook and spun, trying to dislodge him, but Cedrin gritted his teeth and held the grip.

'Now what, half-Blood?' growled Raziin.

'I'm no half-Blood,' hissed Cedrin. He let his right hand drop from the haft of his greatscythe, relying on the Force Matrix to continue to pin Raziin's weapon. Cedrin's hand swept to his harness.

Raziin had time only to widen his eyes as Cedrin snatched a long knife from his harness and drove the calv down at his throat.

At the last instant, Raziin surged back with a bolt of Force, partially dislodging himself. Instead of driving down into his throat, the calv embedded itself deep into his shoulder and into his lung. The blade wedged itself against Raziin's collar bone. 'That's for Jaso.'

Raziin shuddered and backed away, losing his grip on his greatscythe.

'My Lord!' The giant Merceth fought forward with two Armon warriors and shielded Raziin.

Cedrin lowered his greatscythe and looked down at the trapped form of Bovosan, who watched him silently.

It was time to end this.

Cedrin looked across the Hall to where Raphal and Valnis stood behind the turmoil.

'Raphal!'

The old Priest turned his head towards Cedrin and saw him

standing alone above the prostrate minitil and the Spear.

'Release Bovosan!'

There was no reply from the spare Priest, but the net that pinned Bovosan vanished. He was ready. Cedrin used the Matrix of Binding to pin the minitil in place and snatched the Spear from his rigid hands.

Kalyth and Belin came forward to shield him as he backed into the ranks of the One Hundred.

He took his time, searching through Jykor's memories for a Matrix that could channel the Spear's power into Force. As before, scores of conflicting images raced through his mind. Now, though, he knew what he needed. At last he found a memory where Jykor used a Matrix to lift huge blocks into place on one of Raynor's bridges. He built the Matrix in his mind, mentally comparing it against the Force Matrix he had come to know. It shared enough similarities for him to know where he could manipulate it, and that made sense. His forebears would have had to work from what they knew.

The Spear's golden blade flared to brightness.

Through the Spear, Cedrin opened himself to the Realm of Fire. He let the Fire flow through the new Matrix into a single bolt of Force.

A column of silver appeared before him like a colossal ram. It slammed through the ranks of the Eathal, smashing them into blood and bone. He felt his stomach twist in revulsion, but used the discipline of the Way to distance himself from the emotion. This was no time to shrink from attack.

He made a slight change to the Matrix and sent a scything blade through Raziin's ranks. Dozens of the cavern dwellers and remaining Armon troops were sliced in two. All at once, Raziin's defence collapsed. The melee had become so confused that he dare not do more.

'Get everyone behind me!' called Cedrin.

Orders rang out. The One Hundred disengaged. Raziin and his men looked back at Cedrin – his whole body alive with power – and ran for the open Iris. The last of the One Hundred and the Daughters ran back through the retreating enemy, Ellen and Spider with them. Raphal and Valnis followed more slowly.

The Behemoth struggled inside its Essence net.

Cedrin's teeth ground together. His warriors would soon be in the clear. Raziin and his men would not make the Iris. He readied to tap into the power of the Spear again. To end this.

The light coming from the Iris dimmed. The tiled roof of the Temple exploded upward. Tiles and stone rained down on them as an armoured form pushed its way through. A massive, wedge-shaped head appeared above the five columns.

'Black drakon!' called Kalyth.

Cedrin fought panic. Was their no end to the servants of the Behemoth? Three of the five columns crashed down onto the Hall of Dreams as the black drakon dragged its way free of the Iris Temple.

He released the power of the Spear. A scything blade of Force sliced into the side of the Black. The air was filled with the acrid stench of acid. The bodies of fallen warriors below the Iris leapt into flame and the stone hissed as the drakon's blood ate into it. The drakon roared and twisted its body free of the Temple. Cedrin adjusted the Matrix and shot a spear of Force the size of a tower at the creature, but the drakon leapt aside.

'We have to run!' called Kalyth.

'No!' Cedrin was done running.

He cleared his mind. He needed a Shield. His own powers would do little to stop a creature of this size. The very first wound he inflicted on the drakon was mortal, but that alone would not save them.

The black drew itself up on his forelegs. The mammoth lungs expanded. Raphal and his scholar friend finally reached them and scrambled behind the One Hundred.

There!

Cedrin channelled the Fire into a Shield that covered all of his warriors. A cloud of acid hissed across the space between them and the drakon. It swept harmlessly around the wide dome of the Shield.

Blood gushed from the drakon's wound. Gaping fissures opened in the Hall as the gushing blood carved channels through the rock. Some reached the ancient well and the waters there exploded into clouds of hissing steam.

Cedrin shot at the creature again. This time the huge spear of Force struck deep into the creature's breast, punching through its armoured hide. It lifted itself up, and for a moment its huge eyes glittered with the same darkness he saw in the Behemoth. Then it collapsed.

The air of the cavern was filled with steam and acid vapours. Erioth, the Eathal Sorcerer and Veltricus and his bodyguards were gone.

Cedrin ran to the Iris. Raziin and his men had already passed through the portal. He saw a single figure outlined in the magical whirlwind of light that turned at the centre of the Temple. Bovosan.

Cedrin ran to the Temple and up the steps, followed by the One Hundred, Ellen and the Daughters.

'Wait!'

Bovosan turned.

'Tell me why?' demanded Cedrin.

'You should have let him take it,' said Bovosan.

'But Raziin would use it for untold evil,' responded Cedrin. He blinked, his eyes still stinging from the acid vapours that pervaded the cavern.

The minitil bowed his head sadly. 'May Yosini protect you.' Then he turned and disappeared through the gateway.

At the centre of the Iris, he saw the glowmetal in its niche. The small fire was burning down. It hardly mattered. The knowledge of Jykor included the Opening Matrix of the Iris, the magical signature that the glowmetal mimicked.

'Cedrin!'

Ellen pushed through the ranks. She ran into his arms and for a long moment they were lost in each other's embrace. He felt the rigid bonds that held his heart captive break and a new warmth emerged. Against it was a distant voice of rage. His head snapped up, and he looked directly at the Behemoth, still trapped in the net of Essence. He had won the Spear, but would be forever linked to the Behemoth's dark presence.

He kissed Ellen, then they separated. Seeing her was like a miracle – one that had saved them all.

'How did you get here?' he asked in wonder.

'Through a long volcanic shaft – it leads directly to the surface,' said Ellen. Of course, the skyshaft Bovosan had spoken of.

He needed to follow Raziin and end this, but first he needed to be sure the Behemoth was contained. He searched through the crowd for Raphal.

'Can you rouse Dagon and Esmelle?'

The old Priest's bushy eyebrows drew together. 'I will need to release the Behemoth to use my powers.'

Cedrin swallowed. 'Do it.'

The last of the lug fire burned out at the centre of the Iris. Soon afterward the cyclone of light in the Temple collapsed into a faded rainbow of colours and vanished. Belin walked to the centre of the Temple and reclaimed the opening glowmetal. He lifted it into a sack and slung it across his back.

The One Hundred and the Daughters moved to deal with their wounded and he and Ellen sat together on a fallen section of one of the Iris' columns. Content to be together.

When Raphal released the net that contained the Behemoth, they both felt it. They shared a glance as the dark pressure began on their minds. Darkness rippled beside them, issuing from the Spear. Dark streamers ran from the shaft below the blade and linked it to the forming shape. The Behemoth appeared to them both, its strange mismatched eyes triumphant.

I am free now. There is no resisting me.

'Do you hear it?' asked Cedrin, knowing that she did.

'Yes. It is a creature of Earth Essence. It will always be strong near the holy places,' said Ellen.

Cedrin held himself back from saying what they both knew. As long as the Spear existed, it would always be between them, around them. A malicious third presence.

He could feel the creature's pressure on his thoughts, driving them to darkness. All he had achieved now seemed like failure. Despite everything, Raziin had slipped through his fingers again. More than half of the One Hundred lay in cold graves. And still the continent was divided, the Eathal slaying thousands as they advanced. And he was nothing but a pretender to a vanished throne. An ancient order that had no place in Kelas, founded by a slayer. A destroyer who forever tainted the Cinanac line with the blood of thousands . . .

He felt a cool hand on his cheek.

'Come back to me,' said Ellen. Her voice was soft. Warm.

Cedrin stared into her beautiful green eyes and wondered how he had survived without her at his side. The bond between them was a tangible thing, built of love, of shared fortune.

'I've missed you,' said Cedrin.

Something snapped. A dark thread. At once, the Behemoth was once more outside him. He could still feel the pressure on his mind, yet now it remained at a distance.

She tilted her head up to him, her lips parted and wet.

Cedrin kissed her softly, closing himself to the rancid touch of the Behemoth's mind. He leant back and looked down at her. Lights shone in her eyes, dancing like twin seabirds on the winds of Athria's wild harbour. They could survive this, become each other's refuge. Cedrin laid his hand on her stomach, feeling the slight swell of her abdomen, a tight knot beneath her skin.

'I swear I will find some way to end this curse before he holds the Spear,' said Cedrin.

It cannot be done.

They ignored the voice as it spewed its well of vileness. As they sat close, the Behemoth prowled around them, the rotted hide of the Beast's stomach rising and falling in parody of breath. Sometimes two sets of eyes looked out from the chameleon's face – one golden, the other grey-blue, so much like his own. It paced back and forth, restless, like a wild animal in a cage, longing for release. Driven by lust. It desired ultimate power – control of the Spear through its wielder. That must never happen.

The ranks of the One Hundred parted.

A drawn Dagon walked across the darkened mural of the Iris Temple, Esmelle behind him. The Priestess had cut her head as she fell and her hair was matted with dried blood. Red drops splattered the shoulder of her robe. Her eyes were haunted as she approached. He understood. She was a Priestess of healing and this deep cavern had become a place of death.

Dagon bowed his head. 'My Lord.'

'We need to pursue Raziin through the Iris. Are you ready to continue containing the Behemoth?'

Dagon nodded. 'Yes. Of course.' The big Priest waved Esmelle forward. Together they closed their eyes and began a low chant.

There was nothing visible, yet when they finished a weight lifted from him. Not from only his mind, it seemed it had been crushing his whole being. He almost laughed in relief. Truly Dagon and Esmelle had been sent by Larus herself.

'Kalyth. Gather everyone,' he said.

'Yes, my Lord.'

They had wasted enough time. He walked to the centre of the Iris and searched Jykor's knowledge for the Opening Matrix. He carefully constructed it, checking it against his new memories. Then he opened himself to the power of the Spear.

Light flared around him. Slowly at first, then with increasing pace the energies of the Iris turned around him. There was a flash of rainbow light, then it was as though he was standing in six places. There was a grand pattern, a five-fold symmetry that danced around a nexus. Five Faces and a Centre. Within each of the six parts, the pattern was repeated again, then again within them to the limit of his vision. It was as though he glanced into infinity. He saw immediately that the pattern was dull inside Three of the Faces. He channelled more power from the Spear, energising the whole Matrix in a way that would have been impossible for a single Sorcerer, no matter how powerful. One by one, the dulled Faces grew to life. Now all six of the Temples were open to him.

He searched each. High on a mountainside he saw a fallen Eathal and other discarded gear that showed Raziin's path. Further up on the mountain, he could see Raziin's men struggling up towards Riven Peak. He was about to signal to Kalyth and the others when he caught something else in the corner of his vision. Flame.

He turned. At once he saw not Riven Peak, but the streetscapes of Raynor. The city was in flames. Eathal marched in the streets, thousands of them. A great shudder passed through the ground and he saw part of the huge wall of Raynor tumble into the darkness. The Palastrada was burning and the streets were littered with dead.

Raynor was falling. Yet it was not too late. It could still be saved. The Eathal could be turned back. He knew that if he chose this, it would mean losing his chance to destroy Raziin. But he could make no other choice.

He was the Emperor.

Cedrin stepped back from the Iris. He was back in the Hall of Dreams, surrounded by his faithful followers.

'We must forget Raziin for now. Raynor needs us,' said Cedrin. 'Prepare yourselves for war. The Eathal have breached the walls. Pass through the Iris while I hold it open.'

Cedrin concentrated. He knew how to manipulate the Opening Matrix so that those who passed through the portal would be directed towards only one of the five other locations rather than be lost amid the bewildering landscape of light and power.

'As you will, my Lord,' said Kalyth.

Belin and Kalyth hustled the One Hundred and the Daughters up the stairs and through the Iris gateway. Many supported wounded comrades. Spider and Ellen were among the last to pass through. Belin passed through next, his face wistful as he looked around the strange cavern that had been his prison for so long. Then he turned away and strode through the magical opening with a smile.

Last of all, Cedrin stepped through. He let the Iris fall shut behind him.

As his eyes adjusted, he saw they were in a large circular room. The Raynor Iris. The mural under his feet was perfect. The floor was cracked outside it, but within the pentagonal Temple the design was flawless. The power of the Opening Matrix and the Spear had recreated it anew. He knew instinctively that the Olcis Iris and another – perhaps the Athrian Iris – had also been restored to symmetry through the power of the Spear.

Cedrin felt a hand on his shoulder and turned to see Belin looking up at him.

'Much has changed since I carried you from this room,

Cedrin. I never thought to see it again alive, yet here you stand with the Spear. Heir to Riin. I cannot tell you what it means to me to see my journey complete.'

Cedrin nodded, looking into the face of this powerful, yet charismatic stranger. Kalyth's teacher, as Kalyth had been his. He could hardly imagine the determination of spirit required to stay sane as a prisoner of the Ward – trapped in your own body. Yet Belin had not only survived it, he had triumphed.

'Thank you for saving my life. For sacrificing so much,' said Cedrin.

'It was my honour.'

'Even though I have the Spear, there is still much to be done. I am Emperor of nothing until we can push the Eathal from Raynor,' said Cedrin.

'We are with you,' said Belin.

A concussion shook the tower. A wave of anxious talk rose through the ranks. Dust fell from the ceiling.

Cedrin cleared his throat to address them. 'We stand in Raynor. The Eathal are here and the city is in flames. This is where our fight is,' said Cedrin. He searched their faces. All were ready to follow wherever he led.

'I must find the Warlord. Who can lead me out of this tower and down into the palace?'

Ellen took his hand. 'This way.'

Chapter Twenty-Four

Daran made his way through the palace towards the Great Hall. He had walked through this corridor thousands of times. Away from the heat and chaos of the forecourt, he could almost imagine the Eathal invasion had been a bad dream. The regular tremors from Hukum's Wallbreakers ran through the marble under his feet. He passed a wounded Legionnaire, slumped against a fine tapestry. Blood oozed from a cut to his side. He leant to touch the man's throat. His eyes flickered open.

'We show'd 'em, milord,' whispered the man.

'Yes, we did.' The man's eyes drooped closed.

'We have to keep moving. This part of the palace will soon be in flames,' said Uran.

Daran gritted his teeth in frustration and left the dying man. He stalked through the hallway in silence. Uran, Nacius and his aides followed along with the most senior living commanders of the First and Second. Both Legion Generals, veterans Daran had known since the Empire, had fallen.

Scythemen stood guard in the corridors. An odd touch of the familiar. He must pass the command for them to leave their posts. His mind went blank. He struggled to formulate plans, yet failed. A noise grew ahead, distracting his thoughts.

As he entered the Great Hall, he was brought up short.

Thousands of men and women were packed into the place. As they saw him, they surged forward, shouting a cacophony of panicked questions. He was surprised so many had remained here. Yet where else was there for them to go? Some of the upper balconies had collapsed, and the broken dome was open to the sky. Shards of shattered glass littered the floor.

His Legionnaires pushed the crowd back. He had planned to take his men to the rear of the palace, as far from the gates as he could, and ready himself to defend to the last. Yet that would mean leaving his Suul to the mercy of the Eathal.

Daran turned to the dais. The Emerald Throne sat empty. He walked up the first steps of the dais and raised his hands for silence. Gradually the crowd quieted.

'The Eathal will take the city,' said Daran. He was pleased to hear the resonant strength in his voice. Some wailed in despair, but others grew grim with resignation, the news paradoxically calming.

'But we will not yield without one last fight. Will you stand with me? Will you meet them with the dignity of Raynor Suul?'

His words made their way past their panic and touched their pride.

'We will!' It was one of the Suulvey, still mounted on his narsiit. A dozen others on their narsiit were behind him, many with wounds from the fight in the courtyard.

Daran had held court in this room countless times. Now he could sense the sentiment of the crowd shift. There was a crack from the balcony above. Tongues of flame licked out of one of the upper stories of the palace. Even so, there was no panic.

'Get the fires out,' he commanded one of his aides. 'Stop them from spreading through the palace.'

'Yes, my Lord.' Orders were relayed.

There was a commotion at the other end of the room. The Suul shuffled aside as a large group forced its way through the packed crowd. His Legionnaires tried to bar their way, but the men assigned to controlling the crowd were stretched too thin . . . and this was no group of Suul.

Daran blinked as he recognised the tattoos of the One Hundred. He knew some of the men too, first rate warriors all of them. Duro had been one of the finest of the First's Honoured.

'Ellen Cintros,' hissed Uran. 'And the upstart Emperor. It must have been they who activated the Iris. Yet again I pay for revealing my secrets. And there is the Olcis Priest she spirited away. As if we ever needed proof.'

The Warlord looked at the tall Anacian beside Ellen and realised immediately who he was. He felt a chill run down his spine. The years vanished, and he was kneeling at the feet of Riin, looking up into those same grey-blue eyes.

'Should I order the men to take them, my Lord?' asked the First commander.

'Cedrin.' The name was torn from Daran's lips. Kalyth Orin walked at his right, and on the other side . . . 'It can't be.' The thickset warrior with the silver hair could be none other than Belin Kaidell. The man had been a legend throughout Daran's youth, and he had met him twice as he received new military honours in official ink. The man had not aged a day since the last time he saw him. If anything, he looked younger.

Up on the balconies, Suulqua and palace guards battled the flames with buckets of water. It was a breath of wind against the tempest.

'Warlord?' prompted the First commander.

He held up a hand to forestall his commander. His reports indicated both Cedrin and Ellen were Sorcerers. The last thing he needed was a battle of magic here in the palace. Cedrin carried an archaic Spear. The spearhead was not lanedd. It looked like mought, painted gold so that it rippled and shone in the light. He squinted at it. The thing was glowing. It was shaped glowmetal. Impossible. That defied nature. Besides there were no bands of light. *Forged metal.*

'Uran.' Daran's voice was harsh with tension. 'That spear . . .'

The golden-skinned Sorcerer's eyes widened. He took an involuntary step forward, his jaw dropping in shock. 'By the Sisters. The goddamn prophecies were real.'

A flame of hope rose inside him. The Spear of Carris. Legends spoke of its immense power, but how much was truth and how much fiction? Could it equal the power of Hukum's glowmetals? Could it overtake them? Like a dying man brought back from the brink of death, his mind came alive again.

'Send runners. Get all the elements of the First and Second back here. Go. *Go!*'

Cedrin saw Daran and made directly for the dais.

Daran's bodyguard blocked their progress. The grim

warriors of the One Hundred – many wounded from a recent battle – squared off. There was no compromise there.

Daran stepped off the dais and walked to meet them.

'Stand aside. Let them pass,' commanded the Warlord.

Cedrin and Ellen stopped three paces away from him. Another detonation shook the palace, and the flames grew higher despite the efforts of the frantic functionaries. The Suul remained silent and intent. These were the bravest and brightest of his court. Suulvey, and those others who had stayed despite the danger. Some determined to fight, others out of sheer highbred stubbornness. All sensed the world was about to change.

'Cedrin Cinanac,' said Daran. His voice rang clearly through the room.

'Warlord,' said Cedrin.

'Have you come to demand allegiance? Is this how it is? Shall we kneel to the power of the Spear of Carris?' said Daran. A ripple of talk spread through the Suul at mention of the legendary Spear.

There was a roar of falling masonry and the walls shook. Another tower had fallen. No one moved.

'I have not come to demand allegiance, Warlord. I've come to save Raynor from the Eathal.' As he spoke, Cedrin's presence grew to embrace the room. Tall. Stern. The Suul were entranced. 'As Emperor of Bulvuran, that is my duty.'

The Suul waited for Daran to reject Cedrin's statement. He was past that now. Raynor itself was at stake.

'Can you? Can you save us? What power does the Spear possess?'

Cedrin's eyes grew unfocussed for a moment, his mind directed inward. He lifted the Spear. The radiance of the blade grew to a blinding brilliance.

'All the powers of Legend and more!' A pulse of energy radiated out from the Spear. A distortion in the air like waves rippling outward on the surface of a pond. The fires that raged through the place extinguished with a *whoof*.

Uran and Nacius shared an amazed glance.

Daran's legs grew weak. Larus be praised. They had a

chance.

'Then, my Lord. Save us,' he said.

Daran sank to his knees.

Chapter Twenty-Five

Cedrin looked around the Great Hall. Even though he had not asked for it, the Warlord had knelt to him. The Suul of Raynor and the thousands of Legionnaires in the Hall had followed. Then his own warriors. Even Ellen had sunk to the marble, her eyes misted with tears of pride.

He looked around the room, lost for a moment. He felt no glory. Only a sense of isolation. This fealty was a tangible trust. In return for his promise to save them. The dark voice of the Behemoth squirmed in a corner of his mind, glorying in the power. *Take the Emerald Throne. Release us.* He looked over at the dais and the empty throne of the Cinanac. It was carved from a single massive gemstone, the headrest shaped into a phoenix.

'Rise!' said Cedrin. There would be time enough for the ceremonies later. Provided they prevailed.

He leant down and helped Daran to his feet. His face was lined with exhaustion. Cedrin only had to look at the grim, soot-covered faces and bloodied armour of his Legionnaires to understand how desperate their struggle had become.

There was no time for the Warlord to brief him in all the intricacies of the struggle to date or the disposition of the enemy forces and their magical strength.

'You are the Warlord of Raynor, Daran. This is nothing more than a weapon for you to command,' said Cedrin, holding up the Spear. He looked at Uran, recognising him from Ellen's description. 'I need you both to advise me how to proceed here.'

The Warlord's eyes lit with calculation. 'The combined elements of the Silver and Black are on the Palardos with three powerful offensive glowmetals and one of Hukum's Sorcerer-Lords. It is the glowmetals that have turned the tide of any encounter with them, and which are destroying this palace.'

'Lead on, Warlord. We shall deal with them first,' said Cedrin.

Uran looked back at the group who followed Cedrin. 'Perhaps you should leave the Priest and Priestess here.'

Cedrin's hand tightened on the haft of the Spear. 'No. They remain with us. Always.' He shared a quick look with Ellen. The Behemoth had to be contained at all costs.

'Very well . . . my Lord,' said Uran. The honorific sounded strained. Beyond this night, he would have a whole snake-pit of politics to deal with here in Raynor. Who would not kneel to save themselves? Keeping the Emerald Throne when the threat was passed would be another matter.

'This way,' said Daran.

They passed through the ornate corridors away from the Great Hall. Orders were shouted from commander to Captain and from Captain to Razor. The Legionnaires smoothly formed up and filed behind them. The Suul came behind them – all of them.

'Send riders. Recall the Third and the cavalry,' commanded Daran.

'Should we not . . . wait, my Lord?' said the Warlord's aide with a glance back at him.

'No. If we do manage to break the Eathal's hold on the city I intend to take every advantage from their confusion.'

The walls around them showed more damage now, and the blackened soot showed where fires had recently been extinguished by Cedrin's fire-quelling Matrix.

They emerged into a courtyard. Here the ground was littered with bodies, human, Eathal and Tahistil. The wall of the Palastrada had crumbled. Out on the street were thousands of Eathal warriors, drawn up into lines behind three huge glowmetals.

A single Sorcerer-Lord was channelling lightning into a silver glowmetal.

'That is the one that started all the fires,' said the Warlord.

More flames had grown in the palace, the result of recent attacks.

Beside him, Ellen and his men waited expectantly. Spider looked at him with wide eyes from the ranks of the Daughters. It felt strange to have come so far.

He stilled his mind, embracing the Way.

First, he crafted the Great Shield. He touched the Spear and the Realm of Fire opened to him. Fire roared through the Matrix. He let the power continue, reinforcing and growing the Shield.

The Sorcerer-Lord ceased his lightning. A shaft of heat radiated out from the glowmetal. It met the Shield only thirty paces from its wagon. The intense heat cascaded back onto the Eathal. The enemy ranks hastily backed away, while the Sorcerer-Lord raised a Shield of his own against the heat. His slitted green eyes widened beneath his heavy brow ridges.

Kill them all. The Behemoth urged him on.

Cedrin hesitated. He knew what power he had at his command now. Enough to engulf the whole Eathal legion in a firestorm so intense not one of them would survive. Was that degree of death justified? As conquerors, had they forfeited the right to mercy? He used Sorcery to enhance his vision and studied the Eathal faces. He could not help but remember the simple Eathal who had joined him against Raziin.

First he had to end the threat to Raynor. It had not been men who started this war, despite what had happened in history.

He carefully constructed a new Matrix. Then he unleashed the power of the Spear.

A blade of Force grew, as broad as the Palardos itself. It solidified, then sped to its deadly purpose. The Behemoth howled with glee. Its voice echoed at the borders of his mind.

The front ranks of the Black were cut down like ripe baal. The blade of Force hesitated for the briefest of moments at the Shield of the Sorcerer-Lord. The Eathal's protective barrier collapsed with a flash of silver, then the Eathal Sorcerer and his jakkund-mounted bodyguards were sliced into steaming meat. The teams of jakka were slain. Blood splashed the great glowmetals in weird patterns.

Finish them!

Matrices swept past his vision. Memories of power. Of heat and victory. So much. He could kill every Eathal before him in moments.

'Dagon,' called Cedrin, turning back to see the big Priest and Esmelle behind him.

'The Essence is weak here, my Lord. We have it contained as well as we can.'

Uran and the Warlord exchanged a puzzled glance.

'I understand,' said Cedrin. He would have to accept the presence of the Behemoth, yet not acknowledge it. Not give the Beast's voice a force in his thoughts. Once he took possession of the Spear, this moment was inevitable. The more he drew on its power, the stronger the Behemoth would become. His dark partner in power.

The decimated Eathal legion reformed its lines. Without the Sorcerer-Lord, they retreated, abandoning the three offensive glowmetals.

'Defeated in a single strike,' said Daran in wonder.

'And three of their glowmetals abandoned,' said Uran, his voice tight with some unknown desire.

'Shall we press the attack, my Lord?' asked the First commander.

'No. Wait,' said Cedrin.

Using the Great Matrix, Cedrin sent a ram of Force through the Eathal ranks. Hundreds of the enemy were crushed as it shot through the middle of the retreating force. Their eerie howls of pain rose through the night in a discordant symphony.

With an adjustment to the Matrix, he created a giant silver whip. It swept down. Its lashing bulk smashed armour and bone as it drove them into the cobbles of the Palardos.

Cedrin held the Spear high in his right hand, his left extended in balance. The golden blade blazed, illuminating the ruined square and the thousands of silent dead.

Under pressure, the Black broke. Not even the discipline of the elite Eathal warriors could counter the terror of the overwhelming assault of Sorcery.

'Now, Captain. Drive them from the city,' commanded Daran.

Horns echoed through the night. Legionnaires jogged into the Palardos, mixed units of the First and Second. They drew together smoothly under the urging of their Captains and Razors and advanced across the Palardos. The Eathal fallen were dispatched without mercy, and were soon lost under marching feet as the swelling ranks of the Legion pushed on.

Cedrin, the Warlord and their combined entourages followed behind.

Suul on narsiit and amelak galloped through the night, ranging out on the flanks and darting in and out of the side streets, clearing small pockets of Eathal who had been separated from the shattered Black and Silver. Behind them marched the assembled Suul of Raynor. There to bear witness to the rebirth of an Empire.

The Black and Silver had left the Palardos now. They had regained some semblance of order. By the time the reformed Raynor Legion engaged them, they were in a fighting retreat. Men and Eathal both fell as the lines clashed.

Their deaths are on your hands. You have to power to save them. Destroy all the Eathal. Burn them to ash.

A tremor ran through Cedrin. Images of slaughter confronted him. His stomach flipped as he saw what the Spear was capable of and the death the artefact had delivered in the hands of his ancestors.

Men are dying, weakling.

Cedrin used the Force lash to smash into the Eathal lines. Holes opened in the Eathal ranks. The veterans of Raynor surged forward, phalanxes driving deep into the Eathal. The long spears shot forward and back in a frenzy of death. Then, abruptly, the Eathal lost all cohesion. They turned and ran.

The way opened before them as the Eathal fled to the eastern gate as fast as their solid legs could carry them.

'Yes!'

Cedrin flinched as Daran gripped his shoulder in triumph. 'By the Sisters. You have done it!'

'Hukum remains. And the defensive glowmetal,' said Uran.

Cedrin cleared his vision. His breath was ragged, hot with the flames that pressed in on them from the burning city. Ellen was beside him. She was deathly pale in the night, eyes fixed and wide.

'Do not yield to it,' she said.

He released the power of the Spear in a gigantic wave. A broad front of power rippled out through the city, extinguishing the flames of the Eastern Quarter in one stroke.

The distant booming that had continued since he emerged from the Iris ceased.

Uran gave a surprised laugh. 'The Wallbreakers fall silent.'

'At last,' said Daran.

Warriors emerged from the side streets, men who had been cut off from the Legions as they retreated towards the Palastrada. The ranks of the Raynor Legion swelled as units returned from the Western Quarter.

Around them the four to six storey dwellings of Raynor were silent and empty, roofs collapsed, windows cracked and melted. Here and there were buildings that had been miraculously saved from the flames. Hundreds of Raynorians, clothes singed, faces blackened with soot, emerged to watch them pass. They were too stunned to cheer. The sheer miracle of their survival wrapped them in joyous silence.

Eventually they emerged into the flattened wasteland that had been the area behind the eastern gate.

Eathal were filing in through the ruined walls, forming ranks. There were thousands. The fleeing warriors of the Black and Silver joined them.

'The Yellow. And the Wallbreakers,' said Uran.

'Stop the advance,' commanded Daran.

Horns rang out. The Raynor Legion stopped in place, the warriors in precise ranks. Each man eyed the Eathal across the levelled ground with the tense ferocity of the survivor.

Cedrin was stunned at the devastation. Marken and he had entered Raynor through the eastern gate. They had approached through the Outer City, already awed by the magnificence of the old capital. The walls themselves had towered above them like red cliffs, the huge mought blocks something from another age when men were giants. Many bribes later, they finally won their entry. Inside the walls, the tall buildings had loomed over them like disapproving grandparents, dressed in a finery they could only dream of. Crowds had pressed on all sides. Now all was in ruins, the crushed and broken remnants scattered to make room for marshalling ranks of Eathal.

Daran touched Cedrin on the shoulder to get his attention. 'All the remaining Eathal are forming up here. Most of them are the Yellow Drakon Legion. They have linked with the remnants of the Black and Silver legions. Perhaps thirteen thousand in all. Still a formidable force. The combined ranks of the First and Second give us the strength of a single Legion – a little more than ten thousand men. The Third would give us another full Legion, but they are some hours away.'

'And that big zinc glowmetal with the green light. That is a defensive weapon with a sphere of influence that extends almost half a league,' said Uran. 'It has defeated all Force or conventional weapons.'

'Electrical forces pass through it,' said Daran. 'And . . . more insubstantial energies.'

'Insubstantial?' queried Cedrin.

'The Warlord is talking about the ghostly fire of the Firebolt, one of our offensive glowmetals,' said Uran.

Cedrin looked at the gathered enemy. Three more glowmetals were being dragged through the ruins of the wall and back inside the Eathal formations to stand behind the zinc one. These must be the Wallbreakers.

A Great Matrix floated into his vision. One that would enable him to create a lightning storm so intense it would incinerate the entire Eathal force. His head swam.

Use it.

He gritted his teeth in silent determination. He would never follow the will of the Behemoth. He would not start the reign of Bulvuran with a bloodbath. Neither could he allow the unneeded deaths of Raynor's own. First he must deprive Hukum's legions of their primary weapons.

Carefully, he crafted the Great Matrix of Force. The terrible beauty of the Spear was that it could channel unlimited power. Only the vessel, or the magic focus, that channelled it constricted its potential. He touched the Spear with his mind.

The Realm of Fire opened. The magic roared as it rushed through the golden blade and into the Matrix.

Two vast arms of silver appeared. They descended like huge tentacles towards the assembled Eathal. There was a flashing discharge of light as first one, then the other encountered the edges of the defensive Shield. Inside it, at the heart of the assembled Eathal host, he could see two Eathal Sorcerer-Lords pouring Fire into the zinc glowmetal. The bands of green dwindled as their power recharged it, strengthening it.

Cedrin growled deep in his throat. In a contest of power, the Spear would always triumph. He had absorbed enough of Jykor's knowledge and memories to know that.

The two arms flattened out, spreading across the unseen surface of the defensive Shield like oil on water. Soon the whole Shield was revealed, a dome covered in translucent silver. Cedrin increased the flow of Fire. The crushing power of the Force Matrix was now being applied to the whole Shield. The silver thickened, blanketing out sight of the Eathal within it. Before they passed from sight, Cedrin could see the two Sorcerer-Lords struggling to keep pace in the magical battle. He smiled grimly as he saw the bands of green light expanding on the zinc glowmetal. The draw on the defensive weapon was outpacing their power.

The sphere of silver Force covered the whole area behind the eastern gate. As it grew more solid, its surface became as reflective as a mirror. Their assembled forces, the blackened buildings, all were reflected in strange, distorted images.

Then all at once the dome collapsed. The sphere of Force contracted rapidly. Thousands of Eathal were knocked off their feet. It shrank until it contained only the zinc glowmetal. Cedrin ripped the glowmetal from its wagon and lifted it high into the air. The last of its power discharged and it lay inert in his mental grip. Carefully he moved it through the air and dropped it onto the cobbles behind the Raynor Legion.

Cedrin closed off the flow of Fire that streamed from the Spear and the Great Matrix collapsed.

'That . . . was astounding,' said the Warlord.

Uran's eyes gleamed. 'With power such as that – you could

crush Hukum's entire force.'

Yes!

'No.' Cedrin lowered the Spear, using the haft to brace himself as a wave of dizziness passed through now. His vision swam as tears stung his eyes. Across the open space, the Eathal had reformed ranks. Silver blazed as Force was directed into one of their other glowmetals.

Too late, Cedrin realised he had no Great Shield in place.

A powerful bolt of directed Force slammed into the front ranks of the Raynor Legions. Hundreds were crushed. The wounded howled in pain. His heart tore at the realisation that if he had given in to the Behemoth's demands for blood, these men would still be alive. Their blood was on his hands. His own decision to extend mercy had killed them.

'Now this ends,' said Cedrin.

Once more he created the two arms of Force. This time he reached forward to grip the three Wallbreakers. He felt some of his directed Force sucked up by the offensive glowmetal that had struck them. He countered by releasing more Fire into his Great Matrix. He lifted the glowmetals up above the Eathal forces. This time, in his anger, he had been less precise. One of the Sorcerer-Lords was pinned against a glowmetal, along with hundreds of Eathal and the teams of jakka. They were crushed in the vast grip. The cries of the trapped Eathal and animals were brief. Cedrin threw the three glowmetals behind the lines of the Raynor Legions. The ground shook as they tumbled through the debris-strewn streets. Blood and crushed bodies flew through the night as he released his magical grip. Cedrin had no time to consider what he had done. It was time to drive the Eathal from the city.

He adjusted the Great Matrix, this time creating three vast whips of Force. He lashed down at the stunned Eathal. This time there was no attempt to hold the lines. The dark-skinned warriors fled through the broken walls into the Outer City.

'Shall we see them out, Warlord?' said Cedrin.

'Yes . . . yes, my Lord,' said Daran. His voice was subdued, yet there was no doubting his determination. Cedrin could only guess at the desperation the man must have felt as his city came so close to final destruction.

Twice more the whips fell, filling the air with dust and ash and howls of pain.

'There! That must be Hukum,' said Uran.

Cedrin saw the Sorcerer-Lord, fleeing with a strong detachment of jakkund cavalry. They moved fast, the strange beasts leaping between broken masonry and tumbled mought blocks with uncanny precision. Here and there Tahistil ran with the rest.

'You can destroy him. Right now. Cut the head off the beast,' said Daran. 'His men will be leaderless. Easy prey for our pursuing Legions.'

The Warlord speaks the truth. The voice of the Behemoth hissed into his mind. Once more Cedrin's determination flared. He had to find another way.

'To sow the seeds of hatred in another generation? So that Hukum's heir will come in his turn to burn Raynor?' said Cedrin.

The Warlord rounded on Cedrin. 'But we have them! You cannot let them run when we have bested their magic. They are defenceless. We have a chance to cripple them.'

Belin and Kalyth stepped forward to flank Cedrin. 'You will address the Emperor as 'my Lord'.'

Daran's eyes flashed dangerously. Cedrin felt the Fire rise in Uran. They hovered dangerously on the brink.

'I will not let him flee,' said Cedrin. 'I intend to take him prisoner. I will forge a treaty with Maht.'

'A treaty? With those murderers?' said Daran.

Belin extended the blades of his greatscythe. 'I will not warn you again, Warlord.' The old warrior turned to Uran. 'And if you value your life, you will release your hold on the Window.'

Uran's eyes widened at that. The Fire in the golden-skinned Sorcerer leaked away.

'Yes,' said Cedrin. 'Order the Legions to follow me. I will lead from the front.'

The ranks of the Raynor Legionnaires parted before him.

You are a fool. Hukum will laugh at your weakness. Cedrin closed his mind to the rants of the Behemoth.

He meant what he said. The Jakir had been more than just a legend. And somewhere – hidden in Kelas – the order still persevered. In antiquity, they had forged a civilisation where all four ancient races of Yos came together as equals. That was in the past, but in the knowledge of that truth came the seed of a promise. He could rebuild those ancient bonds. Begin anew. It was time for a true peace between Eathal and human. They, no more than any human, were capable of good and evil. A brutal history of ancient wrongs separated them, but there was hope. The simple Eathal of the caverns of Ranmyden had shown him that. Men and Eathal could find their brotherhood if they tried.

The Warlord and his entourage had followed Cedrin, Ellen and the One Hundred through the Raynor ranks. Now at the head of the Raynor troops, they set out after the fleeing Eathal.

The web bridge across the Asgod was choked with Eathal troops, all trying to cross.

'Hukum is already on the other bank,' said Uran. Once more, Cedrin sensed the Fire in him. This time he knew it was only the Lens Matrix.

The fleeing Eathal warriors must have parted to allow the Sundar to escape. Cedrin enhanced his own eyesight. He saw the Sundar and his jakkund troops making for the last glowmetal in possession of the Eathal – one with a speckled silver and grey metal intertwined with bright yellow light. Apart from the copper Wallbreaker he had torn from the Eathal at the eastern gate, this was the largest glowmetal they possessed.

'A defensive glowmetal?' asked Cedrin.

'Arsenic. I can only assume it was defensive, otherwise it would have been used in the attack on Raynor,' said Uran.

The sight of the strange glowmetal gave Cedrin a sense of unease. One of Jykor's memories struggled to take form.

'We will never get across the web bridge,' said Daran.

The memory slipped from his grasp.

Cedrin lifted the Spear and let the Fire flow through a subtle Matrix. Above them, the three intact drawbridges of Raynor gave a chorus of low groans as he gripped the spans. They fell into place with a boom of interlocking mought. He grinned despite himself. At last he experienced the use of the Spear's power without causing death. That too gave him hope.

'My lord. Do I have your permission to harry the Eathal while we pursue Hukum?' asked the Warlord.

'Yes. Of course.'

Orders were given and horns rang out. A small detachment of some three hundred Honoured closed around them. Cedrin, now protected by the Raynor Honoured, the One Hundred and the remaining Daughters moved to the closest of the working drawbridges. The other Legionary forces were split into three, with two detachments moving across the other lowered drawbridges and another marching to the river to hit the rear of the fleeing Eathal. The First and Second commanders left to take charge of the assaults across the bridges.

Cedrin was soon high over the Asgod. From here the vast bulk of Raynor spread out behind them. The Outer City was still on fire. Most of the Suul had followed them as far as the ruined eastern gates and watched the unfolding events from there. Some of the bolder mounted Suul followed behind the Honoured. He took a bearing and fixed his sight on the group of fleeing jakkund cavalry. They had surrounded the arsenic glowmetal.

Cedrin and his small force descended to the eastern bank of the Asgod. The fleeing Eathal and their web bridge was some half a league north along the river. The smashed and smoking ruins of the Docks District stretched out to north, south and east, redolent with the smell of pitch and smoke. They pushed through the debris until they reached one of the cleared alleys that the Warlord's men had prepared, then increased their pace. Behind him, the bulky Dagon and willowy Esmelle struggled to match the pace of the warriors. Slowly they fell behind.

When they emerged at the edge of the ruined Docks, Hukum and his small group of fleeing warriors were half-way to the horizon and increasing their lead.

'Behind us, my Lord,' said Kalyth.

Eathal had swarmed from the web bridge and now emerged from the ruins of the Docks in their thousands. Cedrin and his small group were cut off. Soon they would be surrounded by

414

fleeing Eathal warriors. He had to use the power of the Spear to take Hukum.

Cedrin paused to concentrate. He drew the Great Matrix he had used before and carefully touched the Spear with his mind. The Realm of Fire opened up as before, yet instead of rushing into the Matrix, the roaring flow disappeared.

A column of brilliant light soared up from the arsenic glowmetal. It broadened into a cascading aurora of rainbow light that filled the night sky.

In shock, he closed off the power of the Spear.

'The glowmetal blocked the Fire,' he said, stunned.

'No. No! Hukum is going to escape,' said Daran, his fist clenched in fury.

Cedrin tried to access the power of the Fire again. Again the Fire began to flow, yet remained always beyond his reach. Again the lights flared above them. Memories and Matrices crowded his mind. Too much to take in. Perhaps the answer was buried somewhere in Jykor's knowledge, but now, right here on the eastern outskirts of Raynor, there was nothing he could do. Cedrin watched, aghast, as Hukum and his men disappeared into the night.

'My lord. Eathal!'

Daran and Cedrin both turned.

'Shock troops. From the Black,' said Daran.

Some three hundred Eathal warriors were closing on them. They were big, some of the largest Eathal Cedrin had seen. Each was equipped with twin axes of darkglass.

Cedrin turned to Ellen. They had been through so much together. And now he had brought her into danger. If he had destroyed Hukum and his warriors at the eastern gate, she would be safe now.

'Get back,' he said to her. Cedrin looked up at Spider, who was standing behind Ellen. 'Protect her with your life.'

Spider nodded grimly and grabbed Ellen's shoulder.

Ellen shook off the hand. 'I can fight! Let me stay with you.'

Cedrin met the fierce determination in her green eyes. 'I cannot risk you. Not now.'

He lifted his greatscythe off his back and hung the inert

Spear there in its place. It was only as he activated the mechanism that he realised one of his blades was gone – shattered in the combat with Raziin. Then it was too late.

The Eathal roared out a battlecry and engaged.

Cedrin embraced the Way.

The Honoured linked shields and formed a phalanx, shielding them from the onslaught. Yet here they were not protected by a broad line. The Eathal swept around the Legionnaires, coming from all sides. Kalyth was forced to circle away to give himself room. Cedrin ducked as a darkglass axe cut at his head. He took the blade of the second axe on his greatscythe haft, with no memory of even moving the weapon to block the strike. Elthar's greatscythe blade took the Eathal in the back, but the tall warrior had sacrificed his own defence to take him down. Another big Eathal warrior leapt at Elthar. Before he could turn, twin darkglass axes buried themselves into Elthar's collar bones, cutting deep into his lungs. Cedrin stabbed the Eathal warrior through the eye with his remaining blade, but it was too late for Elthar. The tall warrior's eyes fluttered and he sank to the ground. Dead. Belin leapt in to defend Cedrin.

The Honoured had abandoned the phalanx, repositioning into a circle formation to protect them on all sides. But half a dozen Eathal were still inside the shield wall. Ranis took an axe to the side of the head. He screamed and went down. Duro counterattacked. He used his bulk to slam into Ranis' assailant. As the Eathal tried to recover his balance, Duro's blades cut his legs from under him.

Cedrin's blood froze as he heard Ellen's shriek.

He turned and time stopped.

Ellen was down. An axe had opened her shoulder, cutting down into her left arm. Spider fought over her in a fury. Her greatscythe moved in a blur. An Eathal gave a howl as a blade stabbed through his armour into his heart. Two more Eathal moved in on her. Spider's stocky lieutenant Jeth raced in. Together the two Daughters forced the Eathal away from Ellen. They were soon surrounded. The two women fought back-to-back against four of the hulking Eathal warriors. Other Daughters came to their aid. Two more of the Eathal fell, then another. Soon Spider faced the last warrior who had pushed through the Honoured lines. The Eathal roared and surged forward. Spider stabbed into his heart with her left blade, but the Eathal grabbed the haft of her greatscythe, trapping the weapon. The Eathal raised a darkglass axe high, ready to cut down at Spider's unprotected head.

'Spider!' howled Jeth. The stocky woman slammed into the Eathal, grabbing the warrior's right arm. The Eathal pulled away, wrenching from her grip and releasing Spider's greatscythe. His axe rose again. This time it cut through Jeth's throat. The Eathal warrior fell under the blades of the Daughters, but Jeth was already down.

Cedrin rushed to Ellen. His greatscythe tumbled from his grasp as he sank to his knees. He reached for the Window and felt the Fire once more at his command. He drew the Matrix of Form and inserted the Key that would heal Ellen.

'No,' gasped Ellen. 'The Matrix will heal me, but it will be as though the baby never existed. You cannot.'

Esmelle knelt at Cedrin's side. 'I can heal her.'

He could see nothing but Ellen's blood. Around him men grunted and swore. Eathal howled amid the carnage. Spilled guts and severed limbs littered the ground. Spider leaned over Jeth's still form. The stocky fighter lifted a shaking hand to touch Spider's lips, once, then it fell limply to her side. The lean warrior kissed Jeth's forehead as the fallen woman's glazed eyes stared unseeing at the night sky.

Cedrin felt the Priestess' hands on his face.

She forced him to turn and meet her eyes. 'I can heal her. *Trust me*. Deal with the Eathal.'

Cedrin rose to his feet.

You have killed her. Failure.

His heart boiled with rage. He turned to the east. There was no sight of Hukum or the arsenic glowmetal.

He hefted the Spear and drew a Matrix of Burning Fire. The first that had ever been created for the Spear. One that had been designed by Carris himself before the Spear was even forged. He touched the Spear. He growled in fury as he felt its power once more at his command. *They want Death? Here is Death!*

Light blazed from the golden blade.

Eathal drew back in shock, shielding their eyes.

And Cedrin released the power of the Spear.

He left the One Hundred, the Honoured, Dagon and Esmelle behind him. He walked back to Raynor through the ruins of the Docks at the centre of an expanding cloud of white flame. Nothing withstood its touch.

Eathal opened their mouths to scream, yet became a silent flame before their screams were made real. Cedrin's vision was lost in glorious power. Fire became flame and was rebirthed into the world in a glorious conflagration of revenge. No one threatened Ellen and lived. Deep in a hidden corner of his heart, the desperate youth of the Athrian Docks emerged with a snarl and a broken blade. At the last, he would defend all. He would keep his own safe against the bullies and the scum who wanted to harm them.

They ran. Yet there was no escaping the power of the Spear.

Yes. Yes. At last . . .

At the Asgod, Cedrin paused on the brink.

It was no longer Eathal he faced, but the Legionnaires of Raynor. He turned. Behind him, through the blaze of white-hot power, he saw the trail of burnt destruction. The fleeing Eathal had been utterly destroyed. Finally, what he had done sunk in. With a cry of pain, he shut off the power of the Spear. His mind ached with the void of its passing. The ground around him hissed and spat. Behind him was a path of glowing red heat. The very ground itself had grown molten with the power of the Spear.

No. Unleash us!

The bank of the Asgod was crowded with Legionnaires. They cowered back from him. They had been trying to retreat across the web bridge away from the terrible heat. His stomach twisted in nausea as he saw burnt human skeletons at his feet amid the Eathal.

'Ellen!'

Cedrin ran back through the ruins of the Docks. He skirted around the red-hot trail of molten ground. He saw the ranks of the Honoured first. The grim warriors parted and behind them he saw the survivors of the One Hundred and the Daughters. Ellen walked with them, supported by Esmelle and Spider. Pale but alive.

'Thank the Sisters,' he said, reaching for her.

She shrank away from him, and he looked up to see tears staining her face.

'Is it you? Or is it the Behemoth?' Her eyes searched him, in desperation.

It was a blow to the heart. He let the Spear drop to the ground and opened his arms.

'It's me. Just me.'

Us.

Chapter Twenty-Six

Kranor walked his narsiit through the streets of Olcis. Xyanthius rode at his side, a head-and-a-half lower on his sturdy amelak. The lack of a Suul mount did not diminish the Eleventh General's commanding presence in the least. If anything, Xyanthius' battered appearance made him look even more fearsome.

Xyanthius' eyes narrowed as he studied the ruined houses on either side. 'Nothing moves.'

'No,' said Kranor. After the furious days and nights of battle, the quiet was a strange thing. Broken glass and shattered tiles littered the cobbles. The doors of burned buildings yawned wide as though in death.

Kranor and Lempar had worked in concert. The Olcis general pushed from the south-east as Xyanthius' Eleventh and the Exdor Tenth attacked from the north. Together they had forced the Eathal back into the outskirts of the city. Yet there the Eathal had managed to entrench themselves, using Sorcerer-Lords' magic and their offensive glowmetals to good effect.

Kranor had come to respect the Eathal general Yeffrij. He was careful and clever. Yeffrij had been persistent in his push to retake the city. The battle had moved into a rhythm of nighttime attacks by the Eathal and daytime counterattacks from the Olcis and Imperial Legions.

Last night, well short of dawn, all enemy attacks had ceased. The suns had risen to find the Eathal in full retreat. Xyanthius' scouts reported that their camp across the river was deserted.

The Eathal legions in the north had withdrawn back into Tupur.

Kranor heard hoofbeats and turned to see a rider on a narsiit approach. The man was covered in dust and soot. Even so, the Suul mark stood out clearly.

'My Lord. A message from Raynor.'

'Go on.'

The Suulqua's face spit into an infectious grin. It made the young man look boyish – and made Xyanthius feel even older than he was. 'Victory at Raynor! The Emperor has crushed them with the Spear of Carris.'

Kranor exchanged a look of surprise with Xyanthius.

'You are sure?' asked Kranor.

'Yes. No less than three birds confirm it. Hukum's forces are utterly destroyed, although the Sundar himself escaped.'

'So the Emperor has won the Spear,' said Xyanthius in wonder. 'No wonder Yeffrij is in retreat. He goes to shield his master.'

Cedrin had triumphed. Kranor had no idea how the Emperor had managed to transport himself from Ranmyden to Raynor, but these were days of high magic. With the Spear in their possession, all became possible.

'Yeffrij will retreat all the way to Maht itself,' said Xyanthius.

Kranor bowed his head, pausing for a small moment of thanks. The retreat of Yeffrij meant that Olcis had now been claimed for the Emperor. In his desperation to save his city, and in anger at the Hesguit, Moren Cinlar had agreed to swear allegiance to Cedrin. Kranor had the perfect messenger to bring the word of their victory to Raynor. A man who had earned the trust of the Emperor twice over. 'Bring Osterac. I have a duty for him.'

'Yes, my Lord.'

* * *

The Great Hall was packed with Suul.

The broad dais had been set up with tiers of seats for Cedrin's entourage, although they were only occupied by Raphal and Valnis at the moment. The two scholars looked in the prime of health and were cheerily engaged in some obscure debate. The buzz of conversation filled the Hall. It held a note of tension as all these powerful men and women tested the waters of this new world. Cedrin scanned the faces of the Suulvey, those given prime position up near the dais. Despite the hours of tutoring by Daran's Suulqua functionaries, he could recall only a handful of names. The rest of Raynor's Suul waited behind the scarlet ropes that sealed off the two halves of the Hall, leaving the centre free for the ceremonial procession. The court Steward waited patiently at the other end of the room, a pleasant smile fixed to his face. Sensing Cedrin's eyes on him, he gave an elegant bow, which he acknowledged with a nod.

Cedrin shuffled his feet, uncomfortable in the stiff shirt with its golden embroidery. The Suul sported jewelled harnesses and gossamer dresses of the finest silk. There was so much wealth on display here it made his poor calvanni eyes ache. He looked up at the tiers of balconies that rose high above them. Most were crowded with Raynor's elite, all eager to secure a view of the ceremony. Other balconies were blocked off, still damaged from the Eathal attack. Some were missing entirely, having either burned away in the flames or collapsed under the weight of fallen debris. Glassmiths had carefully replaced the shattered panes of the main dome. A bright pillar of sunlight came down from the suns above, illuminating the dais and the Emerald Throne.

Ellen was dressed in a green gown that accentuated her eyes, matched with a set of pale emerald earrings and necklace. Her poise was perfect as she chatted with the other Suul, displaying an ease that he could only dream of. She sensed his gaze and turned. Her eyes sparkled and the corners of her mouth curled up in a private smile.

They were free. Despite everything, they had succeeded. He and Ellen had reconciled at last. They were both eager to heal the divisions between them. Tonight – not that loveless night in Beslin – would be their true wedding night.

The Spear was secured in the Eastern Tower. After that night of power and death beyond the burned Docks, Cedrin had searched Jykor's memories for a way to lay down the terrible power of the Spear. They had sacrificed so much to win it, he dare not lay it aside where anyone could take it. As he searched for a solution, the Behemoth dogged his thoughts. He struggled to contain a growing terror of being forced to always carry the terrible artefact like some dark partner in his own marriage bed.

Then finally he had discovered the elaborate ways that his ancestor Emperors had dealt with the problem. It was for this reason that the Wards were first created. Sustained by the power of the Spear, each Ward was given life through the mind of its creator, charged with certain powers and clear instructions. Each was commonly crafted with clear guidelines on who the Spear should fall to in the case of its creator's death. The Ward of Jykor was the last in a long line of Wards created to protect the Spear. It had been the most powerful and elaborate Ward ever conceived. Jykor had worked on it for close to a decade until it took the semblance of its own sentience. Cedrin had no need for something so sophisticated – at least not yet. The Ward he created to protect the Spear was like a ghostly version of himself. It was defensive. His Ward had the power to Shield itself from all Sorcery and other magic, and would only yield the weapon to him.

Dagon and Esmelle had been given rooms in the Eastern Tower. They had been questioned about Veltricus' accusation of allegiance to the ancient Anan-Ac, a Temple infamous in myth as the home of the dark Priest Moscran and his warriors of the Red Feast. Dagon had explained that this was a common aspersion cast on Earth Essence practitioners from Thilil, nothing more than an insult from Veltricus. They had volunteered for Testing at a Raynor temple. The local Priestess had fallen ill at the ceremony, yet recovered quickly. Afterwards all agreed that the northerners were beyond reproach. Now that they had regained his full trust, he and Ellen could truly relax. Dagon and Esmelle now used the power of Temple of the Iris itself to contain the Behemoth. At last the darkness was gone from their minds.

The survivors of the One Hundred surrounded the dais, their numbers supplemented by the Warlord's own bodyguard. Six of them had fallen to the Eathal in Raynor. The laconic Elthar would be sorely missed. Ranis had led them well and had survived his wound to the head at a price – he had lost the sight of his right eye. Healing with the Matrix of Form had come too late. Like his father before him, he had regretfully resigned his post as one of the One Hundred due to an injury in combat. Duras now took command of the One Hundred in his place. Ranis stood with them all today though, as a last honour.

The Daughters waited below the dais, arrayed in new clothes. Spider was stern as she stood at their head, the stocky Jeth noticeably absent. Although they had no official part in the proceedings, Cedrin and Ellen insisted that they be given a place of honour.

Kalyth and Belin walked through the crowd, chatting with older Suul. They represented a bridge to a time when his own father Riin sat on the throne. As did the Warlord.

The news from the north was good. The Eathal General Yeffrij had withdrawn from Olcis. Both Lempar and Xyanthius pursed him, reclaiming Tupur in Cedrin's name. Their scouts reported that the Eathal had abandoned all their camps and had already crossed the Yasser on their way to Maht.

Marken and Skye's mission had been a success. Even now they were on their way to Raynor on an Athrian war galley. Thenia's mother, Suul Cinlos, had taken possession of Leygen, and the fleet of Ellen's brother Torren blockaded the harbour of Swebas. Cedrin longed to see his old friends again and start a new life here in Raynor. At last he had found his place. Thenia had reached Beslin safely and was also on her way south.

A Suulqua entered the far end of the room and passed a message to the Steward. The elegant old man looked back across the room and gave Cedrin a nod. This was the signal.

Cedrin walked over to Ellen and touched her arm. 'Perhaps we should take our seats, my Lady.'

She tilted her head up and gave him a radiant smile. 'With pleasure, my Lord.'

He turned to the Suulvey she had been conversing with. 'If you will excuse us?'

They bowed in unison, they faces fixed into an array of pleasant countenances. 'Of course, my Lord.' Who knows what they were really thinking? He took Ellen's arm, more grateful than ever to have her at his side. At least he had one person in this vast Hall he could trust.

Ranis and Duro gave him short bows as they moved up on the dais. A second carved throne had been set up beside the Emerald Throne. This was called the Rose Throne, carved from a single block of rose-coloured marble. It was smaller than the Emperor's throne, yet was also elaborately carved with phoenixes. This was the seat of the Empress. It had last been used by his mother Evylin. He watched Belin and Kalyth move up to take their places on the dais. He had agonised for so long about the identity of his father, yet his parents seemed more like creatures from some storybook. It was time to reclaim his true past and move into the future.

He looked down at the first finger of his left hand, where Belin's signet ring still rested. On impulse he pulled it off.

'Belin,' he called.

The old general walked to him and bowed. 'Yes, my Lord.'

Cedrin held out his hand. 'I believe this is yours.'

Belin reached out slowly to take the ring. As his fingers closed over it, he looked up. 'Kalyth told me about your life in Athria. I regret you had to suffer that, so far from your true family.'

Cedrin felt Ellen's warmth beside him.

'I regret nothing.'

Belin gave him a genuine smile. 'Spoken like an Emperor, my Lord.'

'Did your nephew Linnas accept the invitation?' asked Cedrin.

Belin shook his head. 'No. He did not take the news of my miraculous survival well, I'm afraid. He has refused to leave the Delta. It's time I paid him a visit.'

A hush fell on the crowd.

Ellen's hand tightened on his arm. 'We best take our places.'

They turned to face the far end of the Great Hall. Cedrin stood in front of the Emerald Throne, Ellen in front of the Rose. Kalyth and Belin stood on Cedrin's right, Ellen's Suulqua Mendor at her side.

The Warlord entered with his wife and two sons, tall warriors who dressed simply like their father. He had met them twice now, both were reserved in his presence, although he sensed their anger. It was understandable. His arrival had removed them from the succession. Although without his arrival through the Iris with the Spear, they would be heirs to nothing but a few cities in the Delta and a war with Hukum they could not win.

'The Warlord of Bulvuran,' declared the Steward. He followed with introductions for the Warlord's family and his entourage.

It had been traditional for the Cinanac Emperors to appoint a senior military commander to the post of Warlord, to oversee strategy and deployment of the military. Although many Suulvey urged him to start with a completely new leadership, Cedrin considered it important that Raynor have some continuity. It was important that the Warlord be made part of the new Raynor. He needed his experience. That did not mean he would not be alert for treachery from him – or his family.

'Uran Cinnel, Suulvey of the Raynor Court and Sorcerer,' declared the Steward. His was followed by his First Consort Ersta, and his children. Ersta had light honey-gold hair, with dark eyes. She had been delighted when they told her that her brother Marken was alive. Even so, her first loyalty was to Uran himself. Cedrin was less sure about the Sorcerer than Daran. His knowledge of Sorcery was extensive, and his Druidin would be crucial in the years to come as he established a new order.

The golden-skinned Sorcerer was intent on Cedrin as he advanced across the marble. His face gave away nothing. He and the Warlord had been the undisputed power in Raynor for decades. This must indeed be a strange day for them both. All that was in the past now. The choice was now theirs. They could kneel to him or take their chances outside the reborn Empire.

The Warlord and Uran came to a stop before the dais with their families. The Steward had followed them up the aisle between the assembled Suul and now came to stand at the edge of the dais. The ever-present hum of talk stilled as he turned to the crowd.

'We are here to swear allegiance to Cedrin Cinanac, true heir to Emperor Riin Cinanac!' declared the Steward. 'Any who would challenge his right, speak now!'

Cedrin tensed. Even though he knew he was Riin's son, part of him would always be the Athrian calvanni. On some level, that was still more real to him than this. He turned his mind to the future. To the good he could achieve as he rebuilt the Empire; as he forced back the Eathal, as he loosened the stranglehold of the Temple of the Sisters and freed magic and religion from its grip. One of his first decrees would be to once more legitimise the practice of Sorcery. Then he needed to have a long conversation with the Suul of Herath and one Veltricus Cineth.

There was silence across the vast room.

'All kneel and declare your allegiance to Emperor Cedrin Cinanac.'

There was a shuffle of fabric as the Suul sank to their knees. There was no hesitation as the entourages of the Warlord and Uran knelt with the rest.

'Declare your fealty!'

As one, the Suul spoke words that had not been heard in Raynor since his own father had succeeded from Jykor.

"Under the Light of the Sisters, I pledge allegiance to Emperor Cedrin Cinanac. I swear faithful obedience to the Emperor, never to cause him harm and to assert his right against all others in good faith and without deceit."

Cedrin took a step forward. 'I accept your oath!'

The Steward hit the marble three times with the fluted end of his staff. 'All rise as subjects of Emperor Cedrin Cinanac!'

The Suul climbed to their feet. As they did so, Cedrin and Ellen turned to the thrones behind them. Together they climbed up two more steps on the tiered dais until they reached the top.

Cedrin sat down in the Emerald Throne. Beside him, Ellen seated herself in the Rose Throne. She looked pale and elegant.

The room burst into applause. Cedrin blinked as spontaneous cheers broke out across the room.

'What are they cheering for?' he asked.

Ellen's jaw dropped. 'They are cheering the saviour of

Raynor.'

Cedrin sank back into the chair. Eventually the cheers settled down and the formal proceedings continued. One by one, his new Suulvey were invited up onto the dais to sit in the honoured positions before the throne. Daran and Uran took their places there, along with many other Suulvey from the Warlord's regime. Some others had been recommended by Kranor and Belin and represented the more traditional royalist faction that had been such a thorn in Daran's side. He would have to get used to them now.

Cedrin took a deep breath and prepared himself for the continuation of the ceremony. Other senior Suul were formally introduced before the throne. Each introduction was an important honour, and a public recognition of their place in the new Bulvuran. As such, the ceremony was vital. It did not make it any easier to bear.

His anxiety and nerves drained away, and he found himself drowsy as the day wore into afternoon. The speeches and introductions blurred into one another.

He felt Ellen's hand on his arm. 'Not long now,' she whispered under her breath. He brightened at that. Tonight they would have the chambers to themselves. A welcome piece of privacy after the long months of travel, battle and struggle.

Cedrin snapped to alertness as the Steward's staff slammed into the marble, cutting short the latest introduction. The minor Suul was ushered back into the crowd, indignant at the interruption, while a Suulqua messenger rushed into the room and bowed.

'Suul Moren Cinlar, leading a delegation from Olcis,' my Lord.

The Suulqua paused, he and the Steward waiting for his command.

'Let them in.' The Suulqua rattled off a list of names in a hurried whisper to the Steward, who nodded in understanding. Then the Suulqua exited the Hall. Soon after the delegation entered.

The Olcis Suul were dusty from travel, yet held themselves with pride as they advanced to the Emerald Throne. Cedrin leant forward as he saw Osterac with them. The once false-Scion had been true to his word. The Olcis Suul had embraced a chance at breaking free from the Eathal in return for allegiance.

'Suul Moren Cinlar, Sarlord of Olcis. With him . . .' The introductions continued. Cedrin watched the senior Olcis Suul as he came forward. He had the same Anacian looks as Osterac, olive skin with thick, dark hair. His face was lined with fatigue. He understood from Kranor's reports that Moren had fought tirelessly to rid the city of the Eathal and save his people. He was well respected by the Suul and loved by the common people.

'Sarlord, what brings you to Raynor?' asked Cedrin. He wanted to give the man the respect he was due, despite their agreement.

Moren knelt, followed a moment later by his entourage. Osterac knelt with the rest, his face alive with fervour.

'No. Not Sarlord. Merely your loyal subject,' said Moren. 'We are here to give our allegiance.'

'That is most welcome,' said Cedrin, waving at the Steward.

Like the court before them, Moren, Osterac and the other Olcis Suul recited their oath.

Cedrin rose from the throne and walked down to the edge of the dais. 'I accept your allegiance. All Kelas – and the people of Olcis – owe you a debt of gratitude. Rise.'

As they climbed to their feet, he turned to Osterac. He had to admit that he had misjudged the Olcis Suul, his suspicions given fuel by the man's role as false-Scion for the Hesguit. All that was in the past now. If not for Osterac, Olcis would be in ruins now and thousands more would have died under the heel of the Eathal.

'Osterac. You have faithfully completed your commission and served the throne well. What reward do you desire?' Cedrin looked down into the man's cultured face. He looked the classic Suul. 'You are respected by the Olcis Suul. Do you want to govern Tupur in my name?'

Osterac shook his head. 'The restoration of the Empire is my reward, my Lord. I would not rob my uncle Moren of what is justly his.'

'Then how can I reward you?'

Osterac's face was composed. Solemn. 'I seek nothing more than a place at your side, my Lord. Let me rejoin the One Hundred.'

Cedrin nodded. 'And so you shall. As its commander!'

Osterac's face flushed red, and he could not suppress his smile. It seemed this is what he wanted after all.

'Come. Take your place,' said Cedrin, waving Osterac up onto the dais. The other members of the One Hundred remained impassive as he took his place on the dais. Only Ranis looked at Osterac, nodding to him gravely as one commander to another.

Cedrin turned to Moren. 'Moren Cinlar. Will you take up the post of Governor of Tupur?'

'With pleasure, my Lord.'

'You will have your work cut out for you. Is the Hesguit still barricaded inside the inner Citadel?'

Moren's smile grew thin. 'I am afraid so, my Lord. Although more of his Druids come to our cause each day. Soon he will find himself with no more than a handful of supporters and nothing to eat.'

'Come and join me on the dais,' said Cedrin, walking Moren to a seat with the Warlord and Uran. A buzz of conversation flowed around the room at the events.

Cedrin resumed his seat. He indicated to the Steward for the ceremony to continue. A muscle twitched in his neck. As he turned his head to massage it, he caught Osterac's gaze. The man's pale blue eyes watched him with a strange type of hunger. Osterac turned away to watch the room, slipping easily into his role as bodyguard.

* * *

Raziin longed to curl his fingers around the Seer's throat.

'You said the Spear was to be mine,' he growled.

Marina took a step towards him, searching him with her crimson eyes. The interior of the temple was filled with dank shadows.

He hissed in frustration and turned away from her gaze.

That was hard enough, even though her power slumbered.

'The future has shifted, that is true. Yet your ultimate destiny remains unchanged. You will have the Spear, Raziin.'

He wanted to rip at her, destroy her. Such thoughts were useless. Her power was overwhelming. He had learned that too many times to his peril. Heeding her will had always saved him in the past, he reminded himself. She had given him the means to free himself from Hukum. Her directions had led him beyond Faivel's reach and into the arms of his countrymen. Her whispering voice had guided him and his men down from the slopes of Asgod-Ki as the Eathal melted away and had drawn him back into the green depths of Thilil, to this ruined temple where she had appeared once more.

'What next then?' He rubbed his shoulder. Although healed, the calv wound continued to trouble him. On the slopes of Asgod-Ki, his dulled mind had fumbled the Matrix of Form.

'You must return to Armon. To your family. In time, Armon will be forced into a treaty with Bulvuran.'

'Cedrin.' The name was torn from his mouth like a curse.

Marina reached out to touch the side of his face. He shivered, aware of a terrible emptiness inside him. A void that he did not want to know. His eyes lifted enough to see that her belly swelled with child. His heart seemed to labour under some heavy weight as he counted back the months.

'When the call comes, you will beg your brother to go to Raynor as ambassador,' said Marina.

'Cedrin will kill me,' said Raziin. 'The Spear —'

'He knows the Spear enough to fear it. No. You will be safe. Cedrin will have become the magnanimous ruler by then. He would never murder a legitimate ambassador. You will be protected by all the rules of diplomacy.'

Raziin laughed at the audacity of the idea. 'Yes. It could work.'

'You will go to Raynor,' said the Seer, her voice resounding with power. 'There you will wait for my signal.'

'He will be too well protected. None of his men will betray him. They all swoon for him like lovers,' said Raziin.

'Not all of them,' she whispered.

431

He felt her power grow. His arms tensed as he tried to resist, but inch by inch his head tilted up until he was lost in a sea of crimson.

'What will you do?' said the Seer. Her voice was around him – inside him – through him. A darkness yawned, threatening to spill into his mind. Its vastness threatened madness.

'I will go to my brother in Armon. To serve him. Then to Raynor as ambassador.'

She released him. 'Go,' she whispered.

He did not need a second invitation. He ran from the temple and into the damp Thilil forest where his few remaining men waited. He had weeks of hard travel before he could rendezvous with Kethis and the small guard that secured their Ranmyden camp.

* * *

The Seer sensed movement behind her.

'And what of me, Great One?'

Bovosan had served her faithfully, but that did not ease her anger. Her schemes had failed. Cedrin had proved to be far more resourceful than she had anticipated. He seemed to have the uncanny knack of inspiring loyalty and ultimate sacrifice in others. It was a shame.

'Why must we ally ourselves with a snake like Raziin? The Spear will truly be a force of evil in his hands.'

'It is necessary,' said Marina. She felt the weight of her burden heavily.

'We could enlist Cedrin's aid. Tell him the truth –'

'No. It must be Cinnor. The blood of Osellen will never willingly forego the Spear. He must be the one to pay the price.'

Her hand rested on her womb and she gently touched the swelling life within. Already, this far from Ciofran-Ac, her ancient body had begun to disintegrate. To have new life within her – after so long – was a miracle.

The minitil stepped silently from the shadows. 'Then what of me?'

'You must return to Raynor. To Cedrin.'

432

'He will never accept me now.'

'Nevertheless. You must be at his side when the time comes. Go to him. Tell him who you are and where you come from. Tell him all your actions were motivated by a need to protect him.'

Bovosan bowed. 'I obey, Great One.'

The minitil backed out of her presence.

She closed her eyes and reached through the fabric of Kelas to its heart. She stepped through the portal and passed through to Ciofran-Ac. She would not be able to survive too many more trips from the crucible of her power. She had to hold her fraying essence together long enough for her daughter to be born.

Then all of this, finally, could end.

* * *

Ellen gasped. She blinked in the dark.

For a long moment she did not know where she was. Then she felt Cedrin's warmth and his slow, deep breathing and she settled back under the covers. She had been in the strange dream-Athria again. This time she had wandered through the empty streets, looking for something. Yet all was silent as a tomb. The Behemoth was gone. Yet also was the Raptor, the being she had come to see as her secret ally against the darkness. She came to the plaza where the Iris tree grew with its five twisted limbs. It was still. Frozen. Movement in the upper branches drew her attention. There was a flash of wings and she saw the Raptor fly away, his wings pushing hard for his tower.

'Wait!' she cried.

Two small objects fluttered from the branch where the Raptor had been perched. She snatched at them. They were carved figures. A Priest and a Priestess in formal vestments of white. As she watched they changed to red, the colour expanding across the figurines like a spreading pool of blood. *They are not who they seem.* The voice of the Raptor had whispered in her mind.

She shivered and wrapped the blanket around her shoulders.

'Don't be foolish,' she chided herself. They were safe in Raynor, at last at the end of their journey. Osterac and a dozen

433

other senior warriors of the One Hundred guarded them. All with proven loyalty. The Behemoth was contained and all was well.

She propped herself up on an elbow and reached across to the oil lamp. Turning the spigot, she lengthened the wick. A soft light swelled across them. The night had been glorious. Together they had rejoiced in their reunion, in the miracle of touch and the ecstatic pleasure of lovemaking. She never wanted to let him go again. Never wanted to let anything come between them.

She watched his face in the lamplight. He looked younger, his features softer as he slept, his habitual intensity drained away by the release of sleep.

Ellen shivered as she remembered his face that night on the Asgod's eastern bank. He had emerged from the steaming landscape of burned flesh and charred skeletons, his face twisted into an unrecognisable mask of fury. She had feared him then. He was a stranger, capable of anything.

As she looked into his eyes, she saw a strange light behind them. At that moment of their victory, her heart had torn with grief. She had been convinced the Behemoth had taken him, possessed him like the scores of Eathal who had swarmed to do its bidding in the Hall of Dreams, like the black drakon that had ripped its way free of the Iris.

Ellen lowered a hand towards his face, wanting to stroke his cheek as he slept. Her hand never touched his skin. It hovered there, a finger's breadth away. Fear touched her. It had scarcely been a week. What would happen in a year? A decade? When would the Eathal or some other foe bring the Spear from its resting place? The Behemoth would rise like acid to eat into his sanity, taint his thoughts. They had won the Spear, yet they had never defeated their greatest enemy, the Behemoth itself.

Her eyes stung with tears. She dabbed at them with the corner of a sheet, crying silently. The Behemoth would always be there, ready to invade their minds.

Ellen gritted her teeth. They could not live their lives in fear. The Empire was rising again, just as she had always hoped. As her father had dreamed. They were the future now. She refused to allow her fears to poison the time they did have together. No matter what happened, they had to face it together.

She slid the back of her hand gently down his cheek, already rough with morning stubble. His eyes flickered open.

His body went rigid with tension before he recognised her and relaxed into a drowsy smile. He was always jumpy like that.

'Morning already, Empress?' He ran a rough hand up along her side and she shivered in pleasure. They had been apart too long.

'Not quite.' She leant forward and nibbled his ear. 'And for now I'm just Ellen. The Empress can wait until dawn at least.'

She shrugged out of her sleeping shift and swept back the covers. Then she slipped into his arms.

All the worries, all the fears, just drifted away.

About the Author

Being able to escape into the realm of the imagination was handy growing up as the youngest in a family of eleven. Chris continues his fantasy and SF writing habit from his home town of Brisbane, where he lives with his lovely wife Sandra and three children, Aedan, Declan and Brigit. He has a third-dan black belt in Moon Lee Tae Kwon Do and also enjoys movies and exploring narrow alleyways. Chris is very passionate about music, if a little inconsistent, and loves singing and playing classical guitar.

Website: www.chrismcmahon.net.

Lightning Source UK Ltd.
Milton Keynes UK
UKOW04f0042050915

258083UK00005B/871/P